RISKY ASSETS

RISKY ASSETS

CELESTE DONOVAN SERIES
BOOK 2

RACHAEL ECKLES

APHRODITE
BOOKS

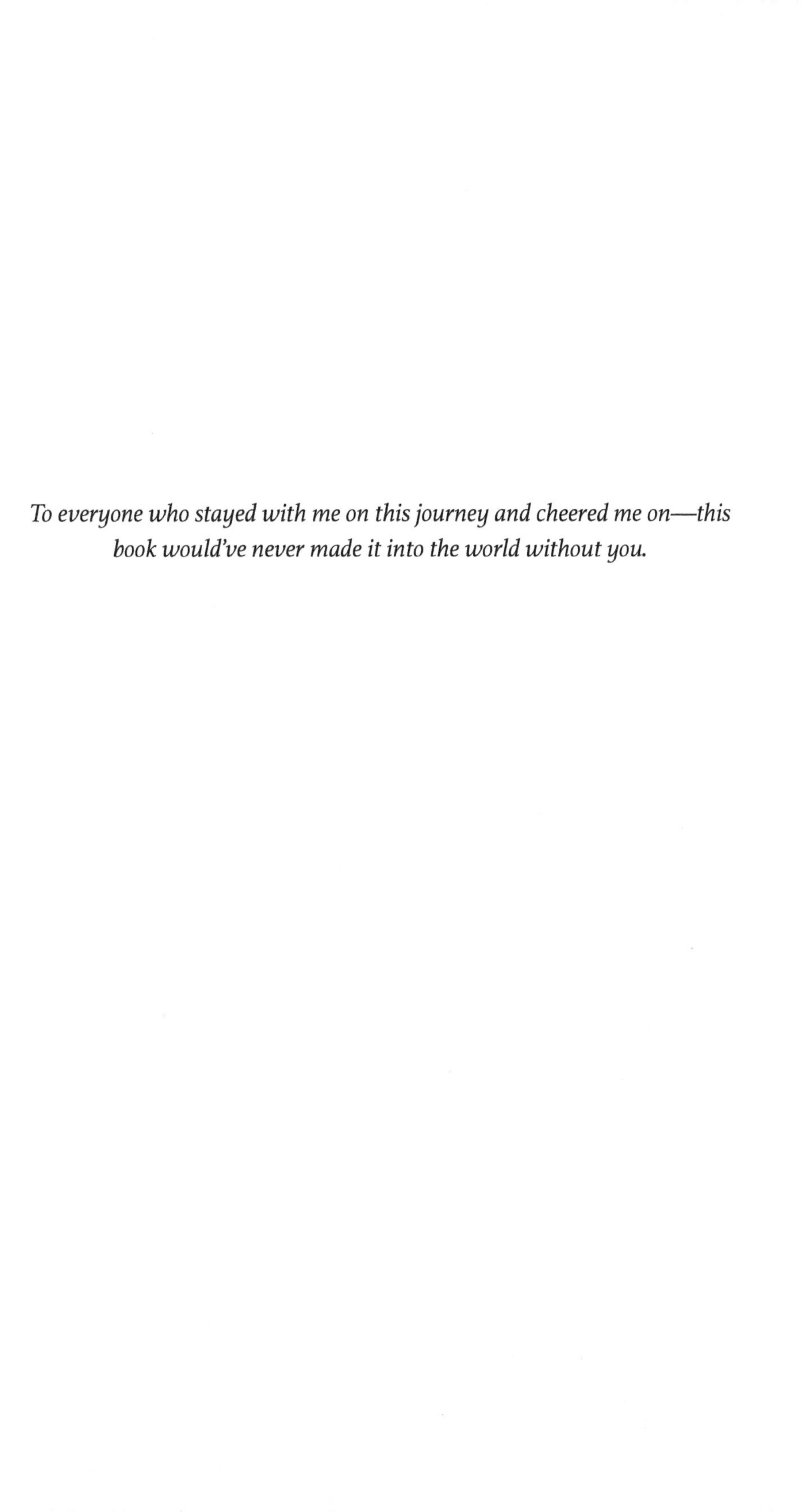

To everyone who stayed with me on this journey and cheered me on—this book would've never made it into the world without you.

she burned from end
    to end, becoming the
    fire she once tried
    to put out, and now
    the world would finally
    see how dangerous it
    could make a woman.

— A. J. LAWLESS

PROLOGUE

It was almost time to leave, yet Celeste Donovan felt unrushed. She sat on the tranquil terrace overlooking the idyllic Tuscan countryside, sipping tea. She'd awoken before the sun to meditate—she needed to be clearheaded for the day ahead.

The sky was a brilliant explosion of pinks and yellows as the sun peeked over the horizon. Rows of pristine Cypress pencil pines dotted the meticulously manicured rolling hills, on the highest of which lay the town of Montepulciano.

Even at this early hour, the staff below bustled about in the courtyard preparing the already immaculate grounds for the week's festivities. The air of old Hollywood romance that Jack's villa provided was the perfect backdrop to marry the love of her life. Only one thing—or person, as it were—stood in the way of the new life beckoning her.

Back inside, she dressed quietly in a camel tank dress and espadrilles, adding an Hermès scarf and wide straw fedora. Her soon-to-be husband was snoring softly in the lavish California king bed. *He deserves his rest after last night's performance,* she thought, smiling devilishly. She'd slept soundly also, her usual nightmares at bay.

"Good morning, beautiful," Theodore murmured sleepily. "Can't we stay in bed all day?"

She learned over to kiss his cheek and laughed when he pulled her on top of him. He gave her a heady kiss.

"Don't tempt me, sexy man," she said when she felt his morning erection against her body. "I'll be late for my pampering."

Celeste had told everyone she was spending the day at a lavish spa to assuage wedding jitters. Even after so many lies, she still hated deceiving Theodore. But some things a woman must do on her own.

He let out an exaggerated sigh. "I guess I'll have to keep myself busy without you," he said with a grin.

"I'm positive Savin will keep you entertained," she replied. Her best friend and business partner, Savin, had introduced her to Theodore, his childhood partner in crime. "And you know how irritable I am when I miss a massage!"

Celeste slipped into the en suite bathroom before he asked more questions and locked the door. The Chanel tote she'd hidden in the vanity the previous day was still there, seemingly untouched. She rummaged through its contents to make sure nothing had been disturbed.

My final day as Mia Blosch. Hopefully.

She returned to the bedroom. Theodore had already dozed off again by the time she was ready to leave. She made her way through the sprawling villa to the foyer and out to the Alfa Romeo waiting to take her to the heliport a few miles away. A handsome young man tipped his hat to her and rushed to grab her bag. She pressed it possessively against her.

"No, thank you," she said, waving his hand away and slipping into the back seat.

Celeste stared out the window, lost in thought, not fully seeing the rolling hills and lush greenery. She mentally walked through the agenda Michel had laid out for the day. There was no room for error, but they'd paid off enough people to have confidence that everything would go well.

When her driver began chatting, she replied, "*Il mio italiano è pessimo,*" and he promptly snapped his mouth shut.

The car ride was quick, and in no time, she had exchanged pleasantries with the helicopter pilot and was buckled in with her headphones on.

"Our flying time will be about forty-five minutes, miss," he said. "The weather is perfect."

And it's a perfect day to put an end to this nightmare, indeed. "Yes, it does look that way, doesn't it?" she replied, at once feeling at peace.

ONCE THEY LANDED AT URBE, Celeste climbed into the back of the awaiting Mercedes Sprinter with blackout window tint. The driver would not arrive for another ten minutes, so he would not see her before the transformation into Mia.

She scrambled to change her clothes and rummaged through the black case that held everything she needed to ensure it was in order. She had checked it obsessively since leaving New York because she knew its contents would be nearly impossible to replace in Rome. She wouldn't risk any deviation from the plan.

Celeste tucked the last of her golden locks into the wig cap and retrieved a chic brunette wig, purchased at an upscale boutique in Brooklyn (rumored to be the artist behind Bey's locks), and a nose prosthetic from her bag. She added silver Chanel eyeglasses, then secured the final touch of her disguise into place just as she saw the driver walking up. *Here we go.* She took one more cursory look in the rearview mirror and frowned at her reflection. *Safe to say I'll never be getting bangs IRL.* The driver only nodded in greeting and let her sit in silence for the fifteen-minute drive to the hotel.

She had reserved a suite at Hotel de Russie for the week as a home base. Theodore and the others had no idea that she'd slipped away as Mia to Rome once already since they'd arrived in Italy the week before. Everything had needed to be organized. *Good luck is when opportunity meets preparation, as they say.* No one could ever accuse her of being unprepared for this moment.

It had been a long journey. Unbeknownst to her friends and colleagues, she'd broken ranks with the illuminati after they failed yet again to deliver justice. She had been moving around for months undetected. When she'd caught wind of what was being planned, she had no choice but to act. The only way to get anything done was to do it herself.

After she made her way to her room, she stood looking in the mirror of the master bath in her hotel suite, ensuring her disguise was still in place. Once she was certain she was unrecognizable, she smiled to herself.

Voilà! Celeste Donovan becomes nondescript Swiss woman once again. It amazed her how easily she could transform into an entirely different person. She'd had a lot of practice of late. A glance at the hotel room clock indicated it was time to go downstairs. She checked the contents of her bag for the final time, ready to face what the day had in store for her.

A life for a life, isn't that right? She and Theodore would be married the next day in the most beautiful of places with their closest friends and family. But first, retribution.

PART I

NINE MONTHS EARLIER

1

ALL THAT GLITTERS IS NOT GOLD

"**I** have her."

"Does she know?"

"She knows nothing."

The cryptic text exchange she'd seen on Zari's phone after she found him murdered in their Dubai safe house had haunted her for the past six months. *"Does she know?"* Do I know what? Who was Zari texting mere hours before he died? *Did Omar turn him against me by threatening his family, only to have him killed?* She held back tears at the thought of his wife, now a widowed mother of two young children who was tormented by his mysterious and untimely death.

But Celeste Donovan was supposed to be on vacation, not playing at being Nancy Drew. Outwardly, her life was enviable. She lay languidly on a chaise behind a luxe private villa in the Masai Mara safari park in Kenya. Up until her thoughts had turned to the past, she'd been engrossed in the latest beach read as she sipped from a fresh coconut to cool down and hydrate after a morning game drive. She ran one of the world's most successful hedge funds, Donovan & Clarke Capital, or D&C for short; had a luxurious Manhattan penthouse; and was engaged to the love of her life, Theodore Prescott.

All that glitters is not gold.

Lifting a hand to shield her eyes from the intense East African sun, she watched as her fiancé sauntered toward her. Theodore was breathtakingly handsome—tall, fit, jet-black hair, and twinkling ice-blue eyes. But Celeste had bedded plenty of beautiful men. What kept her enamored with Theodore was his zest for life, his commitment to making the world a better place (she was hoping some of it would rub off on her), and the fact that he made her feel loved every day.

In that moment, he was smiling ear to ear. She knew that grin—he wore it when he had manipulated someone into doing his bidding. Two days prior, he had finagled them into the sold-out five-star safari camp he'd decided on. Putting his pilot's license to good use, he'd rented a small plane and flown them to a private airstrip. He'd secured the most opulent villa, complete with an outdoor claw-foot tub and a bedroom that opened into the park. She could quite literally watch elephants, giraffes, and zebras graze while relaxing in a bubble bath. Theodore's adventures were always straight out of a fairy tale.

There was no denying that Celeste was in love with him, but the past year had been the hardest of her life. Theodore had vanished for several months, believed to be dead, and she'd been inconsolable. Her reckless attempt to avenge his death had gotten her tortured and nearly killed. And then he'd reappeared like a white knight. Despite her confusion and hurt upon his return, she knew firsthand that she did not want to live a life sans Theodore. So when he proposed, she said yes without hesitation. Now here she was with him, amid Africa's lushest surroundings. *I would've killed for this very moment six months ago.*

She smiled as Theodore sat on the adjacent chaise. "What'd you manage to pull off this time?" she asked.

"It's a bit cheesy, darling, but I've committed us to an aerial safari tomorrow, which is simply a sunrise hot-air balloon ride, complete with Champagne. It's truly the best way to see the herds."

Theodore was referring to the annual great migration, when millions of wildebeest, zebras, and gazelles left their homes during rainy season. The animals were now crossing the Grumeti River, bordered by Kenya and Tanzania. He'd been buzzing with childlike excitement since he first suggested the getaway a month earlier, proclaiming everyone must experience the migration at least once. As an Englishman, Theodore had been coming to Kenya on holiday since his youth and apparently had missed it terribly the past few years.

"OK, twist my arm. I'm in for the bubbles and balloon," Celeste said, laughing. She had to admit Theodore's enthusiasm was infectious, and she was enjoying safari far more than she'd expected. "What's next? You'll only have me all to yourself for a few more weeks, ya know, so you'd better make it worth it."

"Oh yes, I'm aware, and I'm going to take advantage of every second with you," he said, leaning over and kissing her passionately.

"We'll fly out from here tomorrow afternoon to Lamu," he continued, sitting back. "The Kenyan coast is perfectly paced for the last leg of our trip. Imagine it—you, me, sunset sails, catch-of-the-day meals by our own chef, making love until all hours of the night in a private villa with stunning Swahili architecture overlooking a channel of the Indian Ocean. Wi-Fi is spotty enough that we'll have to unplug. I can't wait to show you around where I spent so many holidays as a child. Poppy and Teddy were quite the adventurous pair when I was young." Celeste smiled at the mention of his parents—she'd grown close to them over the past year.

"Plus," Theodore added, "we're going at the right time of year. August is perfect because it's not overcrowded. Lamu is good for the soul."

Celeste laughed at his pitch and relented. "I can't wait to see this magical island where you've spent so much time. It sounds quite special—and we all know my soul could use some goodness after everything that's happened."

She felt his eyes on her and wondered if he'd seen the cloud descending over her face. Celeste had received the best of care in the aftermath of Omar's abuse. But the psychological injuries hadn't healed quite as nicely as her broken ribs. She'd been struggling for months to find an antidote to her night terrors that didn't involve anesthetizing herself with pills. Despite her best efforts, she awoke nearly every night, in turn, waking Theodore next to her.

"She knows nothing."

So many unanswered questions. Zari couldn't be much help these days. When Theodore first returned, she'd demanded answers from him, but now—now she had to balance the risk he'd discover what she was hiding if she probed too deeply. And Ace and the others— she didn't even bother asking them anymore because they regurgitated the same vague information. *The wise forgive... but they do not forget.*

She let her smile brighten her face as she looked up at Theodore.

"Now that our trip itinerary is settled, are you up for a swim?" Celeste asked.

THEODORE WAS RIGHT—KENYA was soothing on a soul level. The afternoon dip in the infinity pool had been serene, watching the majestic animals in their natural habitat. Now, the two lounged on the terrace after their swim, Celeste scrolling on social media for the latest anti-aging science (she was determined to age backward like J.Lo), and Theodore sneaking in work and Twitter when he could. His commitment almost made her feel guilty for leaving her partner, Savin, to manage D&C alone yet again. Almost.

"Ooh! I forgot to tell you about Jack's offer!" Celeste said.

Theodore looked up from his MacBook.

"He closed on the Tuscan villa. He'd been morbidly waiting for that elderly couple to die, and they finally did. He offered their kids fifty percent above market value. He insists we should use it for... for our party! He sent photos. My jaw dropped—it's gorgeous!" She grabbed her iPad and opened it to pull up the photos.

Jack, one of Celeste's best friends, had retired when they were in their twenties and had been roaming the globe since. No one was ever quite sure what he was up to, but it sounded like a lot of chasing women and using recreational drugs. Jack was like a brother to Celeste in many ways, even looks. They were often mistaken for siblings—same blond hair (though she had long, flowing waves, while his was much shorter), dark brown eyes, lithe build, and he was only an inch taller than her five-foot-ten frame.

"So you're calling our pending nuptials a party these days, are you?" Theodore teased. "Jack's villa sounds like a fantastic option. Have you set a date yet?"

Theodore was leaving the details up to her. *Bold move, bro, and quite a leap of faith since I've never once dreamed of a wedding.* She had delegated nearly all the planning to Meredith, originally her personal stylist but now so much more—Celeste's life manager, a true friend and confidante.

"Meredith said spring is the best time for an Italian wedding. So, spring it is! What do you think of May?"

"Jack's place and Meredith as our social chair—we're in great hands. Honestly, though, the only thing that really matters is that you'll be my wife." Theodore leaned over and kissed her, then trailed his hand down her abdomen and paused in between her legs. The lust in his eyes mirrored hers. Wordlessly, the two walked into their bedroom and, once behind closed doors, peeled off each other's swimsuits.

She lay back on the bed while Theodore stood over her, looking over her body adoringly.

"You're so beautiful, Celeste," he said, leaning over to caress her neck and breasts. He had that hooded gaze with which he always regarded her during lovemaking. No man had ever made her feel so loved, so seen, as he did. He knelt on the floor between her legs and slid two fingers inside her, gently massaging her G-spot and licking her clit with his tongue. She sat up to watch him, leaning on her elbows.

"Oh, Theodore, how do you... oh my G—od," she whispered as her body tensed up in orgasm. He reduced the pressure to allow her to relax into the feeling and began rubbing her clit with his other hand. She arched her back and let the tingle spread throughout her body. She watched as he stroked his erect cock slowly, seeming satisfied that he'd made her come twice in as many minutes.

"I need you now," she said in a husky tone. She put her arms over her head, and he slid inside her.

The two held eye contact while he methodically moved in and out. Their chemistry never ceased to amaze her—it was like nothing she'd experienced before. It was not long until she felt another orgasm, and his dick throbbed as he came with her.

I'll never tire of this, she thought later as they fell asleep in each other's arms.

"I MUST SAY, when I finally got your attention that night on Savin's terrace, I never took you for the adventurous type. Outside of the bedroom, of course," Theodore commented, walking into the dining room the next morning. He took in the dusty James Perse slub shirt and khaki shorts she'd donned for their hot-air balloon ride. "You are as gorgeous in safari gear as you are in a ball gown, darling." He walked over and kissed her, then gently sucked on her tongue. She pulled away, laughing.

"Our driver is going to be here in like five minutes, and we have no time to sneak back to bed," Celeste replied. She piled perfectly ripe mangoes, bananas, passion fruit, and scrambled eggs onto her plate from the huge spread prepared by an invisible staff who had taken care of them the entire week.

"And yes, you're right—this has definitely taken me out of my comfort zone. But truly, babe, it's been magical," she said.

When they first met, she wouldn't have been caught dead on safari. Too much roughing it, even at a five-star resort like this. But the past year had changed her priorities. After NYPD had told her Theodore was dead, she was convinced that Omar was involved and went on a whirlwind revenge tour. She'd challenged herself in more ways than one, staying in third-rate hostels coated in stale cigarette smoke and semen.

"I honestly didn't expect to enjoy myself this much. Thank you for bringing this into my life and for making it so special," Celeste said, leaning over to kiss Theodore on the cheek in a rare display of affection. He put an arm around her shoulder.

"I've also noticed that you've been... well, it seems you've been sleeping a bit better lately," he said.

You mean I haven't awakened you with my frightened screams and thrashing about these past few days.

She resisted the urge to run and hide. "Yes, I've been sleeping like a baby lately," she said lightly as she twisted out of his embrace. "I attribute it to the white noise of the forest. I could've left the sound machine at home," she joked.

Theodore looked hurt. "It's understandable that you'd... what you went through—"

"Nope," she interrupted, shaking her head. "You promised this trip would be a reprieve. I'm done talking," she said. "On to happier things. Tell me a little more about Lamu."

Theodore grinned. "Wait until you eat the food on the coast. Fresh tuna, lobster, crab. We'll live like kings! We'll stay in a beautiful villa, Forodhani House, that my family used to stay in. The owners have deep roots in the community."

"After the, uh, climate here, I'm very excited for an ocean breeze and four walls," Celeste said. Being in the safari van all day could get a bit stifling.

"And I'm ecstatic to have you to myself a little longer," Theodore growled, then pulled her close for a kiss.

Even now, a light touch from Theodore still sent sparks coursing through her body. She refused to ruin their trip with talk of her dark past.

"Theodore! This is... it's... special doesn't begin to cover..." She trailed off, flabbergasted at the migrating herd of thousands of wildebeest, zebras, and gazelles. Other than the occasional relighting of the gas in the hot-air balloon, it was near silent that high up. *So peaceful.*

Their eyes met, and suddenly everything she'd been preoccupied with for months—Omar, Zari—was forgotten. This moment, together with Theodore in the most magical of places, this was all that mattered to her. Her many surgeries, his disappearance, the ultimate villain—so much of what had happened felt as though destiny had been determined to tear them apart. And yet, there they were. Together. Their love had transcended. She fought the urge to jump into his arms.

The pilot poured them Champagne, and Theodore insisted they toast to new beginnings. *Yes, on some days I'd love nothing more.*

By midafternoon, the two were situated on the plane they'd take to Lamu. Theodore strapped in Celeste and then himself. After fiddling with a bunch of knobs and buttons, he announced they were ready for takeoff.

Once they were at cruising altitude, Celeste was struck by the aerial transition from the plains of the Mara to the slums and cityscape of Nairobi and finally to the expansive coast off the Indian Ocean. After what seemed like twenty minutes but was closer to a three-hour flight, Theodore expertly landed the plane on a dirt airstrip and brought it to a halt. He removed his headset, then hers, placing them in the console.

"And this, my darling, is my little piece of heaven," he said.

The two exited the plane and were greeted by a local man wearing the traditional kikoy popular on the island. He was barefoot and pushed a small luggage cart.

Theodore and the man exchanged greetings. ("Jambo" was a Swahili greeting in Kenya, though English was also an official language, Celeste had learned the other night on Google.) The man retrieved their bags and then led them through the tiny airport down a winding path to the water. As Theodore had promised, small speedboats and traditional wooden dhows waited to pick up travelers. Dozens of men moved about with luggage and situated people on the waiting transportation.

A man driving a small speedboat stopped close by them and waved them over. He introduced himself as the captain and helped them into the boat while two men transferred the bags.

When they were settled, Celeste commented, "I don't believe I've been somewhere with absolutely no cars. It's surprisingly efficient."

She and Theodore sat close together, though they refrained from hand-holding due to the norms of the conservative Muslim culture (also the reason for her uncharacteristic attire—a long muumuu dress with a pashmina over her shoulders). In a matter of minutes, the boat arrived in front of a charming, whitewashed hotel with a bougainvillea-woven lattice covering the terrace.

"This is it, Celeste, Shela Beach," Theodore said, gesturing toward the shore. "I can't believe you're here with me. That's Peponi, like I was telling you." He pointed to the cute hotel. He jumped out of the boat and reached up to help her. She put her small bag over her shoulder, lifted the hem of her dress with one hand, and managed to exit somewhat gracefully with Theodore's assistance.

The captain placed their shoes on the sand and then shuffled their luggage to the handlers.

"Are you up for a cocktail here before we head to our house?" Theodore asked.

"Sounds perfect, babe," Celeste said.

Theodore guided her up to the restaurant, where the two were seated at a table overlooking the water.

He was typically so refined, a proper Englishman with an unrivaled mixture of sarcasm, wit, and skepticism, but here he was a child, chattering nonstop about his travels with Poppy and Teddy.

Over a bottle of South African wine and some of the best vongole pasta Celeste had had, Theodore regaled her with stories of holidays spent swimming and learning to speak Swahili with the local children, his sailing lessons (of course he knew his way around a sailboat, like he could easily maneuver his way around a plane, the bedroom, and a Michelin-star menu; it would be annoying if it wasn't so sexy), and adventures among the sand dunes of the village.

"I know I've alluded to it a bit in the past, but Mum and Dad weren't always so happy. With their constant shouting, it sometimes felt like the walls of our London flat were closing in on me. I didn't have any siblings and asked Savin's parents if they'd adopt me when we were in middle school. Can you imagine? That didn't go over well with my parents."

Theodore took a swig of wine and then continued. "But this place always had the same effect. On holiday, we were a real family. They were in love here, holding hands and laughing, and it's where all my fond memories from childhood were created.

"I want to share everything with you, Celeste." His expression turned somber. "When I saw your broken body... saw what Omar had done to you... knowing that I could have lost you—I've never been so afraid in my life. I'd die without you."

Celeste was touched at the glimpse into Theodore's past; the more she learned about him, the more she loved him. But that didn't mean the last six months had been easy on her. Quite the contrary. She had cried, shouted, accused Theodore of unspeakable betrayals, dragged him to therapy only to close herself off. And lingering beneath the surface was her resentment—that he had left her, let her believe he was dead, and watched from afar while she unraveled. Whenever he spoke of his reaction to seeing her injured, she struggled to keep her temper in check.

You didn't actually have to experience what it was like to lose me, Theodore. You, my darling, were the lucky one.

She'd never asked Theodore where he'd been, not really. Her therapist, Anne Marie, often reminded her that whenever he tried to bring it up, she changed the subject. "The truth may be less scary than whatever you're imagining," Anne Marie would say, "and then at least you would know." Celeste wasn't sure she wanted the truth, though. What if it meant she had to leave him? What if he'd done something unforgivable? What if he'd intentionally let her suffer? No, it was better not to know the specifics, as much as the unknown drove her crazy.

Now, she plastered a smile on her face. "And I couldn't live without you either, my love," she replied truthfully. "Mmm, what is this incredibly tasty pastry?" She motioned to the three-sided puff filled with camembert cheese.

If Theodore was disappointed with the change in subject, he didn't let on. "Samosas," he replied, blowing on one to cool it off and then feeding it to her.

She chewed slowly, enjoying the decadent flavors, then looked around at the crowd. "Where is our server? We'll need a few more orders of these!"

THEY REMAINED in Lamu for two weeks—at least, Celeste thought it was two weeks. Theodore was spot-on when he said that time seemed to stand still there. Their days had a lazy rhythm, despite being jam-packed with activities. Mornings were spent looking out at the ocean from their terrace, making love, enjoying breakfast in bed. They distributed toys, clothes, and school supplies to children in the surrounding villages (yes, Theodore had somehow thought ahead to pack such things), had massages and did daily yoga, and lounged at Peponi. They sipped wine while watching breathtaking sunsets on *Hippo Dhow*, a beautifully restored old wooden sailboat, and had mouthwatering seafood at their villa or a local spot like Kijani or Majilis Hotel.

The ultimate escape.

Finally, on their last night there, Celeste powered on her iPhone and began scrolling through the messages. Most of the correspondence was business as usual, and her mind wandered back to Zari's wife. The grief Nasrin must be feeling was all too familiar to Celeste: the mornings when she didn't even have the strength to stand in the shower, the days when she sat on the sofa, eyes unseeing, numb with pain. Celeste had to get to the bottom of Zari's murder, and she had to do something to find O—

No, not now, not before this beautiful vacation is even over.

She was accustomed to dozens of texts from Savin, even if she was away from her phone for a day. She couldn't ask for a better business partner and best friend, but his normal state of mind was hysteria. To his credit and Celeste's astonishment, he'd limited his outreach to one update every few days. *Wow, Sav must be in love again. Nothing else distracts him long enough to put his phone down.*

What gave her pause and made her breathing quicken was a single text. It came from her co-conspirator, Michel, a man from her college days that not even her closest friends knew about. The time stamp was two hours prior.

"It's time."

This was code meaning that something had gone wrong and Celeste needed to get herself back to New York as quickly as possible for an in-person meeting.

Fuck.

2

A LOOSE FUCKING CANNON

Celeste tried to cool herself down with a silk fan she'd picked up in Chinatown, willing the sweat dripping from every pore of her body to disappear. *Apparently, the subway wasn't gross enough before, so they decided to do away with air-conditioning and cleanings in the hottest August on record. Fucking climate change.* When the train entered the South Street Ferry stop, she exited, walked up the stairs to the street level, and headed to the meeting spot, a bench by the ferry entrance.

Michel was waiting for her; to an observer, he looked preoccupied with his smartphone. He was as handsome as ever. She still didn't regret breaking off their tryst all those years ago when she learned he was married with children—she wasn't the mistress type—but she owed him for saving her life in Frankfurt. And now he'd become her partner in her attempt to finally bring Omar to justice. She left space between the two of them as she sat.

"You're late," he said without looking up.

"I also have sweat pooled in every crevice of my body. The subway isn't exactly a Gulfstream. Anything else you'd like to give me shit about?"

Michel raised his eyebrows slightly without looking up. Celeste interpreted this to mean he wasn't used to seeing her on edge. *Well, this is the new me. No more Ice Queen of New York.* The pain of losing Theodore, believing him to be gone forever, had liberated the Celeste who had been so tightly wound, so composed. Now she was the woman who threw things at her fiancé and made him sleep on the couch. Now people walked on eggshells around her. *Now I'm a loose fucking cannon.*

"Your instincts were right—about everything. We need to pivot a little and move up the timeline."

Celeste's pulse quickened. *So Omar is alive and the Feds have moved on from him.* "Could you be a little more specific?" she asked.

She didn't want to be right. She'd wanted desperately to hear that her friends had made the right decision getting in bed with the FBI and CIA.

"It's worse than we thought. The Feds are cutting a deal with Omar."

Celeste had spent months playing out scenarios in her head of how Omar would continue to roam free, slipping through their fingertips. She knew it would be difficult to find him, especially with the Feds distracted by a host of other geopolitical crises. But this— Omar getting protection from any government, but especially the US —she'd considered to be outside the realm of possibility. He was a criminal, a violent one at that. The information her colleagues had turned over when she was away tied him to murders, sex trafficking, arms dealing, cyberterrorism. Not only was he not an American citizen, he didn't even live in the United States. How could Omar possibly be more useful...?

It wasn't fear in the pit of her stomach. No, years of therapy had helped assuage that. This was something else entirely. Rage. She flew from her seat, her handbag crashing from her lap to the ground. "What. The. Fuck!" she nearly shouted, enunciating each word slowly.

She looked around and noticed people glancing her way, slightly curious about her outburst, but then, in typical New York fashion, going on with their business. She scrambled to pick up her purse and the few items that had spilled. *Get ahold of yourself.*

Once she'd sat back down, Michel continued. "They won't extradite him to Saudi Arabia—never had any intention of doing so."

Celeste swallowed. The injuries she sustained, those months in the hospital, losing Theodore—had it all been for nothing?

"What about the arms dealing? The other crimes? We gave them everything they need to put him away. And what about…?" she asked.

What about me?

"He was promised immunity if he cooperated. He won't go to prison." Michel finally turned to look at her, the pity in his eyes apparent. "You and I made the same mistake, I'm afraid. Omar is merely a pawn in a high-stakes game of chicken."

Nerve pain shot from the scar on her wrist, a phantom reminder of the irreparable harm Omar had caused. She massaged it unconsciously.

"So he's what? An asset now?" She almost laughed at herself for using a phrase she'd heard in spy movies. "Cooperated? With whom? Who is he working for?" She couldn't bear the thought of him living without consequence, destroying more innocent people. A lifetime of worrying whether today was the day he'd finish off Theodore for real. No, she couldn't, wouldn't allow this.

"I've told you everything I know. He's still in hiding, from what I can tell. But this changes our next steps."

"What do you propose we do?"

"We expose them. The Feds, Ace, all of them. Except Omar. We must take care of him ourselves, unfortunately."

On the one hand, she knew Michel was right—her friends and colleagues had miscalculated when they'd joined forces with the Feds. *But these people are my family, my whole life.* She didn't expect Michel to understand that.

"Get more information. And trust no one. I'll be in touch." Michel stood up and walked away without a backward glance.

Celeste sat still for a long moment, staring out at the Statue of

Liberty and the ferries on the river. Her burner phone vibrated with a text notification.

"West Fourth and MacDougal in ten," it read.

She hailed a yellow cab on Front Street and rattled off her destination to the driver. The heat was sweltering underneath her wig and nose prosthetic. *New York in August is not conducive to disguises.*

The woman was waiting, a hoodie covering her face and making her appearance indistinguishable. Celeste handed off Zari's phone wordlessly, then kept walking.

She stopped in a nearby public restroom to switch from Mia back to herself.

To AVOID questions from her coworkers as to where she'd been for lunch, Celeste took the subway from the Village to SoHo for a quick shopping trip, then arranged for her driver, Monty, to pick her up outside Chanel. No one was the wiser when she arrived at the office with several shopping bags around 3 p.m.

"Hi, Rani," she greeted their office manager at the front desk.

Rani whistled under her breath. "Looks like you dropped a small fortune today, Celeste," she said, nodding toward the bags.

Rani exuded an air of professionalism, tolerating no nonsense from the high-fiving finance bros and continuously shutting down Savin's old boys' club mentality. No matter how many times Celeste chastised him, Savin still regularly shouted, "Rani, get in here!" But Rani seemed to enjoy antagonizing him in return. "Watch this," she'd say, ignoring him and not lifting a finger until he'd come out to her desk and request what he needed nicely in front of the entire office. The more junior members of the team quickly figured out what Savin had not. Rani had a pulse on the entire D&C operation, and nothing could get done without her, so they'd better mind their manners.

Today, her dark hair was pulled back in a tight, high ponytail, and she was wearing a crisp white blouse and tailored pencil skirt. She was quite beautiful with high cheekbones and a chiseled jawline flawless enough to look artificial, though they could be attributed to her Eastern European roots. She was one of the people who had witnessed Celeste falling apart the prior year, but she was kind enough never to bring it up.

"I'm supporting the local economy," Celeste protested. The two women laughed, and then Celeste kept walking. She nodded to some of the analysts, who shared a long table in the middle of the trading floor, and went to her office. She normally had an open-door policy, but today she needed some privacy.

If Michel was right, and he usually was, Omar had some sort of ongoing arrangement that offered him immunity for his past crimes and potentially his future ones as well. Whatever information Omar was feeding federal law enforcement and the intelligence community was valuable, more important than... *than my life.*

Savin barged in then, oblivious to her wiping away a stray tear of frustration, and closed the door loudly behind him.

"Celly, the quants have uncovered something. It's good." He sat down at the conference table, buzzing with excitement. His moods were always palpable, which was sometimes fun but more often intolerable.

"Do you ever knock?" She walked over to join him, hoping whatever this was would take her mind off Michel's earlier reveal.

Savin had a dreamy look in his dark eyes, and a wide smile spread across his face. Though Celeste had never been attracted to him, she had to admit he was objectively handsome. Lebanese, tall, broad-shouldered. He drove women crazy with his English accent and good looks—that is, until they realized he was a stage-five clinger.

"Wait, what's going on with you? Something's different... you're..." Celeste raised an eyebrow suspiciously. "You're *happy*. Spill it. What's her name?"

Sav seemed pleased she noticed his demeanor, though his ear-to-ear smile in place of his usual scowl was hard to miss.

"I'll have you know I'm growing up. I've decided to keep this one to myself until we... until we make it past three months. But I've had a magical six weeks with her, and that's something, right?"

But who's counting, anyway? Celeste bit back a laugh. They'd been best friends for over twenty years, and in that time, he'd had his heart trampled on countless times. The most sensitive of her friends, he never became disillusioned by love. He remained her and Theodore's number-one cheerleader. His optimism could thaw the hardest of hearts. *Even mine.*

Celeste smiled, choosing to offer "I'll be rooting for you two" instead of the more cutting remarks she was tempted to say.

"I know what you're thinking, but it's different this time, Celly. You'll see."

"OK, OK, I get it. You've joined ranks of us poor fools who've chosen love. Now what were you saying about our genius quants?"

The quant team, composed of PhD computer science and mathematician types, was the brain power behind the algorithms D&C used to consistently outperform their competitors. Celeste and Savin were impressed time and again with their collective ingenuity.

"The Feds are gonna love this," Savin said, rubbing his hands together excitedly.

Celeste's mood soured at the mention of their strange bedfellows. "Out with it!"

Savin explained that a major fintech company valued at $100 billion market cap on the day it went public had falsified some of its SEC filings, and one of D&C's more inquisitive quants had discovered the discrepancies. What was noteworthy, though, was that the SEC investigator who had nosed around D&C many times was implicated in the scandal.

"And guess who tracked this down and filed an anonymous tip with DOJ so that we can laugh at his demise?"

Celeste stared blankly at him. *If only this were news about getting rid of Omar.*

"Ace! He's your best decision to date, Celly! Well, besides choosing me as your business partner," he said, chuckling.

She let him chatter on excitedly about how this was their chance to emerge as leaders in the cryptocurrency world. "In a real way, Celly, not the dabbling we've been doing."

"And how do you propose we do this?"

"Simple. We take advantage of the fact that we know about the SEC action. Double down on our crypto holdings and buy up all of it, becoming the hedge fund of the future and knocking everyone else out of the running."

Celeste frowned, mostly because she viewed this as a harebrained idea Sav had floated several times that was once again going to result in a long discussion between the two of them, ending with an agreement to disagree. Besides the business risk, their foundation would take a reputational hit. They'd been receiving positive media coverage since launching their nonprofit, D&C Philanthropies, but Savin's scheme would garner an enormous amount of flak ("Not all press is good press in this situation," Celeste had pointed out again and again) for the detrimental carbon footprint of data mining that verifies cryptocurrency transactions—much like China already had over the past few years. And wasn't the very idea of one large entity owning every single coin at odds with the philosophy and foundation of decentralized finance anyway?

"Imagine how quickly the narrative will shift from us being the hedge fund with a conscience," she reminded him now, "to us being the big bad finance giant suffocating the environment. I don't see another way around this. Do we have to keep going over this?"

"Never fear—your questions will be answered. Mark's on board and apparently has plans for us to buy a startup to significantly reduce the footprint. And he's in town tonight. Have dinner with us, and before the amuse-bouche arrives at the table, you'll be a convert."

"Fine, I'll listen with an open mind, but you'd better be taking me somewhere fantastic," she replied.

Sav laughed and rolled his eyes. "It always goes back to food with you, doesn't it? I assume Daniel works for you for dinner? Monty's driving, so don't worry, you won't have to make the trek uptown alone."

~

"Surprise, surprise, you fuckers! Did you miss me?" Jack said, breaking protocol at the elegant Upper East Side restaurant by strolling over to the table carrying a chair he'd snagged from a table where a couple was about to be seated. He squeezed in between Celeste and Mark before anyone could object. Celeste glanced over to see the server and Philip, the maître d', in a tizzy and smiled. Jack was irreverent, hedonistic, and unpredictable. Friendship with him meant tolerating his disappearances for months at a time and dropping everything when he decided to pop in. Yet he somehow always showed up at the exact moment when Celeste needed him. He was one of her favorite people.

Philip interrupted the group as everyone was exchanging quick hugs with Jack, inquiring haughtily, "I hadn't realized you were expecting another. Shall I move you to a more appropriate table large enough for your tardy guest?"

Jack looked around the table at Celeste, Mark, and Savin, choosing to ignore the disdainful tone, and replied, "Actually, this is great for me. We'll stay right here."

The man wandered off, visibly annoyed with the arrogant group. *Comes with the territory when we're all together.*

Celeste eyed Jack. "You're surprisingly sober this evening," she remarked.

"He's just getting started, I'm sure," Mark said dryly. "Probably carrying enough coke to make a horse's heart explode."

"Nah, not tonight. Is it a crime to want to spend a low-key evening with my best friends? Where's that fiancé of yours, Celly? He seems like Prince Charming in the flesh, but he's quite an enigma, always jetting around."

"He's out with clients tonight, so I'm flying solo," Celeste replied.

"Jack'll understand my crypto vision," Savin chimed in optimistically.

"Ugh, please don't make me discuss this anymore. Jack's here, and isn't once enough for a day? Let's have a little fun. And I've barely had a chance to catch up with Mark. How're Jin and the baby?"

Mark beamed and handed his phone to her. His screensaver was a family photo of him, his wife, Jin, and their little girl. Celeste felt the familiar twinge in her chest from seeing a child. She'd been pregnant once, but it had ended before she'd even been aware, thanks to Omar. The aftermath of the miscarriage was so traumatic that she'd subsequently written off children. But even Celeste had to admit Mark's baby was beautiful, her skin was a mix of his chocolate and Jin's olive complexions, and she had a head full of dark curls and a wide grin.

"Mazel. Such a gorgeous family," Celeste remarked warmly.

"Hopefully they can come next trip. How were the Seychelles and Kenya, by the way? The photos looked incredible," Mark said.

"Pure magic" was all she had time to say before Jack jumped in with an outlandish story of his latest trip to Beijing. "Had a little run-in with the police because I was caught on CCTV buying coke, and apparently that's frowned upon or something."

"Unbelievable, man. I'll never understand how you're not in prison or dead yet," Savin said.

"C'mon! It was a little misunderstanding and nothing a wad of cash can't clear up."

Celeste laughed and rolled her eyes.

CCTV, closed-circuit television or video surveillance, existed nearly everywhere, but the places with the most tracking were London, Beijing, and New York. Celeste was acutely aware of the video monitoring. She exercised extreme caution now that she was moving around everywhere as Mia but was especially careful in high-tech cities. Jack, on the other hand, wandered around without a care in the world.

The rest of dinner went the usual way, the group fighting over airtime while consuming copious amounts of booze and busting each other's balls. Heads turned to stare at the table with so much laughter.

The restaurant was clearing out when Celeste noticed Savin and Mark exchanging a look. Mark cleared his throat and began talking in a hushed tone.

"So... there's, uh, something we need to discuss."

Refined Mark with his impeccable style and calm, collected exterior. Celeste noted his chocolate skin had a pink flush to it. *Mark? Blushing? This oughta be good.*

Savin jumped in. "Celly, we won't beat around the bush. We're at a breaking point. We can't make excuses for you any longer. It's all in or we must separate out the business you're working on from what we're doing with the illuminati."

Celeste narrowed her eyes. *Blah blah blah.* Hearing that term, *illuminati*, pulled her back to a night at her apartment shortly after she was told Theodore had died. It was the first time her friends had approached her to get involved. Her lawyer, Johnny Carolo, had explained that it was a network of hackers, lawyers, traders, and intelligence officials from around the world who had joined together to be part of something good—taking down bad guys. She'd been annoyed with the name of the group since they first brought her in. Calling it illuminati suggested its association with the Eye of Providence Illuminati of deep state conspiracy theories, though in reality, the illuminati she was part of seemed to be quite ineffective than the storied Illuminati, consisting of a handful of financiers and government employees.

It was one thing for her friends to continue this ridiculous sham, with the Feds pretending they had the best interest of D&C in mind; it was wholly another for it to impact her work. She was used to making the rules by which others played, not the other way around.

She took a deep breath before speaking, though it did nothing to assuage her anger. "You've *got* to be fucking kidding me," she spat. "You guys promised me, *promised me*, when I returned from Nice that I wouldn't regret what you guys did while I was away. And now here we are, and I'm one hundred percent regretting whatever the fuck it was that you did."

"Celly, we did what we had to do to save you. And we'd do it again." Savin lowered his voice and continued. "And if I recall, you weren't exactly lining up to return the billion-dollar prize we got for it."

Sav had a point, but it still didn't make any of this OK. Yes, she'd enjoyed the money that had bankrupted Omar and made her a bona fide billionaire. But she refused to believe that enlisting the Feds had been the only way to bring her back unscathed. She hadn't needed saving when Omar kidnapped her. And she would've figured out an escape one way or another. She bristled at the memories of their meddling.

"You're doing it again, goddammit!" She hit her fist against the table, rattling the glasses and silverware and commanding the three men's attention.

"You're treating me like I don't have agency. I'm not some little woman who jumps when those guys snap their fingers. I run one of the world's top hedge funds and also a five-and-a-half-minute mile. I'm one of the richest women in the world, and I'm determined to be one of the richest *people* in the world before I die. I'm a fucking force. And I'll be goddamned if I have one of those chodes in the FBI calling any more shots in my personal or professional life. You got us into this, and you can keep me out of it—but I won't be cut out of *any* of our business dealings.

"Furthermore, why are you even allowed to discuss any of this in front of Jack? I'm pretty sure party boy over here hasn't agreed to walk the straight and narrow, signing his life away on those contracts you've been putting in front of me."

"Hey! I resemble that remark," Jack said, smiling mischievously.

Mark chimed in. "Celly, Jack did sign all the requisite paperwork, and Chet—"

"Who the fuck is Chet?"

Savin jumped in. "The FBI agent you've met several times, Celly. Surely by now you can recall his name. Omar murdered his wife while she was trying to bust a ring of arms dealers." He sighed and continued. "They aren't giving us a choice, Celly. Many of our holdings overlap with their investigations; they're willing to let us operate freely if you'll get on board once and for all."

Right then, Roberto, a jovial Brazilian with a larger-than-life personality and a few extra pounds around his midsection, and his girlfriend, Samantha, a petite brunette whose slightness was pronounced next to Roberto's heft, strolled up. Rather, Sam (as her friends called her) waddled, struggling to keep up. She was very pregnant and very short of breath. Mark stood to give her his seat, and her relief was evident. Savin went to find additional chairs for the newcomers.

Roberto was D&C's biggest client and had given Celeste and Savin $400 million as seed money when they were in their twenties to start their own shop. He was their sounding board to pressure test new ideas, a trusted confidant. Celeste would've been furious that Sav and Mark had called in reinforcements if she didn't love Roberto and Sam so much.

"Hi, friends! I didn't know you'd be in town!" Celeste exclaimed, rushing to hug them. She seized the opportunity to discuss something other than crypto and the FBI once they were all seated.

"How was your trip? Wait, how are you flying this late in the pregnancy?" she asked Sam. "Isn't there some rule about this?"

"We flew up from São Paulo at the end of my second trimester and have been mostly upstate the past month for some quiet. We were in town for a checkup today, and coincidentally, Sav mentioned dinner. Of course we were a yes, but I'm moving a bit more slowly these days."

Once the server brought Roberto his Scotch, he took a sip and then looked pointedly at Celeste.

"Celeste, we do need you to be read in with the Feds. I personally stand to profit handsomely from the arrangement, and as your biggest investor..."

Celeste's eyes widened in disbelief. Never in their fourteen-year business relationship had Roberto ever held his position as a client over her head. She knew he, they, were right—she was too involved in the day to day at D&C to be cut out of major deals, and as the others jumped in to back up Roberto, she found herself up against a wall. She wouldn't risk Roberto's portfolio, and they all knew it. Nor would she be able to stand being firewalled from their big projects; she ran a tight ship and kept a pulse on every major holding.

They countered every objection she had during dinner, and by the end of it, she was spent. The time had come to meet with the Feds. She resolved to make it worth her while.

"OK, OK, I'll do it. I want to be on record that I still believe this is—"

"A huge mistake. Yes, yes, we're well aware of your position on this, Celly," Savin said.

"And no more of these poorly staged interventions, got it?"

She looked around the table. Mark's expression was sheepish, but no one else wavered. *Pricks.*

While they were settling the tab, Jack perked up. "Well, now that my work here is done, anybody up for some dancing?"

The group chimed in with various versions of no, and they made their way to their waiting cars.

"You take Monty, Cell. I've got... somewhere to be," Savin said.

Celeste didn't have the energy to inquire about his cryptic post-dinner plans. She nodded, waved good night to everyone, and slid into the back seat of Monty's Mercedes. *Michel.* Maybe he'd have some ideas on how to limit the Feds' reach into her life. She shot him a text from her burner phone, then watched the city whiz by as they sped along the FDR. She needed to refocus on what was important, not get bogged down with distractions.

In bed with Theodore an hour later, she fought sleep as he shared one of his grand bedtime stories, usually a recap of some hilarious interaction he'd had that day. Tonight, it was a phone conversation with the chef of a six-seat restaurant that had a two-year waiting list, resulting in his scoring them a reservation next month.

"So, baby, if you can squeeze it in, looks like we're going to Copenhagen soon," he said, shifting in bed to look at her. But Celeste's mind was elsewhere. She ruminated on how quickly her plans could get foiled if the Feds were snooping around. *I won't stand for it.*

"Sure thing, darling. I can make that work. You're leaving for Europe tomorrow, right?"

"Duty calls, my love. I'm off to Zurich, but I'll only be gone for a few days."

"We only just got back. I'll miss you." She wanted to keep an eye on him with this business pending.

"I know, babe, I'll miss you too. The scene is really heating up, which is a prime opportunity to persuade everyone to leave the dark side."

"What'll tie up your time?"

"Well, as I said, this surge is creating a lot of opportunity. But it's also creating a lot of unexpected problems as the big players try to figure out whom and what they should invest in. I'll swoop in to show them my strategy is always best."

Theodore called himself a "modern-day Robin Hood," in that he redistributed wealth by convincing ultrahigh-net-worth individuals that infrastructure in developing countries was always the sound investment choice. He'd even persuaded Celeste and Savin to diversify a bit from their traditional holdings, and now D&C owned a property development company with infrastructure programs in South America and Eastern Europe.

"Oh! I forgot to mention one thing, darling. Mum called me earlier and said she's coming to New York the day after tomorrow."

"Wonderful," Celeste said warmly. She loved Poppy. "Is Teddy coming also?"

"No, apparently Dad is bogged down in London. If you have the time, I'm sure she'd love to see you."

"I'll do one better. She and I will meet with Mere to discuss the party this weekend, and I'll take her shopping. I certainly have no idea what the hell I'm doing, and I have a sneaking suspicion that Poppy is the ultimate party thrower."

Theodore kissed her on the cheek. "You're an angel. Mum will be over the moon with excitement."

"I need to send Sav a quick text, babe," she interrupted as reality descended upon her once more. She squirmed out from under Theodore's arm. "Need anything from the kitchen?"

"Some water would be great, honey."

She filled two glasses in the kitchen and then retrieved her burner phone from her handbag in the living room.

Exactly as she'd hoped, Michel had agreed to talk with her tomorrow. *Now I'll have a plan before meeting with Chad or Clit or whatever the hell his name is.*

Once back in bed, she rolled back over to Theodore and began stroking him slowly. More than anything, she had to quiet the incessant hum of her thoughts, and getting lost in his body always did the trick. His dick responded in her hand, and he kissed her hungrily. With other men, Celeste had rushed through sex, but early on with Theodore, she noticed a shift in herself, perhaps because of the way he looked at her, the way he was her match, not prey for her to conquer. She'd never admit it, but she'd begun to enjoy intimacy that came with a meaningful connection.

She removed his boxer briefs, keeping eye contact as she ran her tongue along his abdomen. He let out a low growl and caressed her face while she took the length of him in her mouth. His breathing quickened, and she was wet at his arousal.

"Baby, suck my dick another time. I need to be inside your pussy," Theodore said huskily.

"Happy to oblige," she responded, keeping eye contact while slowly mounting him. His eyes shone with an emotion that could only be described as love. It had made her uncomfortable for the first few months of dating, as though he'd been staring into her soul. She'd been afraid of what he'd see, that his gaze would penetrate the wall she'd so carefully constructed around herself, revealing the darkness she'd taken great care to hide. But that was the past. Now much of it was out in the open. He'd seen the injuries she'd sustained and hadn't left her bedside in Nice for more than an hour or so at a time for the month she was there. He never once treated her with the pity she saw on others' faces after they learned of the horrors of Omar's abuse. He'd never even raised his voice despite her hurling every insult she could think of at him when they'd first returned to New York. He had only expressed remorse that he hadn't gotten to her fast enough and fear that he'd made the wrong decision by letting her believe he was dead.

Then time passed. And she started keeping secrets from

Theodore, from everyone, for fear that they'd let Omar slip away again or get themselves killed. They didn't know about her self-defense training, the disguises, her friendship with a chatty retired NYPD detective, Petey. And she'd wanted to keep things going well, so she swept her questions about Theodore's disappearance and details about her own scheming under the proverbial rug for another day.

He lifted his hips so that he was deep inside her, shaking her out of her reverie, while moving her body forward and back, stimulating her clit. She moaned in pleasure but wanted to feel his body envelop hers. They rolled over so that she was on her back, and he rhythmically thrust in and out until her body tensed and then released. In that moment, Omar, Michel, all of it was forgotten. She focused only on him throbbing inside her as he came with her.

It had taken her a while to admit she was in love with Theodore, but there was no denying it anymore, especially in the afterglow of her orgasms. She felt things with him that she'd never felt before.

They took a quick shower, and then they were back in bed, their bodies intertwined. He ran his fingers through her hair absentmindedly and cleared his throat.

"Are you still angry with me, baby? For when I was away? We'll be husband and wife in a matter of months, yet we barely speak of what happened anymore." He looked at her to gauge her reaction. "I wanted to discuss more on our trip, but the time never seemed right."

She recalled the months after Omar had kidnapped her. Theodore had consistently stuck to the same story—he'd been trying to get Omar out of the picture for nearly a decade, and he felt his very presence in her life put her in grave danger. He couldn't have known that his plan would so badly backfire. But it didn't change what had happened, and she concealed a deep sense of resentment, only to have it creep up at inopportune times.

Let's not forget how much is at stake. What if he expected that she divulge what she'd been hiding? No, it was safer to keep him in the dark.

"I'm not ready to go back there, Theodore. I will be. Soon. I promise. But not yet." And just like that, the moment of bliss passed, and she rolled over to her side of the bed. He let out a sigh, and not long after, she heard him softly snoring.

Everything felt out of control. The Feds. Theodore wanting to reopen a chapter of her life she'd rather forget. The recurrent nightmare of Omar cracking Theodore's skull that continued to haunt her. Michel dropping the worst news possible on her. Resigned that sleep would not come, Celeste went to the kitchen for a drink. She wandered over to her floor-to-ceiling windows and gazed at the twinkling New York City skyline. She must be strategic now. She would get it right this time. No matter what it took.

3

"FINE, I'LL MEET CLIT. AGAIN."

"Celly, no more fucking around. I know you're free tonight."

Ugh, here he comes at seven thirty a.m. with this crap. "Really, what's the rush anyway? It's been months, and we've survived without me meeting any of them."

Celeste and Savin were seated in their secure (soundproof, regularly swept for bugs) conference room in their Midtown Manhattan office suite. She was exhausted from saying goodbye to Theodore at 5 a.m., definitely not in the mood for Savin cashing in on the previous night's conversation.

"You've already met one of them, and you promised, Celly. We can't afford to cut you out, and you know it."

"Fine, I'll meet Clit. Again."

Savin rolled his eyes and then shot off a quick text.

"It's settled then. We'll meet *Chet* and Gabe at my place. Eight p.m."

Her phone vibrated. She frowned. It was beginning to feel as if she were being surveilled by everyone.

"When/where?" Michel's text read.

"54. 6. 14," she typed, their code (not particularly sophisticated, but it seemed to be working) for "meet me at Fifty-Fourth and Sixth Avenue at two p.m."

"Is it too much to ask for us to discuss a little business now? Our staff meeting is in ten minutes, and we haven't aligned on our position on the Shu deal," Celeste asked, annoyed.

MICHEL WAS LOOKING DOWN at his phone when he collided into her in the crosswalk. He was dressed in a suit and aviator sunglasses, toting a fashionable leather briefcase, a deviation from his usual tech-bro jeans and sneakers.

"Excuse me, asshole. Watch where you're going!" she said loudly and kept moving along, playing up their routine.

She walked to the St. Regis and was seated at the King Cole Bar before she allowed herself to retrieve what he'd slid into her Fendi peekaboo.

"A glass of Perrier-Jouët will be great, thanks," she rattled off before the bartender could speak.

"I will put this in now," he said and walked away.

She dug through her purse and pulled out what Michel had slipped in. *Invite to a Chinese New Year celebration?* She perused the front of the red card, looking for clues in the gold text. *No date, time, or place.* The back was mostly blank as well, with the outline of a rat and "Year of the Rat" in small type at the bottom. *This is supposed to prep me to meet the Feds tonight? Useless.*

A quick Google search revealed that the Chinese New Year was in early February, five months away. Celeste committed the contents to memory before putting the card back into her bag. She could hardly ask Michel for clarity with his annoying affinity for cryptic theatrics.

Back at the office an hour later, Celeste was sifting through the Shu financials. It was a holding company of tech assets, and she and Savin were scheduled to meet with its CEO and COO tomorrow. They'd not been able to finalize their position earlier that day.

"Rani, can you send Lorraine in?" she asked from her speaker phone. The reports prepared by Brett, one of their most talented analysts, had significant gaps, which was uncharacteristic of his usually thorough work product.

"Knock, knock." Lorraine stood in the doorway.

"Hello. Come in," said Celeste. She moved to the conference table and sat down.

Lorraine looked polished in a pearl Chanel tweed blazer, an ivory slim skirt, and nude Aquazzura heels. She was carrying a bound document. Theirs was not an easy industry to navigate as a woman, and Lorraine had acclimated quickly. She was the full package: brains, beauty, femininity, and sophistication.

Celeste and Savin had hired Lorraine as an analyst about two years prior. She quickly distinguished herself from the others when she correctly predicted that several countries would default on loans from the Chinese, a catch that made D&C handsome profits. She became one of their savviest team members, and they felt she was invaluable to their mission—and their bottom line. They would have gone to nearly any lengths to make her feel appreciated. After she demonstrated her commitment to and passion for philanthropy, Celeste and Savin created a role for her as president of the newly launched D&C Philanthropies. Yet her razor-sharp insights were unmatched at the firm, so they still consulted her from time to time on deals.

"What's all this?" Celeste asked, gesturing to the document.

"It's the gaps in Brett's analysis that you wanted to discuss, right? I got some intel you'll love. Whipped up a nice little summary for you and Savin." She sat down across from Celeste and handed her the report.

"A woman after my own heart," Celeste remarked. "Thank you. This is obviously way outside of your current responsibilities with the foundation."

Lorraine smiled. "No problem. It's fun to be able to give away money to help people, but I still like the sexiness of the deals every once in a while. And this one in particular is *very* interesting indeed."

"Ooh, now you've piqued my interest. Do tell."

"Well, it's all in there, but I won't bury the lede. It's a setup."

Celeste frowned.

"The whole deal. I haven't exactly figured out who wants what, but I've gotten the gist. And there's some shady shi—something strange is going down." Lorraine divulged everything she'd learned the past several days. Celeste was impressed. *At least someone at this firm was working while I've been gallivanting around Manhattan like a modern-day Mata Hari.*

Celeste let Lorraine finish and then asked her usual question. "What do you recommend?"

"Take the meeting. Feel out what they want. Then decide."

"Who knows about this report besides us?"

"No one. I assumed you'd coordinate with Savin, so I pulled it together as quickly as possible."

"OK, I'll brief Savin. Let's keep this between us."

"Sure thing, Celeste." Lorraine stood up to go.

"It... actually... there's one other thing." Celeste swallowed. "How did you know?"

Lorraine looked at her quizzically. "Know what?"

"Riyadh? How did you know what I'd planned?"

The alarm on Lorraine's face would have been imperceptible to those who didn't know her well. She recovered quickly. "Savin came to me the day after you said you were going to a spa in St. Moritz, which I knew was bullshi—was a cover for something else. You and I had been working such long hours, he said, and he thought maybe I'd noticed if you'd been behaving out of the ordinary. I didn't tell him much because I wasn't exactly sure what was going on, but I decided to do some snooping of my own.

"One of the last nights we worked late at your apartment, you'd taken a lot of something before I showed up—downers and Macallan, I'd guess. You were speaking gibberish at first, but it wasn't hard to piece together that you intended to frame Omar for a crime, knowing that when the charges were announced, he'd lose his fortune."

Blitzed out of my mind in front of an employee must be a new low.

"Of course, I had no idea you'd go to the Middle East and pull off such a dangerous..." She paused, seeming to remember she was speaking to her boss. "I figured you'd frame him for a crime in Europe and hope for the best."

I'm not one to leave things to chance and certainly not where Omar is concerned. "And then?"

"I alerted Ace." Lorraine's face reddened. "Celly—Celeste, I'm so sorry. I didn't want to meddle, but you have to understand—I was so worried about you. You... you seemed like a shell of your usual self. And I could hardly talk to you—or... or to anyone else, for that matter—about it..."

"Goddammit!" Celeste shouted, slamming her hands down on the table while pushing her chair out from behind her. She turned on her heels and walked to her wall of windows.

People bustled about far below, racing to catch a cab or to pick up a latte from their favorite coffee shop, wrapped up in their own problems.

"Who do you all think you are to interfere with my life?" she asked over her shoulder.

She heard Lorraine open her mouth to speak, then her employee seemed to think better of it. Celeste couldn't blame her.

I am completely out of control. Inhale, exhale, then stop with the fucking outbursts. Act like the managing director, for Chrissakes. But her rage would not be quashed with mindful breathing. She fought the urge to run far away from the concerned tone in her friends' voices or the knowing looks they gave each other when Theodore's disappearance or her breakdown came up in conversation. She wanted everyone to... *leave me the fuck alone.* She rubbed her temples, then walked back to the table and sat down.

"That was... uncalled for," Celeste said haughtily. "I appreciate you for bringing the Shu issue to my attention. You're truly an asset to us, and I'm embarrassed by my behavior."

"Consider it forgotten." Lorraine looked at her watch. "I have a call in five minutes. Another media interview about the good things D&C Philanthropies is doing. Let me know if you need anything else on this. Can't wait to hear what you find out." She left breezily as though Celeste's outburst had never happened.

AT 8 P.M. SHARP, Celeste's driver Monty texted that he was downstairs waiting. Celeste smoothed her Wolford bodysuit, zipped her jeans, and stepped into her nude Manolo pumps. She added a white Balmain blazer and put her keys and essentials in a camel Chanel crossbody bag. *Here goes nothing.*

She was quiet on the short ride from her West Village apartment to Savin's place in Tribeca.

"Thanks, Mon," Celeste said when they pulled up in front of Savin's building. "I shouldn't be too long, but please send someone else to pick me up. No need for you to stay out late." Monty was D&C's longtime driver. Celeste and Savin had helped him buy a fleet of vehicles, and he now had a roster of drivers and a booming business. He no longer actually needed to drive but insisted on transporting the two of them when he could.

The concierge sent Celeste up, and she was met at Savin's behemoth penthouse door by D&C's head of security, Angelo. After a career-ending injury, he'd left the NFL many years before. He'd been Jack's security outfit, but Celeste had borrowed his services when she left Omar and then refused to let him go back to working for Jack once she realized how talented he was.

"Celly!" Angelo's usual scowl transformed into a smile when he saw her. "I need to hear all about your safari adventure, but it'll have to wait because you're the last to arrive. Everyone's inside. The place has been swept."

If only you could detect everyone's intentions like you can detect a bug, Angelo. She recalled Michel's words the other day—"I haven't been able to confirm your security firm's involvement." But she and Angelo, the man who'd protected her, the man who'd sent Omar into exile so long ago, went too far back. There was no way he could be working against her.

"It was magic. I'm sad to be back, especially for this bullshi—er, for this work stuff." She winked when Angelo laughed at her slip. "And Theodore has already left me for a work trip," she said, frowning comically.

"I've seen the way he looks at you. He'll be back at his earliest opportunity," Angelo pointed out.

"Yes, he's a doll. Now on to whatever this meeting is."

Angelo pushed the door open for her. She was surprised to see a formal dining area set up in Savin's enormous ballroom, complete with a self-service bar and gourmet buffet. *Must've wanted to ensure no staff was around to overhear our convo.*

"Celly's arrived. Always late, but always fashionable," Savin remarked loudly. She surveyed the room while walking over to him, counting seven people total—close friends, business associates, and a couple of unknown faces.

"Seeing as I only found out about this little soiree a mere"—she glanced down at her diamond Cartier watch, a gift from Theodore—"day... well, no, mere hours ago, I'd say it's a miracle I was available. Seems the others were given a bit more notice," she remarked coolly, noting that everyone was already settled in with half-drunk cocktails in hand.

"Celly, always bringing the drama," Savin joked, handing her a glass of Champagne.

"You can blame the impromptu nature of this meeting on me," said a voice from behind her. She turned to see a man she didn't recognize. He thrust his hand out. "Gabriel Gutiérrez."

"Celeste Donovan," she said, shaking his hand firmly while keeping eye contact.

"I'm Chet Connolly's counterpart at the CIA. Counterterrorism, officially. Unofficially, we work with you guys."

Gabriel was about her height, five ten or so, dark hair and olive skin. Probably late forties. He was dressed in a bespoke blazer, jeans, and loafers, the perfect foil to Chet the FBI agent with his wrinkled khaki trousers and crooked tie. *Chet. Clit. Same thing.* She decided she would call Gabriel "Gabe," hoping it would annoy him to use the less formal version of his name. She was determined to regularly remind the agents that she wouldn't kowtow to them like the rest of her crew. She resented their presence in her life.

"We needed everybody together for a little transparency." Gabe cleared his throat to get the room's attention.

Savin nodded and called to order, gesturing to everyone to take a seat on the enormous sofas.

Celeste smiled and nodded in greeting to Sam, Roberto, Mark, and Fred Warren at the other end of the sofa as she sat down.

"I'm not one to beat around the bush," Chet began. "It seems that the US financial markets have become vulnerable to cyberattacks in ways we'd never imagined five years ago. We're operating at a disadvantage because we're playing catch-up."

"To whom are we vulnerable?" Celeste asked.

"We've identified an extensive underground network of terrorists obsessed with devaluing the US dollar in order to fan the flames of civil unrest and send a message that democracy doesn't work."

"Russia and China have been orchestrating this for as long as I can remember," Fred interrupted. "How is this anything new?"

"Our intel suggests that they'll go to any lengths to make this happen and that they'll hack into the central bank systems, electrical grids, Wi-Fi, airline traffic control, paralyzing them. It would mean a freeze on the stock market, a plummeting dollar, and people taking to the streets. We can only assume that there will be a run on the banks, and everything will shift to decentralized finance. I can't stress enough that this is a doomsday scenario."

Nothing like easing in with some fearmongering as a nice little icebreaker.

Decentralized finance, unlike traditional banking, leveraged digital currency like crypto and peer-to-peer financing. It took out the middleman, such as a large bank, relying instead on software to deliver services with no human interaction. It remained largely unregulated across the world and had been criticized because it could put a consumer's assets at risk. Translation: The US government and entities like D&C could lose control overnight. A bloodbath.

"Why is DeFi the scapegoat here? Couldn't that potentially be good for the global economy?" Mark asked.

"You guys understand a lot of this better than we do. But we've seen the fallout where movements like this have been successful," Chet reasoned. "Destabilizing the dollar even more than it's suffered in the 2010s will have sweeping effects around the globe. Our foreign aid keeps entire continents afloat. Without us importing, the Chinese and Indian economies will burst. Europe is already fucked with Brexit and the ineffectiveness of the euro. And don't get me started on South America. China is bastardizing many African countries with debt, and without our aid, entire economies could be upended."

"Back to my earlier point—it's not like this type of cyberattack has been outside the realm of possibility," Fred interjected. "We've known of these risks for decades." Fred had always been somewhat of a nemesis to Celeste until the past year. He was the one who had alerted her to the fact that Omar was completely unhinged and still stalking her after such a long time.

"True. But we've never seen anything like this," Gabe chimed in. "We suspect involvement at the highest levels of the US government, and I'm not talking a senator or two. I'm talking traitors on Pennsylvania Avenue and in the Russell Building who want to teach Americans a lesson. We think they're working with the Russians and that we're facing all sorts of diplomacy risks."

"So why tell us?" Celeste asked, alarmed. "Not that I'm an expert in counterterrorism, but it seems extremely irresponsible to share this intel with a group of private citizens who have no reason to keep this to ourselves and no background in any of this outside of reading scripts and attending premieres of movies we've financed. And how do you expect us to trade without acting on this knowledge? I can think of a thousand investments I need to change course on if there'll be a recession or depression—and ten thousand opportunities."

Gabe was unruffled. "This isn't like the 2008 crisis or even the crash of 1929. This is like nothing we've ever seen before. And we,

Chet and I, have nowhere to turn but here. We believe you to be the brightest minds and to have the greatest reach of cyber experts who can prevent this."

"Wait, what?" Celeste looked around at the group. "I'm all for playing Wonder Woman here and advising you on ways to put guardrails in place with cryptocurrency, for instance, to mitigate whatever these rogues have planned. But this isn't something the few of us in this room can redirect or prevent. You need cooperation and collaboration from the EU, the Russians, the Chinese, Japan, India, the Brazilians. You need to catch and replace the traitors in the US government. Et cetera et cetera et cetera. We're fucking brilliant, you're right about that. But we're not omnipotent."

They spent the next hour going over scenarios. Chet and Gabe were insistent that they, Celeste and her friends, were the only hope. They talked strategy and theory, but Celeste found the tactics weak.

She took out her phone and texted Savin.

"Where is Ace on all this? Involved?"

"Aware, tangentially involved, and agrees with the threat level," Savin's text read.

Ace was certainly capable of derailing a cyberattack on US banks if anyone was. She used to trust him implicitly, but since Nice, she'd begun to question his loyalties. Whether that meant she was willing to let him go from their organization to work with the Feds was another issue.

She put her phone down, and as she scanned the room to gauge reactions to the news that the world as they knew it could be in imminent danger of collapsing, she noticed no one was surprised. They'd been planning for this moment, hearing the news of an impending attack on the US economy, for as long as they could remember, and none of them would have any real money at risk. So it boiled down to whether they gave a shit about the future of the planet and wanted to be part of the solution.

Goddammit, why are all these assholes forcing me to have a conscience? I was perfectly happy when my life was full of my favorite things—money, fashion, food, fucking—with none of this save-the-world business.

"Let's eat and discuss over dinner," Savin directed.

Gabe approached Celeste on her way to the table and gestured her to the side. "Celeste, not to single you out, but to be able to speak freely with you, we need you fully involved. I know Chet's been lenient with you, but I can't be. These are issues of national security, and we have to know you're on our side. You have more money than you know what to do with, and you have the opportunity to do something good, something great even. Chet and I have been following your work for years, and you're the brains behind D&C. We need you."

Creepy, but yes, flattery will get you somewhere with me.

"What exactly does 'fully involved' mean? I'm not clear why my friends jumped on board so quickly, but I've never seen working with the US government as part of my job."

"They saved your life after your Riyadh stunt," he said, making air quotes with his hands. She hated him.

"You need to sign the cooperation agreement to work with us," he continued. "It may seem silly to you, but it's protocol. We protected you from the reaches of Riyadh, and we protected you in countless deals to ensure you stayed out of trouble. Now we're calling in the favor."

I've been backed into a corner way too often lately. "I hope you'll understand that I'd like to discuss this with my attorney."

"That's fine, but we must move quickly. The illuminati, all of us here and a few others, will expect your confirmation by Monday. If it's not for you, we won't try to pull you in again. But your friends will no longer be able to involve you, which I expect would be difficult given your relationship with Savin and Roberto. There could be future implications as well—your lack of cooperation may require your recusal or theirs from any number of deals because of the confidentiality requirements. The Shu deal, for instance."

Intimidation and threatening to disrupt my business. Fuck. You.

"I'm sure we'll work out something that's mutually beneficial," she replied icily and turned to walk to her seat.

Dinner was a truffle-themed feast, with black truffle caviar, truffle pasta, and lobster tail with truffle. The conversation was less interesting than the food, and Celeste found herself torn. On the one hand, she wanted to be involved with this loose coalition of Wall Street magnates and spies, hopeful she could learn something along the way to help take Omar down; on the flip side, she felt as if she were signing away another of her freedoms.

Working for the very men we spent so many years evading? I'm nothing more than a caged lioness.

Celeste excused herself for a restroom break and made her way down Savin's long corridor to the guest bathroom. She heard someone behind her and turned to find Sam, ethereal with her pregnancy glow, struggling to catch up. Celeste slowed to see what she wanted. Once they were out of earshot of the group, Sam began speaking in a hushed tone.

"Celly, do you feel a little better about being involved now that you know how much is at stake? It's"—she sniffled as her eyes welled with tears—"I can't stop thinking about the kind of world I could be bringing my kid into."

The state of the world is something to consider preconception, I would think.

"Celly, I... I need to talk to you about something, and now is not really the right time. Dinner tomorrow?"

Celeste softened. "Of course. I'll have Rani make some resys for us. How's Italian? Every pregnant woman loves pasta, right?"

"Sounds wonderful. You're one of my closest and—let's be honest —only friends." Sam put her hand on Celeste's arm and smiled sadly. "Thanks for making the time. It's really important to me. I'll see you out there." And with that, Sam slowly made her way to rejoin the group.

Celeste took plenty of time in the restroom, using the reprieve to gather her thoughts. *There's no turning back now,* she realized as she washed her hands.

After she returned to the table, it was more of the same—dark scenarios and even darker proposed solutions. Finally, when she thought she couldn't possibly take any more, Chet and Gabe made moves to excuse themselves. She almost collapsed with relief. She'd received a text notification from her building that a courier had delivered a package. She was sure it was the contents from Zari's phone, which would hold the answers she needed.

As everyone stood, she promised Gabe she'd be in touch with a decision by the next evening and texted Monty to pick her up after exchanging goodbyes.

Roberto approached her as she was walking to the door, Sam not too far behind.

"You're not your usual self these days, Celly. We miss your edge. Is everything well on the home front?" Roberto asked.

Celeste was taken aback. "Nothing a glass of Barolo and eight hours of sleep can't fix, darling."

"Can you believe I'm going to be a father again? At this age?"

Celeste laughed. "You're not a day over forty in my eyes," she said. She and Sav often talked about how many of Roberto's life milestones they'd experienced—three marriages, three divorces, children, grandchildren, and now fatherhood again.

Celeste bade good night to everyone on her way out.

"Angelo, darling," Celeste said once in the hallway, "could you track someone down for me?" She opened her Notes app, typed the name, and handed her phone to him.

"Indeed, Celeste," he said, committing it to memory and handing the phone back. His brows furrowed in concern.

"No, no, nothing to worry about. I want to say hi to an old friend, that's all," she explained. The truth was, she needed Hadid's help to fill in some of the gaps from the past year—and she needed to get to him fast before the Feds started nosing around.

She was quiet again on the way home, lost in thought. It felt as though the pieces here were from different puzzles, not destined to fit together.

"Miss Celeste, you seem... out of sorts," Monty said when they arrived at her building, the only sleek high-rise in the West Village. She had been ecstatic when she found the perfect apartment years before—grungy chic of downtown living with the chichi amenities and high-end security she required.

For fuck's sake.

"No complaints here. Tired, and I already miss Theodore, but other than that, everything is fine."

Monty, not one to pry, nodded, then got out of the car and walked around to open her door.

"Oh, let's discuss Poppy's visit. Are you prepared to pick her up from JFK tomorrow afternoon? She insists on flying commercial over Theodore's protests," Celeste said.

She and Theodore's mom had become quite close when they believed him to be dead. Celeste was looking forward to sharing their wedding plans with Poppy, the closest person she had to a real mother, as her parents had been killed in an accident when she was in college.

"Of course. She'll be staying at the Four Seasons as usual?"

Celeste gathered her things and took his outstretched hand, gracefully exiting his Mercedes sedan.

"I insisted she try the Baccarat. She'll love the La Mer spa." Celeste yawned. "I'm heading upstairs and off to sleep, Monty. Good night."

Jonah, her favorite doorman, held the door open as she approached. "Evening, Miss Celeste. I have a delivery for you."

"Great, I was hoping it would arrive tonight," she said as they walked toward the front desk.

"Here you go," he said, handing her a sealed ivory envelope, luxury card stock from the looks of it.

She frowned. "I was expecting a larger package. Nothing else here?"

"Nope, this is it."

"OK, good night, darling."

She made her way upstairs and placed her handbag on the foyer console table. After pouring herself a glass of water, she sat down on the sofa, slid a finger under the envelope's seal, and pulled out a notecard and a photo. *What the...?* Her heart sank. The photo of her was recent, yesterday in Manhattan. There was a brief message on the notecard written in calligraphy, which would make it impossible to match the sender's handwriting. "They're not who they think you are," it read. She frowned. Michel's warning echoed in her mind: *Trust no one.*

Unbelievable.

She could have the photo and card dusted for prints, though she was sure there were none. Whoever sent this would have covered their tracks. Omar had pulled these shenanigans plenty of times, but she had a hunch someone else was behind this.

OK, so someone was following her, maybe even knew of her reconnaissance with Michel. That same person was snapping photos of her handing envelopes to strangers in hoodies. It wasn't the first time someone had spied on her. She recalled a night not long before when Fred had pulled up dozens, if not hundreds, of photos of her found in one of Omar's homes seized by the Feds. She had felt so violated when she found out Ace had bugged her devices the previous year and spied on her. But so what? They wouldn't be able to piece together what she was up to now. Or would they?

A chill ran down her spine as she considered the different characters who could have sent the photo. The list wasn't short. *Déjà fucking vu.*

She jumped when she heard her cell ringing in the foyer. She retrieved it and answered.

"Hi, Jonah."

"I think the package you were expecting has been delivered."

"I'll be right down." *Don't let it out of your sight*, she wanted to add.

FORTY-FIVE MINUTES LATER, Celeste looked around at the neatly piled stacks of paper. She was seated on the floor in her living room, trying to figure out where to begin. Jonah was right—this was what she'd been waiting for. It contained everything in Zari's phone and hopefully answers to many of her questions. She took a sip of the

Bordeaux that she'd opened to calm her nerves. It felt like such an intrusion to snoop around in a man's personal effects, especially when that man had lost his life protecting her. But she had to know whom Zari had been texting with about her right before he was murdered.

It had taken Celeste months to find someone she could trust to hack Zari's device. The woman she'd hired was somewhat of a legend on the dark web, rumored as the best forensic scientist on the planet many years back. She'd been difficult to track down because she basically went into hiding when she left the field. For a handsome fee (seven to eight figures), she would come out of retirement to do odd jobs without asking a lot of questions. Fortuitously for Celeste, the woman was willing to travel for pickup.

Given that Celeste's hard drive had been compromised in the not-so-distant past, she'd also asked the woman to print out the device's contents, deliver them to her building, and destroy the phone once and for all. She was growing tired of these clandestine errands, but necessity prevailed. The photo taunted her from the coffee table. *And the precautions aren't even working.*

Please reveal something—anything—useful.

The contents were clearly labeled: "email," "phone calls," and "text messages." She started with Zari's final messages—the ones that were about her:

"I have her."

"Does she know?"

"She knows nothing."

She skimmed the preceding messages impatiently:

Unknown: "She dodged my guy in Frankfurt. Slipped out undetected."

Zari: "Should I stick to the plan?"

Then a series of texts from an unknown number before Zari responded:

Unknown: "New plan."

"Keep her in Dubai."

"Do NOT let her leave Dubai."

"Understood?"

Zari: "She'll never agree to that."

Unknown: "Do whatever it takes."

Then nothing. Celeste tried to discern what the texts meant. She had always assumed Omar was behind the kidnapping attempt in Frankfurt, but the possibility that Zari had been working with Omar seemed far-fetched. Unless he was being blackmailed.

Damn Theodore for being gone when all I need is sex.

No mysteries would be solved at this time of night, but she kept digging, mostly because there was no other outlet for her nervous energy. She divided the email and text files into the subcategories "work" and "Nasrin," Zari's wife. Celeste read about the minutiae of their daily lives—pediatrician appointments and grocery lists—then perked up when she saw mention of her initials dating back to mere days before she arrived in Dubai. *Voilà!*

Zari: "CD contacted me."

Nasrin: "And? Is it what you expected?"

Zari: "Yes. Arrives in 2 days."

Nasrin: "So you'll leave with her?"

Zari: "Maybe. They'll be in touch."

And then more texts dated right before Celeste arrived in Dubai:

Zari: "Idk if we'll leave. Seems they want me to stop her."

Nasrin: "So she doesn't know?"

Zari: "No."

Celeste stood up and stretched, at once confused and excited. Nasrin had information. The question was... well, there were so many questions. Would Nasrin share what she knew? Celeste walked into her office and sat at her desk to pull up the diagram she'd been constructing. She added the night's developments to it.

Gabe. Nasrin. Mystery postcard. The Fed recruitment.

Celeste would go to Dubai and track down Nasrin.

The first real lead I've had in months.

Suddenly, she was exhausted. She texted her lawyer, Johnny Carolo, confirming their breakfast the next morning to discuss the illuminati proposal, and rushed through her bedtime routine.

The apartment felt empty without Theodore. *Maybe it's time for a puppy. Or a fish.*

She looked at the clock on her phone. It was midmorning in Geneva.

"Good night, darling xx. Can't wait to see you," she texted Theodore, then set her phone to Do Not Disturb.

Her dreams were a mishmash of Zari's face morphing into Omar's ominous smile and the image that she could never shake—Theodore's lifeless body twisted into odd angles from broken bones—over and over again. The warnings iterated by Michel, Chet, and Gabe were the soundtrack.

She awoke with a resolve: *No more living in fear*.

4

———

NEVER HAVE I EVER

"I'd advise you to take the deal," Johnny said.

Celeste sipped her matcha latte. "But can they force me into this? I'm not a criminal—why am I being treated as if this is a plea bargain I can't refuse?"

She was annoyed with the loud Friday morning breakfast crowd at Sadelle's and more annoyed with everything Johnny was saying. Her phone vibrated with a notification.

"Are we still on for dinner tonight?" read the text from Sam. Celeste shot off an affirmative reply and turned back to Johnny.

"Take the deal, Celly. It's little burden for you and a lot of upside."

Now that Omar is an asset, seems like very little upside to getting into bed with the very entity protecting that piece of shit.

"I'll take it under advisement. Was there anything concerning about the paperwork?"

"No, it's straightforward. The illuminati collaboration is giving you an opportunity."

"They're giving me my back against the wall is what they're giving me," she snapped.

"Frankly, I've had a lot of clients handed much worse options after the kind of stuff you've been able to pull off with no repercussions.

Keep the money, enjoy the fact that there'll be no more SEC or DOJ types nosing around, and rest easier at night knowing that you're helping put some very bad guys away."

BACK AT THE OFFICE, Celeste was scouring Lorraine's intel before she and Savin met with the Shu guys later that morning.

Lorraine's right. Something's off.

Savin popped his head in.

"So? I'm waiting with breath that is bated," he said, entering the room and closing the door behind him. He sat down at the conference table and put his feet up.

Celeste walked over and took a seat next to him. "I think Lorraine's right. This is a setup. But I can't figure out the play."

Right then, both of their burner phones vibrated with text alerts.

"Calling in ten," it read. *Ace is back.*

"I wonder what he has to say," Savin pondered.

"Guess we'll find out," Celeste replied.

They gathered their documents and made their way to the war room. Immediately after they closed the door, the secure phone line rang.

"Do you ever get the feeling they're watching us?" Savin asked in jest. "Whoever 'they' is."

Absolutely, yes. Because they are. Aloud, she said, "Feels that way sometimes, doesn't it?"

"Ace, tell us the news," Savin said in greeting.

Ace spoke with a voice changer and had kept "his" identity concealed since being hired by D&C a couple of years before. Celeste had always assumed Ace was a man, but lately she'd begun questioning a lot of her assumptions and determined that there was really no reason to believe this.

"Chet and Gabriel want you to move forward with the Shu deal."

The ink isn't even dry yet and already they're making demands. "So this is how it works? They call our shots?"

"Yes, for the most part. The irregularities you're seeing in the financials—the Shu guys haven't caught them yet. They've been too wrapped up in the money to see that their CFO has been siphoning money left and right to fund some militants. With you two on the inside, we'll have more access to information to find out who they're working with and cut Shu and their friends off at the knees."

Celeste rolled her eyes. She hadn't spent her entire life building a fabulous career to now have to worry about cutting someone's legs off, figuratively or otherwise.

And with that, Ace dropped the call.

"The motherfucker still never says goodbye," Celeste muttered.

"You ready for this? Your first real deal—"

"My first real deal since I've been recruited for Amway? No, I'm not ready, but we've been given orders, so I'll play the game." *At least for a little while, until I can figure out who I need to blackmail to get out of this shitshow.*

"Is Shu or its subsidiaries facing any current or reasonably foreseeable criminal or civil proceedings of any kind?" Johnny asked the Shu team.

Futile to ask such nonsense since we have to say yes either way.

Celeste, Savin, and Johnny were seated in D&C's large conference room, and the Shu team was projected on the video display. The Shu chief compliance officer droned on in an attempt to assure D&C that no illegal activities were occurring on his watch. Celeste, who'd usually shoot off tough questions, was holding her phone in her lap, texting with Poppy about Saturday's wedding planning errands. She'd chime in once in a while with a question like "What level of investor approval is required to make changes to the firm's strategies?" but otherwise let Savin and Johnny do the speaking.

The illuminati arrangement was taking the allure out of the job she loved. There was no kill anymore when her positions were dictated by men who knew nothing about strategy or business.

Wait, what just happened?

In a complete break from protocol, Shu's CFO, the guy apparently behind the illegal use of funds, was saying that he could no longer support the deal as it stood. He urged his Shu colleagues to abandon the deal. In real time.

Celeste's jaw dropped, and she looked to see Savin and Johnny wearing the same astonished expressions.

Never have I ever...

Everyone began talking at once. The Shu team was shouting at one another, and Savin yelled over them, "Do you mind telling me what the fuck is going on?" The video screen went blank, indicating the Shu team had disconnected the meeting.

The conference line rang then, startling the three of them in the room.

"Yes?"

"Let it go. He got spooked. I'll be in touch," Ace's disguised voice boomed.

"But how—" *Oh.* Now Michel's warning made sense. *A rat.* Who could it be? There was no way anyone at Savin's last night was a double agent. *Unless the leak is one of the Feds.* Celeste wouldn't be surprised.

The three spent the next half hour debating scenarios.

"I'm not sure we're getting anywhere without any further information, and I'm late to another meeting," Johnny said, sounding as frustrated as they all felt. He gathered his briefcase and laptop, and the three went out into the hallway.

"I'll be in touch," Johnny said and left.

Celeste and Savin walked to the war room, and Savin began pacing, seemingly on the verge of hysteria.

"What the fuck was that, Celly? How could he have known? I'm calling Chet."

She was surprised the Feds hadn't called them straightaway. "How often are you in contact with them? The Feds?"

"Not often. They usually communicate through Ace."

"So a game of telephone?"

"Something like that. But I trust Ace more than those guys."

A rock and a hard place.

She became more frustrated as the day wore on. Finally, it was time for dinner. "Go home, have a drink, and relax. Everything will be OK, Sav," she said.

He looked relieved and actually smiled. "You know what? That sounds lovely. I'll order some Mr. Chow. Maybe my lady will even join me."

"Perfect." She looked at the time. "Now I have to dash. Later," she said breezily as she scrambled out the office door before Savin could begin again.

"Sam, you look positively radiant!"

"Thanks, Celly, though I haven't felt very radiant during this last trimester. I can barely dress myself with this giant mass on my body, and don't even talk to me about my feet. I haven't seen them for at least two months. I had to wake Roberto up to put my heels on this morning."

Celeste laughed, picturing a disheveled, groggy Roberto scrambling on the floor to secure Sam's shoes. She hadn't realized it could be possible, but Sam's belly was even bigger than it had been at Savin's.

The two women were seated at Don Angie in the West Village and had ordered the signature lasagna dish for two, a glass of Champagne for Celeste and Perrier for Sam.

Sam was a white-collar defense lawyer who worked closely with Johnny to ensure Celeste and Savin were operating within the confines of the law and not drawing unnecessary attention to the firm's activities. Sam was extremely intelligent, beautiful, kind, a force of a woman. It was no mystery why Roberto was smitten. But despite his repeated attempts, Sam had refused his marriage proposals at least ten times, according to him. "I have no desire to be the fourth Mrs. Roberto Barbosa, thank you very much!" she'd announced over dinner one evening. But their love for each other was apparent. Celeste enjoyed both of them immensely and had never seen Roberto happier.

Though Sam had seemed uncomfortable getting situated in her seat, she now relaxed. "Well, enough about me," she said. "My conversations are now only about babies. Pregnancy this, motherhood that. Boring. I was so happy you and Theodore could get away for a bit after those tumultuous few months... well, you deserve a holiday. Anyway, tell me everything!" She regarded Celeste with the same cautious cheerfulness everyone did these days.

Tumultuous.

Celeste recounted their East African adventures and ended with "It was so nice to see Theodore in his element. Like a kid in a candy store."

Sam chimed in with questions about the food ("so fresh!"), the accommodations ("divine"), and safari ("the greatest adventure!"), then turned serious. "I'm so glad we got to catch up today without the guys, Celly. Roberto and I were recently discussing how much I missed girl time with you. But I wouldn't be a good friend if I didn't pry a little."

And here it is. What she came for.

"How are you managing... well, managing all of this? You walk through life with such poise and grace, but it... must be so hard."

Celeste plastered a smile on her face.

"Oh, that's an easy one! Meditation, lots of therapy, and—I can't stress this one enough—booze and Xanax," Celeste said. Sam smiled sympathetically but didn't laugh.

Celeste's therapist, Anne Marie, had repeatedly assured her, "The people in your life who love you will not think differently of you for your trauma," urging her, "Let them in." *But they do think differently of me.* She saw the pity because of what had happened and the guilt because they hadn't stopped it register on everyone's faces whenever Omar was mentioned.

OK, here goes nothing. "Honestly, it's been a bit difficult," she admitted to Sam. "On the best days, a big part of my coping is that

I've separated myself into two parts: the me I was before Theodore's dea—disappearance and Omar... capturing me and the me I became after. My life is so full now with Theodore, our friends, and D&C's success that I have little time to dwell on the past. That's not to say I haven't had my moments. On the worst days, I cried and shouted at Theodore and made him sleep on the sofa. Then I'd wake up screaming from nightmares because he wasn't beside me, and I'd go yell at him to join me back in bed. All in the same night."

Sam laughed. "In fairness, Theodore deserves a few nights locked out of your boudoir for what he did"—she stopped herself, seemed to weigh whether to proceed, then continued—"Roberto says it's not my place to say anything, but... if I were in your shoes, I'd be furious. I know I shouldn't meddle. But I can't imagine how lonely and alone you felt. I guess I want you to know I'm here is all."

"Thank you. Truly." Celeste was touched. "And believe me, I'm no stranger to being angry. I've been to hell and back, and the only thing I can think about is—"

Careful.

"The only thing I can think about is justice for our business associate who was murdered in Dubai and his young family, as well as for everyone else who has been discarded. There's been too much destruction already. And what I want, what I *really* want, is a time machine to go back to my old life."

Sam reached across the table, took Celeste's hands in hers, and squeezed softly. "What you did to protect us all... when I think of what you went through, not only the physical but the psychological injuries you've sustained... well, I'm not sure I would be sitting here right now if I'd been through the same. Please promise me that next time, you'll let us help. You don't have to take on saving the world by yourself."

Celeste was no fool. She *had* to handle Omar herself. Someone high up in the US government thought he was valuable enough to keep out of prison—which meant he was a danger not only to her but, more importantly, to everyone around her. She knew she would now go to any length necessary to end Omar. *Without hesitation.*

"It was always me he was after. I couldn't let anything happen to anyone else. No more casualties. Anyway, it's over now," Celeste assured Sam. She took a sip of her Prosecco for effect. "Oh! I have news! We've decided on a venue for our... party."

Sam squealed and clapped. "Oh, wow! You've started the wedding planning? When? Where? I need details!"

I knew that would get her. "Jack's letting us use his new toy, a breathtaking villa in Tuscany. It's perfect and remote enough to not be a media circus. We're aiming for May. And yes, your child can come, but a nanny is required."

The two laughed.

"Oh my God! This is so exciting. It's hard to imagine not being pregnant, but I'm happy to think of life on the other side of this big belly," Sam offered while the two women devoured what could only be characterized as the best lasagna on earth. "Béchamel in lasagna? Why didn't I think of that?" she commented. Then she straightened up and her expression turned somber again.

"Celeste, I—well, I came here to discuss something. Roberto didn't think I should say anything to you because of everything you've been through—the man is nothing if not opinionated, though it comes from a good place—but I disagree. You have a right to know, and so much has been kept from you already. It didn't feel right to keep you in the dark. I will understand if it... well, what I'm about to tell you may change your opinion of me. And it's totally deserved. But I hope that you won't write me off."

He seems to have a lot of opinions about me, but maybe Roberto's right. I really don't need any more information these days.

Sam swallowed and continued. "Do you recall when we met that I told you I practiced white-collar litigation?" Celeste nodded. "Well, that's true—sort of. And I'm sure you've figured out I have some sort of affiliation with the illuminati, though the extent may not be clear."

Celeste realized in that moment that she'd never actually thought about why the others had gotten involved. She was always singularly focused on Omar. If past was precedent, it had proven to be a poor strategy the last time around.

Maybe I should listen up. I might learn something that would help me.

"You see, I was very good, the best actually, at what I did—keeping rich men out of prison for insider trading, fraud, tax evasion, you know the deal. So good in fact that the SEC and FBI wanted me. Banana Republic Chet? It was literally he who knocked on my door and asked me to flip my loyalties and work for them."

Wow. That wasn't exactly what she'd expected to hear.

Sam seemed nervous. "You may recall the Walter Radcliffe scandal?"

Celeste remembered it well. "The billionaire involved in sex trade in India. Yeah, it was big news five or six years ago, right?"

Sam nodded vigorously, still on edge. "It... it was yours truly who kept him out of prison in an insider trading case." Sam's eyes teared up. "I knew I wasn't working for the good guys, Celeste, and I enjoyed the money I made. But on my honor, or what's left of it, I had no idea he was involved in anything beyond being a snake who always paid my fees in advance.

"I'll never forget how I felt that day, watching the news coverage and seeing the images of the rescued women and girls. Some of those girls were so young, Celeste. The look of terror and sadness in their eyes still haunts me. It was as though a mirror appeared to show me the type of person I'd become. I was repulsive, abhorrent, as much of a monster as he was because I helped create the system for men like him to thrive.

"And quite literally, the very day the story broke, Chet was knocking on my door, saying they needed me to help them get inside the minds of men like Walter—they needed me to help catch Walter and others like him. He said the sex trafficking charges would never stick, but he wanted to expand the RICO laws to treat certain financial institutions the same way the mob was treated—as criminal organizations. I probably would've agreed to anything he asked based on my self-loathing, so when it was merely to help Chet and his friends investigate financial fraud to provide evidence for their cases against guys like Walter, I said yes without hesitation." Sam stopped for a moment to take a sip of water.

Celeste furrowed her brow slightly, the closest thing to a frown her plastic surgeon Dr. Smythe's Botox regimen permitted. "But he was put away, right? I thought I remembered his office closing up shop?"

"His was an unusual case, and yes, he was put away. Luckily, New York State got him on trafficking, so he was sentenced to life without parole in Rikers. There's some satisfaction in knowing that men like him aren't treated well in prison, but I still wish I hadn't had a role in keeping him free for so long. Think of how many women's lives have been ruined because...because these guys chose the right lawyer." Sam paused and took a breath. Her face wore the shame Celeste was sure she'd been tormented with since Walter's story went public.

"So hopefully you can see why it hit so close to home that I, we, those of us in the background, didn't save you from Omar. We tried, we really did, but you were always one step ahead of us, and he was two steps ahead of you."

"Sam, none of this..." *It's not your fault.* But Celeste knew that wouldn't assuage Sam's guilt. "The world isn't black and white. Walter was a monster long before you represented him. As tempting as it is for you to feel responsible, you didn't know he was victimizing young women. And frankly, there's nothing you could've done to stop Omar. It was our own security guard who held the chloro—who drugged me. We could've never predicted that."

"Thanks, Celly. But I keep thinking it could've been Omar I kept free."

"Nonsense. You were Walter's lawyer, not his Ghislaine."

This can't be all. This was old news and something Celeste could have found out on her own if she'd tried.

"I was the original recruit, Celeste," Sam spit out, her relief from coming clean almost immediately visible. "But I needed you to know why."

Celeste's heart sank.

"The Feds formed the illuminati, if you can stand the terminology, because of me. They thought if they could turn me, there would be many others willing to change sides. In fact, that's how Roberto and I met. We were investigating him, and I approached him to see if he'd flip. His one condition was that any business with you and Savin be off-limits. So of course I had to meet the only two people in this world to whom Roberto had any loyalty. I remarked to him after I'd met the two of you at Savin's party last year that I completely understood the draw." Sam stopped and smiled apologetically.

"I knew you were a part of it, I suppose, but I haven't spent much time thinking about the origins of the illuminati," Celeste said. *Because I never wanted to be involved in the first place.* "So you joined forces with the Feds when? Five years ago?"

"Around that time, yes."

"Mark made a comment a while back that he'd been a part of it for over a year. Is everyone I know involved now?" *Is Theodore more involved than I've considered?*

Celeste reached down and slowly twisted her engagement ring around her finger several times. She did this often to remind herself that Theodore was alive. She wondered how much he knew of what was going on. *The sorts of things fiancés normally discuss on a monthlong vacation.* She recalled Theodore's recent comments and had to admit she was to blame that they didn't talk in more depth.

"Naturally, you and Savin were on my and Chet's radar because of your remarkable profit margin and your questionable media practices. We—Chet and I—were waiting for the right time to bring you in, and in the meantime, we'd crossed paths with Mark. Your friends know you well—they advised against discussing things with you and, by extension, Savin from the beginning. They said you'd refuse, wouldn't trust our intentions, and that Savin would take your lead. Of course, at that time, we could've never predicted Omar's moves and that your involvement would flow naturally from... from Riyadh. Anyway, I thought you should know, and I wanted to give you a chance to ask questions. In many ways, you're the only one who's made any progress with Omar."

Celeste let everything sink in. Maybe the woman with the answers had been right in front of her all along. She considered her most burning questions against the likelihood of Sam answering each of them and in light of the information Michel had passed along.

Who sold me out to Omar, and who continues to protect him? How did Alexsandr find me in Riyadh? And on and on and on. *No wonder I hardly sleep at night.*

"Did Theodore know what I was going through while he was... when he was away?" she asked.

Sam shook her head sadly. "Though I was the first one in our little alliance with the Feds, we each have our own arrangement. Theodore is a bit of a black box for us. I'm not even sure he has any involvement outside of being engaged to you and knowing your friends. So, unfortunately, only Theodore can help with that. He's never provided me or Roberto with a straight answer about—about anything."

"OK, how about an easier one? Who is Alexsandr, really?" A memory had resurfaced in Kenya last week. She remembered that she'd heard someone call Theodore "boss" on the boat—"Everything's all cleaned up down below, boss"—and again when she was in and out of consciousness in the Nice hospital.

"Well, at this point, I suppose it seems I'm fairly useless because I don't know much about him either," Sam said, laughing. "Celeste, I've seen the way Theodore looks at you. He loves you. He sees you. If not knowing the details surrounding his disappearance or his work is causing you angst, tell him. It will matter to him."

Celeste nodded and then motioned to the server for another round of drinks and their dessert. "The tiramisu here is. To. Die."

"I'll eat anything sweet these days! Regarding Alex," Sam offered, "I don't know much about him except that he got you safely to Cairo."

Celeste's mind raced. Nothing was as it seemed.

"OK, this is a lot to take in. Do you mind if we discuss something else?" she asked.

"Of course, darling," Sam replied.

On a whim, Celeste said, "I'm hardly the traditional bride, but this wedding thing is growing on me. It would mean the world to me if you'd be... well, like... be involved in the wedding. Like a bridesmaid." Celeste had never been asked to be a bridesmaid, not even when her brother married her sister-in-law. She wasn't sure of the protocol.

"Oh my gosh, Celly! I'd love nothing more than to be a part of celebrating you and Theodore."

Life hack—if I ever want to change the subject, I only have to bring up my wedding.

~

"CELESTE, I can't tell you how thrilled I am to be a part of your nuptials," her future mother-in-law said. "Having only a son who never seemed to have any interest in marrying until he met you, I never allowed myself to consider I'd have a daughter someday." She sipped her cappuccino.

Celeste laughed, always appreciative of Poppy's candor. "Well, as you'll see soon enough, I don't possess the bride gene, so I'll take all the help I can get."

Pastis was bustling with its usual weekend highbrow crowd. Celeste and Poppy were seated inside to beat the summer heat. After brunch, they were meeting Meredith to look at some of the dresses she had pulled for Celeste to try on. Celeste didn't understand the rush, but Meredith had told her it takes many months to perfect a couture gown.

"They're backordered for ages, Celly!" she'd explained, exasperated.

Celeste savored her eggs Benedict while Poppy told the story of her own wedding many years before. "Teddy and I were so young, so in love. He looked at me then with the same passion evident in Theodore's eyes when he sees you. Nowadays we're just an old married couple."

Poppy, with her raven coif, impeccable skin, and Dolce floral sheath dress, could've passed for a woman half her age. She and Teddy still played tennis three times a week, and she never missed her morning Pilates.

"Ours was the high-society wedding of the year in London, which was incredibly intimidating for me. I wasn't used to running in Teddy's family's circles, so I left much of the planning up to his mother—a mistake on my part because the entire venue was filled with wilted hydrangeas. I still shudder when I see one of those dreadful flowers. So I won't meddle too much, I promise. I'm absolutely thrilled to be a part of it, and that's enough for me."

If anyone actually knew what I was planning...

"I welcome your thoughts, Poppy. Truly. Meredith has lined up two or three of the best wedding planners specializing in Tuscany, but even with all the help, I'm afraid I'm forgetting something. I think the invitations are already overdue for a May wedding—here it is August, and we've only just decided on the venue. Speaking of, would you like to see photos?"

"Yes, of course! I love Italy in general, but there's something special about the countryside."

Celeste pulled out her iPad and opened the album with the villa photos. By the end, Poppy seemed as enamored with Jack's place as Celeste was. It was perfection.

"Wait until you see what Mere has planned. She even has a binder, which I guess is a standard bride thing?"

Celeste chatted on about the details, grateful for the distraction and Poppy's party-planning expertise.

After they finished their brunch, one of Monty's drivers dropped Celeste and Poppy off at an atelier. Meredith rushed toward them excitedly, grabbing a hand of each and practically dragging them into the elevator and then into the showroom. Her long, auburn hair was sleek and smooth, and she was always dressed impeccably. She had an enviable athletic figure from boxing and spinning. Celeste appreciated her attention to detail. Meredith's phone screen saver was something aspirational like "I will make everything beautiful. That will be my life." And Meredith did just that—she made everything beautiful and magical while maintaining an air of luxury and sophistication. Celeste knew she was in good hands.

"Celly, you are going to die—DIE—when you see these dresses.

There are ten altogether, and I'm trying to find a way for you to wear them all." Then Mere shrieked—an outside-volume shriek that made Celeste jump—when one of the designers wheeled out a rack with four dresses.

"Ooh, my favorite one is on that rack!" Mere turned to Poppy. "Should I tell her which one I LOVE? Or let her decide on her own? I don't want to influence her choice, but *ohmygodohmygod*, it's the most amazing dress I've ever seen."

Celeste rolled her eyes. "Mere, I already know which one you're talking about. You've been styling me for years—don't you think I've figured out how you like to dress me by now?"

She nodded to the designer, introduced herself and Poppy, and smiled apologetically.

"You'll have to excuse my friend. She's been like this ever since I asked her to head up the planning. It's going to be a long couple of months!" Even Meredith joined in the laughter.

"Make as much fun as you like, but I'm planning the wedding of the century—it's going to be *the* wedding to end all weddings, and then we'll see who's excited!" Meredith said, feigning hurt feelings.

And now for the fun part. As cynical as Celeste was about marriage, one of her favorite pastimes was finding precisely the right outfit for an occasion. Choosing the perfect dress for her wedding would be no different. She clutched the champagne-colored dress she intuited was Meredith's favorite (resulting in another shriek from Mere) and walked toward the fitting room.

"I can do it myself. Thanks, though," she said dismissively to the three women rushing to assist her.

Five minutes of maneuvering later, she could see why it was helpful to have an extra set of hands. *These dresses are no joke.* But even without it being zipped, she was floored. It was better than any gown she could have imagined. She admired herself from every angle in the mirrored room.

"Celly! Are you ready yet? I'm dying to see. Can't you come out now?" Mere urged from the showroom floor.

Celeste opened the dressing room curtain and sashayed into the middle of the room. She stepped onto the platform surrounded by mirrors. The room was still, and everyone stared at her blankly.

Crickets. "OK, at first glance, I thought this was the one," she said sheepishly, "but it's not getting the reactions I—"

Suddenly, Meredith let out an ear-piercing squeal and shouted, "The *most beautiful* bride in all of eternity!" She began jumping up and down.

Celeste's eyes widened in surprise, and then she burst out laughing. "Oh my God, I think you have literally destroyed my eardrums."

"Oh Celeste, oh my," Poppy said. The older woman walked over to Celeste and took her hands. "I've seen a lot of brides in my day, but never one quite as spectacular as you. I feel I may not be eloquent enough to describe how exquisitely beautiful you look in this dress."

Well, I guess they're in agreement. This is the dress. "My vote is also yes, so it's unanimous."

"No, Celly, it's a FUCK YES," Mere corrected.

"Theodore, darling, are you home?" Celeste called when she walked into her apartment. She slipped off her heels. Silence. "Babe, are you here?"

Poppy had dinner plans with a friend, and Meredith had a date, so Celeste had called it a night in the event Theodore made it home early. She wandered through the expansive apartment and then heard his voice coming from their bedroom. "I'll take care of it. Thanks for letting me know. No, I thought I was clear. I want to know everything where she's concerned. Everything. And next time don't wait so long."

Her heart started to beat faster as she heard him coming toward the door. She ran soundlessly into the living room and was draped on the sofa reading the latest issue of *Harvard Business Review* by the time he arrived.

"Hi, beautiful," Theodore said nonchalantly when he entered the room. He leaned over the back of the sofa, and their lips met for a passionate kiss.

"I just got off the phone with Mum. She's smitten with you. You're the daughter she never had, she said. Thank you so much for including her."

Celeste grinned widely through clenched teeth. *Your mom, my ass.* But she wouldn't let on that she'd heard him, at least not now. "It was my pleasure. She helped me narrow down a dress and gave me a lot of advice about flowers."

"Oh no, that means you've heard Mum go on and on about the hydrangeas, then," Theodore said, hanging his head in jest. "She'll never let Gram live that one down."

Celeste laughed. "Yes, I heard all about them. Luckily for everyone involved, I find hydrangeas to be beautiful, but they were not what I was eyeing for my own... wedding. Your mom is tied up with a dinner tonight. Date night?"

"Shall we check out the latest creations at Rakuen?" The maître d', Hiroto, was a close friend of the couple and would always find them a table, even now that the restaurant had joined the Michelin Guide's two-star ranks. Rakuen was where the two had had their first date, and they returned often.

"Perfect," Celeste said, smiling. "But how about we have dessert first?" she asked suggestively. She needed to silence her brain for a while.

"I thought you'd never ask." His hand caressed her neck and continued down to her breast, sending shivers of desire up her spine. Right as she was contemplating taking her clothes off, he hopped over the back of the couch, scooped her up, and carried her to their bedroom.

He laid her on the bed slowly, caressed her cheek, then her breasts. His hand made its way between her legs, and he rubbed her clit. When her breathing sped up, he removed her thong and began suckling her clit while sliding two fingers inside her. She reached for him.

"No, baby, I'm focused on you. You can please me later."

He rotated his wrist and massaged her G-spot with his index and middle fingers. Within moments, she was reeling. She gripped the down comforter as her body shuddered. She let out a moan. "Theo—oh, Theodore, you're so fucking amazing," she whispered, out of breath. Her body went slack, and she reveled in the feeling of her mind finally being quiet.

"That was exactly what I needed—thank you," Celeste purred, then kissed him hungrily.

"I'll fuck you all night long if you'll let me, honey. But now it's time to get to dinner," he whispered.

"I'm cashing in on that promise later tonight," she said and kissed him once more.

THREE HOURS LATER, the two were seated at their favorite corner table with a round of dirty martinis.

"I don't know what I did to deserve you, baby, but I hope we'll never be apart again," Theodore trailed off and sniffled.

Celeste felt the familiar pull. She wanted to comfort the man she loved, but... *Will I ever be able to forget the pain and betrayal of him leaving me?*

"I'm sorry, I don't mean to be dark. Mum got to me earlier after she saw you."

"I want to know everything where she's concerned," she recalled overhearing. She knew it wasn't Poppy. Theodore would never speak to his mother in that tone.

"Oh? What did she have to say?"

"Her usual motherly stuff. She's been asking a lot of questions about how you're doing."

Theodore's tone was nonchalant, but she knew this conversation was anything but. Everyone danced around questions about her well-being, these people who made up the mosaic of her life, afraid she would shut down and withdraw completely, and rightly so. She recognized what was happening, but there was no real way around it except through it.

"So what did you tell her?"

"I said I thought you were doing better."

"Better?" *Meaning I wasn't doing well before. And still not doing great.*

"Honey, she was asking because she cares. We all do."

"I'm fine. Anne Marie says I'm making tons of progress." *I mean, I haven't asked her, but that's what she'd say.*

"Well, the nightmares improving must be a good sign."

Their regular server, Mitch, walked up then with their first course. *Saved from this convo.*

"Celeste, Theodore, so great to have you back," he said. "Chef sent this out, prepared especially for you. He'll be out when he can get away to say hello." Mitch set their small plates in front of them with a flourish. "*Meshiagare*," he said, then walked away.

Celeste picked up her chopsticks. "This looks amazing!" she said excitedly. Slivers of raw scallops molded into flower petals surrounded artfully sliced asparagus, and a delicate vinaigrette completed the dish. She plucked a bite into her mouth and closed her eyes. "This is beyond, darling."

Theodore hadn't touched his chopsticks. He was frowning. "As I was saying, you're sleeping better."

The drama of the past couple of days was wearing on her. "Please, babe, Chef is preparing this beautiful meal for us. Can we not ruin it by talking about how it's noteworthy that I don't wake up screaming in the night like a child?"

"Anyone would have—"

"Please, it's embarrassing enough that you see, but the fact that your mother knows... is mortifying. I'm glad I didn't know earlier today, or I wouldn't have been able to face her."

"You've pushed off any talk of this for months. Can you stop treating me like a casual lover and let me in?" Tears welled in his eyes.

Oh, fuck. The guilt set in. *I'm an actual monster sometimes.*

"I'm sorry, OK? I haven't been sympathetic to how hard it must be for you to watch me suffer. But I don't think it's unreasonable to want to postpone this discussion until we aren't in a public place. Is that possible?"

Theodore muttered something under his breath about being together for a month straight but it was never the right time, then softened. "Yes, of course. But promise me we will talk... and soon."

"I promise." *Double fuck.*

The rest of the dinner went without incident. Part of her wanted to tell him everything, while the other part of her had no idea where to begin. Michel thought there was a rat among her friends, and the Shu debacle made that seem more likely. Theodore had someone keeping tabs on her. Nasrin knew something. And there were the Feds' ominous warnings. It was all distracting her from the one thing she actually cared about—stopping Omar before he got to Theodore.

Let's see if mi amor will show his hand. "I had some interesting meetings this week," she said airily.

Theodore furrowed his brow. "Really? What happened?"

"I can't go into too much detail, but we were ready to close on a deal, and the company backed out at the last minute. In real time. On the line with *us*, their executive team split, argued in front of us, then aligned on pulling out of the deal. I've seen some crazy shit, but this was beyond." *And my confidentiality agreement prohibits me from telling you the Feds forced us into the deal in the first fucking place.*

"Wow. How do you feel about it?"

"Disappointed." *Half true.* "We had a good feeling about it. It would've been a strategic addition to our portfolio."

"Do you think it can be salvaged, or is it a done deal?"

"Eh, I doubt it can be fixed at this point. But the whole thing was so odd... it felt very... suspect. Like someone knew our play ahead of time. But what troubles me is I can't fathom anyone on our team being a double agent. Only a couple of people were involved."

"Strange. I can't imagine anyone on D&C's team sabotaging a deal."

"Yeah. And the *why* is what really gets me." She sighed. "Nothing we can solve tonight, I suppose. How was Zurich?"

"Baby, you would've loved the tub at the Baur au Lac. We'll have to stay there next time. I'd love to have my way with you in every inch of their Presidential Suite." He recounted his meal at The Restaurant, his favorite dinner spot in Switzerland. "A five-course amuse-bouche. Imagine!"

"Sounds yummy."

"Nothing exciting. Walked along the water. Missed you. Other than the hydrangea discussion, did you, Mum, and Mere make any progress?"

"Didn't Poppy tell you? I found my dress! Well, I guess Mere found it, but I have a dress, there will be fittings, and I can get back to work." She laughed and continued. "I had no idea when I said yes to you how much work a wedding was. Though who can blame me? No one could say no to this ring."

She held up her hand, moving it around so the light caught the impeccable diamond, and for once didn't think back to how she'd felt the first time she saw it. At eight carats, cushion cut, and perfect clarity, it was a showstopper.

Theodore laughed heartily. The corners of his eyes crinkled, and he'd never looked more handsome. "A beautiful ring for a beautiful woman," he said and kissed her tenderly.

Sleep didn't come for Celeste that night, even after two martinis and a bottle of sake. *I have work to do anyway.*

When she was certain Theodore was asleep, Celeste crept out of bed and went into her office. Angelo had tracked down Hadid in Riyadh and had sent her his contact information. It was midmorning in Saudi Arabia. She grabbed one of her burner phones from the locked drawer and texted Hadid. It wouldn't hurt to see a friendly face (if he still was after what she'd pulled) on her upcoming trip. After some time researching, she stumbled on the right business opportunity to justify visiting the UAE. She'd duped Savin a couple of times before, but he wouldn't fall for a fake business trip again.

Maybe I should bring him with? It wasn't a terrible idea, but it could cause some complications. He had known Zari. She could hardly sneak past him to meet with Nasrin. There was also the possibility that Theodore would want to join her, and then what? Two chaperones?

It wasn't hard to track down Nasrin. She had a high-profile position at a telecommunications firm, and she was still based in Dubai. She had no social media presence, but Celeste was able to track down some photos of her and her children. Once she had a rough plan of how she'd arrange the trip, she logged off her VPN (a must after Ace's hacking) and went to bed.

I need some answers soon.

5

———

"WE ARE GETTING MARRIED, MOTHERFUCKER!"

On Monday morning, Celeste and Savin were seated in their war room. They'd outfitted it when they first began working with Ace ("You can never be too careful," Ace had warned) and only rarely invited others in.

"I canceled my morning so we'd have time for a proper catch-up," she said. "What should we do about this Shu issue? Are the Feds going to tell us what happened? How has this worked in the past?"

"Honestly, we've never had anything blow up like this," Savin said. "Ace will have some intel."

Celeste rolled her eyes. "I didn't realize Ace was going to filter everything when I agreed to this insanity."

"Celly, Ace saved your life. Your harebrained Riyadh plan would've gotten you killed if Ace hadn't sent Alexsandr to rescue you."

"Bullshit," Celeste retorted. "I arranged for my own safety. Ace's intervention is what nearly cost me my life and definitely... probably cost so many others theirs." *It cost Zari his—one of Omar's many casualties.*

As she'd hoped, Savin dropped it and suggested they hold off on discussing the Shu deal further until they heard from Ace. She decided it was time to spring the Dubai trip on him.

"We have a significant business opportunity with a fund in Dubai. It's time for us to make an acquisition. You and I should meet with them on their turf, tell them why they need us."

The look on Savin's face suggested he was unconvinced.

"If we're going to go to the next level, we need to seize more business development opportunities and not wait for the Feds to bring things to us."

"I feel a pitch coming on," Savin said, smiling.

"We need to take meetings in the Middle East. And what's happened to our European stronghold? No more excuses—it's time to ramp up. We can check out our Paris operation too."

Savin's head jerked back to make eye contact. "Are you... sure?" he asked.

"Of course I'm sure."

She launched into a long motivational monologue about the next phase of D&C, knowing full well she could get Savin to agree to nearly anything if she spoke long enough.

"OK, OK, I get it. You're ready. I'm in. Honestly, it feels like you're back for the first time in a long time, and I'm here for it." He grinned mischievously. "But let's make these trips quick. I'll miss my lady."

"Great! I'll arrange everything. We'll leave next week."

CELESTE SPENT the next couple of days getting everything in order. Thanks to Angelo tracking down Hadid so quickly, she had been able to arrange a clandestine meeting in Paris with him. Savin would never suspect anything related to Zari there.

Dina, Celeste's chef and a celebrity in her own right thanks to Celeste's investment in her business, was bustling around in the kitchen on Friday night when Celeste got home from working out. Theodore would arrive back from a day trip to Philadelphia in an hour or so. She'd asked Dina to prepare one of their favorites—

mouthwatering braised short rib with roasted vegetables and a lemon sorbet for dessert. Tonight she'd tell Theodore about her trip. She only hoped he'd be unable to join. Breaking free from him *and* Savin would prove difficult.

She wandered into her bedroom closet, touching the beautiful fabrics of the couture she'd acquired over the years. To her, the clothes represented the life and image she'd so carefully curated. She was a disruptor, a changemaker, a trendsetter—the epitome of the modern woman. Not someone who followed orders from some poorly dressed bureaucrats, floundering around and caught off guard in the middle of a deal because someone in her trusted circle had tipped their hand. And then there was Omar. She'd had enough of looking over her shoulder.

It was time. Time to hunt him down, find out who he was working for, and destroy all of them. But there was something else nagging at her—Sam's words about the young girls in Walter's trafficking ring. "The look of terror and sadness in their eyes still haunts me," she'd said. Celeste had rewatched the footage of the rescue the other night, and it had shaken her to her core. Yes, she'd had to withstand Omar's abuse more than once. But she was an adult, and she had resources at her disposal. These were children brutally victimized by men and women who treated them like commodities. She was fed up with all of it. These monsters thinking they were above punishment.

Why stop with Omar?

"Celly, your phone's been ringing off the hook," she heard Dina call from the other room. "Could be important."

Savin's hysteria, I'm sure.

An unknown caller. *202. DC. Ignore, ignore, igno—unless this could prove useful.*

"Celeste Donovan," she greeted the person on the other end.

"Mizz Donovan, Gabriel Gutiérrez here." He pronounced "miss" as "mizz."

It's like he's trying to make me hate him, she thought as she walked into her office and closed the door for privacy.

"Who tipped off the Shu team, Mizz—?"

"Please call me Celeste. We were told to go all in with the deal and that that's what you guys wanted. Despite our significant hesitations with the deal, we obliged. And then chaos erupted. So I'd ask you the same thing. What the fuck happened?" She was unable to keep the snarkiness out of her tone.

"Mizz Donovan, I assure you I have no idea who wrecked the deal. It was one of our last chances to find out who was behind a terrorist attack close to one of the US military bases in China."

Celeste laughed. "You do realize Shu is a tech company, not one of your doomsday arms dealers, right? A few guys who launched a good idea many years back. They consistently deliver. Perhaps they weren't even involved." Even as she said it, she knew this wasn't true.

"These aren't good guys. I've been watching you long enough to know you're very thorough, and you surely would've caught the abnormalities in their financials. You know they're laundering and probably involved in a host of other crimes as well," Gabe countered.

"I don't know anything except that it's the weekend and my fiancé will be home soon for dinner. Was there something specific you wanted, Gabe, or did you call to shoot the shit?"

"I know you found out about Omar."

Hedging, Celeste asked, "Found out?"

"You have to trust me that there's a reason behind it. And keep it to yourself. The others don't know."

Click.

"Has anyone seen my beautiful future wife?" Theodore called from the foyer.

Gabe knows I know.

"Yes, darling, in here. I'll be right out."

DINA HAD PREPARED A FEAST. The table was beautifully set with their good china, usually reserved for dinner parties, and Theodore poured them red wine from a decanter. Celeste was suddenly starving.

"Smells delicious!" Celeste commented as Dina walked past her with the serving platter and then went back to the kitchen to retrieve the other dishes.

"Hi, my darling," Celeste said to Theodore. She kissed him on the cheek before sitting down across from him.

The two recapped their week for each other, Celeste leaving out most of what had actually happened. After a glass of wine and some sustenance, she was ready to spring the news.

"Sav and I have some business to explore next week, babe." *Please don't make a thing of this, darling.* "That means we're going to Europe and Dubai for a couple of days."

"Oh, wow." Theodore's expression was thoughtful, likely weighing the best reaction to her returning to places where she'd experienced so much pain. "It's... so, it sounds like you're ready for this. Not that I'm... surprised. You've made so much progress lately."

Progress. Such a sexy term to hear your lover use. His clinical assessment of her mental well-being made her feel all sorts of ways.

"Yes, it's time to get back out in the world," she said brightly, hiding her annoyance. "I haven't visited my Paris apartment for months."

After the breach in security at her pied-à-terre the previous year, everyone seemed to think it would be too triggering for her to return. She avoided the conversations altogether by traveling to other places. But the time for hiding out was over.

"I'm only disappointed the trip is a little too early for Fashion Week next month."

"If it goes well this time, we could stop over for a few shows before or after Copenhagen. But only if you're up for it."

Celeste's face reddened. "Theodore, fuck!" she shouted, then remembered Dina was still hanging around the kitchen. She lowered her voice. "I'm not a delicate flower. I can handle being back in my own apartment."

He would usually back off when she was this angry, but tonight he seemed particularly hell-bent on pushing the issue. The two had a whispered heated discussion until Dina said loudly from the kitchen,

"Everything is cleaned up. I'll see you next week." She was gone quickly after.

When Celeste was sure Dina had left, she said, "I won't have it, Theodore! Why must you bring up what happened with Omar in every fucking conversation? I thought we were past this months ago, but you won't let up since we've been back."

"You're shutting me out. I can feel it."

"You're bugging the shit out of me! Something bad happened. We don't need to discuss it every day." A meddling Theodore could wreck everything.

I need to shut this shit down now, right fucking now.

"I've lost my appetite. I'll see you in bed." She stormed out of the room and slammed the bedroom door. She grabbed her burner phone from her locked drawer in the closet.

Five missed calls from Michel. He never called her; the risk of being overheard was too great.

She shot off a text: "What? What do you want?"

His reply contained another meeting spot and time.

Six a.m.? Ugh.

"Fine," she texted.

Exhaustion set in and she fell fast asleep. She didn't stir when Theodore came to bed later.

"A LITTLE BALLSY meeting in my 'hood, isn't it?" Celeste said as she sat down on a bench next to Michel in Abingdon Square Park the next morning. As far as she could tell, she hadn't been followed on the quick walk over from the shady sublevel apartment she used to store supplies and change into Mia. She paid cash for the apartment, and it had no cameras or concierge staff to monitor her coming and going. She'd stopped by there to pick up a SIM card. She changed it often and also used a phone number scrambler—all in an attempt to stay under the radar.

But does anything ever really go undetected in New York?

Celeste had spent months researching surveillance systems before venturing out as Mia. Cameras were on every corner, part of the fabric of large cities. She'd trained herself to look away from the cameras and learned techniques to blend in, with a nondescript walk and no distinguishing characteristics or accessories—that is, unless she wanted to be seen.

To understand more fully what she was up against, she had decided to learn from an expert. She had tracked down Petey, an expert in counterterrorism programs after 9/11, shortly after his retirement from NYPD. Starting a friendship with him could fast-track her learning and help her identify more ways to successfully dodge law enforcement. When she told Michel about her idea, her friend had Petey followed to get a sense of his routines. Celeste learned that he hung out every Tuesday at a dive bar in his neighborhood. One night, disguised as Mia, she began chatting him up.

Petey was a first-generation Irish American who loved his city and his job. He took great pride in all he had achieved, and in retirement —lost without his work—he found joy in retelling stories from his old beat to anyone who would listen. Fully embracing the role of Mia, Celeste became the attentive audience he craved, and as she had hoped, Petey inadvertently revealed tricks of the trade that would've otherwise been difficult for her to find out about as a civilian.

He schooled her on how reliant law enforcement had become on facial recognition technology and that FRT made it possible to detect anyone nearly anywhere in the world at any given time. While she recognized that FRT could endanger her life if someone ever released the footage from Riyadh to the Saudi government, she appreciated that, in the future, there might be opportunities for her to mitigate its threats and harness FRT to her advantage.

Yes, Petey was proving to be quite useful. She couldn't tell him, though, that it wasn't a surprise to her that someone was always lurking, always watching. The photos people took of her and sent to her as threats served as proof of that. Well, they could watch her all they wanted as long as they didn't figure out her game plan.

Sitting with Michel now, she took in the sun peeking over the buildings to the east, casting a warm glow over the park. She marveled aloud that she loved early mornings, when the world was still quiet, yet a new day had begun.

"I know about the Shu deal," Michel interrupted.

"Don't bury the lede. I know you didn't leave the comforts of the Four Seasons to discuss Shu. But since we're on the topic—what does it mean?"

Michel took a sip of his bodega coffee, a pensive look on his face, then asked, "What do you know about Fred Warren?"

"We have a complicated past. But at the end of the day, I think he has a conscience." She remembered the lengths Fred had gone to when he found out Omar was after her. "Why?"

"I can't find the leak. I'm not sure who's been compromised."

"So there's no rat? Then what happened with Shu?"

"Must've gotten spooked, I suppose."

"Bullshit. What did your sources find out?"

"Nada. But you're right, that's not what I came to discuss. Thought you'd like to know in real time—he's back and is apparently not worried about showing his face."

"Who? Back where?" But she knew who. Omar had resurfaced for the first time since Theodore shot him.

Michel raised an eyebrow.

"So he's alive and well then. Made it out unscathed. Protected by the US government. Brilliant," she said. "When do you think he'll show up? He won't be able to stay away for much longer; he'll want to take credit for"—she gestured vaguely to the expansive garden—"all the chaos he's caused."

"Probably planning a run-in with you soon. He was spotted in Zurich a few days ago."

Theodore. Her heart sank as she thought about how many things could have gone wrong if Omar and her fiancé had crossed paths in Zurich. "Wow, Omar has donkey-sized balls." The complications that could arise with Omar out in the open were difficult to assess. "I'll be traveling next week. What if he does show up? Should we expedite the plan? Will we be ready?"

"You're right to worry, but it's too risky to move the timeline this significantly. We need months, not days, to pull this off." Michel stood up. "I'll keep digging. Be careful on your trip."

He left without a backward glance.

She shot off a text to Angelo, then made her way to her and Theodore's favorite coffee shop. A croissant and cappuccino run was the perfect cover for her early morning absence.

Celeste roused Theodore from sleep twenty minutes later. "I brought you your favorite," she said. "Let me know when you're up." Theodore peeked out of one eye, then closed it again.

"Way too bright in here," he said, pretending to fall back asleep.

"I thought we could talk before I go to the gym."

Theodore stretched through his fingers and toes, then hopped out of bed. "I wasn't sure you'd want to. Wait, hang on..." He walked to the closet and looked inside. "Aha! My things are still here hanging up and not out on the front lawn, so that's a good sign."

She laughed, shaking her head.

"I'm going to take a quick shower to wake up. I'll be right out."

She took the opportunity to go to her office and review her most important file, a digital grid formatted like a prosecutor's suspect wall or murder board, her beloved road map containing all the unusual, suspicious, and criminal things that had happened lately and the people she believed to be involved—now with the lens that Omar was likely following both her and Theodore. *Maybe it was Omar who sent the photo after all?* But with whom was he working? Someone in her circle? Surely not.

Theodore came in minutes later, looking handsome in a light-blue cashmere sweater that brought out the blue in his eyes and black jeans.

He kissed her on the cheek, then sat in the chair opposite her.

"I didn't get to sleep until you left this morning," he said softly. "I had a lot of time to think about what you said, and I'm truly sorry."

He raked his hands through his hair and sighed. "I'm sorry for probing so much yesterday... and over the past few months. I'm sorry that there are things I haven't been able to let go."

He sniffled. "I... I want to understand what's going on. I... something... something has changed recently. I'm afraid I'm losing you." He blinked quickly to hold back tears.

"Losing me? No, no, of course you're not losing me, babe." She softened. "I need you, but I also need you to let me navigate through this at my own pace. I know you were trying to be empathetic about going to Paris, but I need you to trust me when I say I'm ready. It makes me..."

Tell him, Celeste.

"It makes me feel like you don't think I'm your equal when you say things like 'But only if you're up for it.' I go to therapy twice a week, for fuck's sake. Surely at this point I can appropriately evaluate what I'm ready and not ready to do."

Theodore nodded. "Fair enough. Look, baby, if I'd known... well, I didn't realize that I was making you feel small, weak. In fact, you're the strongest person I know. All I want is to be the best fiancé and soon husband to you that I can. What's the best way I can support you through this? I'll do whatever you need, baby."

Twenty years of therapy to be able to say "It makes me feel..." one time and here you are with the perfect response. How about you could make it less apparent that I hog all the crazy in our relationship?

"It's... give me some time to feel everything out. I'm excited to go back to my apartment, and I'm excited for our new business opportunities in the Middle East. I had a lovely time with Poppy. I'm back in shape. I feel like I'm bouncing back. So please let me navigate this and trust that I'll let you know if I need your help." *And let me handle things on my own.*

"I'll agree to that if you'll let me in a little more. I sleep next to you, Celeste. I hear your nightmares night after night. You've never even really told me about them. Why do you only let me share laughter with you and not any of the pain? Do you not really trust me? Do you not want to share a life with me? Do you think that I'm too weak to handle it?"

Tears welled in Celeste's eyes. "No, I... it's not that at all. I don't want to... to burden you with my shit."

Theodore's eyes bulged. "*Burden* me? I *caused* your fucking pain. I didn't get there quick enough to stop what that monster did to you. I fucked everything up. And my penance is a hell loop—I have to watch you suffer day after day, night after night, with the pain that resulted from my fucked-up judgment, and the icing on the fucking cake is that you won't let me support you through any of it." He threw his hands up, then put his head in his hands and sighed. "I don't deserve you. Point-blank. I have no business marrying you after what I've put you through."

"Wait, what?" she shouted. "Oh, that's fucking rich! You're going to dump me now? After all this? No, we are getting married, mother-fucker! Now there's a dress and invitations, and I never would've even wanted to get married in the first place if I hadn't met you. But now I love you too much to lose you, and I can't imagine surviving life without you again, so you are stuck with me FOREVER!" At once she realized the absurdity of her reaction but refused to acknowledge it.

At least I didn't throw anything at his head this time. Baby steps.

Theodore acquiesced. "Of course I still want to spend my life with you, baby. The only one who would be calling off the wedding is you. What I meant was that I don't feel like I deserve you, and I feel so much guilt and regret because I am to blame for so much." He walked over and pulled her to her feet. He embraced her.

She inhaled his scent. It was then that she realized home wasn't an apartment or a city. Theodore was her home, her family, and she wouldn't let Omar or anyone destroy it.

"I don't blame you. For any of it, OK?" She considered her words. "Well, that's not entirely true. I'm still pissed beyond words that you didn't tell me what was going on. And that you left me. And that they all—" *Heard me falling apart every day.* "And that my pain was on display like I was a circus animal.

"But ultimately, it was Omar's actions that caused most of my suffering. I can recognize in my best moments that you did what you thought was best for me, for us, at the time. In my lesser moments, it's much harder to wrestle with.

"As for my nightmares... it's... I haven't shared a lot because on some level, I'm worried that if I talk about them, give them airtime, they'll come true."

"It kills me to watch you tossing and turning," Theodore said tenderly. "I feel completely helpless."

At Celeste's request, they moved out to the living room and situated themselves comfortably on the vast sofa.

Celeste began to describe the nightmares and how much pain it caused her to watch the scene over and over again—Theodore's broken body, Omar cracking his skull. The recurring dream of Omar, not Theodore, waiting for her at the altar. How violently each of the dreams ended, waking time after time with the same feelings of loss, fear, anger.

"Oh, honey, I'm so sorry. I can't imagine how awful I would feel, having to see the same visuals of you over and over. My poor baby."

After a bit more discussion, Celeste was spent. "Babe, look, I'm glad we talked," she said. "I don't want you to feel shut out. And now I need a good workout to clear my head. Can we continue this conversation later? This has all been a lot."

"Of course, darling. I'll be around when you get back."

She changed into her athleisure and walked back out into the living room. Theodore was still in the same spot where she'd left him.

"I'll be back in a bit," she said and kissed him on the lips.

"Enjoy, honey."

On a hunch, she stopped and turned around. "Babe, did anything unusual happen while you were in Zurich?" she asked, attempting a nonchalant tone.

"Hmm, not that I can think of," he replied and turned back to his phone.

"OK. Gotta run. Love you!"

～

Celeste had to remain focused, patient, stable. It hadn't been easy sharing so much with Theodore. Yet she knew it was necessary to assuage his growing concern with her suffering. She knew his concern was genuine, could feel his love for her. *But there is such a thing as too much honesty in a relationship.*

She was close, so close. The timer on the elliptical read forty-five minutes in, and still she hadn't decided whether to expedite her plan. She didn't want to rush anything—yet how realistic was it to think she could protect everyone from Omar now that he had free rein? It was safe to assume that Omar would be consumed with plotting. She thought back to the volumes of photos he'd had taken of her over the course of a decade before he pounced. He would be patient, biding his time. His revenge would be symbolic and catastrophic.

She had to flip the script. While she may not know why Omar was now protected, she still knew *him* better than anyone else did. No one could get under his skin the way she could. Now she had to use that valuable knowledge to her advantage.

"You have to trust me that there's a reason behind it. And keep it to yourself. The others don't know," she recalled Gabe had said.

Fuck you, Gabe. He'd had months—months—to make some progress. Instead, he and Chet had pivoted to another shiny object. *Nope, this is not how this is going to be.* The plan needed a little tweaking, but it wouldn't be difficult to set in motion. In fact, she could begin the very next day. She would need to find someone to replace Ace.

6

———

"IT'S A TRAP"

"I must say, you've done an excellent job with the design of the Paris office," Savin remarked. "And doing the hiring from New York—well done!"

The two were eating lunch in La Cour Jardin at the Plaza Athénée. It was a balmy September afternoon, and the courtyard was stunning with ivy spanning the entire facade of the building and red accents all around. It was one of Celeste's favorite spots in Paris. Though Celeste had offered up one of the many guest bedrooms in her palatial pied-à-terre, Savin had insisted on staying here. Not that she could blame him. She loved the balcony views of the Eiffel Tower aglow at night, though she'd never admit that to anyone local. The French snobbery was over the top.

Celeste took a sip of her martini. "It was a nice little project to keep me busy." She'd had a ruse going for a while about the D&C satellite office the previous year, but once she'd recovered, she'd thrown herself into making the Paris outpost a reality. Savin completely deferred to her on decision-making, so the process had been quite smooth.

"Look at the time," Savin commented.

"Yes, yes, I saw your new Patek, Sav," Celeste said, laughing. He was forever in search of the perfect vintage watch, and this one was his latest prize. *Probably dropped a high six figures on that.*

"No, it's not that. I actually do need to go."

Celeste narrowed her eyes. He was usually so needy on their trips. "Go where?"

"I have... an appointment. With a tailor... for a... new suit."

She rolled her eyes. "You have more clothes than I do, and that's saying a lot."

"I'll call you in a bit." He threw a $50 bill on the table and was off before she could comment.

Can't I have one normal man in my life? She pulled out her iPad Pro. *At least one of us has a solid work ethic.*

It was 2 p.m. She was set to meet Hadid around 6, close to his hotel, and had decided it was safer if she showed up as Mia. The logistics of the digital age made everything much more complicated. She could assume that Omar had someone on her now, and Ace, the Feds, any number of people were watching. Michel and Petey had each helped her learn the art of blending in, and her practice was paying off because they hadn't found any hits of Mia's face since her alter ego was created.

Hadid had proven quite useful again. He'd found someone in the deep underground of the dark web who was willing to help Celeste track down Omar via the software databases. Hadid said it may even be possible for her to find out what Theodore had been up to in Zurich and whether he and Omar had crossed paths. She didn't like spying on her love, but something about his response the other night was nagging at her. If she'd learned one thing over the past year, it was to listen to her gut.

Well, she'd also learned how to street fight with someone much bigger than her and how to land a bullet between someone's eyebrows, thanks to her trainer, Zed, former Special Forces marine and an eighth-degree black belt. "The subconscious mind picks up on cues that you can otherwise miss," Zed always told her. Or, rather, lectured Mia. He'd agreed to anonymity and had never once asked for her real identity.

After responding to some high-priority emails, she called Lorraine, who answered on the first ring. "Hi, Celeste."

"Hi there. I need your help on something. Do you have a minute?"

"Of course. What do you need?"

"Can you ask Ace to find out everything possible about Shu's CFO? Everything. I want to know where he spends his holidays and his dogs' names. Tell Rani I said you can use my office. I'll need this by close of business today New York time." *That'll keep Ace distracted for hours.*

"Sure thing. But Rani isn't here today. Said she wasn't feeling well."

"OK. Have her assistant let you in. Talk to you later."

It went without saying that Lorraine would keep this request to herself. Lorraine had learned how to manage sensitive information and required very little direction at this point. She was still the D&C associate Celeste trusted the most.

IT WAS NEARLY DARK, the massive Arc de Triomphe looming large and backlit by the setting sun. There was minimal traffic on the roundabout and along the usually bustling Champs-Élysées. Celeste hid in the shadows along Rue de Tilsitt and watched for Hadid. Her heartbeat drummed in her ears as the different scenarios in which this clandestine meeting could go south played over and over in her head. Michel had urged her to send someone else or to use a more traditional method like chalk marks on a mailbox.

"It's not 1964, for Chrissakes," she'd protested. She thought these hands-off information exchanges removed a critical piece of the puzzle upon which she relied—the intelligence gathered by being in someone's presence. Darting eyes, shortness of breath, shaking hands, calm facade—all were clues as to a person's trustworthiness, and in that moment, she needed to see what Hadid was up to.

Michel was right. Trust no one.

It would be jarring to see Hadid. He looked almost identical to

Omar, which was why she'd hired him for the Riyadh operation in the first place, despite his being Egyptian and Omar being Brazilian. She had so many questions for him, but this wasn't the time nor the place. She needed information—and fast.

Her pocket vibrated. *Fuck.* She'd forgotten to leave her iPhone at her apartment, guaranteeing someone now knew where she was. She worried that the phone screen would illuminate her face and give away her location if anyone were watching. She shoved her hand in her pocket and held the side buttons down to power it off. But the damage had been done. It was time to go.

Come on, Hadid!

At last, she saw him approaching their agreed spot from the Avenue de la Grande Armée on the other side of the Arc. She adjusted her ball cap to ensure her face was fully concealed. The Glock was warm against the small of her back, held in place with a secure strap.

Just in case.

She was about a hundred yards away from him, using her peripheral vision to spot whether they had company, when something caught her eye: light reflecting off an object on the rooftop of a nearby building. She squinted to make out what was up there. It was—

Oh, fuck.

Someone was up there. She could make out the frame but couldn't tell if it was a man or a woman. The lights from the street below were reflecting off glass. *The scope of a sniper rifle.* Her blood turned ice cold. She knew from her research that a rifle scope worked much like a telescope, allowing a shooter to zoom in on a subject so that it appears closer for accurate aim at long ranges. The sniper seemed unaware she was close by, focused on the spot where Hadid would be in mere seconds.

Seeing Zari only minutes after he'd been murdered was the worst moment of her life. Was tonight going to end the same way? She felt frozen in place. Her burner vibrated then with a text. She glanced at the phone.

"It's a trap."

There it was in type from an unknown number. The verification she needed to get the fuck out of there before whatever was going to happen unfolded. She shoved the phone back into her jacket pocket.

Go!

It was a balmy night, perfect for a run, and she had dressed the part in a matching magenta jog set and white sneakers. Building up speed, she changed course when she realized she couldn't go to her apartment as Mia. Fueled by her racing thoughts, she crossed the miles quickly, flying past the Place Vendôme and Angelina toward Le Marais, praying she was not being followed. She listened for footsteps following her, took unpredictable paths, and kept her head down.

Silence.

She turned a corner and ran smack into a woman. The impact nearly knocked both of them to the ground. Celeste's eyes bulged with recognition. *Rani?* It took only a brief moment to confirm it was indeed her.

After both women had recovered, Rani gave Celeste a dirty look and scolded, "Watch where you're going," then continued walking. A quick exchange between two strangers, one inconvenienced by the collision, the other in disbelief that her disguise was able to conceal her identity from even those closest to her.

There was no time to ponder whether Rani had recognized her. Celeste kept running as fast as she could until she finally reached her hideout. She ran into the building and took the stairs two at a time until she reached the third floor (really the fourth floor in France, which drove her crazy). No neighbors in sight. Once inside the apartment, she ran straight to the bathroom, making it to the toilet just in time for the vomit to project out of her mouth. She heaved for several minutes until there was nothing left to throw up.

Was Hadid the one who had texted her? Or had he been hurt—or worse—because of her? Had another life been taken, another person who'd been helping her carelessly tossed aside? She turned on the shower faucet and stripped out of her workout clothes, then sat on the floor with her head in her arms. She waited until the room filled with steam and then immersed her body into the scalding shower.

Truthfully, she felt spared, relieved, fleeting emotions before the guilt set in. Hadid was once again working to help her, and she'd put him in an enormous amount of danger, possibly cost him his life. She did not recognize the number that had warned her, and she knew better than to text Hadid directly because someone could intercept her text or trace her location.

She needed to get out of there. She dried off and transformed back into herself, putting on a pair of jeans and heels and rushing through the application of what little makeup she had there.

She packed a handbag, then locked up the apartment. The landlord had confirmed before she moved in that there were no cameras in the building or on the street immediately outside. She could only hope that she remained anonymous coming and going, but to be safe, she walked in the shadows for several blocks before hopping into a cab. She spoke to her driver in French and paid him in cash when he pulled in front of the Tour Montparnasse, the second-tallest skyscraper in Paris and home to one of her favorite lounges, Le Ciel de Paris. She had frequented the place often enough the prior year. The staff would recall her presence if she ever needed an alibi for that evening.

Only when she was settled at the bar with a glass of wine did she dare to return Theodore's five missed FaceTime calls. He answered on the first ring.

"Hi, darling," she said.

"Hi, sweetheart," Theodore replied, the smile in his voice softening her.

"Sorry I couldn't talk earlier. I was... out for a run. I'm at Le Ciel as we speak but wanted to give you a quick call before dinner. How are things back in the city?"

Theodore babbled on about his day. Celeste nodded and inserted "Mm-hmm, really?" and "Wow, that's incredible!" when appropriate. She didn't process a word he said.

"Wait, are you out alone?"

"Yes. Savin said he had some sort of appointment. I don't know, he's been more bizarre than usual lately. Oh, and get this. When I was run—" She caught herself. "Er, I love Paris in the fall. It was so beautiful along the Seine tonight."

There was so much she couldn't say, so much she wanted to share but knew she could not.

Her first course arrived, so she was able to excuse herself before she spilled all the secrets she harbored.

"Baby, dinner's here. I'll text you good night when I get back to my place."

"OK, dear. Be safe. Love you."

"Of course, darling. Love you too. Bye."

She was nauseous again thinking of what might have happened earlier. Her nerves were frazzled, and eating was a challenge. Her burner phone vibrated repeatedly in her bag, but she would have to wait to look at it until she was back home.

I need the one thing I don't have—information. Is Hadid OK? Does Michel know what happened? How will I get the information Hadid promised me? She ate her meal in silence, only nodding when the staff asked her questions. When she was ready to go, she signaled to the bartender to close her tab. He dropped off the receipt and her card.

"I'll take care of this one," came a man's voice from behind her.

She turned and was inches away from a familiar face. *Antoine.* Shortly before she met Theodore, she and Antoine had had a brief tryst. He was still quite the heartthrob, but Celeste no longer felt a sexual pull toward other men.

"Long time, no see, mademoiselle!" he exclaimed. They exchanged the obligatory cheek kisses.

"You've changed restaurants," she observed.

"Yes, yes. How could I say no to this view?" He gestured grandly at the dining room. "What's new?" Then he moved his head in closer to hers and lowered his voice. "I'd love to see you later tonight."

Celeste was taken aback. She realized it was the first time a man had openly hit on her since Theodore's return.

"I, uh, well... I do have news. I'm engaged. To be married. I'm a fiancée!" She held up her hand with the ring as though he'd need proof.

He looked around. "Yet you dine alone?"

"He's back home in New York and... well... I'm not free tonight to see you. Or any night anymore. Sorry."

Antoine stepped back a bit to create more space between them. "I'd still like to take care of your dinner."

Celeste refused, insisting it was unnecessary. *Need the credit card swipe so anyone who is monitoring me knows I was here tonight.*

He shrugged. "It's no problem. If you ever change your mind, you know where to find me." He gave her a light kiss on the cheek and walked away.

She signed the receipt and left the restaurant via the express elevators to the ground floor. She caught a taxi waiting outside and gave her address.

Back at her apartment, she read and reread the two texts she'd received that evening on her burner. "You were the target," the first one read, taunting her from an unknown number, a faceless sender. "You're lucky to be alive," the second one said.

She laughed ironically. *How could I have been so arrogant?* Hopping into an unmarked taxi? Frequenting a hot spot? Wandering around freely as if she were going to save everyone from some of the world's most depraved souls, moving around safe and undetected?

Idiot.

It had not even crossed her mind that she was the mark, the preordained victim of a sharpshooter who'd gone to great lengths to remain concealed.

"WHAT DO you think about having Brett spend some time in the Paris office?" Savin asked. "It's not a terrible idea to have our teams integrated."

They were sitting at a café the following morning, and Celeste was trying to act like nothing was awry. But truthfully, she didn't give a shit if Brett or any of them took off for good. She had almost been killed the night before, and she still hadn't heard from Hadid. Was it time to pull the plug on her Dubai trip? *Am I playing with fire?*

"Hmm, maybe. We still haven't spoken with him about his Shu analysis. What if Lorraine hadn't done her own research? What if we'd gone into that meeting blind?"

Not that it would've fucking mattered, since Gabe and Clit call the shots now.

"Yeah. You're not wrong. Who else could we send?"

"I don't know... maybe one of the quants," Celeste replied noncommittally.

"What's going on with you lately? Trouble in paradise?"

"With Theodore? No, of course not. Simply a bit distracted with the wedding, and I'd really like for us to secure this acquisition in Dubai. I'm getting antsy, and now that the Feds are going to be making decisions for us... well, I still want our own deals, our own successes. Don't you?"

"That's a good point. Yes, I'd like to maintain some independence."

"We've said we wanted to build an empire. Now's the time to expand. I can feel it."

"I've always trusted your instincts, Celly, and I'm not about to stop now. But what should we do about our people in this office? They need some direction, some inspiration."

"Well, we are in Paris. Let's take them out for a night on the town, starting with a pep talk at one of Paris's premier hot spots. I'll have Mere work with her contacts to find something wonderful."

The opening of the Paris office had been a ruse when Celeste was hunting Omar the previous year. Someone in her circle had found her doppelgänger, and the woman had been regularly seen going in and out of Celeste's Paris apartment and office space to cover for her while she was away. She knew the woman had been paid handsomely, but Celeste hadn't given her much thought until this trip. Who was she? Did she do this sort of thing—impersonate—all the time? Was she a regular woman who just happened to be Celeste's height and frame? Or was she in the intelligence industry? Celeste could ask Ace, maybe even Savin. But she feared that revealing she was doing any digging around would raise suspicion.

Back to the present, Celeste. Since her return, she was vested in making the Paris office a success. She'd built it into something she was proud of—and had done it remotely. *Tonight will be a nice distraction.*

She messaged Meredith regarding the group dinner and turned her attention back to Savin. They finished their breakfast and cappuccino, then made their way to the office. The D&C staff meetings in New York began promptly at 8 a.m. She'd learned that no matter how committed and hardworking the Paris staff was, they'd never arrive to work before 10:30 or 11:00 a.m. *The only thing I've seen Parisians on time for is a boozy lunch.*

Still no word from Hadid. Or Michel for that matter, though she hadn't involved him much in this trip.

Eight of their Paris team members were seated with Savin and Celeste around the table in a private room at Restaurant Guy Savoy, a Michelin three-star delight. The last thing she wanted was to mingle with subordinates, but she knew Sav was right—they needed to stay connected to the teams if they were committed to growth. She stood and lightly clinked her spoon against her Champagne flute. Everyone turned her way.

"Our Parisian D&C outpost was merely a dream for Savin and me two years ago. Paris is like a second home to both of us, and we knew it was the perfect place for our first foray into expanding D&C..." She droned on, barely hearing the words she said, but everyone clapped, some even cheering, when she said, "Now let's make some money!" She concluded, "Seriously, though, please know we value your commitment, your best-in-class expertise, and strategic minds. *Santé.*" Everyone clinked glasses, smiling broadly.

The excited energy carried them throughout dinner, and Celeste had to admit she was enjoying herself and the team.

Finally, she and Savin were the last ones remaining. They'd sent the others out with instructions to use their expense accounts. Celeste imagined that meant they'd indulge in a night of dancing to cheesy French pop music.

"That wasn't so bad, was it? I think they may have even been inspired by your babbling," Savin joked.

"Hey, fuck off. I am an inspiration to those who know me and even to those who don't," she countered.

"Well, all kidding aside, it was great, and I really love the team. Maybe my girlfriend slash roommate and I will spend more time here. It is quite the romantic vibe."

"Paris for romance? Groundbreaking," she said.

"Speaking of roman—er, well, it's time for me to call it a night. Need to call the lady and see how the moving is going."

I'd love to have a few minutes to FaceTime with Theodore as well—before I get back to scheming. "You're brave to let her move in while you're away. I micromanaged the shit out of Theodore's move. It's a wonder he still likes me after everything I've put him through."

"It *is* a mystery why he's stuck around this long."

They both laughed, gathering their things and walking toward the exit.

"So we leave the day after tomorrow for Dubai? That's the plan?" Savin asked.

"Yeah, we'll need to leave a bit early—is seven OK?—to arrive in the afternoon. That'll give us time to get settled before our dinner."

Savin's secret iPhone vibrated then.

"See you for breakfast tomorrow," he said, suddenly in a rush after reading his texts. "You have a car, right? I'm going to walk and enjoy the evening."

And just like that, she was pulled back to reality. *You were the target last night.* There would be no leisurely strolls home for her. *More like bulletproof windows.*

After the kidnapping the year before, their head of security felt it best to sever ties with everyone on the D&C Paris security team, including Raoul, their longtime driver. *Better safe than sorry.* "Uh, yes, yes, there's my car. Angelo's always so great about finding me a driver."

Savin looked down at her four-inch pumps and laughed. "Of course, you won't be walking far in those."

"No one will ever take me out of my heels. Ever!"

"Night," he said and waved over his shoulder, walking in the direction of his hotel.

Her driver pulled up the car and hopped out to open the back door for her. *What if it's another trap? No, it wouldn't happen twice.* But she was frozen in place.

"Angelo sent me. He said I'm to escort you up to your apartment." The driver was a large man with a buzz cut and an American accent.

She felt her phone vibrating in her bag. After digging it out, she checked her messages. Angelo had sent the man's physical description and license plate number, telling her, "He's one of my guys, an ex-marine flown out to take care of you until you leave for Dubai."

Celeste exhaled, and suddenly she could walk toward the waiting car.

She needed contact with Michel to see if he knew anything about the events of the previous evening and who had warned her. She shot off a text to that effect and then sent a good-night text to her fiancé.

It's going to be a long night. The list of people she planned to take down was growing, but she wasn't pleased that there was an unknown enemy lurking. Who specifically had tried to kill her?

7

"STILETTO TO THE NUTSACK"

They arrived in Dubai in the late afternoon via the private terminal. Sav was still unaware that anything was awry under the surface, his obliviousness a gift. Once they were settled in the black car delivering them to the Burj Al Arab, he chatted on about their dinner reservation at At.mosphere and after-party plans for the evening.

"Wait, this is the first time you've been to Dubai since... well, since..."

Since I saw Zari's body only moments after he'd been killed? "Yes, it's the first time. I'm fine, don't worry."

Savin shrugged and then turned to his phone. He broke out into a huge grin.

"You have a second burner phone now?" she asked when she noticed it was not one of his usual iPhones.

"Uh, it's for football. Better to watch football."

Celeste frowned. "When are you going to tell me what's really going on with you?"

"OK, fine. I brought up the possibility of getting engaged with my lady friend, and she said she'd consider it."

"That's... great, but... what happened to taking it slowly?"

"Trust me. This time it's for real."

"OK. So is it time to meet her?"

He shifted uncomfortably in his seat. "Soon."

CELESTE LOCKED the security chain on the suite door, then set out to get things organized for the next day. As Hadid had promised before she'd left New York, a bag was there for her in the closet with instructions. Regardless of what had happened in Paris, the plan was already in motion for the meeting with Nasrin. So she would show up and hope that it wasn't some sort of trap. She still hadn't heard from him.

The details were scant. She would enter the Dubai Mall as herself at 10 a.m. There she would change into an abaya and headscarf in the women's restroom on the second floor, third stall. A handler would give her further instructions.

After the bag for the next day was ready, she changed into the plush hotel robe and set out to unpack. The opulent Presidential Suite had panoramic views of the city below and floor-to-ceiling windows. Sunlight splashed across the king-size bed, which was adorned with an ornate gold headboard and a matching mirror on the ceiling. The bathroom was an array of jewel tones, blues and reds, with more gold accents everywhere. The enormous tub with jets beckoned her, and she resolved to relax there after dinner. The dressing room had an oversized boudoir where she hung her clothes.

She reminisced about simpler times when her travels were effortless, when the butler staff professionally unpacked for her and would fulfill her every whim. It was a stark contrast to now, when she always left a Do Not Disturb sign on the door and double-locked the room. She'd had to be insistent that she did not want service staff in a hotel like the Burj, known for its immaculate service, but it would've raised too much suspicion with Sav if she'd booked them in a Marriott.

The itinerary was to stay in Dubai for three days, with a business dinner on the first night, the second day free (Savin had bought her story that her hairstylist was in town), and then business the third day. She hoped things would unfold as planned.

She looked at her watch. An hour until dinner. It was morning in New York. She opened her laptop and sat on the bed to FaceTime Theodore.

He answered on the first ring, their living room in the background. "Darling, hello," he said easily. "How're you? How's East Las Vegas?"

She smiled. "Hi, my love." She paused to take in his face. *Such a nice face.* "Dubai is just like I left it. Shiny and robotic."

"And how's Savin?"

"His usual weird self. We're having dinner with some colleagues tonight at At.mosphere. I'm aiming to expand our footprint in the Middle East and hoping we can find the right team for this." She divulged the pitch she'd been selling Savin on, explaining that their presence in London, Paris, and São Paulo was meaningful, but expansion was how they would maintain their best-in-class numbers. *Sometimes even I believe my own bullshit.* "Anyway, enough work talk. How're you?"

"Lost without you, honey. I ordered Indochine for dinner last night, and I'm having leftovers for breakfast."

Celeste laughed at the thought. "I'm sure Dina would happily prepare something for you."

"I'm not too blue blood for leftovers, my dear."

"Suit yourself."

"I thought about you when I woke up today," he said in a low voice.

"Mm, I'd like to hear about that. Wait, hang on a sec." Celeste put the phone down and retrieved her vibrator and lube out of her suitcase. "OK, tell me more," she said, returning to the opulent bed, showing her toy to Theodore, and turning it on. He unzipped his pants and held his already erect cock.

The two exchanged their intimate talk that made the vast distance between them seem not quite so far. They'd gotten their virtual sex down to a science with all the travel they were both required to do.

Celeste came first, and Theodore followed shortly after. They were both grinning widely while they carried their devices to their respective bathrooms.

"That was so nice," Celeste said. She propped the phone up so Theodore could see her disrobe. "I miss you."

"Yes, you've been gone for quite a while. And by the way, you're getting me hard again, baby," he said.

"I know, it feels like forever since we've been together, and it's only been like ten days." She glanced at the time. She was to meet Savin in the lobby in twenty minutes. "Shoot, I really need to run, babe."

"I love you, honey."

"I love you, too."

Celeste rinsed off in the luxurious shower and quickly toweled dry. Within minutes, she freshened up her makeup, packed her Bottega Veneta clutch, and dressed in a simple black sheath dress paired with magenta Amina Muaddi crystal-embellished heels. She completed the look with an ivory pashmina wrapped loosely around her shoulders. Satisfied, she dashed out the door and walked up to Sav at the hotel bar at 8 p.m. on the dot.

"Well, you're on time. A first for everything, I suppose."

"Fuck off," she replied, laughing.

"The restaurant isn't far, so we have time for one more," Savin said. He was holding a rocks glass of what looked like a Manhattan. "I'll have another, and the lady will have the same," he told the bartender. He turned back to Celeste. "So who is it exactly that we're meeting tonight?"

She explained that they were meeting with the managing partners of a wildly successful Dubai hedge fund, TA Capital. Celeste planned to lure them away from a potential deal, a merger with another firm. What she didn't say was that she didn't care much about the business opportunity; she needed this deal for reasons she could hardly explain to Savin. He couldn't keep a secret to save his life, and she could not risk the illuminati catching wind of her plans. He bought her explanation.

"How's Theodore?"

"Says he's lost without me. You Englishmen and your flair for drama." She did hate being away from him. "Though it does feel like we've been gone for a month," she added.

"I hear that. I can't wait to get back to my lady."

THE VIEWS at At.mosphere lived up to the hype, situated on the 122nd floor of the world's tallest building, the Burj Khalifa. The illuminated city was the perfect setting for the delightful culinary experience, which included an extensive caviar selection and tasting menu. Celeste and Savin were joined by their three guests: the CEO and portfolio manager (PM) of the fund, Tarek Abdullah, a UAE native; the CFO, Kaya Botha from Johannesburg; and the COO, Matthew Duncan from Edinburgh.

The conversation was light at first, vague references to the state of the world. But Kaya quickly shifted gears. Celeste learned they were similar—both women had little tolerance for bullshit.

"Candidly, we took this meeting out of curiosity, but we're committed to moving forward as planned, absent something from which we cannot walk away," Kaya remarked, then sipped her Champagne. She was elegantly dressed, tall and slender, with coveted cheekbones and ageless skin. Behind her beauty was a shrewd businesswoman. Celeste had the impression the other woman was skeptical of her motives, which was fair since they were entirely suspect. She knew Kaya's game: Kaya was pushing for a big deal, an offer to which Tarek couldn't, wouldn't say no, that would position her as next in command. She wore her ambition like she wore her three carat diamond studs—well, but loudly.

Celeste and Savin complemented each other well in business scenarios. She provided the framework for the deal: "We're willing to buy out all the AUM, and you can keep your positions at the firm, the investor relationships. We want to strengthen your presence here in Dubai and provide a foundation for our satellite presence. We have no intention of interfering with the way you operate."

Savin swooped in then in his usual fashion to massage it around the edges. Celeste could read a room—it was clear that Tarek, Kaya, and Matthew were a united front and definitely not interested in the deal. Assets under management, or AUM, were a PM's greatest pride. A typical PM had much too big of an ego to ever agree to the deal she had proposed. Celeste was undeterred.

"Enough business talk for now. Let's enjoy. It's been quite a while since I've been out and about in Dubai," Celeste said lightly. Tarek would need to be blindsided for her plan to work. *All in good time.*

Tarek played the part of a pious man well—a devout husband and loving father of four, who kept a room at the office for his five daily calls to prayer and drank water at dinner while the rest of the table indulged. He wore a dishdasha, the traditional white robe worn by Islamic men in the Gulf, and a headscarf tied with a black cord. Soft-spoken and mild-mannered, he was the perfect foil to Matthew, a hard-drinking Scot with the pink flush of alcoholism-induced rosacea tinging his cheeks and tales of sex workers and hard drugs as table talk.

Matthew, Savin, and Kaya were talking golf. But Celeste was laser focused on Tarek.

She turned to him. "Not much of a golfer, huh?" she inquired.

"No, no. The last time I attempted to play, it was a tournament, and I swung too hard. My golf stick ended up flying through the air and nearly hitting a colleague. It was—how do you say?—humiliating."

She laughed along with him. "Yes, humiliating is a good way to put it. I'm not into golf either. But that—and at a tournament, nonetheless—that must've been a real stiletto to the nutsack, huh?"

Tarek's eyes widened. Celeste knew it was considered offensive in his culture for a man and woman who were not married to each other to be conversing directly, let alone about genitals, but that wasn't the source of his alarm. She could almost see the wheels turning in his mind, evaluating. He recovered.

"It was very embarrassing, yes." He turned his head so it was closer to hers and lowered his voice so that only she could hear. "I've watched you for years and have always found you to be sharp, savvy. What I can't figure out is why you're here. You know I'd never agree to this."

Celeste looked at him thoughtfully. "I'm optimistic that you'll change your mind—and very soon. Have breakfast with me tomorrow." She paused for effect. "We can speak a little more... freely." She stood up then. "If you'll excuse me, I need to take a trip to the ladies' room."

As she was leaving the table, Savin shot her a quizzical look that said, "I know you're up to something, but I haven't yet figured out what it is."

Tarek seemed intrigued—and nervous. Celeste was confident he'd have breakfast with her the next morning. He thought she knew something, so he had no choice.

She used the restroom and freshened her lip gloss, then returned to the dining room.

Savin was regaling the table with a tale of deep-sea fishing from his last Dubai trip, where he'd caught a midsized shark. "I was terrified the big guy was going to bite off my arm! I was shouting for the captain to come over and help while the line was running out of control."

Celeste had heard the story at least seven times, and the shark got bigger with every telling. Now it was a great white shark over twenty feet long. When she'd first heard the story, the shark was vegetarian and ten feet long. *My best friend can be an idiot sometimes.* She could hardly be upset, however, because Savin had successfully kept the conversation away from her acquisition proposal. She was anxious to get back to her room, so she was glad when Kaya suggested, and the others agreed, to skip digestifs and call it a night.

Once the check was settled, everyone stood up together to walk out. Tarek hung back a little to speak with Celeste while the others headed toward the door.

"What time and where shall we meet for breakfast?" he asked.

"Eight thirty a.m. at Starbucks in the Dubai Mall."

Perfect. Their meeting would place her at the mall, and there would be plenty of video footage.

When they were settled in the car that was waiting to take them back to the Burj, Savin asked, "Are you going to tell me what's going on?"

"Let me work my magic. You'll see," Celeste replied nonchalantly.

She looked over to see him juggling his multiple devices again.

"You're still doing a spa day tomorrow, right?" he asked.

"Yeah, a spa day and then a hair appointment."

The driver stopped in front of their hotel. They walked in together and agreed to talk the next afternoon, then went to their rooms.

The following morning, Celeste awoke with the sun. She visited the hotel gym for a vigorous workout and took care to dress in her most modest work clothes, cream slacks and a lightweight taupe blouse. She threw a patterned pastel headscarf over the top of her head and around her neck and added large Cartier aviators.

She had prearranged a car to take her to the mall and arrived right on time. Starbucks was on the first floor, and Tarek was already seated. She approached and when she arrived at the table, she sat across from him, removed her sunglasses, and pulled her headscarf down around her neck.

"Morning. What can I get for you?" she inquired.

"Hello. I don't drink coffee from"—he looked around with disdain—"places like this."

She imagined him sipping $500-per-pound kopi luwak in his garish Italian marble condo and laughed. "One bottle of water coming up." She went to the counter, ordered her tea and his water, and paid with her credit card.

Back at the table, she took a sip of her tea and observed Tarek's body language. He was trying to appear smug, but she sensed his nervousness.

"I'll get to the point. I want this acquisition. And I want it wrapped up by tomorrow. You keep your position as PM, you call the shots; for all intents and purposes, you'll remain completely independent of D&C. We'll throw in some extra cash for you to sweeten the deal."

"Why, exactly, do you think I would agree to this? You've brought me to this *American*," he said with a sneer, "coffee joint, only to insult me once again with this"—he paused, searching for the word—"bullshit offer."

Celeste went in for the kill. She pulled a folder out of her bag, opened it, and placed a stapled document in front of him. He flipped through the pages, giving them a cursory glance.

"My business is clean, and I'm not in any financial bind, Cele—" Tarek's eyes bulged as he looked more closely at the document. He glanced around suspiciously to see if others were watching.

"How is Mistress these days? Seems like you've been a naughty boy."

Tarek was angry but also assessing how lightly he should tread. Outwardly, he kept his temper in check, but Celeste noted the shallow breathing.

"Don't worry; no one besides me knows about this. Well, no one besides me, you, your Domme, and one of my very discreet friends."

It hadn't been difficult to find some leverage on Tarek. He was a finsub, a financial submissive, and had entered into a Dom/sub relationship with a financial dominatrix. Celeste's quick research a few nights earlier had revealed that a financial domination relationship was similar to a sexual BDSM relationship. A finsub sent monetary tributes to their FinDomme in exchange for being humiliated or degraded. The FinDomme controlled the sub through their wallet.

"Imagine how quickly something like this could spread. Front page, above the fold of the *Financial Times*. Or better yet, the *Journal*. Investor panic. Hemorrhaging of assets. And your family's reaction when they find out you're a sub, wiring Mistress money several times a week when she demands it. We haven't had a scandal of this magnitude for a—"

"What do you want? What the fuck do you—?" He took a deep breath.

Celeste smiled widely, her dimples pronounced. "Look, I have no interest in outing you. I could give two shits about what gets your dick hard. I told you what I want. The acquisition, clean and simple. Well, that and two more small things."

He shot her a withering look.

"I want a hacker of my choice to have full access to everything Matthew is involved in, his phone, his laptop, every transaction originated by him or for him, and I want your word—perhaps you could swear on the lives of your beautiful wife and your lovely children—that you'll never share my request or the fact that he's being monitored with anyone. Ever.

"You'll keep him on once the acquisition is final, but I'll be gathering data to set him up to be put behind bars. When the time comes, TA Capital won't take the fall for his... shall we call them misdealings... and in fact, you'll be heralded as the PM who does business honorably and by the book. Or... there's the alternative. You'll live the rest of your life in disgrace when it's revealed that the image you've conveyed to the world is only part of the story and that your sexual appetite for submission clouds your judgment. I didn't scour the records, but my rough math was that almost one hundred million dollars was sent to Mistress over the course of a year. Not what I'd call shrewd money management, but who am I to judge. The choice is yours."

"How did you even get access—"

"Mistress's firewall was easy to hack into when you've got my resources. I can assure you I will take all of this to my grave if we can come to an agreement."

Tarek swallowed as he absorbed everything he was hearing. It wasn't long before he realized he'd been beaten. "Even if I agreed to these terms, how do you expect me to overcome Kaya's and Matthew's objections? They'll go to the board."

"I've seen their contracts. And yours. You have enough control, and if they make any threats, you'll have your counsel remind them that they'll lose everything if they cross you. They're both too power hungry and greedy to risk that. Any other burning questions?" She glanced at the time. *Nine twenty-seven. Time to wrap this up.*

"What's the interest in Matthew? What's your angle?"

"All you need to know is that he's a monster, and I've decided the world needs fewer monsters."

Tarek shrugged. "Fair enough. I've always hated that mother-fucker anyway. I assume you've had the contract drawn up?"

"It's already in your inbox. Run it by your attorneys, and let's close this thing by end of day."

Celeste began gathering her things and adjusted the scarf to cover her head. "I have to run, but you'll be happy to know that someone anonymously alerted Mistress to her vulnerabilities for breach, and they've been remedied. So your secret is safe. Make the right choice —for all of us."

Tarek knew he was defeated, but he seemed OK with it. "I'll be in touch later today."

Blackmail is very efficient. "It's been a pleasure doing business with you, Tarek."

CELESTE TOOK the long way through the mall to the meeting place in the ladies' restroom, exactly as Michel had coached her. She walked past the Dubai Aquarium and the stores beckoning tourists to come in and take advantage of the favorable dirham exchange rate. She even stopped to browse at a few of the kiosks. Then promptly at 10 a.m., she entered the bathroom on the second floor and went to the third stall.

Celeste knew she was in the right place when the door opened and she was face-to-face with a woman who looked nearly identical to Celeste.

It's her.

Celeste quickly went into the stall. Hadid was right—the resem-blance was uncanny. The only discernible difference was their eye color, and even that had been resolved. In the close space, Celeste could see that the woman had light eyes and was wearing brown contacts to match Celeste's eye color. The woman's hair was pulled up in a blonde ponytail, just like Celeste's had been.

Wordlessly, Celeste stripped down and handed the woman each piece of clothing she'd been wearing. The woman changed into Celeste's clothes and added her headscarf and sunnies. Even under the closest scrutiny, no CCTV viewer would ever be able to tell the difference between the "Celeste" who would leave the bathroom and the real Celeste who had entered. The two women had even been careful not to wear jewelry or anything else distinguishing that might be a giveaway.

While Celeste dressed in the T-shirt and long, flowy skirt she'd brought to wear under the traditional black abaya, the woman switched out their handbags. Celeste noticed she was even wearing the same nail polish color, Celeste's signature nude pink, and the Stuart Weitzman strappy sandals Celeste had paired with the outfit. Clearly she'd done her homework. *No wonder no one noticed I was gone when she was traipsing around Paris as me.*

Hadid had proposed to let this woman sub for Celeste in Riyadh the previous year. When all was said and done, Celeste didn't regret having handled it herself, but meeting the woman now, she was quite confident her double could've pulled it off. Celeste had so many questions, but now was not the time to get them answered.

Celeste slipped off her heels and changed into the nondescript sneakers she'd brought. The woman helped her drape the traditional hijab over her hair and adjusted it to cover Celeste's nose and lips.

The woman held up her iPhone for Celeste to read what had been typed into Notes. Celeste was to wait in the stall until 10:15 a.m. A man would be waiting outside the ladies' room for her and would escort her to a car. His photo was attached. The driver would advise her of the next steps. The woman deleted the note from her phone so Celeste could see, then nodded and left the stall. She would spend the day as Celeste Donovan at a spa while Celeste moved around undetected.

The entire exchange of one woman transforming into and the other transforming out of being Celeste had taken only a couple of minutes.

Simple enough.

AT 10:15 on the dot, Celeste exited the stall. There were two Emirati women in the restroom speaking easily to each other in Arabic. They did not look twice at Celeste as she washed her hands and adjusted her hijab. Her blonde hair was completely concealed. She walked out of the bathroom and immediately saw the man waiting for her. He smiled broadly as though they were familiar. She guessed he and her doppelgänger had entered the mall under the guise they were together. She smiled as she would if it were Theodore waiting for her. They began walking through the mall toward one of the parking lots, while he spoke in Arabic. From the outside, they looked like an Emirati couple enjoying a shopping trip.

They arrived at a black Audi A8 with opaque windows. The man opened the back passenger side door for Celeste. Once she was settled, he slid into the front passenger seat.

Click.

The driver, dressed in plain black clothes and with a full head of dark hair and a dark beard, locked the doors and then turned around to look at her. He wore a scowl on his face. She held his gaze and watched in shock as his hand whipped from his lap. She squeezed her eyes shut and braced herself for a blow.

Instead of his hand on her face, she felt cold steel pressing against her forehead.

Was this a trap after all? Only two people knew about this little rendezvous—Hadid and Michel—and they didn't know each other. Hadid had coordinated with Nasrin and had assured Celeste that her movements would be undetectable under a variety of different safeguards.

It's a bit late for cold feet.

She took a deep breath and slowly opened her eyes. The man's forefinger was steady on the trigger of the .45 caliber pistol, and his facial expression read that he would not hesitate to pull it.

Celeste kept as still as possible, moving only her mouth. "Nice piece. Would you mind telling me what this is all about?" she asked, sounding calmer than she felt.

"Do you have any idea how much danger you've put Zari's wife, my sister Nasrin, in just by being here?" the man roared. "Haven't her children lost enough? Will you not be happy until she's stoned to death for treason? Zari's death should be left in the past, yet here you are trying to dig him up. Do you even know who you're messing with? Or are you the arrogant American who thinks of no one but herself?"

Oh. Hadid hadn't mentioned that her handler for the day was a grieving family member.

No one moved for several seconds. Celeste's senses were heightened. She could hear his breathing—steady, even. His colleague in the passenger seat was more agitated, tapping his foot against the floorboard and taking rapid breaths.

Maybe he's seen his friend kill before. Her heart pounded in her chest.

"I assume you have no intention of killing me, at least not yet, or you would've already pulled the trigger. So would you mind putting that thing away?"

He frowned deeply but pulled the gun back to his lap.

The guy who'd escorted her from the mall spoke up then. "We're taking a little road trip. Nasrin refused to meet in Dubai. Too many eyes around."

These men did not like nor trust her, and her instincts told her Michel would urge her to get out of there. But she was so close to getting some answers and wanted to meet Nasrin. She also doubted they'd let her go at this point even if she demanded.

"OK. Is there any other information you can give me?"

"No," growled the driver. He put the car into gear and began navigating through the parking garage.

Celeste sighed. She didn't want to press the issue. They hadn't blindfolded her or taken her phones, so it wouldn't be hard to track where they were going.

Wait. She'd been so distracted with changing into the disguise that she hadn't watched the swap. She dug around in her look-alike's handbag, and to her dismay, neither of her phones was there. *Goddammit.*

She kept her face neutral. Two sets of eyes studied her in the car's mirrors while they made their way through the midday traffic.

The two men spoke quietly in Arabic while Celeste's mind raced. *Has Hadid been compromised? Will Michel know how to track me? Did my twin intentionally take my phones? Yes, of course it was intentional, Celeste,* she scolded herself. How had she not noticed? She sighed again. *Nothing I can do now except watch this play out.*

It wasn't the first time she'd traveled through the Middle East. She recalled when Alexsandr had driven her through the desert from Saudi Arabia to Jordan a lifetime ago. At that point, she'd still believed Theodore to be dead and had witnessed Alex killing two men handily. The men were soldiers and certainly would've captured her, if not worse. But it had been a bit disconcerting to watch how easily Alex could dispose of another human life.

Zari. Poor Nasrin. The driver was right. Celeste had been selfish when she'd planned this trip. She'd been laser focused on what Nasrin could do for her, excited to have a lead from Zari's texts, but now she could see that his widow would want answers of her own. Celeste looked down in shame. She knew all too well what Nasrin was going through, and yet she'd been blinded by her own self-centered motives.

I'll make this right. She'd find out who killed Zari. If Nasrin was willing to go to such lengths to meet with her, the least she could do was give the grieving widow information to move on. She turned her attention to the city whizzing by. They were now on a highway.

"This is the way to Abu Dhabi, no?"

"Yes," the driver responded reluctantly.

"I'm... look, I'm so sorry for your loss. Zari was an exceptional man, and he didn't deserve to die any more than Nasrin deserved to be widowed."

"If you hadn't been nosing around, he'd still be here today."

Fair. How many times had she told herself the very same thing? "Maybe you're right. And for my role in all that, I'm truly sorry."

"Tell that to my niece and nephew when they ask where their father is," he snarled.

"Go easy on her, bro," the other man muttered under his breath. Celeste had to strain to hear him over the blast of the air-conditioning. "She didn't know. She still doesn't."

The driver shrugged.

What the fuck don't I know?

They sat in silence for the next forty-five minutes.

"Nasrin insisted on a public place. You'll meet at the Louvre. There's a café there where you can speak freely."

NASRIN'S FACE broke into a wide grin when she saw Celeste walking toward the museum entrance. The building was a combination of traditional Arabic and modern architecture and housed some of the world's most coveted art. Under normal circumstances, Celeste would've relished having a day to browse the collection, but today was meant for other things. She looked around out of habit to see if anyone was following her, but she knew anyone watching her would be a professional at hiding in plain sight.

"Habibti!" Nasrin greeted Celeste with an Arabic term of endearment. "I feel like we've known each other forever," she exclaimed as she embraced Celeste affectionately. "It's so nice to finally meet you." Celeste had nearly forgotten her concealed identity when Nasrin added, "Perhaps next time you'll be able to wear some of your fabulous clothes. Zari always remarked how fashionable you are."

Nasrin had a distinctive scent, embodying luxury and femininity at once. Everything about her oozed sophistication and culture, seeming much more mature than her thirty-one years. She was stunning, with olive skin, long dark hair, and doe eyes, just like the photos Zari had shown Celeste. She wore a pleated multicolor maxi skirt, orange silk blouse, matching headscarf, and gold wedge heels.

"Have you been here before?"

"No, I haven't, but I'm dying to see the Versailles exhibit."

"I figured we could browse and talk. This space is an oft-overlooked treasure in my country. I come here one afternoon a month to immerse myself. It's become the perfect place to clear my head. And less likely to have a tail than in Dubai," she added in a hushed voice.

They walked through the lobby, and Nasrin paid their ticket fare using Emirati Dirham. She led Celeste through the early civilizations exhibits on the ground floor.

"Zari and I came here together several times before he died. We had two date nights a week, devoting the rest of the evenings to our kids. They're the sweetest—a bit too young to appreciate all this, though," she said, gesturing to the artifacts. "Shah is six going on seventeen. He reminds me so much of Zari. And Samar—she isn't even four yet but is quite the handful. I never thought I could love anyone more than Zari, but a mother's love—well, there's nothing like it."

"Zari always made sure Savin and I saw the latest photos of you and the kids"—Celeste paused, searching for words—"I was going to reach out, but things... got a bit complicated in my life for a while, and then so much time passed that I... well, I didn't know exactly what to say or how to say it."

Nasrin frowned, and instead of responding, she glossed over Celeste's apology and continued talking about her children, proudly sharing their accomplishments ("Shah is quite the soccer player" and "Samar is the smartest in her class and wants to be a doctor!"), while they browsed the exhibits for the next half hour.

"I've had enough art for today. What do you say we go to the café? We can sit outside, have a drink. The water is beautiful, although the cranes from the construction are an eyesore," Nasrin remarked.

Celeste nodded affirmatively. "That would be lovely."

"YOU CAME ALL this way to speak with me. There must be an important reason. What is it that you would like to discuss?"

Celeste pulled her headscarf down a bit to sip her green juice, then put it back in place. Nasrin's brother's scolding had hit hard earlier. Suddenly, she felt guilty and childish for making this trip, for putting Shah and Samar's remaining parent in danger. Nasrin had certainly gone to great lengths to keep their meeting concealed. She must have felt it would be dangerous to be affiliated with Celeste.

What came next would be the most difficult part of the conversation. Celeste had waffled back and forth but finally decided that, at the very least, she owed Nasrin the truth.

"The morning I found…" She let out a muffled sob at the image. "When I discovered that Zari had been killed, I had only moments to think. It seemed safest to take anything identifying from his body. I was in shock and was afraid. I realize now how strange it must seem that I—"

Nasrin put her hand on Celeste's. "Celeste, it's OK. I know you fled that morning, and I know you took his phone. I'm glad you did, and we were pleased you thought to destroy the SIM card. I assume you had it wiped?"

"Yes," she replied sheepishly.

"Smart lady. Zari had it backed up on one of our secure servers, so I, too, scoured his last words."

"I'm looking for answers—you are correct," Celeste admitted. "But now that I'm here, it feels shallow to come to you searching for answers after all that you've lost. And to jeopardize your safety after I've already caused so mu—"

"Oh dear. My brother must've said something offensive. I could kill him sometimes. Look, I'm glad you're here, but if I may—you have this all wrong. We should be apologizing to you, not vice versa."

Celeste looked at her quizzically. "Why would you possibly owe me an apology? Your husband was murdered be—"

Nasrin shook her head. "No. Zari and I were charged with

keeping you out of harm's way. It's what we do. We are... associates of some people motivated to keep you safe. And we failed. All of us." She looked at Celeste pointedly.

"Do *not* ever feel that Zari's death was your fault. We knew our line of work was dangerous, and we learned early on that it was only a matter of time until one of us was compromised. Of course I miss him desperately—I randomly start sobbing in the grocery store sometimes—but he and I were both committed to making the world a better place for our children. At any cost. We knowingly and willingly assumed that risk."

The words Celeste had memorized from the text messages between Zari and his wife and between Zari and the unknown number danced through her head.

Zari and Nasrin. Ace and Lorraine. Ace and the Feds. People committed to protecting me, willing to risk their lives for me. Yet they are as elusive as ever.

Nasrin was savvy, possibly a member of the intelligence community. She would have been expecting Celeste's questions, would have memorized the texts, and would be prepared to keep anything from Celeste that others didn't want her to know. *I need answers.*

"For what it's worth, I was very uncomfortable reading your and Zari's personal messages. I felt very invasive..."

Nasrin shrugged nonchalantly. "Oh, Celeste, don't even give it another thought. Just some texts between two people in love and probably lots of boring parent-child logistics. Besides, we've had an audience to our correspondence for many years. Even in the beginning stages when everything was brand new. I miss those days, our bright-eyed innocence and convictions, believing we could take on the world and win! I envy the people we were, not yet hardened by the harsh realities of the world."

Nasrin's eyes teared up, and she retrieved a tissue from her next-season Birkin. The old Celeste briefly surfaced when she felt a twinge of jealousy. The bag was impossible to get. *Focus, Celeste.* She wasn't here to admire Nasrin's taste in handbags or connections to get them before release.

Nasrin sniffed and continued, "My apologies for my emotions. No matter how many days go by, it still always feels like the morning I found out that he was—that he'd been killed. Now, a trip down memory lane wasn't what you wanted to discuss. How can I help?"

"Several people in my life have gone to great lengths to conceal things from me. Even your brother's colleague referenced something I didn't know. And Zari knew things I hadn't told anyone—like about the guy in Frankfurt who tried to kidnap me. Zari was also told not to let me leave Dubai, and the next thing that happened is... is that he ended up dead." She winced, imagining the pool of blood around his head. "So it raises the question—what is everyone hiding from me? What don't I know?"

Celeste noticed something moving over Nasrin's shoulder—a man walking several yards away on the outdoor terrace. She squinted.

Hadid. She was relieved to see him—he hadn't been harmed in Paris after all. Celeste nearly clapped as she tried to catch his eye. He wasn't looking her way and seemed to be searching for someone.

Wait.

She saw it then.

Omar.

The most obvious distinguishing factor between Hadid and Omar was the facial expression—Omar's face was neither inviting nor kind. She watched him in disbelief. Omar was in the UAE.

But he can't be... it's not time yet.

She panicked. Had he seen her? She looked down, grateful that the headscarf somewhat shielded her eyes. He seemed to be satisfied that the person he was looking for was not on the patio and began walking away from her again. *Has the Omar gait.* She didn't exhale the breath she was holding until he was out of sight. She must have blended in well, though it was too close of a call. Her heart pounded. It was time to move before... *Before what, Celeste?* Would he really chance hurting her? In broad daylight? Omar worked for the Feds now. *So do you,* she reminded herself. Her thoughts were jumbled. Hadid had arranged this meeting with

Nasrin, who knew her whereabouts. But it was Omar who was in Abu Dhabi.

"Are you OK?" Nasrin looked around at the pedestrians, Omar nowhere in sight. "You look like you've just seen a ghost."

Celeste forced a laugh that sounded empty even to her. "No, I'm sorry, I... thought I saw someone I knew." Her mind raced. Was it too dangerous to be this close to Omar? Would Nasrin be suspicious if she abruptly made an excuse to leave? She straightened up, aware that a timer was now ticking on this little meet and greet. Information is what she'd come for, and that's what she'd get, Omar or no Omar.

"Level with me, Nasrin. What don't I know? Was Zari compromised? Was it Omar's people who"—she swallowed and continued—"killed him?" She blushed. "I don't mean to suggest you were being dishonest, but please don't think you have to sugarcoat anything for my sake." She had already resigned herself to the idea that she was responsible for Zari's death.

"There's a lot that I can't share. But I can say with certainty—Zari didn't die because of you. As I was saying earlier, we were in the middle of an operation entirely unrelated to you, and he was compromised. He agreed to help you out in a pinch amid all the chaos, and honestly, his plans being derailed by picking you up probably kept him alive longer. So please know that you are not at fault, and moreover, the last time I spoke with him, he relayed how lovely you are and how concerned he was for your safety."

After months of carrying the weight of Zari's death around with her, Celeste should have felt relieved. Instead, she was confused.

"You may also be surprised to learn that the man who was chasing you in Frankfurt was sent to stop you, to protect you," Nasrin continued. "We knew Omar had insights into your location. That guy was sent to extract you—to get you safely out of Frankfurt. He was one of us."

Extract? Celeste had only heard the phrase in military or spy movies. Perhaps her instincts were correct that Nasrin and Zari worked in the intelligence community.

She thought back to the brute who had smacked into her on the

S-Bahn platform in Germany. It wasn't difficult to conjure the fear and panic she'd felt in those moments as he chased her through the airport. She'd finally lost him and escaped on a jet chartered by Michel. Frankfurt felt like a lifetime ago, and looking at it with fresh eyes was disconcerting. She didn't know what to think anymore.

"Us?"

"Yes. As I mentioned before, we have loose ties to some of your... colleagues. We have, shall we say, common enemies."

"So who do you believe was behind Zari's death?" Celeste asked.

"It isn't a matter of belief. I know exactly who did it, and I know why. Our culture is not so pure like the Americans. It's—" Nasrin struggled to find the right words. "Well, you see, Zari was a stubborn man, and he refused to look the other way once he uncovered a money-laundering ring with deep ties to radicals all across South America and Africa.

"But you have to understand—neither of us was particularly great at our job once we had children. When you're a parent and see the photos of casualties from ill-gotten automatic weapons... those are no longer just stacks of bodies. They're daughters and sons, fathers and mothers. Zari was tormented by the tragedies from Venezuela to Syria. He was told to stand down, to keep his cool, and he fucked up. He let his emotions drive his decision-making, and he acted against orders. So he was disposed of.

"I was angry with him at first, leaving me with two kids to raise and the heaviest of hearts. But I knew who he was when I married him. I loved him, still love him, for all that he was—empathetic, kind. But hot-headed and impulsive too. He was furious at being asked to look the other way, enraged that the entire intelligence community was always waiting for the right time to act, turning a blind eye to the children, women, and men being brutalized, starved, and enslaved all across the globe, while the right time never seemed to come."

I can relate to that.

"He took matters into his own hands in this particular instance by hacking into the money-laundering system and draining accounts of some of the key players that every Allied force in the world was monitoring. And that is why you found him with"—Nasrin dabbed at her tears with a tissue and continued—"a bullet between his eyebrows."

Celeste remembered every detail of those few moments when she'd discovered what had happened. How eerie the silence had been when she wandered around that Dubai apartment, calling out to Zari to prepare breakfast. She shuddered at the realization that they— whoever "they" was—could've killed her too. *My nine lives are bound to be up soon.*

Nasrin stood abruptly and gathered her things. "I'm sure this is a bit overwhelming for you to learn, but I'm afraid we have to move you —and quickly." Taking hold of Celeste's arm with a gentle but firm grip, she shuffled Celeste out of the café and to the museum exit. They continued down the pathway toward the parking lot where Nasrin's brother had dropped Celeste off.

"Omar's lurking around the museum security offices, having paid off a corrupt guard to find video footage of you. Won't be long before he's back out here."

Celeste's eyes widened. *How did she...* Her mind hadn't been playing tricks on her. Omar had been mere meters away from her, right inside the museum doors.

Right then, the car pulled up. Nasrin's brother hopped out and moved toward his sister to embrace her. She brushed him off. Before he could speak, she said, "Thank you, brother, for coming on short notice. She knows the truth now, so don't torture her with your lies and toxic propaganda. He's gone; let him rest in peace."

In no time, Celeste and her escorts were on the highway heading toward Dubai. She'd dodged Omar once again.

8

INFORMATION EXCAVATION

Celeste lay on the California king, spread-eagled with her eyes closed. She had dimmed the lights and drawn the shades, preferring the silence over her usual background music. Omar was in the UAE. Of course, she'd known that he'd survived his fall into the Mediterranean after Theodore had shot him. It was wholly different to see him walking around in broad daylight —and processing that he was still a free man was extremely distressing.

On the drive from the Louvre to Dubai, Celeste had begun to realize that Nasrin hadn't given her much information at all—no illuminating insights into what she didn't know, no names of anyone with whom Nasrin was working. Celeste was embarrassed. Why had she been so naive to think she'd hop on a plane and surprise Nasrin into answering all her questions? The entire trip had been a foolish attempt to trick a woman trained in espionage to spill the tea.

Idiot.

At least she'd recruited Tarek and was building her own team.

Since she didn't have her many monitors to look over her grid, she was visualizing all that she'd learned in her mind's eye. The interplay of so many events, so many motives, was mind-boggling. Frankfurt had been a rescue attempt? Zari's death was not her fault—or Omar's for that matter. The return to the hotel had been a major ordeal. The men had worked out a swap for her phones, and she had changed into herself once again at the Dubai Mall. This time, her doppelgänger wasn't there, but the bag of Celeste's things with instructions was in that same bathroom stall.

She'd bailed on dinner with Savin, saying that she wasn't feeling well and she'd be taking dinner in her room. Surprisingly, he said he was lying low that evening as well.

Shit. She realized it was time to call Theodore. She'd dodged his calls all day. She opened FaceTime on her laptop. He answered when she rang.

"Babe!" Theodore exclaimed with a huge grin. His face filled the screen, and she could feel the warmth in his expression even with the distance between them. "When will you be back? I'm going crazy without you. If you stay away any longer, I'm getting a puppy."

Celeste laughed. "If there are any puppies in that apartment when I get home... well, they'd better be adorable." She straightened up. "I miss you, too, darling. Desperately. This trip has been a lot of work."

"Tell me everything. How was your day?"

Where do I begin, my love? Omar's back. Nothing was as it seemed in Frankfurt. I'm willing to ruin a man's life if he doesn't cooperate with me. I still don't know what's happened to Hadid. But other than that, everything is the same.

"One of my hair stylists was in town, so I spent the day at the salon. Sav was annoyed at having to fend for himself for a day."

They laughed, both aware of Savin's peculiarities. "You and Savin makin' some deals?"

"Of course. You know us well," she said, then changed the subject. "Oh! I forgot to tell you—Mere and I have made some progress on the party planning for our—"

"Wedding, darling. It's called a wedding. And that's wonderful!"

Celeste dove into a make-believe story about candle hurricanes and flower arches, then further distracted Theodore by letting the strap on her slip gown slide down, revealing a nipple. His eyes darkened with desire, and all questions about her day were replaced with his talk of what he wanted to do to and with her in that moment. There was a knock at her door. *Dinner is served.*

"Oh shoot, babe, I hate to cut this short, but my dinner's here."

Theodore frowned in disappointment. "You never seem to have any time on this trip. When will you be back?"

"Day after tomorrow."

"Breathlessly awaiting your return," he replied with an English flourish. "I love you."

"Love you too. Good night."

She closed her laptop and went to the door. A look through the eyehole revealed a man in a hotel concierge uniform, but she could not see a food cart.

"Who's there?" she inquired.

"Good evening, madame. I have a delivery for you." He held up a large Hermès shopping bag with a signature orange box inside for her to see. *If this is a trap, at least the sender knows my love language.* She opened the door an inch.

"Thank you. Next time, please call up beforehand and announce any deliveries."

She weighed the risks of taking the bag. She could probe as to who had made the delivery, but they would've covered their tracks. She'd learned from her own training how easy it was to avoid being identified on CCTV: head down, hat covering face, nondescript clothes, no accessories.

"Of course, madame, but the man who dropped it off asked for it to be a surprise. He said it was your birthday." He smiled broadly. "Happy birthday! Please let us know if we can make your celebration more special."

Celeste nearly rolled her eyes. *Whatever. This should be good.* She took it from his outstretched hand, thanked him, and closed the door, locking the chain.

On the bed, she pulled the large box out of the bag carefully. A card on creamy ivory stock was tucked under the black ribbon. Omar had pulled similar tricks over the years, but her instincts told her this wasn't from him. She jumped at the unexpected shrill of the hotel room phone ringing.

"Hello?"

"Sending you a new cell, arriving tomorrow morning. Yours have both been compromised." The line went dead.

Fucking Michel, always with the bad news. Not that she hadn't considered that her body double could've accessed her phones while she was in Abu Dhabi. But why would the woman who had gone to such lengths to protect Celeste both in Paris and in Dubai do something so duplicitous?

She opened the Hermès-branded card.

I saw you eyeing mine. Zari would be so happy knowing we met. This should help us stay in touch.

xx Nasrin

Celeste gingerly untied the ribbon—it wasn't every day someone gifted Hermès—and lifted the top off the box. She gasped. Next season's Birkin lay on a bed of tissue paper. A color she'd been eyeing, but which seemed to be sold out worldwide. She fingered the rich epsom leather. The Gris Meyer marbled gray was the perfect neutral. An extremely generous gift.

"This should help us stay in touch"? She frowned and dug through the tissue paper. *Nothing.* She threw some of the tissue aside and shook the box. Something rattled. She removed the rest of the tissue. *A phone!* She flipped it open and found five waiting text messages.

"You asked about what you didn't know."

"We knew he was alive."

"Never a good time to tell you."

"Please be careful. Your life depends on it."

"Loved meeting you today. Hopefully under better circumstances next time."

Celeste was short of breath, feeling as though she had received a blow to the gut. So. There it was. Theodore's deception on display.

Many people had known he was alive. They'd watched her unravel from afar, just as he had. They'd watched her flailing for any way to make sense of the situation. And yet... none of them had told her. Why? Part of her wanted to believe it was solely for her safety. But she feared there was more to it. *And this, Anne Marie, is exactly why I didn't ask Theodore more questions.* Could going down this path, doing this information excavation, possibly reveal anything helpful? Hadn't she learned over and over again that some truths were best left unearthed?

She awoke some time later with the feeling that someone was watching her. She looked around the luxe room for an intruder, finding no one. *Must've dozed off.* Her new bag lay neatly beside her.

She walked to the restroom to splash cold water on her face. If Nasrin knew Theodore had been alive, Zari had also known. How could he have kept that from her? She brushed her teeth and went back to the bedroom. It was then she noticed a food cart close to the door. *So someone was in here after all. Dammit. I told him not to come up without calling.*

The food was still piping hot, so it must've been the hotel worker who woke her a few minutes before. Her stomach growled. She sat down and began eating the salmon and steamed vegetables she had ordered earlier.

The meeting the following day was perhaps the most important of the entire trip, but of course, Savin didn't know that. At a designated bench on the promenade in front of the Dubai Mall and Burj Khalid, Celeste would recruit the world's most elusive hacker. They didn't know it yet, but this person would help her track down the traitors—Omar, Matthew, the Feds, Ace, and whoever else got in her way —and she'd deal with each of them on her timeline, not theirs. And it would all happen before her wedding, the day in which her new life would begin, when she'd be rid of all this unpleasantness.

Time was of the essence. Omar was growing more bold, more

confident, now that he was out of hiding. *What must my fellow Americans have promised him that makes him feel he can roam freely around the world?* It was an inconvenience that he'd resurfaced so soon, and it also indicated that Celeste's security measures needed to be ramped up. Only Hadid and Nasrin's team should have known she was in Abu Dhabi—yet Omar was there. She couldn't risk having him move in on her before it was time, and she certainly wasn't willing to jeopardize Theodore's or anyone else's safety in the interim.

What the...? A piece of paper stuck out from under her plate. "All's clear if he's wearing green."

In a moment, she finally understood the game her opponents were playing. They meant to overwhelm and distract her. This was all a way to prevent her from figuring out what was really going on. Get her all worked up with these trivial bits of information while the real action was happening right under her nose. Well, she was not some novice. She was brilliant. A step ahead of everyone—the US intelligence agencies, hackers, her friends—since day one. Had any of them taken a minute to think about *why* she'd been able to slip away from them so many times? Because she understood her opponents better than they understood her. *Two can play this game—and I'm playing to win.*

SHE COVERED her golden locks with a dark scarf and pinned it into place to ensure her hairline wasn't revealed. She was once again in the mall bathroom the following morning, this time alone. She had thrown a black abaya over the suit she'd wear for her meeting later, but first she must meet with the person she hoped would be the newest addition to her surveillance team. She washed her hands, then donned her oversize sunglasses.

At exactly 7:10 a.m. Dubai time, she sat down on the bench outside on the mall promenade, amazed at how many tourists were already out and about, oohing and aahing at the immensity of the Burj Khalifa's profile. But they weren't her focus. The past few weeks, it had become less and less clear who her real opponents were. She recalled the words with which Alex had taunted her: "You may want to consider the possibility that Omar and Ace are not the only people involved in your little game of cat and mouse." *Fuck you, Alex.* Glancing down at her watch, she bristled when she discovered that the person was over twenty-five minutes late. How long was long enough to wait?

Admittedly, she'd been careless. Michel had warned her there was a rat, and she'd brushed off his words. Who had she overlooked as a potential enemy? Someone who'd been compromised? She let her memory take her back to that night at Savin's right before someone tipped off the Shu team. *Savin, Roberto, Sam, Fred. Mark, Gabe, Chet, Angelo.* She thought through the past year, scouring her brain for more obvious adversaries.

Anyone who'd had a major stake in Omar's holding company that she'd essentially gutted would love to see her head on a platter. No one was as successful as she and Savin had been without breaking a few people along the way. But losing out in business was wholly different from committing any number of crimes. *Unless...* Unless whoever it was knew that she and Savin were now working with the Feds. If anything would up the ante in a conflict, it was knowing that a nemesis was protected by law enforcement.

Forty-five fucking minutes I've been waiting. Inexcusable. If she didn't leave soon, she'd be late for her breakfast meeting. She gathered her bag and was prepared to storm off.

"Miss, miss! Would you like a photo in front of the beautiful Burj Khalifa? Miss! I will take your photo!"

She was set to spew a cutting remark when she saw it. The little man with the big camera was wearing an ivory polo shirt and a linen jacket. But what caught her eye was the small green pocket square. "All's clear if he's wearing green," the note had said. *This spy shit is getting old.*

Going along with him in case he actually was the guy, she said brightly, "Yes, a photo would be wonderful." She stood in front of the massive building, and the man walked several meters away to take the pictures. As he snapped away, she considered the situation. *If this is a trap, my cover is completely blown. Again.*

He took several, then remarked loudly, "Miss, the photos are magnificent!" He walked over to her and turned the camera screen toward her, seemingly to review his work. But there were no photos on the screen—only words scrolling rhythmically as though on a teleprompter.

Matthew's files will be delivered
To you in New York
Within the week
Look beyond Omar
And Ace for someone
In your inner circle
Your plan will work
If you find the leak
Do not reach out
I'll be in touch
You're still in danger
Stay vigilant
Walk away now
Inshallah.

She looked the man in the eye, sizing him up. He stared back blankly, as though he had no idea what had scrolled across the screen. Perhaps his English was limited and he didn't actually know what was on it.

"These are lovely, but I really must go. I have an appointment that I'm late for."

She hurried back to the mall to change, keeping her head down to avoid being seen by anyone on their way to the breakfast meeting. Thankfully, she made it back to the bathroom with no encounters. She stripped off the abaya, folded it into a small square, and stuffed it into a zippered side pocket of her tote for safekeeping.

Within minutes, she was wandering through the mall boasted as being the largest in the world (*Who cares?*), lost in the sea of stores and infuriated with the commercialism on display. Signs pointed in nearly every direction for an exit or a restaurant or the aquarium, yet she kept ending up where she'd begun. She finally stumbled back outside after she referenced a map and discovered the breakfast meeting wasn't *inside* the mall but was across the way in the Armani Hotel. Even at the early hour, Celeste felt enveloped by the heat and smog like an unwelcome blanket. She was already sweating.

For fuck's sake. Her flight out of Dubai could not come soon enough.

AFTER EXCHANGING introductions and placing orders, Celeste and Savin were now seated with brother team Enzo and Nico Ricci.

"We like what we see with D&C's portfolio and growth trajectory. Your strategic vision seems aligned with ours, as expansion into the Middle East is our number-one priority in the near term." Enzo Ricci was polished, poised, and not at all sleazy, unlike the typical Italian businessmen Celeste had encountered. But he was not her target. His brother, Nico, had captured her interest.

Nico was a piece of work. She suspected and wanted to confirm that he ran in Omar's small circle of cronies. She was determined to infiltrate Omar's business operations, and to be successful, she had to expose every vulnerability she could. Nico's entire act was not only insincere but concerning. It was industry standard to be prepared for a meeting like this, but Celeste discerned from Nico's remarks that he had done more than his homework. He'd been investigating D&C. From her research, she'd concluded that Nico was someone she needed to keep an eye on, and what better way to do so than to gain control of the purse strings of his fund. Savin didn't seem to have picked up on anything unusual.

"Remind me... where is your operation based?" Celeste asked, then took a sip of her latte.

"Well, Rome, technically, but we each have several homes. I'm currently spending most of my time in Capri, soaking up the last rays of this Indian summer," Enzo replied.

"And I split my time between Dubai and Miami," said Nico. *Of course you do.* He probably trolled South Beach on the daily for young girls he could add to his sad little harem.

"A presence in Rome would certainly be nice for us. As you know, our only satellite office in Europe at the moment is in Paris," Savin commented.

Celeste tuned out. She didn't need any further proof that Nico was a dirtbag; that much she could read from his demeanor and words. She wanted to know his motivation—to find out why he was so fascinated with the D&C portfolio. Perhaps he was cash strapped, but her gut told her that she was right—there was something more sinister behind the enthusiasm. To ensure that Nico didn't catch on to her and also that Savin remained in the dark, she moved the meeting along until finally it was time to close out their bill. She was pleased that the breakfast ended with a verbal agreement to collaborate.

"Our lawyer, Johnny Carolo, will be in touch," Celeste said. She and Savin turned to leave.

"Something's not right with that dude," Savin whispered. "Let's get the fuck out of Dubai." *So maybe he was paying attention.*

"Yeah, I caught the same. Can't wait to be home."

"WELCOME BACK, Celeste! It's been such a long time!" Rani said by way of greeting two days later. She walked around her desk and embraced Celeste. "How was it? Lunch soon once you're settled back in?"

Celeste searched Rani's face for any signs of deception. *Had she really not recognized me in Paris?* It seemed so long ago, and a small part of Celeste doubted that she'd even seen Rani. She'd been quite upset that night, having just left where she was supposed to meet Hadid after receiving the warning text that it was a trap. *What if I didn't really see her? What if it was just some woman with a strong resemblance to Rani?* No, she mustn't doubt what she saw with her own eyes.

She knew Rani's gait, knew her style. It was Rani that night. *Unless it wasn't.*

"It was a fabulous trip, but I'm very excited to be back—and in time for the weekend! And yes, lunch early next week should work," Celeste replied nonchalantly. "Buzz my office phone if anything arrives for me. You'll never believe it, but I cracked my iPhone in that hideous city. My new one should be delivered any minute."

"A cracked screen is the worst," Rani said, groaning.

Celeste began to make her way to her office.

"Oh, Celeste, Lorraine asked that I find time for you two ASAP. I told her you'd be free in thirty minutes. Is that OK?"

She and Savin would break the news to the team later today that they'd be expanding and that new opportunities would be available. They'd want eyes and ears in those satellite offices. Before the meeting, Celeste had hoped to discern the best way to reach out to her various new recruits. *Guess it'll have to wait.* Lorraine never requested a meeting unless it was important.

"Sure, send her in at"—she looked down to confirm on her watch —"nine oh five." That would give Celeste time to do a little digging.

In her office, she closed the door, hung up her coat and handbag, then walked over to her corner desk. She stared out at the tall buildings, knowing that someone somewhere had the answers she needed. Sighing, she sat down and powered up her computer. She navigated to her encrypted remote file folder and opened the grid. The previous night, after Theodore fell asleep, she had made a list of everyone she needed to check in with, and it was long. Ace was number one on the list. They had tentacles in nearly every new development, it seemed. *As they say, keep your friends close and your enemies closer.*

She opened the address book on her computer and dialed a number on her landline.

"Fred, darling, how are you? It's Celeste." She nodded. "Yes, I'm calling from my office phone. Yes, we just returned from what was quite a journey."

Once she was finished answering his trivial questions, she took a breath and continued. "Are you free for a drink tonight after work? I need to, uh, discuss a few things."

"Sure." If he was put off by her cryptic words, he didn't let on.

They arranged to meet at Polo Bar at 5 p.m. "I have a standing reservation," Fred had boasted.

Excuse me while I swoon.

"That sounds great; see you then."

Now she had to spend the day digging out from all the messes accumulating from her trip. She dialed Ace from her new flip phone.

"What?" Ace asked sharply. Ace had always spoken with a voice changer, so it was impossible to discern their identity.

"It's Celeste."

Without missing a beat, they replied, "You've been avoiding me."

Not wrong. Celeste needed information, and there was only one way to get it. "Yes. Frankly, you've lost my trust. But given our long-standing relationship, it seems fair to talk things through, rather than write you off."

Silence.

Then Ace responded, "You hired me to keep you safe and to keep your network secure. There have been some breaches that have had sweeping repercussions for you, I realize, but all the vulnerabilities have been repaired."

Celeste recalled the cryptic postcard and photograph and the other recent developments that she hadn't reported to Ace—or shared with anyone, really.

"I hired you to make me money, which admittedly you've done times a thousand. To expect anything more was... short-sighted." *Idiotic, an epic failure, stupidity.* Whether she was referring to herself or Ace, she didn't know.

"No, I promised to keep you safe, and I've failed you more than once. I'm sorry for the errors on my end that may have caused you any harm."

"Any harm"? Theodore disappearing for months, Celeste nearly losing her mind with grief, Zari's death, Omar almost killing her, the

surgeries, the rehab, and everything that had happened since. *Any harm.*

She had to let it slide to get what she came for. "I need your help."

"Shoot."

"I have reason to believe that Omar was in Dubai when I was. I need confirmation it was him." *A softball. Let's see what you can do.*

"Done."

She hesitated. *Maybe it's safer if more people know.* "Also, there was an... incident in Paris. I was supposed to meet Hadid, but... he never showed... and never reached out. It was uncharacteristic. I want to know what happened and also confirm that he's safe."

"Hadid? May I ask why?"

"He was helping me with some business in the Middle East."

"OK, done."

"Thanks."

"I aim to please."

Click.

"Knock, knock" came Savin's voice from the other side of the door. As usual, he barged in before she responded.

"You do know it's pointless to knock if you're not going to wait for permission, right?" she scolded.

"Cheer up, buttercup." He whistled while he crossed the room to her conference table. Savin's good moods were really starting to grate on her nerves.

"What's going on with your phones?"

"Oh, I broke my iPhone screen, and my burner battery is fucked. Of all the luck, they happened at the same time! Fucking Apple. When will they ever make a good product?"

Savin moved on, satisfied with her explanation. "What do we do about the Italian greasers? Their numbers are stellar, but I don't like Nico's vibes."

"That's a good question. Dirtbag that he is, he makes sound investments. What do you recommend?"

"Keeping him away from women, for one," Savin replied with a grin.

Celeste laughed along with Savin. "Yeah, that's a lawsuit waiting to happen. Maybe we keep him in Dubai chained to a cubicle?"

"He'd fit under my bed, though he'd probably get a little weird when my lady friend sleeps over."

They laughed even harder as they exchanged scenarios. *It's so nice to laugh.*

"In all seriousness, he's sharp, but a loose cannon," Celeste said.

"Yeah. We'll have to ensure there's some sort of protection in the acquisition agreement," Savin affirmed. "By the way, when were you planning to tell me about Omar?"

Celeste nearly spit out her alkaline water. "It... what?" she stammered. "Omar?"

"You're scheming. It's not like I haven't noticed all your secret outings. This whole world tour was a ruse. Promise me you're not doing something insane like last time."

Shit. She was shocked. She had underestimated Savin's ability to read her. She'd have to be more disciplined.

"Well, you're half right. I did ask Ace to track him down, keep tabs on him, so we're not blindsided like last time. Ya know?"

"Celly, I'm your best friend and business partner. And I'm more than just a pretty face. I can tell when you're hiding something. Don't make me regret looking the other way."

Please, let me do what I need to do until my wedding day, and then you can interfere all you want.

"Gotta run to a meeting. Think about what I said." He left her alone and closed the door behind him.

Her computer dinged with a notification. Tarek had sent her an encrypted email at the secure address she'd given him. He wanted assurances that his secrets were safe. *Oh, darling Tarek, I have no interest in sharing how you get your rocks off as long as you hold up your end of the bargain.* She sent him instructions on how to provide her with remote access to Matthew's devices. She was anxious to see if Matthew had tipped off Omar that she was in the UAE. Were her instincts correct that Matthew was one of Omar's many evildoers?

Would following the Matthews and Nicos of the world help her infiltrate Omar's circle? She'd soon find out.

"FRED, darling, thanks for meeting on such short notice."

He nodded and held up his Scotch in greeting. "The same?" He caught the server's attention and waved him over.

"A dirty martini for me. Extra dirty, extra olives. Thanks." She turned to Fred. "Dinner."

He laughed. "So how can I help?"

"I need your take on a couple of people. The Ricci brothers—Enzo and Nico."

"That Nico is a motherfucker. Evil little fuck."

Celeste looked sheepish.

"Uh-oh. What did you do?" Fred asked.

"Well, Savin and I wanted to expand our Middle East operations, and you know Nico's strategy—"

"Is it a done deal? If not, get the fuck out now. He's bad news. I doubt anything he does is legal. You'll end up in trouble—or dead."

"Wait, really? Everything seemed solid."

"Celeste, he's as bad as Omar. Maybe worse. Mousy little weasel."

She frowned. *Doubt that.*

"That was insensitive. I'm sorry." Fred reached across the table and awkwardly patted her hand. "Look, you didn't hear it from me, but..." He dove into the specifics, reciting a litany of Nico's wrongdoings. Nico's rap sheet was typical of a wealthy man with an affinity for sadism.

Bingo. Exactly what Celeste was looking for. She knew Fred would get fired up and point her in the right direction.

"Thanks, I appreciate your perspective. It does sound like it would be a risky business partnership. I'll talk to Savin. In other news, how have you been?"

"Same old. Honestly, I enjoyed the time away more than I care to admit." Fred had also been a target of Omar's and had fled town for a month or two when Omar was on his rampage the previous year. "I'm considering slowing down a bit, maybe buying a vacation home somewhere in the Caribbean."

"You loved diving in Belize, right? Is that a place you could see yourself?"

"Perhaps, though I am quite fond of the luxuries of St. Barth's."

"Aren't we all?" Celeste said, laughing.

"He'll be back soon, ya know. Do you have precautions in place? Real precautions this time?"

"I believe so. We're doing the best we can. Have you heard anything?"

"Only some rumblings that something's about to going down. And rumors that Omar's struck some deal. Maybe he's an informant of some kind?"

"Really? That's… who would want to protect him?"

"I'm not sure. But he's ruthless. He'd roll over on anyone. I wish we could've taken him out when we had the chance. Frankly, I'm tired of looking over my shoulder."

"Yeah. Same," Celeste said mildly. She wanted to keep him talking, feeling he knew more that he wasn't saying. She'd never figured out where Fred got his information, but it was always reliable.

"Eh, hell, I would have a lot of sleepless nights if Omar hurt you again. So I may as well tell you all I know. I have reason to believe he's… well, it seems the US government is working with him."

Celeste feigned surprise. "Wait, what? He's not even a citizen."

"I'm not sure why he's valuable, but like I said, he must be useful for some reason. But he'll be more brazen, more unstable."

Celeste stifled an ironic laugh. *More unstable? Is that possible?*

Fred continued. "I hate to be dark, but you won't make it out alive next time. Is Theodore prepared? What has Angelo done to remedy all the pitfalls from last time? Do you need a referral for new security? I know a former Secret Service guy looking for work."

"I have the illuminati." Celeste looked at Fred evenly to gauge his reaction. To her surprise, he began laughing.

"Those useless fucks? They're nothing more than paper pushers with an agenda. Chet is afraid of his own shadow since his wife was killed, and Gabriel would give up anyone to avoid getting his clothes dirty. You gotta look out for yourself, kiddo."

They had another round, their heads together conspiratorially. The more imbibed Fred became, the more freely he relayed his opinions.

"What did you think of the illuminati gathering a few weeks ago?" Celeste asked. "And don't sugarcoat it this time." They both laughed.

"Eh. Those guys aren't all bad. Their passion is evident, but they're too damn naive. If they're right about some sort of major cyberattack, there's nothing any of us can do to stop it."

"And they're relying solely on us and Ace, it seems? They mentioned our networks, but they don't really reach out to me much." *Except for Gabe telling me to trust him, which is laughable, and that there was a reason the Feds were working with Omar.*

"Understandable. You haven't exactly hidden your contempt," Fred said, smiling widely. "They've contacted me a few times. It's not clear to me what they're actually working on."

After one more round, it was clear Fred had nothing more to divulge, and Celeste was ready to go home to Theodore. They paid their check and went to their waiting cars.

Theodore was snoozing on the couch. Celeste decided to let him sleep a little longer and take advantage of the time to update her grid.

Michel had told her to trust no one, so she needed to assume that anyone could be the enemy. She started with the obvious adversaries. *Omar, his cronies, and his business partners.* If all went well, she'd neutralize Matthew and Nico, but she still added them to the list. Then there were those in what she deemed the gray/unknown space. She added text boxes with each of their names and put them in the neutral zone of her document. *Ace, Clit, Gabe, US govt, Nasrin's bro, Hadid, Shu team.* Were there others she should be considering? She needed an exhaustive list, and she had a nagging feeling she was overlooking someone.

The Ace situation was perplexing. Celeste had been hoping for a sign one way or the other, but it hadn't become clear yet. The Feds didn't seem interested in doing her any favors. In fact, she'd decided that Gabe calling to give her a heads-up about Omar was more to save his own ass than to help her. And just because Omar was responsible for Chet's wife's death did not mean Chet would be loyal to Celeste. Quite the contrary.

Gabe had told Celeste and her friends that his superiors were part of some conspiracy to "teach Americans a lesson." "Involvement at the highest levels of the US government... traitors on Pennsylvania Avenue and in the Russell Building," he'd claimed. Had she become a person of interest to these turncoats?

Nasrin's brother—was he an enemy? He clearly had some pent-up resentment toward Celeste, and he'd had plenty of time to find out about her, while she hadn't known he existed until recently. Could she be wrong about Hadid's intentions? She still hadn't had a real chance to apologize for Riyadh. Alex snatching her had probably exposed Hadid to grave danger.

Was there a disgruntled current or former D&C employee? What bothered her the most wasn't Omar or the Feds or her new recruits— it was that someone inside her circle could be compromised. She ran through the names of those with the most access to her. Was someone being blackmailed? By whom? Why? She was confident that her friends wouldn't intentionally hurt her. But had they known Theodore was alive like Nasrin and Zari had?

Impossible. Savin had to have been in the dark about Theodore being alive, because she'd watched him grieve alongside her. Mark too. Jack. Even Fred had been devastated. And they had her best interest at heart, that was clear. But she wasn't sure she could trust their judgment, especially Savin's and Mark's. Neither of them was great at keeping secrets. And Jack—well, she couldn't imagine him following through on much.

Celeste had never had any reason to question Angelo's loyalty, regardless of what Michel thought. Lorraine had shown herself to be extremely trustworthy. Brett? Rani? How would she determine where Hadid's loyalty lay? Had he set her up in Paris?

Then there were the issues she'd chosen to avoid. The photo, the shooter, Rani in Paris, Omar popping up.

Perhaps the most important task was to identify the people she needed to help her accomplish her revised and expanded plan. She had two new hackers to replace Ace, her new recruits, Tarek and Nico, though Nico didn't know it yet. But she needed more... what had she called Omar? *An asset.* She needed more assets. Answering only to her because she'd either blackmailed them or paid them—she didn't have a preference. Her plan, though brilliant in its simplicity, wouldn't be easy to pull off.

9

———————

HOUSE OF CARDS

"Breakfast in bed for my love," Theodore said softly, waking her the next morning.

Celeste opened one eye and smiled when she saw the spread on the tray he carried over to the bed. "Hi, honey," she murmured sleepily. "Did you stay on the couch the whole night? You wouldn't wake up to join me in bed."

"I was dead tired. I came to bed around four a.m., and you didn't even stir."

He set the tray on the end of the bed and slid under the sheets next to her. He passionately kissed her and then leaned over and grabbed a piece of cantaloupe.

"Mmm, that's a nice wake-up call," she purred. She was suddenly starving. She sat up and helped herself to a croissant and some strawberries. "Thank you! What a treat!"

"Of course. What's on the agenda for today? You've been working so hard lately. I was hoping you'd have some time for me. We could take a walk, enjoy the weather, maybe a boozy brunch?"

The incessant worry that had followed her around like a black cloud faded away, and she found herself looking forward to a day like they used to have. Strolling around the Village hand in hand, nowhere to be, popping into one of their favorite local spots. *Before everything changed.* It sounded dreamy. "You're in luck because I need a day off," she replied, smiling broadly.

"The best news I've heard all morning."

The two finished their breakfast and then made love. Afterward, they showered and got ready. She wore a casual sundress, Chanel slides, and a Maison Michel straw sun hat. Theodore looked fresh and handsome in a peach linen shirt with the sleeves rolled up and khaki shorts.

She heard her burner phone vibrating from the office just as they were ready to leave. "Oh! I left my laptop on. I'll be right back."

"Don't get stuck in there. That office is like a black hole—you go in and I don't see you again for days," he said, laughing.

She grinned and quickly walked out of the room.

Once in her office, she shut the door behind her softly. *Careless to leave the sound on.* She retrieved the phone and saw missed calls and a text from an unknown number.

"We need to meet in person. Tonight," read the text.

Fuck. It was becoming difficult to keep track of everyone coming out of the woodwork.

After replying, "9 p.m. Where," she put the phone on silent and locked it in her desk drawer.

"Sorry about that, sweetie. I'm ready now," she called to Theodore breezily.

"Ooh, let's pop into Sant Ambroeus and see if they have a table outside," Celeste suggested. The two were strolling leisurely along the tree-lined West Village streets, discussing their fall travel plans.

"Of course, darling," Theodore replied, kissing her hand.

They approached the host, who promptly led them to their favorite table. After settling into their seats, they ordered their usuals and a Cioccolato Cornetto to share.

"It's so nice to relax, isn't it? Feels like we've been ships passing in the night lately. I've missed you, baby," Theodore said.

"Yes, my trip was much too long. I felt… rushed in Paris, and you know I've never been a fan of Dubai."

"Tell me everything. We've barely gotten to talk since you've been back." He lowered his voice and looked at her pointedly. "Are you still concerned that someone inside D&C is sabotaging you and Savin? That's kind of a big deal, right?"

There was so much she wanted to ask him instead of lying yet again, but her fear that he'd dodge everything, as Nasrin had, stopped her. Like an unshakable virus, the unanswered questions would forever infect the relationship they'd built. *Built atop a house of cards.* She smiled ironically. *It may not be a perfect relationship, but it's mine, and I'll do everything in my power to protect it.*

"Funny you should ask. I've been a little distracted today, wondering the same thing. We're still looking into it. But it's definitely a possibility," she replied in a noncommittal tone. His inquiry sparked an idea of how she could find out if anyone in her circle had been compromised. *Monday's project.*

"Who are you and Savin thinking? Have you been able to narrow it down?" he asked while signaling the server for another round of Bloody Marys.

"We have no idea. We're looking into every last one of them." *A little emotion would help.* "Ungrateful fuck, whoever it is," she added for emphasis.

He looked pensive. "And the deals? Did they pan out? Were the trips worth it?"

A question she could answer honestly. She jumped on the opportunity and smiled a genuine grin, her dimples appearing. "We closed both deals! Of course, there's paperwork to be finalized, but there was a gentlewoman's agreement in both cases. Johnny will finalize everything with their lawyers. D&C will now have a stronghold in the UAE and a presence in Rome."

She wished she could elaborate. Theodore would find Tarek's

predicament particularly amusing, and he'd agree about Nico. *Nico the douche canoe.*

"Wow, very impressive. I know how hard you've been working to make these deals happen. I've spent many a night rolling over to spoon you, only to find your side of the bed empty." He frowned.

"Oh, honey, I'm sorry I've been neglecting you lately." She kissed his cheek. "You're the most important person in my life."

"Can you still make Copenhagen work? It's in a few weeks. It'd be nice to get away together, and I booked a gorgeous hotel."

Celeste took a delicate bite of her croque monsieur, turning her face toward the sunshine and soaking it in. *Take the easy road when it presents itself.*

"Sure, why not?"

They talked through their plans, and all the while, Celeste's wheels were turning. Copenhagen wasn't a bad place to plan a meetup.

∼

I CAN'T BELIEVE *I've resorted to this.*

She was halfway through the sublevel basement window when she felt the shard of glass slice through her lightweight sweater and the liquid ooze from the gash on her abdomen. *Motherfucker.* So much for not raising Theodore's suspicions. *It's a good thing I'm thin or I never would've fit.*

Earlier that evening, she'd told Theodore she needed to get some fresh air and had attributed her late-night departure to a craving for frozen yogurt.

"I can change and join you," he'd offered.

"No, no, honey, you're already in your pajamas. I'll be back before you have a chance to miss me, my love," she'd said and rushed out the door.

There was—quite literally—no turning back now that her body was half in and half out of the dark apartment. She was still fuming by the time she maneuvered herself inside.

Ew. This place wasn't that different from her West Village apartment, but it was much less clean. An awful stench that had probably settled in the room many years before made her stomach churn. Or was that the smell of the blood that was soiling her sweater?

"Come out, come out, wherever—and whoever—you are." She realized that she hadn't thought through how many ways this night could go wrong. *A bit late to back out, Celeste.*

"Hello? I'm bleeding, so the least you could do is turn on a fuc— turn on a light."

Silence. A chill ran down her spine, and her heart thrummed in her ears. *What if this is Omar's doing?* After all, she knew he was back. He'd figured out how to track her whereabouts again. She tried to gauge whether an escape route was feasible.

After what felt like hours, a small floor lamp in the corner illuminated the room. Celeste gasped.

"You?" Panic flooded her body and dizziness set in. "I—I need to sit." She made her wobbly way over to the sofa, concentrating on not toppling over. "It's... are you... is it hot in here? I can hardly breathe." She'd anticipated that one of her hackers would step out of the shadows, revealing their identity. Now she was certain she'd walked into a trap.

There Gabe stood, looking smug in his shiny glasses and pants with perfect pleats. She half expected him to tackle her and slap handcuffs on her.

"I made sure you weren't followed, Mizz Donovan, though you could afford to be a little more cautious."

The best defense is a strong offense. "Are you going to tell me what exactly you're doing here?" she asked, pleasantly surprised that her voice sounded firm and slightly annoyed.

"You weren't lying about the bleeding. I have some bandages around here somewhere." Gabe retreated down the tiny hallway to whatever hellish bathroom lay beyond the abysmal living area.

The CIA agent was rogue outside of the rogue illuminati he'd formed? *How does a rogue go more rogue?* It made no sense.

"What is...?" she called out, then looked around, assessing with a frown. *Don't touch anything.* The room was bare except for the simple Swedish couch, small coffee table, and floor lamp. A narrow doorway was off to the right. She imagined the bedroom was as depressing as the living area. She had passed through a tiny kitchenette on her way in, which was now situated a couple of steps to her right. It would've taken her three strides to cross the entire living area. No framed photographs, no artwork.

"What is this place? Is this a setup?" she asked loudly. "Are you going to try to arrest me or something?"

"No, this isn't a trap, and I couldn't arrest you even if I wanted to." He suddenly stood in front of her, carrying a large first-aid kit. "The CIA is an intelligence agency, not law enforcement. Take a seat on the couch."

Celeste wrinkled her nose. "I don't know—or care—what you and your co-eds have done in this sad little pied-à-terre, but I'm not interested in catching anything. I'll stand, thank you very much."

To her surprise, Gabe laughed heartily. "I suspected there was a sense of humor behind your steely facade." He looked at the blood soiling her gray T-shirt and gestured once more for her to sit. "That needs to be cleaned—and soon. Tetanus is a real bitch, from what I hear."

Celeste swallowed her disgust and sat down. She watched as he opened the kit and expertly placed the supplies on the small table. Gauze pads, waterproof surgical tape, antiseptic, scissors. *Here goes nothing.* She gingerly lifted up her shirt. "That's quite the gash. Lie back and put your feet up so I can properly clean it."

Perv. It hurt badly enough that she obliged.

Gabe crouched down on the floor beside her. He swabbed the wound several times with antiseptic, using a fresh gauze pad each time. The cold disinfectant stung. She looked at her navel once he was finished and was surprised to see that the cut was small, only two or three inches long.

"That's it?" she asked.

"Don't let the size fool you. This is a deep wound. You'll need to clean it regularly over the next few days and keep it dry."

Great. That'll be a breeze to hide from my fiancé with the libido of a twenty-year-old.

Gabe worked quietly and quickly, and within moments, she was bandaged and seated next to him.

Standing, he said, "Hang on," and then retreated once more down the hallway. He returned moments later with a maroon Columbia sweatshirt.

Celeste found the college gear to be particularly fitting in that moment and burst out laughing. "You've got to be fucking kidding me."

"It's the best I could find. The bathroom is right there—"

"Yes, I see, though I'm sure it's hard to find any of the rooms in this palatial suite." She went to the bathroom and changed out of her shirt into the sweatshirt. When she returned, Gabe was standing in front of the solo cabinet above the two-burner countertop stove.

"Would you like a drink?" He retrieved a bottle and two glasses. *Macallan 25.*

Celeste whistled. "It's as though you were expecting me." She wasn't sure what the protocol was, but she was in pain. "Yeah. Maybe it'll take the sting out of this."

They sat.

Celeste was growing impatient. "OK, Gabe, what am I to make of this odd late-night meeting?" *In other words, what the fuck do you want?*

"Look, Mizz Donovan—"

"I've told you to call me Celeste."

"I'll level with you. I know you've been digging around, and I admit your sleuthing skills are quite good. But you must stop now. Leave it to the professionals. You're going to get yourself killed, and because you're acting against orders, I can't guarantee I—or anyone else—will be able to protect you."

Protect me. Ha!

"I haven't the slightest idea—"

"Mizz Donovan, spare me the bullshit." She shot him a withering look. He pretended not to notice and continued. "I don't know exactly what you're up to, but it's safe to say you're in over your head. What is it that you want?"

"I want information."

"Tell me what you're trying to find, and I'll do my best to provide you with answers."

"Are you working with Nasrin?"

"Nasrin?" He was good at concealing his emotions, but she was better at reading them. His tone and facial expression indicated he knew exactly who Nasrin was.

Celeste stood, wincing, and then straightened. "This was obviously a waste of my time." But she had garnered an important piece of information—he didn't know she'd nearly crossed paths with Omar in UAE, or he surely would've mentioned it.

Gabe sighed. "OK, yes, we've worked with Nasrin and her late husband a few times over the years."

She sat back down and took a sip of Scotch. "We?"

"My colleagues and I." Celeste's alarm must have been apparent on her face, because he quickly added, "A select small group of people at the agency. Don't worry; Nasrin and her family are safe."

But Celeste knew that was not something he could guarantee. "How do you explain what happened to Zari, then?" she snapped.

"Zari's... situation was unfortunate. A tragedy, though nothing we could have prevented."

Unfortunate. "You were supposed to keep him safe. And now... and now..." She teared up. *Pull it together.*

"There's no use ruminating over what can't be changed. Zari was murdered. As I understand it, you were close to him, so I'm sorry for your loss. But I didn't ask you here to discuss the past."

"Why *did* you summon me here?"

"To answer all your burning questions." He smiled, a sinister gleam in his eyes.

She took a swig of Scotch. "Fine. I'll keep a lower profile if you stop bullshitting me. I'm sick and tired of being given the runaround when I'm the only one of us who—" she stopped herself.

"Who got close to Omar," he completed. "Yes, I know. A rather unfortunate sequence of events, but ultimately it ended well, right?"

That word again. Unfortunate. As though Omar's attacks and Zari's death amounted to an annoyance, a minor inconvenience in her life like a delayed flight or a sample sale with no size twos. *And how exactly do you define "ended well," Gabe?* At that point, she was ready to walk out, but her pride kept her planted in place.

"Yes, of course, it worked out well in the end," she said nonchalantly. *Omar remains a free man and is now protected* from me *by my own country. Bravo!*

"Actually, Mizz Donovan, let's not focus on what you want to know. Here's what you *need* to know. Someone who was at Savin's that night we first met alerted Omar that we were all working together. My intel suggests he hasn't told my corrupt superiors yet. But he's clearly biding his time.

"You can imagine what will happen to Chet and me if and when he does. If we're taken off the case—or, worse, fired from our respective agencies—the protection we've provided to the illuminati will vanish. Leaving you—and your business dealings—vulnerable to exposure."

Gabe slammed back his Scotch and poured another two fingers in his glass. He extended the bottle and filled hers as well.

"So, *Celeste*," he sneered, "if you had to guess right now—who was it? Who's the leak?"

The million-dollar question. *And whoever it is, it's the same person who told Omar I was in the UAE and tried to kill me in Paris.* The leak situation kept nagging her on a subconscious level, but she hadn't been able to bring it to the forefront of her mind no matter how long she'd stared at her grid or sifted through the knowns and unknowns.

"I haven't the slightest idea," she answered honestly. "My guess would've been you and/or Cli—er, Chet."

"We're doing everything we can to identify the leak, but it could be a job for one of those hackers with whom you have covert meetings."

"You're having me followed? What the fuck?" *Shit.* He could've been fishing, and like an idiot, she'd taken the bait. She wondered if he was behind the photos. She'd have to be more careful.

He smiled broadly, which Celeste interpreted to mean he *had* been fishing. She continued. "Sav and I have always had cybersecurity... experts we employ. Is that a crime now?"

He shrugged. "I don't much care whom you hire, but you really should be focusing on who within your circle is working against us."

"I'm on it." *But not without a little quid pro quo.* She was determined to get him to answer her most important question and wasn't leaving until he did.

Celeste slammed a heavy plate on the kitchen floor and jumped back to avoid the shards of glass. She peeked down the hallway to ensure the bedroom door was still closed, then set to work. She put the bloody gauze pads and T-shirt she'd saved from Gabe's on the counter. She opened the first-aid kit, placing antiseptic and packages of gauze and tape where Theodore would see it when he walked in.

She'd arrived home from Gabe's the night before to find Theodore asleep. She slipped into bed beside him, wearing pajamas to cover the bandage. After tossing and turning all night, scheming to catch the traitor in her inner circle, she'd pretended to be sound asleep when Theodore awoke that morning. He'd kissed her on the forehead and whispered, "I love you, sweetheart," then went into the bathroom. When she heard that he'd started the shower, she'd rushed out of bed to stage the scene that would explain the wound on her abdomen.

"Honey!" she called loudly when he was out of the shower. "Hey, babe, can you come here?"

He padded into the doorway, and a worried frown crossed his face. "Oh my God! What happened?"

"Wait, there's broken glass. Go get slippers, then I'll tell you how clumsy I am."

He was back by her side within moments. "My God, sweetie!"

"I was trying to get a plate off the top shelf, and it shattered. It's embarrassing how ungraceful I can be sometimes." She frowned theatrically with a hint of flirtation in her expression.

"We need to get you to the hospital."

"No, no, I think I've got it under control." She had dampened the gauze pads, Gabe's dressing, and her T-shirt so that the timing was believable. "See? The bleeding already stopped."

"How big was the gash? What if it gets infected?"

"That's a good point," she conceded. "I'll have the concierge doctor come by a little later today. But I'd rather not ruin our entire Sunday with this mess. We're supposed to meet Savin in an hour for brunch, remember?"

"Are you sure you're up for it?"

"Yes. The pain is nearly gone," she lied. The cut made her extremely uncomfortable, and she, too, was worried about infection. "Sav was dying for us to join him today, and you know how he pouts if we don't show up."

"Oh, wow, I didn't know the whole crew was showing up today!" Celeste exclaimed when she and Theodore walked up to the table at Balthazar's. Jack, Savin, and Mark stood up to greet them, and the server quickly asked for the new arrivals' drink orders.

Celeste noticed they were seated around a table for six. "Are we expecting another?" she inquired.

Mark rolled his eyes. "It's for Savin's mystery live-in. She's apparently joining us in thirty minutes."

Jack grinned broadly and rubbed his hands together, brimming with excitement for whatever drama Savin was bringing. He met Celeste's eyes and said, "Yippee!"

Savin frowned at his friends' antics. "It's different this time," he said, hurt sneaking into his tone.

Celeste laughed. "Poor Sav. We promise we'll take this one seriously. Are you going to tell us anything about her?"

He perked up. "You'll see soon enough. She's stopping by after Pilates."

"So, Theo—can I call you Theo?" Jack asked, turning to Theodore.

"You'd have to clear that with my—" Theodore replied.

Celeste interrupted. "No. We aren't doing Theo."

"That got off the table real quick," Jack retorted, and the group laughed. He turned to Theodore at the other end of the table. "Anyway, my man, Theo*dore*, we always miss each other when I'm in town. Excited for you to officially join our fam. You taking care of our best girl?"

"Best *woman*, and yes, he does well," Celeste interjected.

"Except this morning. I got out of the shower immediately after hearing Celeste scream." Theodore paused and looked around the table.

Celeste frowned. She could've sworn he turned off the shower before she screamed.

"I ran in to see what happened, and there she was, blood everywhere!"

Fuck. Of course Theodore would tell everyone, because he'd have no reason to know she'd want to keep it private.

She jumped in, as nonchalant as possible. "It's true. I dropped a heavy plate and watched in slow motion while it shattered all over the place. A shard of glass sliced my skin. A bloody mess is right."

"Well, sounds super gross, so I must see it right away," Jack demanded.

Celeste wore a flowy summer top and black linen shorts. "There's not much to see," she said, baring her midsection to show the blood-stained gauze. *I really do need to have this checked out.*

Mark recoiled at the sight. "Looks like you need a doctor and a new bandage."

Jack whistled. "How big is it? Is it deep?"

Theodore laughed. "That's what I wanted to know too!" he chimed in, then straightened up. "She refused to get medical treatment. Said Savin may have a tantrum if we missed brunch."

Savin sat back in his seat, eyeing the group, then pointedly asked Celeste, "So, let me get this straight—you dropped a plate and ended up with a gash on your stomach?" The others seemed not to notice the disbelief in his tone, but Celeste caught it. Not long before, when she'd had a bandaged hand, she'd told Savin the truth—that she'd thrown a vase, cutting her hand. *But honesty is too dangerous these days.*

"I know, crazy, right?" she said breezily. "Rest assured, my concierge doctor is coming over later. Now, can everyone stop worrying about me and get back to why we really came? To hassle Savin about his new lady before she arrives and place bets on when she'll be moving out, remember?"

Celeste noticed that everyone was staring at the entrance. She looked over her shoulder, and her jaw dropped. Walking toward them, clearly straight out of Pilates with a fresh workout glow and a bouncing ponytail, was... *Rani?* "Sav, what's *Rani* doing here?"

But he wasn't listening. The same wide grin he had worn when she'd seen him texting with his mystery woman slowly spread across his face as he jumped up to meet Rani. She lit up when he put his arm around her and escorted her to the table.

"Everyone, meet the woman I've been hiding. Celly, don't be mad. We wanted to tell you—well, I wanted to tell you—long ago. But we were waiting until we were sure. And now we are!" Savin turned to Rani and asked quietly, "Shall we tell them?"

Rani nodded vigorously. "Yes!"

"I've asked Rani to—"

Pick up your jaw off the floor. "Yes, yes, we already know you're cohabit—"

"We're engaged!" Sav and Rani said in unison, then kissed each other passionately.

"Congratulations, mate!" Theodore exclaimed. He jumped up to shake Savin's hand and gave Rani a light hug. Mark followed suit.

"So happy for you, my man. Rani, welcome to the family," Mark said.

Jack caught Celeste's eye and giggled. "Don't be such a bitch," he mouthed, then stood up to join the others.

Celeste frowned, but the joyous group did not notice. *An office romance involving Savin is not what we need right now.* Her more optimistic estimate was that they'd have a disastrous breakup by February, but the realist in her believed it would be much sooner.

Right then, four phones vibrated in unison. She looked at hers first.

"Ohmygod!" she shrieked. "Sam and Roberto had their baby!" *Saved by the bell.* She finally stood. "Congratulations, you two lovebirds, and nice work on sneaking around." *This raises the question of what* else *Savin could be hiding.*

"It was so hard not to share this with you, Celeste," Rani admitted. "But I told Savin we needed to be sure this was real before we made any announcements."

"Can I see the rock?"

Savin jumped in. "It's being fitted. A diamond-studded sapphire inspired by Elizabeth Taylor's engagement ring from—"

"Michael Wilding," Rani said, her face shining with happiness. "My grandmother and I have always loved that ring," she added.

Inspired by another love affair with a happy ending. Celeste stopped herself from rolling her eyes and smiled. "Ooh, sapphire! I can't wait to see it," she said cheerfully. Theodore strolled over and put his arm around her waist. She flinched.

"Oh, honey, I forgot. I'm so sorry," he whispered in her ear, adjusting his hold.

"I hadn't the slightest idea of whom Savin was seeing, did I?" she asked loudly, locking eyes with Theodore. "Did I, darling?" She kissed him on the cheek, then turned to the couple. "We couldn't be happier for you!"

"Thank you, Celly, that means so much," Savin said, oblivious to her real reaction.

"Now, let's eat, shall we?" Celeste said. "Rani, you're probably starved from your workout."

The hovering server looked relieved and quickly took everyone's drink orders.

"Champagne is in order today. Bring us a bottle of your finest and six glasses, please," Jack instructed.

"Since when do you need an excuse to order bubbles at brunch?" Celeste teased.

"Touché."

Their phones vibrated again.

Savin read aloud. "It's a girl!"

Roberto had sent Celeste, Savin, Mark, and Jack photos of Sam and their new baby.

"Wow, she's beautiful," Celeste remarked.

"They are in for a lot of sleepless nights," Mark commented. "But parenthood is the most rewarding thing I've ever done. It's all worth it in the end."

"What about the two of you? Do you want children soon?" Jack asked, directing the question to Savin and Rani. Jack never inquired about anyone's personal details, so Celeste knew he was doing it to bug her. He caught her eye and winked. She flipped him a discreet middle finger.

"Yes, Sav and Rani, when will you two start popping out babies?" Even as she said it, Celeste felt a little bad because they both knew her too well to miss her sarcasm. *Well, that's what they get for springing this on me—and the timing couldn't be worse.*

"All in good time, my friends," Sav responded lightly. "We're still in the engagement afterglow, so no babies anytime soon. And don't worry, Celly, we won't steal your wedding thunder. We've agreed to wait until after yours to start planning. We couldn't have the three of us out at once."

How generous of you. Maybe next time, don't lie to me. Or here's a thought: Don't sleep with—and then propose to—the woman who keeps our entire operation running.

LATER, when Celeste and Theodore were home, she was still fuming. What had Savin been thinking? How was this going to play out in the long term? And in the interim, he had blurred the lines between them, as the co-founders and co-CEOs, and the staff. *There goes all our respect.* But it was too late. It wasn't as though she could talk him out of it.

"Doc Mayfair will be here any minute, babe," she said as she and Theodore sat together on the couch, separately scrolling delivery options for dinner. "Let's go with Il Mulino."

"Perfect. Do you want the usual?"

"You know me well, love," Celeste said, then kissed him on the cheek. "I'll open a bottle of red after the good doctor does her magic." She buzzed up the doctor when the arrival was announced and opened the door to her moments later.

"Celeste, whatever happened, dear?" Dr. Mayfair said by way of greeting. She rushed in, nodded in the direction of Theodore, and asked, "Where are we doing this?"

"The couch in my office is fine," Celeste replied. She led them down the hallway and they entered.

"I can't believe you waited all day to call me. Don't blame me if there's a scar."

"You never let *me* in your office," Theodore remarked from the doorway. Then he turned to Dr. Mayfair. "I said the same thing, but she refused to miss brunch." He crossed the room and laid a blanket across the pristine velvet couch cushions. "Voilà! See, nothing will soil this beautiful sofa." He sat down and patted the cushion next to him.

"Fine. Get over here, Celeste," the doctor demanded. "I need to stitch this up quickly."

Theodore moved out of the way to make room for the two women. Celeste lay down and lifted her shirt. Dr. Mayfair removed the bandage and barked orders at Theodore to retrieve a trash can. He left the room.

"Are you going to tell me what really happened? This clearly isn't a cut from a broken plate, and it's at least a day old."

Celeste had feared that her doctor might pick up on this. "I'll tell you another time. But I may need a tetanus shot if you have one," she said quietly.

They kept the chatting at a minimum as Dr. Mayfair first numbed the wound, then cleaned it. She withdrew a syringe from her bag. "This shot is a bit painful for a day or two after. Sit up." She pulled up Celeste's right sleeve, cleaned the injection site with an alcohol swab, and administered the vaccine to the deltoid muscle. After swiftly putting the syringe and swab in a travel biohazard container, she looked at Celeste.

Here comes a lecture. Celeste let Dr. Mayfair finish dressing the wound.

"If I'd seen you right after this happened, I'd have been able to stitch you up. But because of your delay, I'll need to use some skin adhesive. Your body's already begun the healing process, so I can't do full stitches."

"It only happened last ni—" Celeste said in protest, then pivoted when Theodore came back with a trash can. "Babe, I was telling Dr. Mayfair the good news." He gazed at her quizzically. "Savin's engagement," she said with false cheer.

"Oh yes, it's wonderful, isn't it? You know, Doc, I've known Savin since we were young lads, and I've never once seen him lucky in love. Until now. No one deserves it more than he does. And Rani is such a spectacular woman. They'll make each other very happy."

Let's not count our chickens before they hatch.

"Ow, fuck!" Celeste nearly shouted. "It feels like you just stabbed me." The doctor was poking around in the wound with a pair of tweezers.

"Hold still. I can see a tiny shard of glass floating around. I'll get you sewn up right away."

"Is it infected where the skin is bright red, Doc?" Theodore asked with concern in his tone.

"It does appear to be, but nothing that a course of antibiotics won't knock out. You really should've gone to the hospital," Dr. Mayfair scolded.

"You know how important brunch is to me," Celeste joked.

Though if I were going to miss a brunch, perhaps today's was the one to miss.

"And all this from a broken plate. Hard to believe a little plate could do all this damage, isn't it?" Theodore said, then came around and kissed Celeste on the top of her head. She eyed her fiancé.

Does he know?

"You'd be surprised at how much harm commonplace kitchen items can cause," the doctor said nonchalantly. "OK, this is the best I can do tonight. Take good care. I'll show myself out."

"Thanks for the house call, Doc," Theodore said, and then buried his face in Celeste's hair. "Dinner will be here in less than twenty minutes, honey. I got your favorite," he murmured. "Shall I pour us some wine?"

"Oh, I'm sorry, I forgot to open the wine." Celeste said, leaning to sit up. The sharp pain was back. She gasped and then lay back again.

"I'll take care of it. You stay put," he said lovingly.

She wondered if she had imagined the disbelief in his voice before.

"LET'S go see Sam and Roberto one evening this week. Sounds like they're ready for visitors," Celeste suggested. She took a bite of her pappardelle Bolognese. "The Barolo pairs perfectly," she added.

"That would be lovely. Chances are, though, that I may need to be in Europe again for a couple of days."

"What? You've been traveling so much lately, and I was hoping you'd be here until we leave for Copenhagen."

"I know, darling. I don't want to go, either. But everything is a bit of a mess right now, and it's so much easier for me to be on the ground."

Celeste wondered if she wasn't the only one in their relationship with secrets.

"OK, I suppose I'll survive without you, although I'm beginning to feel like a Connecticut housewife, ya know," she said, then puckered her lips. He leaned over and dutifully kissed them.

"I know better than to ever try to move you from Manhattan. There are limits to your love," Theodore said, laughing.

"Yes, indeed."

After dinner, they decided on a movie and settled on the sofa. But Celeste's eyelids were heavy from the many nights spent at her computer and on errands. She dozed off before the opening scene and didn't stir when Theodore turned off the TV and lights after the closing credits and went to bed himself.

Her sleep was tormented. Splashes of blood and a chaotic mish-mash of faces stayed with her even when she awoke in the night. She padded into the guest bathroom and splashed water on her face, then met her own eyes in the mirror.

How am I ever going to get to the bottom of this mess?

10

MOMENT OF TRUTH

Celeste sat at her desk preparing for the D&C Monday 8 a.m. meeting, and she was still trying to make sense of Gabe's reveals. The most explosive was that there was indeed someone on the inside acting against her and the firm's best interest. She'd been shaken when Michel had told her the same thing, when she'd seen it again in Dubai on the camera screen, but the examples Gabe gave her made it imperative that she uncover the traitor's identity—and quickly. If Gabe believed that this person had tipped off the shooter about her recent trip to Paris and alerted Omar that she would be in the UAE, it was definitely worth exploring.

"How did you know about the shooter?" she'd demanded during their rendezvous in the tiny apartment with the rusty broken window. "Did you send me that text? And why didn't you stop them?"

What happened to Hadid?

"My ground team was responding to another crisis, and in that moment, there was a power vacuum in France. It's almost as if they'd known. So if you hadn't received that text..." Gabe had trailed off, leaving her to finish the thought.

"*You* didn't send it?"

"No. Like I said, our ground team wasn't prepared. They—and by extension, I—found out after the fact. A news helicopter got a video clip of the shooter putting the sniper rifle away, oddly enough. Believe me, it wasn't easy to quash the story."

Celeste had wanted the information to flow one way, with Gabe tipping his hand, so she kept to herself that she was supposed to be meeting Hadid that evening. She wondered how Gabe knew about the warning text but pushed on to the higher-priority topic.

"Why is the US government *really* working with him? Protecting him?"

Gabe's face reddened. *At least he has the decency to look guilty.*

"Mizz Donovan—Celeste if I may—I'm not at liberty to release information to a civilian about an ongoing investi—"

She could no longer keep her composure. "I'm sorry! I thought it was I who was recently forced to sign a bunch of fucking papers indicating that I'm no longer an ordinary citizen, but some sort of collaborator with the US government, as explained to me by my attorney. And that you and your pal need my friends and me to save the world or some shit.

"So don't *you* tell *me* that I cannot be in your little circle of secrets after you've exploited me to no end and then gotten into bed with a man who has terrorized me..." She would not cry in front of this man, even if they were tears of anger.

"I hope that you'll recognize how risky it is for me to have you here. And you're not officially working with us. You've basically done little more than sign an NDA. Do you even know what this place is? Whom I usually meet here?"

Celeste kept her face impassive, though her fury was brewing right below the surface. *Don't know, nor do I care.*

"This is where I bring someone who has volunteered to work against their own government to make the world a better place— American agents. People who would be tortured and killed if their home country found out they were spies. People who are willing to die for a greater cause—democracy, providing their family with a better life, fighting corruption—whatever it may be.

"Do you think for one second that I want to be associated with an organization providing any sort of protection to that bottom-feeding piece of shit human being Omar? He had Chet's wife killed. I know for a fact that his organization provided automatic weapons to rebel militants in my family's hometown. Those bastards leveled the shit out of the entire city within a day. It's unrecognizable now.

"So please do not mistake me for an Omar sympathizer. I have the privilege to work with some of the bravest, most principled people I've ever met, willing to give up their lives for the greater good, climbing through that window week after week to feed me information that I then funnel up through our intelligence channels. Until very recently, I believed wholeheartedly in my government, in my agency, and in my chain of command.

"But the wool has been pulled from my eyes. The world is not black and white. I am still doing good, I believe that, but the stakes are high. Every time I send an encrypted communication to Langley, I worry that someone reading the information is going to burn my agent. That the higher-ups who are working against the US are going to make the call to put a hit on someone I've devoted my career to protecting. A compromised agent doesn't have a long lifespan after being exposed." He looked as though he were struggling to get air.

"Please do not insult me by suggesting that my plight is without serious ethical dilemma," he continued. "I want no more to do with Omar than you do. Is your cause noble? Maybe. But your recklessness is not. You think you know Omar better than anyone, and maybe you do. But you're a fool if you don't accept the reality. You're not only up against him—you're in a fight for your life with anyone protecting him if you cross him. Including my bosses."

I'll take my chances, she had thought once he finished his tirade. She jolted herself back to the present moment. *Where I am now two minutes late for my own meeting.*

D&C was a close-knit team, so the betrayal would be felt deeply once she uncovered who was leaking information. She considered those who worked closest to her and Savin—Rani, Lorraine, Brett. A couple of the portfolio managers. The three analysts interested in ramping up the

Paris operation. She and Savin had built D&C from the ground into an empire. It was her home, what she'd chosen to construct while other people moved to the suburbs and built mansions and families.

Celeste gathered her portfolio and tea and made her way to the conference room, where the staff waited expectantly.

"Good morning! We have a lot to cover, so let's get started. Analyst team—you have the floor."

As the two analysts who led the team dove into specifics around some of their research that would drive decision-making around the future of D&C's investments in raw materials, Celeste noted Savin's absence. Rani sat at the opposite end of the table, dutifully recording the minutes of the meeting and projecting slides.

Where is he?

Celeste still hadn't come to terms with the fact that Savin had successfully hidden his budding relationship with Rani from her—and so well too. She'd always pegged him as terrible at keeping secrets, and in the past, she also would've found it outside the realm of possibility that he'd date someone right under her nose without her noticing. Maybe she needed to evaluate the situation with fresh eyes. His betrayal would sting more than anyone else's, which was perhaps why she'd never had the capacity to look at the situation objectively.

Around 8:15, Savin walked in, disheveled and buzzing with frazzled energy. Celeste narrowed her eyes. "Lovely of you to join us, dear colleague," she remarked snidely.

"Everyone, take this as a lesson of what *not* to do," he said. "Never, ever show up late for one of Celeste's meetings. I'll be in the doghouse for weeks." There were nervous giggles from those around the table, everyone careful to avoid making eye contact with Celeste for fear of an eruption.

"Accurate. Now please take a seat and stop rudely interrupting." She noticed him make eye contact with Rani and wink. She looked to the presenters. "I'm sure Savin sends his regards for the disruption. Please continue."

THE MORNING'S theatrics had cemented in Celeste's mind what she needed to do. She dialed Rani on her speaker phone. "Rani, please cancel my day. And arrange a call for me with Fred Warren at eleven a.m. Thanks," she said curtly and disconnected.

She set up a phone call with Ace for that afternoon from her burner phone. Over the course of the next half hour, she worked out the trap that would bring her closer to learning the identity of the leak.

Energized, she shot up from her chair and leaned over the desk to grab her handbag. *Ouch!* Fucking Gabe. If he hadn't insisted on meeting, she would've never had the ugly wound and bruising on her abdomen. She retrieved the Nokia from her bag and dialed the number he'd previously used to communicate with her.

"Gutiérrez," Gabe grumbled on the other end.

"I need your help."

"Make it quick." He didn't mask the alarm in his voice, likely because he wasn't alone.

"I'm going to Europe this evening, but I haven't mentioned it to anyone yet," she spilled out. "I'll tell each person who was at Savin's that night a different story about where I'll be tomorrow evening at seven p.m. Paris time. Is there anyone on the ground who could scope out the spots to see where a tail surfaces? There will be six different spots—for Fred, Mark, Angelo, Rani, Ace, and Savin."

"Simple yet effective."

"Will this field team be competent if Omar shows up?"

"Yes, I'll put my best on it." He lowered his voice and continued, "Send me the list on the encrypted channel I showed you at the safe house."

Click.

In under forty-five seconds, she'd relayed a plot to frame those closest to her. Now the waiting would begin.

Her iPhone rang, and Fred's name popped up on caller ID.

"Hey, can you meet me for lunch?" she asked by way of greeting.

"Sure. How about Benoit at noon?"

"Perfect. See you there."

Now on to Ace. "Calling you in ten," she shot off from her burner.

She gathered her bag and iPad, then went to Savin's office. His door was closed.

"Knock, knock," she announced and peeked her head in. *Now I have to worry about walking in on him fucking our star employee, so I can no longer barge in.* He was alone talking on the phone. She strolled in and sat at his conference table.

"Hey, I've gotta go. Celly just walked in," he said and ended the call. He came over and sat down beside her. He folded his arms across his chest.

"Why do you look so pissed off?"

"Well, Celly, you weren't exactly supportive of me yesterday. I've always been your biggest fan, and I've always been ecstatic when you're happy. It hurt my feelings that you had so little to say."

Savin, the one man in her life who could shamelessly identify and verbalize his emotions, the one who always rooted for love and who had never missed a beat supporting even the craziest ideas she had, wanted her approval.

Maybe I've been unfair.

"I'm sorry. I *am* happy for you two, truly I am. I was a bit caught off guard and a little shocked, I guess, mostly because I didn't notice what was happening right under my nose. Regardless, I'm sorry, and please know that I'm quite happy for you." She plastered a smile on her face. "Engaged, Sav! You're finally coupled up with a woman who matches your kindness. I can't think of anyone who deserves a great love more than you. And Rani is obviously fantastic!"

Savin's body language softened, and a huge grin spread across his face. "Thanks, Celly! We were both really worried to tell you. Rani said to be patient, that you'd come around, but I was still hurt."

Rani said. This is going to be fun. "We should throw an engagement party for you two lovebirds soon. Mere can help with the planning," she offered. "Speaking of, I really should check in and see how my wedding planning is unfolding. I've left literally everything to her."

"So what can I help you with this fine morning?"

"I'm going back to Paris for a day or two. Mere has a few dresses set aside for me for the rehearsal dinner that I need to try on," she fibbed. "And I'd like to check on the office—the Paris outpost must be running smoothly before the acquisitions are finalized."

"That's a good point. I'll keep things going here."

Celeste had an idea. "I was thinking of taking Lorraine. I've promised her a trip with just the two of us, and it would be great to have her as backup there in the event someone left." Celeste was sure Lorraine would be up for it.

There was a knock at the door.

"Come in," Savin bellowed.

In walked Lorraine... and Brett was behind her. *That's strange.* Brett closed the door.

"Your ears must've been burning—we were discussing you, Lorraine," Celeste remarked. "Have a seat." She gestured to the empty chairs.

Once they were all settled, she asked, "To what do we owe this surprise visit?"

Lorraine replied, "Brett and I," at the same time that Brett said, "Lorraine and I," then they both laughed. *Hmm, seems they've been spending a lot of time together. Just what I need—another office romance.* Brett nodded to Lorraine to proceed.

"Brett and I... well, remember how perplexed we all were about the Shu financials?"

Celeste and Savin nodded affirmatively in unison. Their analysts' excitement was palpable. *This oughta be interesting.*

"Well, afterward I asked Brett what had happened. You know, why he'd left out critical pieces of the analysis."

Frankly, Celeste had nearly forgotten about the Shu deal. *The least of my worries right about now.*

"Yes, and?" Savin inquired, looking from one to the other. "I'm assuming if there was a problem, then you two would've alerted us."

"Of course. We didn't think it was strange until we realized what really happened," Brett said conspiratorially.

Spit it out already.

"Brett got the wrong file—or, rather, the wrong documents were uploaded to his shared drive. He didn't mess up the analysis; *he did a different analysis* based on the figures in his files."

It was rare that Celeste was annoyed with these two, as they were D&C's rock stars. But she was losing her patience.

"Can you speak more direct—"

"Someone *in this office* tampered with Brett's files," Lorraine said. Celeste frowned.

Savin chimed in. "That's impossible. We have surveill—"

"Surveillance and security measures in place. Yes, that's what I said. But we printed out the two documents and compared them side by side. It's clear Brett's was altered. And then we began working through other projects where our respective analyses were conflicting—"

Brett jumped in excitedly, finishing her thought. "There were several instances where *we had different files.*"

But how is this possible? If true, this was an alarming security breach. Out loud she replied, "Well, that certainly seems strange. Can you—"

"Make a list of all the discrepancies we could track down? Yes, it's right here." Lorraine pulled it out of her folio, always the epitome of preparedness. She handed copies to Celeste and Savin. Celeste's interest was piqued, and she couldn't wait to dive in.

"OK, nice work," Savin said. "We appreciate your diligence and for bringing this to our attention with speed and a sense of urgency. We'll take a look and get back to you."

"As always, this must be kept completely confidential," Celeste urged.

"Yes, of course," Brett replied.

"Hey, would either of you like to join me in Paris for the next few days? It's a bit of a last-minute trip. I'll be flying out tonight," Celeste said, looking pointedly at Lorraine.

"I'd love to," Lorraine said at the same time that Brett exclaimed, "Count me in!" Then the two laughed.

Yep, they're fucking.

"Great. Meet me in my building lobby at eight p.m. We'll fly out of Teterboro. I'll share the details a bit later, and Rani will arrange hotel rooms."

Once the two had left and closed the door behind them, Savin remarked, "They're fucking."

"Yeah." It was then that Celeste remembered why she'd come. "I'll arrange a dinner with them at L'Avenue. Maybe there'll be a celebrity sighting for them to gush over." She looked into Savin's eyes. He'd been her best friend for so many years. *Are you hiding something more than an office romance, my dear friend?* If he wasn't the rat, he'd be so hurt she'd suspected him. *He must never know.*

"OK, I have a lunch and a lot of packing to do before I leave. I must be going," she said.

"Mere will be doing the heavy lifting, I'm sure," Savin teased, "but good luck getting ready for the trip."

She gathered her things, and Savin escorted her to the door. "Let me know how everything goes while I'm gone," she said over her shoulder. She stopped by Rani's desk on the way back to her office.

"Hi, darling."

Rani was all business. "How can I help, Celeste?"

"I've decided to spend the rest of the week working from our Paris office. Lorraine and Brett will join me. Can you book two rooms for them? Hôtel de Crillon?" *Could've booked one and saved the firm a little money.* "Oh, and one more thing. Could you send a giant baby gift to Sam and Roberto? I won't be able to see them until next week, from the looks of it." *That buys me a little time before I'm officially a bad friend.*

"No problem."

Celeste glanced around to make sure Savin wasn't within hearing distance. "And could you book dinner for four tomorrow night at Le Cinq?"

"Consider it done. Anything else? Will you need a driver?"

"Angelo can help with that. I'm going to do a little shopping as well this trip, for which I'm ecstatic." *May as well test my theory.* "Have you been to Paris lately?"

Rani had the decency to look sheepish. "Not really. A quick trip last spring. I'd like to make it back soon."

I know I saw you there, Rani. What is it that you're hiding? "Maybe you and Sav can plan a romantic getaway soon," Celeste said, smiling cheerfully. "I've offered Mere's services to help you and Sav plan an engagement party—if you're amenable, that is."

"Oh, wow! Really? That would be amazing, thank you," Rani gushed.

That should make up for my dark thoughts. If Celeste were being honest, she *was* rooting for them. And if nothing else, she would get to attend a fabulous party. Mere didn't throw any other kind.

"It's done, then. I'll let her know. I'm off to lunch now and then to prepare for my trip. Have a fantastic week," Celeste said and began walking toward the elevator. "Oh, and Rani—congratulations. Truly. I can't think of two people who deserve love more."

For a man with such refined taste, Fred really has slovenly table manners. Celeste fought the urge to tell him to wipe the butter from the corner of his mouth.

"You scored a table *today* at Plénitude for *tomorrow night*? How in the hell did you manage that?"

"One of my stylists is a miracle worker. She can get me a table anytime, anywhere in Paris," she fibbed. *Halfway done with my traitor test.*

"Hmm. Good for you." Fred finally dabbed the corners of his mouth to remove the distracting food from his face. "I assume you summoned me to lunch to do more than brag?"

"Yes, actually. We've decided to move forward with Nico and Enzo. If you were me, how would you handle?"

"You're playing with fire."

"I'm aware. So how do I get out without getting burned?"

"This must be about Omar. You'd never make a business decision this poor. They're a liability for many reasons. Nico is impetuous and impulsive, not to mention evil, and on top of being extremely unpredictable, he's well connected with the mob. Like actual mafiosos." His face turned beet red, his anger palpable. "Goddammit, Celeste." His voice was rising, and he looked extremely frustrated. "How many lives do you believe you have? Does your fiancé know about this? Does he know you have a death wish?"

"Oh, I'm sorry," she replied sarcastically. "Unlike your wives, all three of whom left you from what I understand, I don't have to ask my fiancé for permission to make business decisions."

"This isn't about business, Celeste, and you know it." Fred sat still for a moment, seemingly contemplating options. She watched as his fury became more apparent and prepared for him to continue his tirade. "No, you know what? I'm washing my hands of all this. I can't watch any more destruction." He pushed his chair back noisily and threw his cloth napkin on the table. "Best of luck to you. It was nice knowing you." He stormed off.

Unbelievable. Gabe's admonishment and now this. Why was Fred suddenly being so unreasonable? What business was it of his anyway whom she decided to work with? Sure, his warnings had helped her fight Omar last time, so she had no reason—until that moment—to believe he meant her any harm. But life was different now that Celeste had to consider everyone as the potential leak, and she wondered if Fred's outburst was a setup.

Back at her apartment that afternoon, she was still fuming. To think that she'd always acted in her friends' best interest, yet Savin had been harboring at least one secret from her for months, and Fred ended up berating at her in a French bistro. Everyone wanted her to stop acting alone, yet no one was willing to help in a real way or make her life any easier. *Perhaps it's time to reevaluate my friendships.*

She stood in her closet, debating what to pack. She'd told Meredith she'd take care of everything herself for Paris because she was too angry to deal with anyone else. *And now someone's calling me to annoy me further*, she thought when her phone rang.

"What?" she barked without first checking who it was.

"Hi, honey. Just calling to say good night and see how your day is going," Theodore kind voice said through the phone. "What's good in your world today?" *He's certainly the yin to my yang.* But even his calm demeanor grated on her nerves that afternoon.

"No complaints, sweetie. Packing for Paris. I'm taking Brett and Lorraine to meet the staff. We really need someone we can trust to fill in there. And who knows? Maybe one of them will someday enjoy running that office." *Or both of them.*

"Paris? I didn't realize you'd be traveling this week as well. We could've arranged together."

She explained that she'd only decided a few hours prior to go to France and that the trip would be mostly work.

"Wait, are you sure you should be going out of town with your injury? What did Dr. Mayfair say?"

"Oh, babe, all is well. I'll be sitting around working the whole time anyway."

"I know you better than to believe that. It's fall in Paris, my darling. You'll be supporting the local economy, buying next season's haute couture and trying all the new hot spots."

Celeste laughed. "Fair, but I'll be fine. You worry about me too much!" She realized she'd been so preoccupied that she hadn't asked him any details about his whereabouts before he left. "I'll be back by the weekend. How about you? I don't even know where you are," she added. "London?" *Note to self: Be a more attentive fiancée.*

"No. Zurich again and trying to make a couple of stops on the way home. Frankfurt for sure and possibly Amsterdam. I'd like to relive some of our days there. Wouldn't you?" he asked, referring to their romantic Netherlands getaway the previous year.

"Mmm, that was a memorable trip, wasn't it?"

Celeste was grateful that the conversation had shifted to their sexual escapades and away from what she'd be doing the next couple of days.

"Amsterdam memories will give me something wonderful to dream about tonight," he remarked in a husky tone. "Which reminds me—you probably need to finish packing."

Celeste sighed. *Back to reality.* "Yes, I do."

They exchanged goodbyes and hung up.

She made the obligatory call to Sam and Roberto, congratulating them, telling them about her trip and dinner the following evening at Guy Savoy, and promising them a visit upon her return stateside.

Then she rang Angelo and told him the details of the trip. He confirmed that security was in place and she'd have a driver. She mentioned dinner at Kei but said they'd play by ear whether she would walk, take a taxi, or need a driver.

Throwing some clothes in her bags, she packed without her usual attention to detail and zipped them up.

She went into her office to call Ace and closed the door out of habit, though no one was there to overhear her. So what if she was a little too paranoid these days? *It's not like it's not warranted.* She kept the door shut anyway.

"What?" Ace said by way of greeting.

"Well, that's quite a greeting; your phone manners are really blossoming. Sorry I'm late. I'm planning a dinner in Paris tomorrow at L'Arpège at seven p.m. and have been swamped. So, what did you find out about Omar? Was he in UAE when I was? Is Hadid OK?" *If you even found out anything at all.*

Ace replied swiftly. "H is fine, and yes, flight records confirmed O was in UAE. Enjoy Paris."

Click.

Next, she rang Mark. He answered on the first ring. "What's up, Celly?"

"Hi, friend! I wanted to remind you to call Roberto with your congratulations on their firstborn! And to brag a little... I have a quick trip to Paris and am eating at your favorite spot tomorrow night!"

"No way! I've promised Jin that we'll go to Epicure as soon as we can make it to Paris again. We haven't been since the baby was born."

The two caught up a little more, and then Celeste claimed she had to go and pack.

"Great chatting, and enjoy the best meal in Paris tomorrow night," Mark said enthusiastically. "Take good care."

After they hung up, her phone vibrated in her hand as she walked to her desk. She nearly jumped out of her skin. She watched as a series of texts came through, one after the other.

"A sample of Matthew's files has been delivered to your door."

"His phone and hard drive partially cloned—his spyware detector kept us out of many files."

"More soon."

And then a lull. She thought the conversation had ended, but then one more text came through.

"Be safe in Paris. Bon voyage."

Her phone rang then. It was the front desk notifying her a package had been delivered.

"Hi, Jonah." Celeste acknowledged she was expecting a package and said she would come down to retrieve it.

"No need, Miss Celeste. I sent the porter up with it."

Celeste frowned. "What is it?"

"It's your Net-a-Porter delivery."

Celeste rolled her eyes. She had no more energy to spend contemplating what was going on.

"Knock, knock! Celly, I know you're here!" Meredith called from the foyer.

Celeste walked out to the living room as her stylist struggled into the room with a giant signature black-and-white bag.

"What on earth is in there?" Celeste asked. She was relieved to have some company—and some help packing. She needed a reprieve.

"I asked Jonah to let me surprise you. I know you can't pack without me, and you also need something new. So I had some pieces delivered."

While Meredith was focused on pulling some of the dresses out of the bag, Celeste noticed a manila envelope underneath all the goods. She turned her back to Mere, scooped it up, and threw it onto the sofa. Mere was none the wiser.

How did Michel's files end up in a shopping bag ordered only hours ago? Would Jonah have known to conceal the documents?

"Earth to Celly. Do you like any of this? I'm beginning to get a complex here."

Celeste looked over to see that Meredith had spread four beautiful outfits across the sofa.

"I love them all," she replied honestly. "We have about forty minutes to pack. Can we make it happen?"

"*We* aren't making anything happen. Go read whatever's in that envelope, and I'll have you packed with time to spare."

"No complaints here."

Celeste nearly ran into her office with the envelope and closed the door. She retrieved her letter opener and sat down to scour the documents. She had one hour to make some progress.

Whoever had compiled Matthew's file was thorough. Celeste scoured the texts and emails. He was an addict and a predator, exactly like Omar. The hacker had also compiled pages and pages of transactions: crypto, international wire transfers, withdrawals of large amounts of cash. Dozens of suspicious exchanges were flagged, many linked to what appeared to be a single shell company, RH Global. She tracked two locations: Switzerland and the Cayman Islands. *Idiot.* Everyone knew the two countries were tax havens. Matthew was going to have to be a little more clever if he didn't want Celeste on his heels. The information in the files confirmed two things for Celeste: It was imperative that she track down RH Global and—perhaps more importantly—now she knew that she hated him enough to destroy him. Right after Omar. *All in due time.*

She glanced at the time. *Fuck.* She had to go, and it would be foolish to leave the file in her apartment while she was out of town. *But more foolish to carry it with me.* There was no time to deliberate. She shoved the papers back in the envelope, which she stashed in her bag, then powered down her computer and went to the living room, where Meredith had her luggage lined up neatly by the door and was typing on her phone.

"There you are! Cutting it kind of close, aren't you?"

"I'll be fine. Monty's downstairs with Lorraine and Brett." She gathered her carry-on and wheeled suitcase, and the two took the elevator to the lobby. Passing the front desk, she said, "Paris calls, Jonah, so I'll be gone for a few days. Can you let me know if any packages arrive for me?"

"Absolutely, Miss Celeste. Have a lovely trip, my dear." Jonah nodded at Meredith in acknowledgment and then turned his attention back to his concierge duties.

When Celeste and Meredith were outside, Mere said, "In case you were wondering, though it doesn't seem like you have been, your wedding planning is going off without a hitch."

The wedding. My *wedding.* Celeste wondered if she were the only woman alive who spent so little time thinking about her pending nuptials.

"When I get back, we'll do dinner one night, just you and I, anywhere you want, and we'll talk through every single detail, k?" *Well, not* every *detail. Some details are best left to me.*

Meredith's face lit up. "Yes, that will be perfect. You're going to be blown away! We'll do next Monday. You're free. I'll make sure Rani knows." She was silent for a moment, then continued, "I, uh, heard her and Savin's news…" She looked at her boss to gauge any reaction.

Celeste smiled broadly. "Isn't it wonderful? I'm beyond happy for them. I can't think of two people who are more deserving of true love than those two," she gushed. *Lying assholes.* She hugged Meredith and then joined Lorraine and Brett in the back seat of Monty's SUV.

"ONLY THE BEST FOR YOU, Celeste. I know you'd dump out anything that wasn't Dom," Cam, the bitchy flight attendant, joked. He poured Champagne for her, Lorraine, and Brett, then distributed the glasses.

"You need a glass, too, Cam," Celeste urged. He had been on several of Celeste's flights of late, and she thoroughly enjoyed his company.

"To last-minute getaways to my *second* favorite city and to having the best team in the business. It's truly a pleasure to work with both of you," she said, then paused for effect. "And you, too, Cammie. How could I ever forget about you?" The four laughed. "*Salud.*" She raised her glass and clinked with the others.

Though they were trying to play it cool, Brett and Lorraine were both brimming with excitement to be flying private. Celeste had grown so accustomed to her lifestyle that she'd almost forgotten what it was like as a bright-eyed twenty- or thirty-something first experiencing the luxuries of the world. She found it endearing. She also begrudgingly found it sweet that they were taking extra care not to make eye contact. They definitely seemed to have a real connection. *Is literally everyone in love these days?*

"OK, so tell us about the Paris team. What's their structure? Who do you want us to get to know? I have so many questions," Lorraine remarked. "I know we'd both love to—well, at least I would love to—spend more time there."

Brett was more reserved, but he echoed the sentiment. "It's exciting to see D&C expanding so significantly. Will we also get to meet everyone at the newly acquired firms in Rome and Dubai?"

Oh yes, I should probably start taking some action to make those sham deals appear legitimate. Some days, she was so focused on ways she could blackmail or entrap Matthew and Nico that she forgot about the massive undertaking the acquisitions were going to be. Celeste suddenly realized she had failed to take advantage of two of her most prized assets.

"Given that Savin is paired up now, he's less enthusiastic about being on the road as often. I'd definitely be open to one or both of you spending some time in our new offices."

"That would be amazing, Celeste!" Lorraine exclaimed. "I was hesitant to ask, but I've been dying to check out what they're all about. TA Capital especially. I mean, I'm sure you offered them a great deal, but even then, it's interesting that Tarek is willing to hand over any sort of control. He's such a powerhouse in his own right."

Celeste was continually impressed with Lorraine's instincts. "You're right—we did give him an offer he couldn't refuse." *Stiletto on the nutsack and all.* "Let me discuss with Savin, and then we can talk logistics," she said vaguely. "You're going to love the Paris team and, more importantly, the Parisian attitude of lots of eating and drinking."

They discussed her vision for integrating the acquisitions a bit more, and then she dozed off. She needed to catch up on sleep if she was going to make the trip worth her while.

THE FOLLOWING MORNING, after Cam served them a breakfast of pastries and fruit, they bade him farewell and exited the plane. A man was waiting for them next to a black Tesla Model Y. She smiled because Angelo had taken to heart her comment that she wanted to stop riding in SUVs because of their environmental impact when organizing her driver. Angelo now insisted on arranging every detail of her transport and security, and she was happy to let him. She'd never blamed him for the kidnapping because she knew it hadn't been preventable. She was sure he'd never again let anyone who could harm her slip through the cracks. Tears still sprang to his eyes if anyone referenced her security in front of him.

"Rani booked you rooms with views of the Eiffel Tower at Hôtel de Crillon." *Close enough to my apartment that I can keep an eye on you if necessary.* "You can drop off your bags and freshen up. The driver and I will pick you up at noon, and we'll meet some of the others for lunch," she said, nodding to the driver and then sliding into the back seat. The other two joined her.

"Hôtel de Crillon!" Lorraine exclaimed. "Its renovation was Lagerfeld's last interior design. I've only seen it in magazines. I'm so excited."

"I'm glad you'll appreciate its history. It's quite beautiful. I also snagged us reservations at L'Écrin for dinner tonight." *The perfect cover so I can do some sleuthing beforehand.*

AROUND 11 A.M., Celeste walked into her Paris apartment with a latte in hand, and the concierge wheeled in the luggage cart. She thanked him and then closed and locked the door when he left. *You can never be too careful.* After all, someone had been prepared to shoot her the last time she'd been in town.

In addition to the suspicious transactions with RH Global, she had found a recent text message thread in Matthew's correspondence that was sure to be with someone close to Omar. There was reference to a "drop" that they were arranging, and she wanted to learn more about it. She pulled the Matthew file out of her Chanel tote and walked quickly to her office to read a bit more in the thirty minutes before she had to leave for the team lunch.

Celeste opened the door. She screamed at the top of her lungs. A man was leaning on her desk, facing her. Without even realizing it, she'd dropped the entire file and papers flew everywhere. It took a moment for her brain to catch up with what her eyes had seen.

"What—what are you doing here?" she demanded forcefully, though anyone who knew her would notice her voice wavering.

"Oh my, I'm sorry, I didn't mean to startle you, Miss Celeste," Hadid said. The man she'd been worried about for months, wondering if he'd been hurt or turned, was standing in front of her plain as day. He sounded remorseful when he added, "It's only me."

"Why haven't you called? I've been beside myself wondering if you were OK."

Hadid explained that one of his friends from the intelligence community had alerted him about the shooter, and he'd sent her the warning text.

He continued, "You did exactly the right thing getting out of there. I feared you'd wait behind for me, but I stayed back at my hotel to be safe. The two of us spotted in the same place by whoever hired the shooter would've escalated the situation immensely. To my knowledge, no one knows you and I have made contact since then, and I'd like to keep it that way."

My mind played tricks on me a second time that evening. She could have sworn she'd seen Hadid walking toward her right before she noticed the shooter's scope that night.

"But what about—Riyadh?"

"Riyadh was no problem. When I realized that man had been sent in to extract you from the situation, I was able to escape. It really was quite the scheme and almost fun to pull off. And watching the news after—man oh man. You really pulled a fast one over on Omar." His nonchalance was surprising, considering how high the stakes had been.

"And recently—why didn't you tell me it was you who warned me?"

"I did. I signed the text with an H."

She had scoured her text messages that night and didn't recall seeing an initial. But it had been a stressful night, and she could have missed it. *Just like I could've imagined Rani.*

"And what are you doing here now? Besides giving me a heart attack?"

"My apologies for the means, but I have some good news. I've found a way in."

"A way into my apartment? Yeah, I noticed. How the fuck did you get in here anyway?" She made a mental note to discuss with Theodore about finding a new Parisian pied-à-terre. Enough was enough.

Hadid looked at her pointedly, his face so much like the man from her nightmares. Nearly identical to Omar's. But the subtleties—the eyes that could shine with hope or convey concern, the smile that appeared as a result of happiness, not from causing other people pain—made all the difference.

This man put his life on the line at least once to help me frame Omar. I can hear him out. "I'm sorry. I'm a bit on edge. Why don't you start at the beginning while I clean up this mess?" She waved him away when he tried to help and quickly placed the papers inside the envelope.

"I've infiltrated his network."

"I assume you mean Omar's? How so?" She wanted to be excited, but it was difficult to avoid the reality of what she knew. *It doesn't change the fact that he's protected by the world's most powerful intelligence community.*

"One of the guys in his inner circle has some, uh, vulnerabilities, shall we say? He's willing to cooperate. And you can connect with him directly—your identity concealed, of course. Imagine what this access will give you."

Suddenly, Matthew's files and Michel's intel seemed less important. She hadn't thought it possible to directly penetrate Omar's network. The wheels began turning as she thought of ways she could take advantage of the situation.

"I... I don't know what to say. I mean, thank you. But honestly, I'd never even considered we could find a way in." *Especially now that Omar's working for the US.* "Who knows about this?"

"As far as I know—you, me, and Nasrin. In fact, she was the one who orchestrated all this."

Celeste was impressed. But she wouldn't, couldn't let this backfire on Nasrin. Her children had lost enough already. "I worry about her safety. Is she willing to stay out of it from now on?"

"Yes, exactly. Once I hand off, it's you and you alone with the access and the knowledge. That seemed the safest, given all that's going on." His tone was cryptic.

"One more thing—who do you think was behind the attempted shooting?" she asked, not sure if she wanted the answer.

"From what I could track down the night the shooting was supposed to take place, the whole thing had digital fingerprints pointing back to the US. It doesn't seem to be Omar-related. Does that seem odd to you? Any idea who would be behind it?"

Chet and Gabe had alluded to the fact that they were aware of some nefarious Americans. Just her luck to have pissed someone off enough for an assassination attempt. The drama was getting a bit dull of late.

"No idea, but I intend to find out."

~

THE MOMENT of truth had arrived. As she sat at dinner listening to her two protégés, Lorraine and Brett, excitedly discuss their ideas for the Paris office, she wondered how she'd feel later when she called Gabe. Would her test tonight reveal who was compromising her? More importantly, would she be able to handle the betrayal? It made her heart hurt to think that someone whom she loved and trusted could put her in danger—grave danger. But she couldn't hide from the truth any longer.

"I can't wait to discuss your ideas with Savin. You know I view you two as integral to the success of D&C, and I want to ensure you have opportunities for growth. That said, I'll be more than happy to keep you where you are. As we expand, though, please know that you are at the top of the list for new opportunities. You are uniquely positioned as our top two performers, and I want nothing more than to see you both continue to grow. To new adventures! *Salud*."

The three clinked glasses, and Celeste closed out the check. They made their way to their awaiting cars out front.

"I hope you don't mind I switched our dinner spot at the last minute. What did you think of Plénitude? Worth the three stars?"

Lorraine smiled widely. "Absolutely. So elegant and cozy as well."

"I can't remember the last time I enjoyed a meal this much. Thanks so much for arranging, Celeste," Brett said appreciatively.

"This is what I love about Paris. Around every corner is an adventure or a tantalizing meal. Thanks for joining your old boss for the best food I've eaten in weeks and enough wine to lend me a perfect slumber. Now I, for one, am going to bed, but that doesn't mean you two shouldn't go have some fun. We don't have an early morning, so feel free to explore."

Celeste smiled to herself as the two separately gave excuses for why they were going to call it a night. *I'd bet my Birkin that you two will be horizontal together in a matter of minutes.*

"That's my car. See you tomorrow!"

Back at her apartment, she was relieved to find it empty. *For once.* She wandered through it, an ode to her former life, before Theodore and before everything had become so complicated. It was opulent and luxurious, and every inch of it had her signature style stamped on it. She'd been holding on to the place out of sentimentality, but she could no longer ignore the danger of the repeated security breaches. Upon her return to New York, she'd have to discuss it with Theodore. A safer building was a must.

In the master bathroom, she cleaned her wound the way Dr. Mayfair had instructed and changed into a La Perla silk gown and matching robe. While going through her nightly skincare routine, she contemplated that whatever Gabe revealed was going to be difficult to process. *But I've handled everything that's come my way to date— I can handle this too.*

She poured herself a cup of tea, and then she could delay no longer. She retrieved one of her burner phones from her safe and went to her cozy sofa, cuddling under her Missoni cashmere throw. At 11:30 p.m. on the dot, her phone rang.

"Celeste."

"Gabe."

"The situation is a bit complex."

"How so?"

"My guys found two of the restaurants swarming with surveillance—roughneck types who associate with Omar."

Those surveilling found the places being surveilled. Got it. She took a long inhale and let out a longer exhale but realized no amount of mindful breathing would make this any easier. Out loud she said, "Which two?"

"L'Arpège," Gabe said, then paused. "And—" *Spit it out already.* "And L'Avenue."

She didn't need to reference her list to know what it meant. *Ace.* She let out a single sob before she could process the second one. *And Savin.*

Celeste had spent the afternoon playing out scenarios in her head. Ace compromising her was not surprising. In fact, she'd almost expected it. With Ace, it was business. They'd probably found a higher-paying client. Celeste was annoyed but not hurt.

But her best friend and business partner? The man who'd been her main cheerleader since she was nineteen, the man whose brow furrowed with concern if she so much as sneezed, her fiancé's closest childhood friend who had orchestrated a meet-cute so the two most important people in his life could fall in love? This—*this*—was the person who had set her up? The person who possibly leaked her location, which could have resulted in her death? She could no longer keep her cool.

Michel, Gabe, Ace, Fred. They'd all been right—there was a turncoat at D&C.

Savin has betrayed me.

PART II

FEBRUARY TO MAY

11

———

THE HUNTRESS BECOMES THE HUNTED

The force of the attack caused her to lose her footing. Celeste steeled herself against the blow a second too late, as her body went airborne and then hit the ground with a loud thud.

Fuck. Tears burned her eyes.

She curled into a fetal position and rubbed her forearm. *I didn't rebreak my wrist, I hope.* It had taken months to heal last time.

"Get up!" Zed shouted.

He was a foreboding figure, massive at six-foot-ten, 275 pounds lean, with a shaved head and tattoos covering most of his body. He bent down, his face mere inches from hers.

"Get the fuck up." The menace was apparent in his eyes. "You're not going to have the luxury of nursing your wounds when you're under attack. You're not taking your training seriously, Mia."

A former marine and the man she'd hired to train her in street fighting and hand-to-hand combat, he did not look like someone she'd want to run into on a dark street. Any normal human being would be terrified of him.

I can't believe I'm paying this asshole to dish out such abuse. She pushed herself to standing.

"I need my brace." She walked off the training floor.

"Do you think you'll be able to hit pause when they come for you? Is that how you think an ambush works—"

Enunciating each word while holding his gaze, she retorted, "I said—I need my fucking brace." She was sure he was used to people cowering to him. *Not me. Not today.* "I'll be right back."

She walked to the locker room with her head held high, hiding her limp. There was no way she'd give him the satisfaction of knowing she'd sprained an ankle.

It had been over a year since that night when she'd intended to kill Omar. But her plan had gone horribly awry, and he'd ended up pistol-whipping her with her own piece and nearly taking her life instead. She had vowed that she would never again be a victim—of Omar's or anyone else's. Now, the more she trained with Zed, the more it became an obsession—engaging in increasingly difficult sparring drills, taking marksman lessons, studying military and CIA training manuals. It was going to take everything she had for the next few months to play out according to plan. She may not have been sure whom she was up against, but of one thing she was certain—she would be ready this time.

She opened her locker and took out the hard-sided wrist immobilizer. Zed was right—she would have to be prepared to fight without the brace. Until then, though, she had to avoid serious injuries.

In front of the mirror, she adjusted her nose prosthetic and wig. Zed had no idea who she really was or what she looked like, and she was determined to keep it that way. She'd kept her training a secret from everyone, paid Zed in cash, and told him very little about herself.

She lifted her shirt gingerly. *That'll be a nice little—or big—black-and-blue mark to explain to my babe. If he doesn't leave me before the wedding.* Theodore had bought her lies—or at least had stopped probing—but she could feel his frustration mounting. She didn't yet know how she'd respond when he finally demanded answers. *Only three more months.*

She walked back out to where she'd left Zed. He was standing with his arms crossed like the drill sergeant he used to be. He was the best, trained to kill, so she tolerated his snide remarks, the long hours, and the physical demands. She now felt confident she could manage against a man twice her size. She had just the right combination of rage, speed, and raw instinct, Zed had told her.

Not only had he taught her the physical components of battle, but she was learning what it took mentally. "The subconscious picks up on cues your conscious mind will otherwise miss," he'd explained. She'd need every possible advantage to stay safe, so she'd been training overtime, sometimes twice a day if Theodore was out of town.

"Back to work," Zed barked. "Unless, of course, you'd like to take another break for a latte or a massage," he added with a snarky tone.

Celeste rolled her eyes. "I'm ready to go again. But easy on the pressure. The injuries raise unnecessary questions." The hardest part of Zed's training wasn't the lessons or the sparring—it was remembering to wear full pajamas to bed or convincing Theodore she wasn't in the mood until her bruises faded. *At least my babe won't be back for another four days.*

At home that evening, she stood naked in front of her bathroom vanity, assessing the damage. Contusions on her abdomen where she'd failed to dodge one of Zed's intense kicks, a sprained ankle, and perhaps a broken wrist. *All in a day's work.* For what felt like the thousandth time, she considered whether the pain was worth it. The answer was always the same. *Yes, yes, it is.* She would go to any lengths to destroy Omar. *And I'll also take down anyone who stands in my way.*

After a quick shower, she retrieved several ice packs from the freezer and situated herself on the sofa to nurse her injuries. She idly flipped through the channels before resigning herself to the fact that she needed to get back to work. *No rest for the weary.* Retrieving her nearby iPad, she opened the grid she'd been obsessing over for months. It really did look like a prosecutor's "who done it" murder board. So many different players, so many nefarious motives, and so many missing puzzle pieces.

Omar hadn't turned up since Dubai. She hoped this meant her

reconnaissance was working. After Hadid and Nasrin had initiated contact, she'd been able to open a line of communication, anonymously, of course, with Omar's right-hand man. For a handsome retainer, the man agreed to provide a steady stream of information about Omar—sometimes his comings and goings, other times interesting contacts or comments he'd made. *Everyone has a price.* It had turned out to be exactly what Celeste needed for her plan to work. Things were in motion the way she had envisioned.

The one wild card she hadn't planned for was that Savin was somehow compromised. It had broken her heart to realize it, but there was no other explanation. The biggest challenge was that she could not let him know she was on to him, just like she could not show her cards to Omar and his guys. With Savin, she had to pretend all was well, continue to read him in on their business deals, and hope that whatever deal he'd struck required him to only occasionally provide information about her.

After repeated security breaches, Celeste had begrudgingly revamped her entire network. Angelo was still in charge of her safety, but she'd upgraded to more sophisticated techniques for communicating with her hackers and the dark web people who'd been assisting her.

It pained her to do so, but she'd also recently sold her Paris apartment after fibbing to Theodore that they'd outgrown the place, and they had moved into a safer building. On some level, Celeste resented the changes she'd had to make. But she and Theodore would never have their happily ever after if they were always looking over their shoulders.

CELESTE WALKED off the elevator and into the D&C lobby, her first day back after a weeklong trip to the Rome office where the Ricci brothers' firm was headquartered.

"Happy Monday! Let me get that for you," Rani said, rushing to meet Celeste to take her coat. It was a floor-length mink fur that Celeste wore only in the dead of winter.

"Thank you, darling. What would I do without you?" *And while you're answering questions, I'd like to know what else you're hiding. Are you in on something with Savin?* Celeste still wasn't any closer to figuring out what Rani had been doing in Paris. She had asked one of her hackers to install spyware on Rani's phone so she could read her messages from that fated night, but for some reason, Rani's phone was impenetrable. The hacker couldn't exactly figure it out, and Celeste didn't want to raise any antennae, so she'd told him to stop trying and said she'd find another way.

Rani grinned. "I'm sure you'd find a replacement, though they'd never be able to fill my shoes. Size thirty-eight to be exact, and I prefer a one-hundred-and-five-millimeter heel."

They were laughing when the elevator arrived once more. Savin came out, balancing a cardboard carrier with four hot drinks and a large bag of pastries.

"How did I beat you here?" Celeste asked, giving him a hand with the bag.

"Traffic was a beast," he said, placing the drinks on Rani's desk and handing her his coat.

Once Rani was back behind her desk, Sav handed a drink to her wordlessly. She barely looked up from her computer.

Must be trouble in paradise.

Savin pretended not to notice, and he and Celeste walked back toward their offices.

"What'd you end up doing last night that was so important you couldn't stay for dinner with our newest business partners?" he asked.

"We spent an entire week with Enzo and Nico in Rome, and honestly, I needed a night off. I went to bed early, woke up in the middle of the night after Theodore fell asleep, and then went to my office. And of course, I worked till dawn." *Alibi cemented.*

She took a sip of her matcha latte, and they sat down at her table. Unbeknownst to Savin and the others, Celeste had used the week in

Rome to prepare for the days leading up to the wedding. *Spectacular achievement is always preceded by unspectacular preparation.*

"What do you think is going on with the illuminati?" Savin wondered. "We haven't heard from them or Ace hardly at all in the past few months."

She thought back to her meeting with Gabe the previous week and her regular touch points with Ace. "I don't have the slightest idea. I never hear from any of them, as you well know."

"I'm still acclimating to the whole thing. I guess that means they don't need us?"

"Guess so."

Since Celeste's recruitment had been formalized the prior fall, the Feds had meddled in only two deals. She'd expected they'd be much more heavy-handed.

"I wonder if they ever figured out what happened with the Shu situation," Savin pondered.

"Who knows? That was a weird one." But Celeste knew damn well what had happened. Chet's and Gabe's supervisors had been meddling in the D&C network. For some reason she still hadn't discovered, they'd had the Shu files modified, just like her clever associates Lorraine and Brett had guessed.

She'd glossed over the issue with the two associates and Savin when she realized who was behind the Shu debacle, telling them the only thing she could track down was that the Shu team had staged the entire deal for their board of directors and had sent two versions of the files that she mistakenly uploaded. She'd figured they would catch on, but they hadn't asked any further questions.

Still, she'd used it as the perfect excuse to demand upgraded security protections at the office. Angelo hired the former deputy director of the CIA's Center for Cyber Intelligence, Sloane Mitchell, who had recently resigned when the agency refused to take her advice to prevent another WikiLeaks debacle. Sloane didn't know that anyone at D&C was aware Angelo had consulted her, but Celeste had looked into her and believed she was clean.

Celeste and Savin transitioned to talk about their upcoming

employee retreat. As a reward for their highest-ever quarterly returns at the end of the previous year, D&C would have its inaugural team-building trip in Grand Cayman in six weeks. Rani had planned what looked to be a beautiful respite for the team at the newly renovated Ritz. It was costing a pretty penny to rent, but they could afford it. They were bullish on D&C's portfolio, especially since the Feds had tipped them off about what was coming—essentially future-proofing their investments.

"We'll have to leave time on the agenda for everyone else to golf," Savin was saying, "and for you and me to taste all the wine."

Celeste hadn't really been listening. She was building her own agenda in her mind so that she would have time to break away from the group to track down more information about RH Global, which she believed held the key to much of what she was investigating. She'd been running into dead ends for months. Additionally, she would use the trip to establish a couple of shell companies of her own.

"I'm so excited that my man—well, I guess he's your man too—Theodore decided to come with us," Savin said. Celeste's head shot up, and she looked at him quizzically.

"Why does it feel like this is the first time you're hearing this?"

She adjusted her face to neutral. "Oh no, yes, of course. It'll be fun for him to join us." *Fuck.* Between the demands of her team and Theodore, she'd have no time for the recon she wanted to do. *Unless...*

"Hey, so Theodore's always talking about how he wants to go deep-sea fishing, but I obviously *never* want to go. Would you be a doll and accompany him one day? You guys can go when everyone else golfs."

"What makes you think I want to go?" Savin whined. He didn't like getting his hands dirty any more than Celeste did.

"Please? For me? I can't bear to see his disappointment on yet another trip. He had to go alone in the Seychelles over the holidays. C'mon!"

Savin relented. "Fine. But consider this your wedding present."

"And quite a generous one at that," Celeste retorted.

Savin flipped his middle finger. "What does one even wear for such things? I'll have to have my lady pick it out."

Celeste couldn't care less about Savin's attire for the outing. She was ecstatic she'd have at least a day to break off from the watching eyes.

"Trust—it's better than climbing the Pitons. He tried to get me to climb *both* of them last time we were in St. Lucia. I was like, 'Cute—but no, babe, I won't even be climbing one.'"

"How has he known me his entire life and is marrying you in ninety days and doesn't know that we don't *do* activities?"

"A mystery. But anyway, thanks. Truly. I owe you one." *Or rather you owe me one for saving our business from the evil reaches of some unknown people.*

"No prob. Now can we get back to business? Always the social calendar with you," Savin joked, shaking his head.

They both laughed. Savin was definitely more of a socialite than Celeste, who merely tolerated most people.

"Where are we on the integration? Do you feel like Tarek's team is stepping up?" Celeste asked.

They discussed Kaya's lingering negativity and Matthew's recent eruptions when he was asked to change course on a business deal. Savin mentioned that he was pleasantly surprised at how well Tarek was acclimating. *Not surprised in the slightest—considering.* Once they'd wrapped up their discussion, Savin left her office and she was alone.

Celeste thought back to the night before, when she'd changed into Mia and negotiated her way into Nico's New York hotel room. It had been a risky move, but she needed more information from his laptop. Her hackers had indicated it would be impossible for anyone to retrieve the files unless they were physically in the room with his device. She called their bluff, and one of them was savvy enough to walk her through uploading the contents of his hard drive to the web in under three minutes. It had been a brilliant stroke of luck all the way around. And now she could confirm what she'd sought to—not only did Nico know Omar, but he was now giving Omar proprietary information about D&C. Celeste wasn't alarmed—in fact, she'd been setting Nico up to do just that since they had discussed merging their shops in Dubai. Ultimately, though, the Nicos and Matthews of the world would never suspect they were being compromised. Their narcissism, much like Omar's, blinded them to any risk of detection, and they refused to believe anyone else was smart enough to pull anything over on them.

THE REST of the week was a blur of work, sessions with Zed, and doing everything she could to help the contusions heal before her fiancé arrived back home. She and Theodore would leave the following week for Switzerland under the guise of a ski getaway—but Celeste had specific research plans for RH Global. She fully intended to find out who ran it and why they'd been exchanging so much money with Matthew. She had a hunch it would expose something useful about him and Omar.

On Thursday night, she met Michel at her basement apartment in the West Village.

"Any news?" she asked him when he arrived. She was certain he'd taken precautions to ensure he wasn't followed, and even if he was, no one knew of their connection or that she had the apartment. Michel was a ghost in New York.

"Nothing great, I'm afraid. Omar was accused of beating a woman he's seeing last week while he was in St. Tropez, and the US, whomever he's working with, swooped in and covered up the charges. A bad day for that woman and for justice overall."

Celeste swallowed her disgust. "Frankly, I'm surprised he isn't hassling me more, but I'm not complaining. Were any of Matthew's files valuable? Do we have enough to frame him?"

"Yes and no. The willingness of the US to step in and absolve Omar is concerning. Given that the higher-ups of Gabe and Chet seem hell-bent on protecting Omar, I'm worried we don't have as much leeway as we'd planned."

I'll make do.

"I managed to track down Nico's files last night. I'll pass them along if I find anything good."

"OK. Anything else you need me to look into?"

"Can you check one more time to see if there's a way into Rani's systems?"

"Sure."

"And don't forget—I'll be out of town next week, so you'll have to keep me posted the old-school way."

"Carrier pigeon?"

"Yes," Celeste replied, laughing.

"Celeste—be careful. If it comes down to you or him, your government is going to choose him."

Only if they see what's coming.

Michel left after they planned their next steps.

Celeste was pleased with how her preparation was unfolding. Petey still proved to be extremely valuable. Their friendship—or, rather, his friendship with Mia—continued to blossom.

Every Tuesday that she could sneak away, Mia would pop into his favorite pub where they'd met. Petey missed the streets, and Mia always seemed interested in hearing him talk about his investigations, what he'd learned in his thirty-year career, the bad guys he'd taken down. "Even though the ends justify the means," he explained, "you still have nightmares. The blank stare on someone's face when their soul leaves their body, when they change over from a person to... a corpse." She knew that look all too well, having seen it on Zari's face.

Petey's tips flowed. She'd buy the beers, and he'd share the ins and outs of the New York streets—where illicit drugs were sold, the patrol frequencies in each neighborhood, the locations of the CCTV cameras, how one flickering streetlight could make a "perp," as he called a perpetrator, unidentifiable and therefore cause a case to fall apart. "No body, no crime, no perp to do the time," he'd said one night, grinning with pride at his dad joke humor. Celeste had giggled along with him, silently thanking her good fortune for finding someone who could spell out for her exactly how to get away with murder.

The best part about going after terrible men was that she would feel no remorse. These men were monsters, and she had proof. After her evening with Fred months before, he had tracked down police reports of women Nico had brutalized in Italy. Four in total had gone to the police (who knew how many had been too afraid to), only to have the investigations dropped without resolution or explanation. Nico's power in his communities reached far and wide, and he was rumored to be protected by the Napoli Mafia. Fred's sleuthing had come with the photos that accompanied the police reports. These women, whose faces were mutilated, rendered unrecognizable from that scumbag's violence, had consumed her thoughts ever since. Women Celeste would never meet who had trusted—and been betrayed by—the very system that was supposed to protect them.

She'd felt rage coursing through her veins, and in that moment, she was more certain that she was on the right track than she'd been since Omar had reappeared in her life the previous year. *The beginning of the end for all these monsters.*

Over drinks one night, Petey divulged a story of the first time he had shot and killed a man. The guy was holding up a restaurant. The perp had already murdered one restaurant employee, Petey explained, and was a known criminal in the neighborhood with a long rap sheet including domestic violence, sexual assault of a minor, rape, battery, and armed robbery. Petey had arrested the man on more than one occasion and said the man had no soul. But the charges never stuck, and he was always back on the streets in a matter of days.

The first kill was difficult, Petey said, even when it was a bad guy. "For months, I dreamed about the expression on his lifeless face as the blood pooled around his body," he recounted. She wondered if she'd have the same experience.

Dreaming of these guys dead sure sounds a lot better than the nightmares of Omar alive.

Because of the nature of his beat in a dangerous part of New York

City, Petey had shot and killed many times over the past thirty years as a cop. He'd never forget the names of the people whose lives he'd taken, he said, but he didn't feel guilty. It was easier, he pointed out, to remember the victims and focus on preventing future crimes.

And so Celeste would accept the repercussions, whatever they may be, of the irreversible acts she would commit. There was no turning back, and perhaps she should have been frightened. But in that moment, she allowed herself to feel victorious. Finally, the monsters would pay the price for their evil deeds. And that in itself was enough to make any resulting pain tolerable.

"Baby, you're home early!" Celeste exclaimed when Theodore walked in the door on Friday afternoon. "Whoa, you look exhausted. Rough trip?"

His face broke into a wide grin. She ran to him and allowed herself to be enveloped in one of his wonderful hugs. She ignored the pain from her contusions. *The bruises are covered with concealer, so I must pretend they do not exist.* Otherwise, Theodore would ask questions.

"I'm so excited for our trip next week that I'm already packed. Can you believe it?"

Theodore laughed. "Honey, I'm looking forward to spending some time with you as well. It feels like it's been months since we've been able to connect."

It was true. Between the acquisitions, training, and research, Celeste barely had time to process how much she and Theodore had been away from each other. He was traveling to Europe nearly every week now, working on some critical projects.

The two went directly to the bedroom and, for the next hour, reacquainted their bodies.

No other man has ever rivaled Theodore. Afterward, she laid her head on Theodore's chest, listening to his heart beat, its steady thrum soothing her nerves.

"In case I don't tell you often enough, you make me happier than any man ever has," Celeste purred while she played with his sparse chest hair.

"I don't know what I've done to deserve you, my love, but it must've been something right. I'm the luckiest man alive."

They decided to go out for dinner that night since the Chef's Table had had a cancellation. She committed herself to being fully present all weekend so that she'd have a little breathing room in Switzerland. The grid would have to remain untouched for the time being.

AFTER WALKING down the aisles of breakfast cereal and frozen lasagna as they passed through the Hudson Yards grocery to get to the restaurant, Celeste and Theodore stood in front of the host stand. It had been a while since the two had enjoyed the extensive seafood-forward tasting menu, and Celeste was ecstatic.

"Some days, I'd love nothing more than to eat my way through this city," Celeste said as the hostess escorted them to their seats at the chef's counter.

"And I'd love nothing more than to eat you again tonight," Theodore whispered in her ear as they sat down.

They ordered the wine pairing and took in the show. Well-timed dishes were brought out simultaneously to all the tables by immaculately dressed servers. Celeste loved the flourish with which the place, in a class of its own, operated.

Course after scintillating course, the delectable food surprised and delighted their senses. Finally, it was time for dessert. While they waited for the frozen soufflé, happily satiated, they debated which course had been the best. "Hands down, the wagyu. It *actually* melted in my mouth," Celeste asserted.

"Honestly, I'd eat every course again, but if I can only choose one, it would be the sea urchin," Theodore countered.

They shared what they were planning for their trip the following week.

"I was thinking we'll leave Sunday night. I arranged early check-in for us," Theodore announced.

"I can't wait for the mineral springs. This winter is going to be the death of me," Celeste said. "Ohmygod, this soufflé is better every time I try it."

After dinner, they were happy wine drunk and made their way to Monty's Mercedes.

"Mon, I tell you all the time, send one of the others when we'll be out late. The missus probably thinks I require you to work nights!" Celeste scolded.

"Miss Celeste, it's a pleasure when you're in town to escort you around," Monty replied, consistent with his usual response.

"Monty, I, for one, appreciate you carting my lady around when I'm away. Thank you," Theodore said.

"You're quite welcome. Someone has to keep an eye on her," Monty said, then laughed.

If you only knew.

When Celeste and Theodore were back in their apartment, Celeste sheepishly admitted she was too full for sex.

Theodore let out a hearty laugh. "I dare say that's the first time I've heard you utter that you were unavailable, and don't fret, my dear. I, too, am perfectly satiated and ready for bed." They walked into the bedroom and began undressing.

"Oh God, is this what marriage will be like? We'll stuff ourselves and stop having sex?" Celeste, half joking, asked.

"Darling, I'm a novice to this marriage thing as much as you are, but I'd guess we'll be just fine in the sex department. Me keeping you in bed for an entire evening is another battle altogether. You don't have to work tonight, do you? I'd love to wake up with you beside me."

"No work for me. I'm going to make an effort to truly unplug this weekend and next week, so we can enjoy our vacation."

It's so nice to be together like this. Maybe I'll be good at marriage after all.

Celeste remained in Theodore's arms while they slept undisturbed and awoke rested, spared the nightmares for once.

THEY ARRIVED IN ST. Moritz midday on Monday. The place was bustling with travelers, the excited vacation energy palpable. Theodore planned to hit the slopes, and Celeste felt a massage was in order. Once they'd checked out their room, she kissed him tenderly and bade him farewell to ensure she made it to her appointment on time.

"Oh, baby," Theodore called before she got to the door. "I may need to go to Zurich tomorrow or Wednesday. Is that OK with you?"

"It's more than OK—as long as I can join. I can always shop, and I want to see this town where you spend so much time."

"Deal."

As Celeste acquainted herself with the massage therapist a half hour later, to avoid any questions, she explained, "I'm working on my karate black belt, so I have some bruises scattered across my body, and please avoid my midsection." She attempted to quiet her mind, but it went to the one place she was not prepared to deal with— Savin. She hadn't yet set another trap because she did not want to believe he was capable of betraying her. Plus, other things had been occupying her mind.

Once she had some insights into RH Global, she would be able to clearly frame Matthew. She bade her time because she wanted an airtight case to present him with an offer he couldn't refuse—though any deal she made with Matthew would be short-lived. *He'll get one last hurrah, and then he won't know what hit him.* She wasn't aware of Nico and Matthew working together, but she was curious to see if Nico's computer would have any evidence of a transaction trail pointing back to Omar, Matthew, or RH. *We shall see.* She shuddered when the images of the women Nico had beaten flashed in her mind. Nico may not know yet what he was in for, but she had every intention of hunting him down and making the rest of his short life very unpleasant.

As for the unknown person or persons who were sabotaging her, she planned to get to the bottom of it one way or another. She had ruled out the idea of a disgruntled former employee because most everyone they'd hired had made a career at D&C and those who hadn't left on good terms to take a job she and Savin had landed them. Michel and the hackers continued to be her eyes and ears. She hoped with their help to track down all her opponents in the months before the wedding.

"DARLING, the concierge arranged a car for us to drive to Zurich. Shall we leave around eight tomorrow morning?" Theodore asked later that afternoon.

"That's perfect, sweetie."

Celeste felt the now-familiar excitement coursing through her body. She fully intended to have some answers within twenty-four hours.

The two were enjoying the view in their villa. She noticed Theodore frown while looking down at his phone, and then he excused himself to make a work call. "Duty calls, baby. I'll be off as soon as possible."

In addition to finding out more about RH, Celeste was going to use this trip to hammer down more of the wedding details before Meredith threw her hands up altogether. She had sent Celeste a thorough to-do list and had given her a deadline for completion— Wednesday afternoon Eastern Standard Time. Celeste had laughed at the specificity, then quickly shut her mouth when she realized Mere was quite serious.

The following morning, Celeste dressed warmly in leather leggings, a bulky wool sweater, and Balmain combat boots. She wished she had one of her Glocks, but she'd left them at home for fear of detection.

She and Theodore grabbed breakfast and hot to-go beverages for the two-and-a-half-hour drive. Once they were settled in the Mercedes, he mapped the directions, and she prepared to sit back and relax. She had made a list of the banks she planned to check out and fibbed, telling Theodore it was a list of shops. *The less he knows, the better.*

They chattered on about the wedding and evaluated potential honeymoon spots. They had narrowed it down to Cocoa Island in the Maldives, Laucala Island in Fiji, or Necker Island in the British Virgin Islands. Celeste had almost forgotten the purpose of the trip when they arrived in Zurich.

"How long will you be, babe?" she inquired.

"Probably two to three hours."

"Perfect. I'll shop, have lunch, and then check in." She gave him a heady kiss, then walked away from him without a backward glance.

She had added a bulky coat, oversized sunglasses, and a cashmere cap, but she wasn't in full disguise. It was too risky—she might pass Theodore or someone else who knew her and be caught as Mia. *Though Rani didn't seem to recognize me in Paris.*

At the Swiss bank on her list, she walked in and asked to speak to the manager for a private banking matter. A tall, nondescript white man introduced himself as the one who could help her and took her into an office in the back.

He sat behind his desk, while she perched on an uncomfortable chair not at all luxurious enough for the clientele the bank kept. Celeste told the man she wanted to open an account that would be kept private, explaining that she required a level of privacy that US banks couldn't provide. The manager described the process, which would take about thirty minutes total, and waited for her approval.

"That sounds lovely. Also, my business colleague asked me to check on his account. I am a registered account user," she added nonchalantly.

"Great, I'll need your passport and wire information for your first deposit, then we can look into the other account for you."

As they completed the paperwork, Celeste was antsy to find out what the man knew about RH.

Finally, he asked her, "What is the company name and your business associate's name?"

"RH Global. Matthew Duncan is his name."

He left her alone and went to speak with another employee.

He returned, an apologetic look on his face. "Miss Donovan, I'm afraid you are not a user on the account, so I cannot provide you with any information."

You just provided me with all the information I needed, doll. Her hackers could compromise the bank's files now that she knew where the account was housed.

When her account creation was complete, she put the documents in her crossbody bag and walked out into the crisp sunshine of the late morning.

She went through the same motion at the two other banks she had flagged, receiving similar responses—no access to the files but an acknowledgment that an RH Global account existed there. *So much for anonymity.*

Now, she looked at her iPhone map to find the best route to the shopping area. Once she had her bearings, she set out to spend some money. But first, she wanted a hot chocolate at the cute coffee shop she'd passed by earlier.

As she turned the corner onto a quiet street, she heard loud footsteps approaching from behind. She wasn't alarmed but was surprised at the speed with which they moved. Then she heard tires squealing as a car rounded the corner. Before she could turn around, her stalker placed black fabric over her head, restrained her arms behind her, and put tape over her mouth. Two people, one on either side of her, escorted her to the car.

The huntress becomes the hunted once again.

12

FAN-HITTING SHIT

The duct tape covering her mouth prevented her from demanding answers. One of the people who escorted her into the vehicle had buckled her in. *Note to self for next time: If you're going to be kidnapped, make sure it's by someone like this who cares about your road safety.*

This wasn't the first time she'd been blindfolded and taken somewhere against her will, but admittedly, the fact that it had occurred before didn't make it any less frightening. Her heart pounded in her chest as she tried to take inventory of the situation. "When one sense is deprived, rely on the information you can garner from your other senses," Zed was always lecturing.

The SUV was in motion, the driver now abiding by traffic laws they'd seemed comfortable ignoring earlier. As they slowed for what may have been a traffic light or stop sign, Celeste strained to hear if anyone in the SUV was speaking. But the only thing she could hear was the steady hum of the heat coming out of the vents. She deduced there were at least three people in the vehicle, likely one on the opposite side of her seat and two in the front.

Now what, Zed? How do I get myself out of this pickle?

Her wrists were bound together with rope, and she knew well

enough not to make moves to wriggle out of it, lest she subject herself to violence. She sat stock still and bit her lip to prevent tears from falling.

Why couldn't she have left well enough alone? Why hadn't she heeded the repeated warnings of Fred, Gabe, Ace? She was in over her head, and perhaps Fred's flippant comment about how many lives she had remaining had been prescient. After what seemed like twenty to thirty minutes, the car pulled into a garage. The driver parked and removed the key from the ignition.

First rule of being attacked: Never let them take you to a second location. She supposed it was irrelevant now, but she strained to recall the statistics Zed had spouted at her. He'd relayed that an abduction was much more likely to result in murder if the victim was taken to a second location.

Extremely helpful to me now, Zed.

Two people assisted her out of the vehicle and into what she assumed was a house. She was placed in a chair, her ankles secured to two of the legs, and a rope was tightly fastened around her waist, binding her to the seat.

Figures that the rope is right where Zed's foot made contact with my rib cage.

She must be alone now. Her body was warm because of her heavy coat and winter attire. She strained to hear the people speaking in another room, but she could only make out faint murmurs. After some minutes, footsteps approached her.

Boots but light footsteps. A woman?

"Miss Donovan, you've been repeatedly warned about your reckless nosing around, and yet you continue to put your own life and the lives of those you care about in danger," said a woman's voice in a heavy Eastern European accent with sharp pronunciation. The voice sounded vaguely familiar, but Celeste couldn't place it. "Have you ever considered that you may not want the answers you seek?"

I'll be the judge of that when I finally get them, thank you very much.

"You can relax. We mean you no harm. But consider this your last warning. Your meddling is dangerous. If you slip up one more time, you *will* be stopped." The woman paused and then said ominously, "We've been given the green light to stop you *by any means necessary.* All this is part of something bigger than you can understand, and the stakes are too high for it to fail at this late stage."

Insulting my ability to understand your shoddy operation is just the icing on this fan-hitting shit sandwich. Fuck you.

"You'll now be taken back to Zurich. I trust you'll keep this little detour to yourself. Please take heed—we won't be this kind next time."

More footsteps. The rope that bound her to the chair was cut, and two people were once again at her sides, helping her to standing and then leading her out to the garage. The ride seemed quicker this time, perhaps because she trusted she was not in danger. These people must not know her well—otherwise, they would've realized that the more they told her to stop, the more committed she'd become to tracking down the answers she deserved.

And just like that, the kidnapping was over. The vehicle stopped in what seemed to be an alley, from the lack of traffic sounds. One of her captors, a man with an unfamiliar voice, whispered to her that he would loosen the rope on her wrists and she was to count to one hundred, then she could remove them. She was escorted to a bench, where she dutifully waited for the designated time to pass. Finally, she removed the rope from her wrists and the cover from her head. She found herself in an abandoned parking lot. Retrieving her phone from her handbag, she opened her maps app and discovered that she was only a couple of blocks away from where she'd been picked up. *What a fucking waste of a perfectly fine day to shop.*

Theodore had tried calling her once, only minutes before, and followed up with a text. "Hi darling, I'm famished. Lunch at the Dolder Grand? Call me back."

She dialed him on WhatsApp.

"Hi, honey," he answered. "How's the shopping?"

"It's a bit of a bust. I forgot how spoiled I am with New York and Paris shopping."

"I'm sorry you haven't had much luck, but maybe a delicious meal and some wine will cheer you up?"

"Sounds wonderful, babe. Where's the car? I can meet you there."

"I'll send a pin drop. See you in a few."

She ended the call and waited for his location. He was close, four blocks away. She pulled a mirror from her bag. She looked surprisingly together, considering she'd just been kidnapped. Her makeup was still in place, though the tape had removed her lip gloss. She applied liner and gloss, smoothed her hair, and then made her way to the car.

"Hey, there, handsome," she called out as she approached Theodore. He looked straight out of a winter wonderland fashion shoot in his jeans, shearling lined coat, and boots. He smiled broadly when he saw her.

"Hi, babe," he said, opening his arms for an embrace. She fell against his chest, feeling safe in his arms. She looked up to him for a kiss, and he obliged with a heated one.

He pulled away and frowned, smacking his lips as though he'd tasted something past its use-by date. "Your lips taste... metallic."

"Oh, oops. It must be my new gloss," she said nonchalantly, pulling it out for effect. "It's one of those plumper brands that you hate," she added, laughing.

"Even with an awful taste, I'd kiss you a thousand hours a day, dear," Theodore remarked. "What do you say we head to lunch? The views at the Dolder are breathtaking, and you'll love the food."

"I'm in." They settled into the car parked on the street, and Theodore began driving. Celeste found a jazz station, and the conversation between them was relaxed.

Confirmed—I live in the twilight zone. Kidnapped at eleven, heading to lunch at twelve thirty with my love, listening to Miles Davis and discussing our Valentine's Day plans.

Theodore was right—the panoramic views at the hotel were something out of a storybook. They kept their conversation light and marveled over the food.

"Tomorrow I'm definitely heading to the mineral springs. I could use it after all the travel…" *And I've had a bit of a rough morning.*

"If nothing comes up with work, I should be able to join." He took her hand. "I've been meaning to ask you—have you and Savin discovered the leak at the firm? You haven't mentioned in a while, but I didn't want to assume it had been resolved."

It's Savin, she thought with a heavy heart. *The one person whose betrayal I never could've predicted.*

"Funny story. After we had several cyber experts look into it, we learned our system had been hacked by some guy living in his mother's basement in Belarus. He had installed a malicious spyware software, but Angelo and his team were able to remove it and provide stronger safeguards."

She lied so often now that she'd actually begun believing them. *The ends justify the means.* At least, she hoped that was true.

Theodore's phone rang then. He swiped to answer.

"Hi, Theodore," Poppy's voice sang through the car speakers.

"Hi, Mum," Theodore said cheerfully. "I'm here in the car with my lovely wife-to-be."

"Where are your travels taking you two this week, dear?" Poppy asked.

"We're in Switzerland. You and Dad have been to the Dolder, haven't you? It'll be Celeste's first time."

"Oh yes, your father raves about that place. And the views—wow."

"Hi, Poppy," Celeste said pleasantly. She had an idea. "Any chance you and Teddy are free the third week of March?"

"I'd have to look, but chances are we are free."

"Theodore and I will be in Grand Cayman. You're welcome to join! It's a D&C retreat, but I fear Theodore will be bored with all my meetings taking time away from him."

"My son? Requiring a lot of attention? Well, I can't imagine that for a minute," Poppy teased.

The three laughed. "There's nothing wrong with requiring that, Mother," Theodore retorted.

"The golf is supposed to be amazing, according to the guys, so Teddy would be entertained as well. And Savin would love to see you, too, I'm sure."

"Mum—did I tell you? Savin's engaged!" Theodore recounted Savin's side of the budding romance between him and Rani.

"Oh, that's wonderful news! He's always been like a son to us. And to answer your question, Celeste, yes, we'd love to come. I'll see if we can make it work."

Celeste contained her excitement. Since Zurich had been mostly a dead end with RH Global, she was determined to have more time to investigate in the Caymans. *Take that, you awful kidnappers.* And now her inquisitive fiancé would be tied up with his parents for the trip, leaving her ample free time to get to the bottom of the RH saga.

While Theodore and Poppy chatted, Celeste looked at her new encrypted messaging app. One of the new hackers had urged her to modernize her communications, and this app, paired with the most protective VPN, was now apparently the safest way to do so.

Three texts from Michel:

"Where are you?"

"I have an update."

"Call me."

There was a missed call and a cryptic text from the 202 number that Gabe regularly used to message her.

The final text arrived then from Ace: "Call me. Now."

Apparently, the troops had heard about her brief stint at being held captive. But this would have to wait until after lunch. If anything was urgent, she assumed they each would've provided more detail.

Theodore wrapped up the call with his mom and then turned to Celeste.

"You're in for such a treat today," he said, licking his lips comically.

"Mmm, can't wait. And perhaps we can have dessert when we get back to our hotel," she said, smiling suggestively.

"Now that is a dessert I can get behind—both literally and figuratively." They laughed.

This—protecting us—is what will make all of it worth it in the end.

THE REST of the trip went off without a hitch, and Celeste was sad to leave the safe haven of their relationship to return to reality. They flew back to New York at the end of the week and decided to spend the weekend inside.

Now, they were seated on the sofa in the living room, sipping red wine in their pajamas and watching the snow come down outside. It was the largest accumulation in the past few years, and they were happy to snuggle by the fire and hibernate.

"It's always so pretty coming down before you actually have to go out into a winter storm, isn't it?" Celeste remarked.

"Yes, and it's even better with you close to me."

"You're the cheesiest man alive, but you're mine, and I love it." She kissed his cheek. "Hey, should we FaceTime with Sam? She's probably dying of boredom right now being trapped at home."

"I'm not sure if new parents describe parenting as dying of boredom, but sure, I'd love to say hi."

Celeste grabbed her iPad from the kitchen island and returned to Theodore. She dialed Sam, who answered on the first ring.

"Ohmygod, Celly, I'm so happy to hear from you. I'm dying of boredom! Valentina is sucking me dry." She squinted and saw Theodore sitting behind her. "Theodore, if I can give you one piece of advice—don't ever breastfeed. It is some bestial shit."

Celeste was laughing at Sam's tirade. "And this is why we're friends. Wait, are you guys still upstate? Or in São Paulo?"

"We're in the city, actually. I had a work meeting earlier this week. We were supposed to leave yesterday for Brazil, but this snowstorm derailed our travel. *C'est la vie.*" Sam sighed. "So how are you? Tell me everything!"

"We just got back from St. Moritz. Never any complaints there. I was actually able to relax for once." *It's amazing how relaxing a trip can be when you get the kidnapping out of the way on the second day.*

The two chatted happily for another few minutes, and then the frazzled Sam reappeared. "Roberto has just texted that SHE is awake again. This little lady runs our lives. She's ruining my tits. Did you know that they learn to bite your nipples? Mine are black and blue. If evolution is not the cruelest thing… I've never seen anything like it. If she weren't so precious, I'd never stand for it. But Roberto and I are both in love, and alas, duty calls. Hugs and kisses." Sam hung up, leaving Celeste and Theodore still laughing.

"She is just too much." Theodore pulled Celeste's shirt aside to reveal one of her nipples. "No black and blue here," he remarked and suckled it. Celeste's body responded with arousal, and she moved the iPad out of the way to lie down. Theodore slipped her pajama pants off and kissed her from head to toe, stopping to give her an orgasm orally.

This man is heaven sent.

~

"EMERGENCY ILLUMINATI MEETING, DID YOU SEE?" Savin said after closing the door in the war room. It was two weeks before they were scheduled to leave for the D&C retreat, and Celeste was getting antsy.

"Yeah. What do you think it could be about?"

"Not sure. But Monday before nine a.m. for an emergency is aggressive."

Their war room landline rang just then. A voice boomed through the device.

"This is Gabriel, and I'm with Chet on a protected line. Everyone present, please announce yourselves."

You called us, weirdo. Shouldn't you already know who's here? Out loud she said, "Celeste and Savin are present."

The others each identified themselves in turn: Mark, Sam, Roberto, and Fred.

"I'll cut to the chase," Gabe continued. "As some of you know, we've been concerned about a leak within this group for some time.

Unfortunately, that meant Chet and I had to open an investigation of sorts into each of you."

Yes, of course I know because you, Ace, and Michel all rushed to tell me while I was out of town. She was grateful for real-time updates, but it was getting a bit repetitive.

Celeste hoped her methods had kept her extracurricular activities under the radar. She looked at Savin to gauge his reaction. He seemed unconcerned. *Funny, since you're the leak.*

"Interestingly, we've been able to confirm that all of you are clean. You have no spyware on your devices, your lines are not tapped, and you're not involved in anything illegal."

"Not that I had any doubts, but woohoo, that's good news!" Savin exclaimed.

"Hold your applause," Chet said. "There's more."

Gabe continued, "Someone in your next degree of separation to us is where the leak or compromise is, and that's where it gets a bit tricky. You see, you volunteered to be surveilled by the US government when you became an agent, but your friends and family have not." *Guess that answers whether Theodore is involved—or not, as is the case.*

"The leaks have been significant and have compromised some of our key investigations," Chet explained, "so we must use every available means to determine who is behind this."

"What exactly does this mean?" Fred asked.

"That your significant others, anyone living with you or working closely with you, will be looked into. We're going to find—and stop—the leak. There is too much at stake, and we are too close to averting impending disaster to risk everything falling apart now," Gabe answered.

"Celly and I haven't heard from you in months. Can you give us some sort of update on how Operation End of the World is panning out?"

"The good news is that we've managed to stall a bit of the attack on the dollar that we expected. Our opponents' efforts were derailed, partly by chance and partly by strategy. Your contacts have turned out to be quite useful, so we haven't needed any of you much. But we have to hold the line, and we can't do that when we can't communicate freely with you."

"So that's why you haven't been in touch? Because of the leak?" Savin asked.

"Exactly. We'll be remotely installing new VPNs on your devices. You're to use absolutely no other means to contact us, and we'll only reach out to you through these safe channels. Do not—I repeat, do not—respond to any phishing attempts. We will never ask for passwords or call you with codes to unlock your account.

"It's all very simple," Gabe continued. "We'll message you on the encrypted app, and you'll only receive communications when you're on the secure VPN. They'll vanish immediately after you read them. It will be a closed, secure network, exactly like what we use for our overseas agents. Do not text each other about any of the information, and do not discuss with anyone outside of this core team. Your lives depend on it."

"Whoa, that escalated quickly! Our *lives*? Could you elaborate?" Mark demanded. "I'm a father and a husband. If there are safety risks to my family, I need to fully understand what precautions are being taken."

"We're offering you the best protection we can. Some of this is out of our hands because, as we conveyed at Savin's a while back, people above our pay grade are involved with some scary players."

"Well, let's get this show on the road then. What do you need us to do?" Celeste inquired.

"Your enthusiasm is appreciated, but it's premature. We need to secure your network first, and then we'll start moving forward. I'd guess the next week or so."

Celeste was afraid she would jump out of her skin by then. Nothing could get in the way of her plans. *Nothing.*

"We'll be in touch," Chet said, then ended the call.

Savin sat back, a pensive look on his face. "What do you make of all this?" he asked.

"I don't know. I want to believe there's some 'there' there, but I'm losing what little faith I had in this operation to begin with. It's been" —she stopped to count on her hand—"six months since I've been involved..." *And they've done nothing to help me deal with Omar.* Celeste gathered her cell phone and handbag. "Let's get back to work and forget about these things for a bit. Cayman is only a few weeks away, so I'd like to make sure we're ready."

After work, Celeste escaped to her secret apartment, where Michel was supposed to meet her before she went to dinner. She'd been keeping as low a profile as possible since the Zurich incident, but she was anxious to resolve everything before her wedding, which was coming fast in two months.

She projected her grid on the wall screen and focused on the lingering questions. The hackers had been unable to infiltrate the RH Global account she'd identified in Switzerland, making her Cayman recon that much more valuable. She thought back to what the illuminati had revealed earlier. Did this mean she could really assume Savin wasn't compromised? No, she didn't think so. After all, Chet and Gabe couldn't be that thorough if they hadn't caught on to all her secrets. For now, she resolved to continue her same level of precaution, but she preferred to think optimistically that her best friend of over two decades was not acting against her.

Hadid and Nasrin had delivered well beyond her expectations by making the connection with Omar's guy. Celeste knew little about him, but he was more helpful than anyone else since this entire debacle had begun. Nasrin checked in every month or so to confirm everything was well with her and the kids. Now that Celeste knew she wasn't responsible for Zari's death, she could rest a little easier, though she was still fiercely protective of his family.

Celeste wasn't sure how she'd ever repay Hadid. Not only had he helped her entrap Omar the first time around, but he'd gotten through to her about the very real security risks when no one else had. She'd seen him two more times while in Paris, and he'd been pleased to see that she was operating more safely now. But there was still no clarity on who had tried to shoot her, just that the person ordering the hit had been in the US. The fear of the unknown enemy had motivated her to train harder than ever, and Zed was more than happy to oblige with her demands for advanced sparring. She'd even learned some tactics for how to escape if she ever wound up in a position like the kidnapping in Zurich again.

Tarek and his firm (with the exception of Kaya and Matthew) had been accommodating in the acquisition, and Celeste had even managed to throw Tarek a bone by allowing some of the more admirable D&C Philanthropies donations to be attributed to him. Lorraine's PR team had been able to deliver very positive media coverage for him, and his resulting cooperation was invaluable. Unfortunately, though, she still had nothing concrete to pin on Matthew until she knew more about RH Global. It wasn't illegal for him to be in cahoots with Omar, especially given Omar's stature as an agent of the US government, nor was it illegal to have multiple transactions to one shell company unless it was funding illegal activities. So until she knew more, Matthew was free to operate as the scumbag that he was.

She'd given Ace a few assignments to see if rebuilding trust there was possible. They'd always delivered on the ask, but Celeste wasn't sure she'd ever move on from resenting the actions of the past.

The unknowns were significant. Who had kidnapped her? Who had hired the shooter in Paris? Who was behind RH Global? Who was Ace and could they be trusted? Who was responsible for the leaks Chet and Gabe kept referencing?

Michel knocked using their secret pattern—two quick, pause, one long. Celeste turned off the screen and went to greet him.

She signaled to take his coat, but he waved her hand away.

"I won't be staying long because I must leave for Europe in an hour."

"OK. Any news?"

"Still nothing on RH. Your Cayman trip is probably the best chance we have, since your Zurich fact-finding raised some red flags. It's entirely possible that whoever is behind RH has Matthew using a new account now." But Celeste knew this wasn't the case because she received weekly readouts on Matthew's correspondence and transactions. He was regularly interacting with RH accounts.

"Thanks for staying vigilant."

Michel sighed. "There's something else. I hesitate to mention, but I know you'd lose your shit if I kept it from you."

"Well, don't keep me in suspense."

"It's Nico."

"Out with it."

Michel pulled out his phone and opened his photo album. He scrolled through a carousel of what looked to be police evidentiary photos.

"This woman was found dead in Rome yesterday morning. Badly beaten, raped, bled to death on the ground mere steps away from the Vatican. They're attributing it to a serial killer, but it has Nico's fingerprints all over it."

"And?"

"He won't even be accosted. Swept under the rug much like Omar's recent slip-up."

A tear slid down Celeste's cheek. She sniffled and wiped it away.

"I'm sorry. I know how hard it is for you to see after what happened to you. We'll get them. I promise. We just have to be patient. Be careful on your trip, and you know how to find me if you need anything." He awkwardly patted her arm and then left.

She sat down on the couch, and for the first time in a long time, she let the tears fall. Tears for the unhealed parts of herself, tears for the women who had lost their lives, their dignity, their sense of safety at the hands of these men. She sobbed for what felt like hours until there were no tears left to cry, and in place of the sadness, her quiet, determined resolve returned. She pulled herself together by splashing cold water on her face and reapplying makeup.

Later that evening with her friends and colleagues, she mulled over what she'd learned about Nico. While everyone else laughed and carried on, she focused her thoughts elsewhere. Over the course of dinner, she came to the realization that she was going to kill Nico. It hadn't been in her original plan, but then again, she'd always prided herself on being nimble. It wouldn't be premeditated—not really. It would be a crime committed in the heat of passion, as Petey would say, as she was feeling quite passionate about her cause these days.

13

____

UNHINGED

"It's obviously too soon to include TA Capital's and the Ricci Fund's teams in our retreat," Celeste said. "What if we host them in New York next week for a dinner? Bring the whole crew together? As leaders of the integrated D&C firm, don't you think it's our role to make everyone feel loved and appreciated?"

Celeste and Savin sat in the Bar Room at the Modern for lunch. He considered her proposal as he chewed his steak tartare.

"It's not a bad idea. We won't want the newbies to feel 'less than,' ya know? I like it! The question becomes, Can we pull it off before we leave?"

"Yes, I believe we can make it happen. Let's rearrange next Wednesday and Thursday. They can fly in Wednesday, have a fun dinner, work Thursday, and then if they'd like to stay the weekend, they'll have the option. Sound good?"

"Actually, yes, it does. I like it a lot. What do you need me to do?"

"Rani can help with logistics. How about you decide on dinner and post-dinner extracurriculars? I have a sneaking suspicion many of them will require a night out on the town."

The plot thickens.

~

"Darling, are your parents ready for their trip? Rani can definitely help with their travel if needed."

Theodore looked up from the stack of papers in his lap. "You'll be happy to know that Mum was so excited for the invite that she booked their flights right away. I'm not sure I've ever invited them to tag along on a trip, and they are thrilled. You're racking up daughter-of-the-year points left and right."

Celeste laughed. "I never thought I'd hear those words out of someone's mouth, but I'm glad they're looking forward to it. The team is ecstatic as well."

"I'm sure. A no-expenses-spared trip to the Caribbean in the most awful March we've had since I've lived in New York? I'd say you and Sav are pretty great bosses, indeed. I've never sent so much as a holiday gift to my team."

"I'm trying to free up my schedule a bit so I can have a night for you and your parents. I'll let you know when I work it out. Did you see Savin's text that he has agreed to go deep-sea fishing with you?"

Theodore laughed. "I could hear his begrudging tone through the text message, so this has your name written all over it! Trying to spare yourself like with the Pitons—I get it."

"You know me—and Savin—too well. But yes, honey, I talked him into it because I didn't want you to have to go alone again."

"I remember my solo Seychelles journey like it was yesterday," Theodore said. "Lonely with only a fishing rod and the open sea, while my babe relaxed at the resort spa."

Celeste giggled. "Life with me is hard, I know. It must be worth something, though, because *you* proposed to *me*, remember?"

"Yes, but only twice, and only once with a shotgun in my back as encouragement."

"What can I say? The world wanted me married, barefoot, and pregnant."

"Mm, I'll take the married and barefoot part, and let's sub out the 'pregnant' with 'naked and aroused.'"

"Deal," Celeste said, extending her hand to shake on it.

"The deal is sealed," Theodore replied, shaking her hand and then pulling her onto his lap for an embrace.

"I can't wait to be married to you," Celeste said in a rare moment of vulnerability.

"Are you calling our special day a wedding yet? You know that weddings are the venues where people marry, right?"

She smiled and kissed him in response.

To prepare for what was to unfold over the next couple of weeks, Celeste booked three extra sessions with Zed.

"I *cannot* have even an inkling of a bruise because now is not the time for anyone to learn of my training. So I'd like to focus on speed drills, agility, and sprints," she told him.

"Have things escalated? Should I be concerned?"

"Nope, not at all. Since I'll be traveling soon, I didn't want to miss too many sessions."

"Understood."

She was sore afterward but happy that she'd made the time to work with him. She'd also sneaked to the shooting range over the weekend to practice. She was ready.

The D&C team was abuzz on Monday morning before the 8 a.m. meeting began, with everyone chattering away about the teams from TA Capital and the Ricci Fund. Celeste had always known D&C would become her and Savin's empire, even before they'd received their seed money from Roberto. But she'd never envisioned that it would be built upon blackmail and deceit. After she reflected over the way the circumstances around the acquisitions had unfolded, she had to admit—but only to her therapist—that it bothered her. It was even more difficult to process because she couldn't be honest with

Savin for two reasons: He could be compromised, and if not, he'd be so disappointed in her for doubting him.

There were worse reasons for business partnerships, of this she was certain. But the person she used to be, with the naivete of youth, would have considered it beyond possibility that she would make such decisions, putting her reputation and everything she'd built on the line to get into bed with bottom feeders like Matthew and Nico.

Too late for regrets now. The ink was dry on the contracts, and permanent moves on the integrations were in place.

"Good morning, everyone," she said, bringing the meeting to order. "I gather from your enthusiasm that you're all looking forward to meeting your new colleagues as much as we are. You have contributed significantly to making D&C what it is today. And now we are on the precipice of something amazing. Your excellence and best-in-class performance have gotten us here, and Savin and I have no doubt that we'll continue to make history..." She droned on and on, boring even herself, but to the team's credit, their faces still shone with excitement. *This is a bunch of bullshit,* she wanted to say, *and I'm sorry to put you in the middle of the war between me and some very bad people.* Once she was done speaking, her employees gave her a standing ovation, to her astonishment. Savin caught her eye and raised his eyebrows and then joined them in cheering her on.

"That's a hard act to follow, but I'm going to try," Savin said, then began delivering his remarks.

Celeste completely zoned out at that point, memorizing her plan for Wednesday evening and figuring out how she would dodge Theodore. The one night she actually wanted him to be away on a work trip and he'd be in town. *Figures.*

SHE SAT at her desk later in the day, reading reports from two of her portfolio managers and their teams, when Rani spoke through Celeste's office phone.

"Enzo and Nico are on the line. I already told them you were busy, of course, but they insist on speaking with you. Is it OK to put them through?"

"Sure, thanks for checking with me." *Dammit, I knew they'd be a pain in my ass.*

"Hey, fellas, what can I do for you? Rani said it was urgent."

Enzo began. "Hi, Celeste. We're thinking of coming in a night early—"

Just then, Savin gave his half knock and walked in.

"Hang on a second. Savin is arriving."

"Hi, Savin," the brothers said in unison. Enzo continued, "We're thinking of coming in a night early so that we can have some time with you two before the larger team meeting. How does that sound? Are you free?"

Celeste rolled her eyes. *My eternal penance.* Savin looked equally annoyed.

"We have a prior engagement on Tuesday for a late dinner, but we could certainly meet you two for cocktails. Can you make it in time for happy hour? Five p.m.?"

"Sure, we can make that happen," Nico chimed in. "Find a nice lounge and send us the information. See you then."

Click.

"That was... interesting," Celeste remarked.

"Indeed it was. This is going to be a long road."

Not for one of us.

SAVIN HAD PICKED out a hot new lounge downtown for drinks Tuesday. Enzo arrived at 5 p.m. on the dot and apologized profusely for his brother's tardiness. Celeste imagined he'd spent a lot of his life dealing with Nico's shortcomings. Enzo was a sharp, tasteful dresser, wearing a bespoke blazer, an of-the-moment slim-cut men's oxford shirt, and dark jeans, pulled together well with a camel cashmere blend trench.

Not surprisingly, Nico managed to be fifteen minutes late and managed to look ridiculous. His obscenely expensive watch had no character, no story behind it, and his three-piece pinstripe suit was something like a villain costume out of a Marvel movie.

While he told outlandish tales that made her hate him more with every passing second, Celeste imagined the emotions the women Nico killed felt when they realized they were going to die. Celeste knew all too well because she'd been knocking on death's door the previous year on Omar's yacht, convinced that his next blow would be her last. She held back tears and swallowed her rage, furious that she had to breathe the same air as this man. She reminded herself that it was short-lived.

Nico got liquored up faster than everyone else, ordering the most expensive Japanese whisky on the menu, no doubt in an attempt to look sophisticated. *Little does he know that Savin hates Japanese whisky and, more importantly, hates the type of pretension Nico puts on display at every possible turn.*

The carousel of the women Nico had hurt—or worse—played over and over in her mind, to the point that she withdrew from the conversation altogether. Savin took notice and made moves to wrap up by signaling for the check.

"Hey, Sav," Nico said drunkenly, putting his arm around Savin. To Savin's credit, he kept his face neutral, though Celeste was certain his skin was crawling. "Can you hook me up with a visit to Casa Cipriani tomorrow? You have the key to Manhattan, right? I heard it was dope."

Argh, this man is such a cheese dick on top of everything else.

"I do happen to be a member," Savin admitted. "We can stop by after dinner."

For the following evening, D&C had rented out a private room at Peak restaurant on the 101st floor of the 30 Hudson Yards building. Besides offering an amazing view of the city, the restaurant had excellent food, and the vibe was chic and upbeat. A trip to Casa Cipriani after dinner made Celeste's plan even easier. Petey had told her the locations of all the "blind spots" downtown, where the CCTV coverage was either scant or nonexistent. She had memorized them because she knew they would come in handy someday. Apparently, someday was a lot sooner than she'd realized.

Celeste skipped out on dinner with Savin and decided to walk a bit on her way home. The only time New York was quiet was on wintry evenings, and the stillness tonight calmed her nerves.

She took her phone out of her bag, opened one of the many encrypted apps she now had, and called Michel.

"I need a favor," she said when he answered on the first ring. He wasn't going to like it, but she knew he'd help.

"Wow, the view is incredible," Lorraine remarked. The D&C team, along with their new colleagues from TA Capital and the Ricci Fund, were having a cocktail before dinner to watch the sun set, and then they would be escorted to the dining room Rani had reserved.

"It is, isn't it?" Celeste wasn't one to gawk, but even she had to admit the view was otherworldly. The floor below theirs was The Edge, the highest outdoor sky deck in the Western Hemisphere. One could see for miles in every direction, and she was always in awe of how well her favorite city showed up for visitors. "And wait till you try the food!"

A server came by with a Champagne cart, and Celeste ordered a glass of her favorite, Perrier-Jouët. She was pleased to see everyone enjoying themselves. Everyone except Nico, who stood off to the side, taking shots alone. He looked pathetic. Celeste would've felt sorry for him if she didn't know the evil he was capable of. She shook the images of his victims from her mind. *Save it for later.* She nursed her bubbles because she had to be alert later in the evening.

Celeste and Savin gave another iteration of their pep talk when they all crowded into their private room for dinner. Tarek, with whom Celeste hadn't had a chance to spend any time, also clinked his glass, and to his credit, delivered an incredibly inspiring speech about how privileged he felt to be joining his family with the D&C family. Of note, Kaya and Matthew were noticeably absent. *They're probably trying to plan a coup. Good luck to them. Johnny Carolo doesn't write contracts with loopholes.* In every way that D&C did not have power over TA, Tarek retained the authority. Celeste had really begun to like him over the past few months and would ensure they protected his portfolio from the likes of Kaya and Matthew. *Maybe entering into business arrangements via blackmail doesn't always have to be bad.*

By 7:30, they'd finished eating, and it was clear that the young associates were itching to have a night out. Celeste and Savin encouraged them to use their expense accounts and celebrate. "Remember when we were that age, full of hope and also full of... energy?" Savin asked rhetorically, and the two laughed.

Finally, the junior staff left, and it was time for Savin to escort Nico downtown. Celeste made up an excuse about having a headache, and Enzo also dipped out at the earliest opportunity.

"Sorry," Celeste mouthed to Savin. He shrugged as if to say, "I can handle it."

Just a few more hours.

CELESTE WALKED in the shadows heading south on Broadway in the Financial District. It had gotten quite cold. Black ice covered the sidewalks, and even with tread on her boots, she had to walk gingerly all the way downtown from her secret West Village basement apartment, which had become her command center. The massive skyscrapers created high-speed winds, and she shivered as the cold bit her skin through the layers underneath her black ski jacket and matching pants. Her blonde hair was tucked into a cap. At nearly 1 a.m., the streets were quiet, with only an occasional taxi or black car passing.

Michel had been keeping tabs on the Nico situation for her so that she could go home until Theodore went to sleep, thereby establishing her alibi. To her surprise, Michel hadn't tried to talk her out of her plan, and in fact, he'd been quite helpful. Maybe he thought it was good practice.

She had time. Nico was extremely liquored up at the Dead Rabbit, drinking through its Scotch collection. She'd arranged for the bartender to be paid a handsome fee to keep the bar open until Nico was too incoherent to know what he had coming. Her instincts had been correct that her Dubai trip wasn't the first time he'd heard of Celeste Donovan. He had known that she was behind Omar's holding company going under. While the money he lost wasn't entirely traceable—offshore accounts owned by skeleton corporations—Celeste had suspected, and rightly so, that crushing Omar's company had also nearly bankrupted Nico. And hence he had launched his vendetta against one Miss Celeste Donovan.

The day they had officially met in person, at that fateful breakfast meeting in Dubai, Nico's demeanor appeared relaxed to a casual observer. But Celeste had noticed his nervous foot tapping. Business success relied on exercising shrewd powers of observation. Celeste never trusted a fidgety person, and so within the first minutes of knowing Nico, her antennae had been up. Her instincts told her he was not to be trusted, and she listened to her gut feeling.

Night after night while Theodore slept, she sneaked into her office and researched, connecting on the dark web and tracing transactions to find where they'd originated. She tracked down everyone Omar had been corresponding with over the months since she'd seen him at the Louvre. She didn't stop there. She raided every record she could obtain on crypto exchanges, Swiss bank accounts, anything tying a number of evildoers to Omar, which is how she'd discovered RH Global. But Matthew wasn't her concern at the moment—Nico was. And Nico would have no problem getting even with her. What he didn't know was that she was committed to eliminating anyone she perceived as a threat and that she played to win.

Her heart drummed in her ears. Even with all the preparation, it was nerve-racking to think of what came next. She had walked through every step with Michel over the phone the previous evening and that morning, and Zed, without even realizing it, had helped her choreograph the attack. The rest had been planning. She'd walked that route a million times when she was younger, as she had worked at firms in the neighborhood. But none of it could have happened without Petey. Knowing where the cameras and dead zones were, learning the trash routes for the neighborhood and where the dumpsters were located in case her plan went awry—these would mean the difference between failure and success. She delivered untraceable payments to the people who helped her. A nice to-do list of tasks that she'd checked off one by one. *No more planning. Now it's go time.*

Coming up on Bowling Green Park, she took the Whitehall fork in the road and pulled her ski mask over her head. The oldest NYC public park was abandoned, too cold for even the highest of drug addicts. Relief flooded over her when she saw there were no police cars patrolling the area. *Petey was right; it's deserted past 6 p.m.*

The rock she'd cleverly hidden at the corner of Whitehall and Stone Streets was waiting for her. She hoisted it up over her shoulder and continued walking down Stone toward Broad. Broad to Water, and there it was, the Dead Rabbit. It had taken a lot of maneuvering and a stroke of luck for Nico to end up there. She had played on his desperation to feel important and mentioned that Savin belonged to an exclusive members-only club the previous week on a call, knowing that Nico would almost beg for an invite. He had unknowingly played right into Celeste's hands.

She had further manipulated the situation, not that it needed much, by sidling up to Nico at happy hour and mentioning that the historic Dead Rabbit had the best Scotch menu in town and was only a five-minute walk from the new downtown Cipriani outpost. As predicted, Nico had demanded that Savin show him the way to the Rabbit after several drinks.

Even though she knew all the CCTV cameras had been switched off or weren't working, she still walked on the opposite side of the street and stayed in the shadows out of an abundance of caution. When a loud garbage truck two streets over interrupted the night stillness, she heaved the rock at the streetlight. The giant bulb shattered, the glass flying across the concrete. Of course, she could've arranged for someone to shut the light off in a less destructive way, but it felt symbolic that on the night she'd rid the world of a man who'd destroyed so many lives, there would be broken glass and trash scattered around his lifeless body.

Now she ran farther down the block and pressed her body against a Manhattan building that housed the White Horse Tavern. A glance at her watch revealed that Nico would be stumbling out of the Dead Rabbit any minute now. The air was crisp, but the wind had died down. Other than her visible breath, she was a ghost.

Her head shot up when the Rabbit door opened. Just as she'd imagined many times that day, Nico came stumbling out alone. He walked down the middle of the street toward her, a drunken grin spread across his face. *He'll never see it coming.* Though maybe she should drag it out a bit, make him suffer, replay all the hideous acts he'd committed in his lifetime. Fear what was next for him. She wasn't a sadist, but knowing how evil Nico was kept her motivated even when she was exhausted, even when she was afraid of the consequences, even when she knew Theodore may never look at her the same way again if he found out that she was capable of taking someone's life.

She silently withdrew the baseball bat from behind her, where it had been tucked into her waistband. Nico hadn't noticed her; he was plastered, and she was well concealed in the shadows. It was too late to turn back now, and she was fine with that. When she'd seen what he'd done to those women, she knew what she would do, what she had to do.

He was within striking distance now. Without hesitation, she swung the bat with all her might, surprising herself with her own strength and steadiness.

Crack!

The sound of aluminum meeting bone with such force bounced from building to building, echoing around her. The volume didn't matter; they were alone. No nosy tenants peeking out of apartment windows, no cops on patrol. No one would even miss Nico. He had no children or significant other, his brother found him repulsive, and his parents had died years before. The world did not need him.

He stumbled backward from the blow but didn't fall. His face registered surprise—and anger. Celeste struck him once more, and he yelped in pain, cowering. Then her rage kicked in. She grew more and more disgusted by him as the women's faces played in her mind, and she swung the bat again and again and again. Blood splattered from his mouth and his ears and his eyes, until finally he was on the ground. Petey had explained it perfectly—she saw the moment the life left his body. A man who took from the world and tortured innocent people, tortured and took, had now met the fate he deserved. Perhaps she'd become unhinged, but she didn't much care. It felt good to get rid of Nico.

There was no time to relish her victory—she mustn't linger. The cleaner would be there soon to collect his body and dump it into the Hudson, weighted down by enough rocks to ensure it would never float ashore, at least not until his body was unrecognizable. Just as she'd planned and instructed. It was a cliché way to go, a mafioso tossed into the Hudson. But she could think of nothing more fitting than for his remains to be devoured by the bottom feeders in one of the most contaminated bodies of water in the world. She couldn't resist the poetic irony.

She pulled the body close to the building out of the street and then nonchalantly walked around the block to Stone Street. About five minutes later, she heard it all. The car coming to a stop, the trunk popping, Nico's body being dragged across the cobblestone, the thud of his corpse being dropped into the trunk. She'd been promised a short video of the disposal of Nico, his body sinking to the bottom without a trace, as though he'd never existed. Once the car pulled away, she was satisfied.

～

THE SCALDING SHOWER warmed her skin after the frigid walk back to her secret West Village apartment. It was nearly 4 a.m. now, only an hour before she normally awoke for her morning workout. Contemplating whether she should head straight to the gym or sneak into bed with Theodore, she massaged the shampoo into her scalp and through to the ends. Nico was gone now; she had the video to prove it. She grinned. *One down, four more to go.*

Celeste had felt nothing but disdain when she had looked into Nico's eyes.

Was she in shock? Would it hit her tomorrow or the next day or three months later that she had taken a life?

She would've preferred to have ended his life in a more civilized way. Alas, the killing had to be untraceable, so it had to realistically look like a random mugging or drug deal gone wrong. The bat had been taken from a high school baseball team equipment room and had dozens of people's fingerprints on it (none of them hers, since she'd worn gloves). The Dead Rabbit employees didn't know who had paid them to stay open late—they'd taken the money without asking questions. Celeste had shed the winter clothes and tossed them into a dumpster going to the incinerator within hours. The cleaner—well, Michel had arranged for him, and the cleaner knew nothing about Celeste. All bases were covered.

"Good morning, my love!" Celeste said cheerfully. She left her bag on the sideboard in the foyer and walked into the living room. After cleaning up, she had headed to the gym and taken a dance cardio class before coming home. *Nothing like a good workout to clear your head after the first time you take a life.*

Theodore was sitting on the sofa and barely glanced up from his iPhone. "Good morning, darling." He was dressed impeccably as always, today wearing a Prada slim-cut poplin shirt in a gorgeous light blue. Celeste had bought it for him because the color was called Celeste and nearly matched his eyes. He paired it with navy Tom Ford wool pants and his Berluti brown leather oxford shoes. Another gift from her. But she noticed dark circles under his eyes.

Had he awoken in the night and noticed her absence? No, that was impossible. Besides, she'd already practiced how she would respond if he asked her. She hadn't been able to sleep, so she worked in her office until the early morning, then went for a jog and to class. It wasn't that out of the ordinary, especially lately.

On her way to the kitchen, she asked over her shoulder, "Have you already eaten, babe? I'm famished. I had a lot of nervous energy, so I went for a run and then to class." She retrieved the blender and protein powder from the pantry. "Would you like a smoothie?" she called to him. *A little less manic, Celeste.* She was overdoing it.

"I wondered where you disappeared to when I woke up to an empty bed," he replied from the other room. "I don't think you've stayed in our bed more than two nights in months. I have to whisk you away on a vacation to have you for an entire evening."

She laughed. "Sounds to me like we need to take more vacations, then," she said, and shuffled around the kitchen, retrieving the rest of the ingredients. She was glad he couldn't see her face in case it revealed what she had done.

"Babe, I didn't hear what you said. Would you like a smoothie?" Before he could reply, she started the blender to reduce conversation opportunity. Even though she had canned responses planned, she wasn't prepared for an interrogation. Surely she could allow herself some sort of grace period.

She poured half of the mixture into each of two juice glasses and carried them into the living room.

"Now, what was it you were saying, my love?" she said in a singsong voice, sitting next to him on the sofa. He took the drink from her outstretched hand.

"Thanks," he replied, taking a sip and then setting the glass on the end table. "I'm curious about what's been keeping you up so often. Is everything OK?" He looked at her pointedly.

From the moment she'd met him, Celeste had always felt a bit uncomfortable when he stared into her eyes so intently.

Can he see the tarnish on my soul?

She searched his face for any sign that he knew more than he was letting on. But he only seemed concerned, with no pretense in his gaze.

Best to own it.

"Oh, honey, I'm sorry. I hadn't thought of the effect this may be having on you. I get in the zone, obsessed with work, and... I forget to think of... well, I'm still learning with this whole relationship thing. I'll get better at making time for us, I promise. Forgive me?" She flashed her dimples with a sheepish grin.

He seemed satisfied with her response. "There's nothing to forgive. I'm missing our late-night cuddling is all."

She closed the gap between them and pulled his face to hers, kissing him hungrily. The months of isolation and scheming were taking a toll on her. She stripped off her sports bra and capris, and he frantically removed his clothes, leaving them in a heap on the floor. They were breathing heavily. Then he was inside her, and the events of the previous evening were momentarily forgotten.

"Oh, baby," he moaned, his hand in her hair, pulling her head back just enough to bite her lower lip. She pressed herself against his body and allowed his love and desire to envelop her, a protective bubble shielding her from the anxiety that had consumed her lately. They continued making love, exchanging whispered sweet nothings, until they climaxed together minutes later. She collapsed against him and listened to his heart thundering in his chest.

After their breathing returned to normal, he rushed to get a towel and some water for them, and when he returned, she needed to feel his body again, so she pulled a blanket over her and laid her head in his lap. He caressed her cheek and then ran his fingers through her hair, an absentminded expression of love and the highest form of intimacy. *His touch is magic.* They sat like this for a while without speaking, each lost in their own thoughts. She even dozed off, the late nights catching up with her.

It wasn't until one of her phones vibrated in her handbag that she awoke and was immediately brought back to the reality of what today was. It was the day there would be chatter of Nico's disappearance, and she'd have to ensure her alibi for the previous night was airtight.

Theodore was gazing at her lovingly when she opened her eyes. She groaned. "Can't I just stay here all day?"

"No complaints from me," he replied, "but your phone seems to have other plans for you."

"What time is it?"

"Almost eight thirty."

She sprang up from the couch. "Shit, I'll be late for my ten a.m. meeting if I don't hurry." She gazed down at Theodore, still naked. *I could look at him forever.* She vowed to stop neglecting him, regardless of what else was going on.

"Are you free for dinner tonight?" she asked. "I think I actually have a night off for a change."

He shrugged. "I can't tonight, babe. Duty calls. How about tomorrow?"

"Ugh, I promised Sam I'd come have a glass of wine with her after the baby was asleep. I think she's drowning in mom duties."

"I'll let you know if anything changes in my day. Wouldn't mind skipping out on dinner for a repeat of this morning," he said, and her stomach flipped.

The vibrating started up again on her phone. "It's probably Sav. He's the only one who calls four times in a row or until I pick up." She laughed and rolled her eyes.

"Maybe you'll have time to join me in the shower after you deal with him," Theodore said and made his way to the bedroom.

A single text and three missed calls. The text was from Ace. "Call me after your meeting." She frowned. Ace was getting careless, not even texting her in their encrypted app. She'd have to have a talk with them.

She was right that Savin was the caller. She dialed him.

"Morning. What was so important that it required three calls?"

"I'm picking up some breakfast from Angelina. Would you like your usual tea and croissant? Are you close?"

She rolled her eyes. *I interrupted my post-sex bliss for this.*

"Uh, that'll be great, I'll have my usual. I'm walking out the door in a few minutes. Be there in forty. Theodore and I had some... some, uh, wedding stuff to take care of this morning." *More specifically, some premarital fucking,* she thought, making herself giggle.

Savin either didn't hear or ignored her laughing. "OK, see you then."

CELESTE ARRIVED at the office at the same time as Savin, and they rode the elevator together. Once upstairs, they removed their coats and laid them on Rani's enormous desk.

Celeste whistled. "Whoa, where'd you get the fancy threads?" referring to the bespoke Italian suit Savin was wearing.

"Arrived compliments of Enzo and Nico last night. I guess Nico likes me showing him around New York."

Celeste raised her eyebrows. "From the looks of it, he had a great time."

The two walked into her office and shut the door behind them.

"Oh, whatever. I know what this was really about. You hate that little shit, Nico."

"It's true he's not my favorite person. But hate is a strong word."

Savin laughed. "Since when do you not say you hate people who suck? Hello, who are you and what have you done with Celly?"

"OK, fine, I do strongly dislike him. But I also really like the idea of the Rome presence, and his Dubai contacts are second to none." *Probably because he's providing young sex slaves for half of the Middle East. Or, rather,* was *providing,* she corrected herself.

The two chatted a bit more, and then Savin left for a meeting with the quant team on a new proposal.

Rani rang her speaker phone. "Do you still have time to meet with me and Meredith right now?"

Shit. Celeste had a biweekly meeting with the two women who kept her life and work running smoothly, and apparently it was happening right now.

"Of course, I always have time for you two," she said and hung up, awaiting the other women to join her.

"Celly, my goodness, you are skin and bones! You look terrible too. Have you been working late again? When are you going to realize that you're the boss and that you can hire other people to do all this for you?" Meredith barely took a breath when she was speaking.

Celeste winked at Rani, who was smiling broadly. They were used to Mere's style.

"OK, slow down a little. Which part are you going to focus on? How terrible I look? Working too much? I need your scolding to be a little more focused," Celeste said, and everyone laughed.

"Well, we haven't even begun to talk about the Cayman trip. I have no idea what you're wearing, when you're leaving. Have you even gotten a keratin treatment? Your hair will be a disaster without it, and you know it. Are we focusing on accessories this trip? Hats? Flowy skirts? I can't work like this, Celly. And we haven't even scratched the surface on discussing your wedding. You don't even know what your colors are! I need you to focus on what's important for once instead of work, work, work."

Celeste had to bite back a laugh at the irony of what Meredith was saying.

"From the sounds of it, I am a disaster!" she retorted. Rani giggled. "OK, you have my undivided attention. Rani will walk us through the trip itinerary, and you can make magic happen with my life that has become so disappointing to you."

"There's no dress perfect enough to get rid of those bags under your eyes. Dr. Smythe may not even have enough filler for that. You need *rest*. A massage. And when was the last time you went to the gym? Huh?"

"This morning, thank you very much. But the point is well taken. I should be able to rest up the next few days before we leave. Now, let's get down to business."

Rani worked out logistics, while Mere set up a keratin appointment and fittings. Celeste was in good hands for the trip, and she wrapped up the meeting with them. When they left, she exhaled. She needed some time alone.

She groaned when Savin burst in for the second time that day.

"To what do I owe this pleasure again?"

"I just got a call from Enzo."

"And?"

"He's freaking out about his brother."

"Yeah, his brother is a sociopath. I suppose that would be worrisome to a sibling."

"No, I mean, he thinks something happened to Nico. Like, Nico never came back to his hotel room last night, and his phone goes to voicemail."

"Doesn't Nico get into coke and strippers a little too often?"

"From what I can gather, yes."

"So how is this your—" she corrected herself. "How is this *our* problem?"

"I may have given him my dealer's number. What if he OD'd and is lying dead in a ditch somewhere? Isn't that like... couldn't I get in trouble?"

"Well, first of all, there aren't any ditches in lower Manhattan, so you can probably rule that out."

Savin shot her a dirty look.

Second, I happen to know he's dead, and it wasn't coke or an angry pimp that killed him.

"Second, there's nothing to worry about. You've met the guy. He's not the poster child for restraint and healthy living. I'm sure he's just sleeping it off."

"He never came back to his hotel room. Enzo confirmed."

"Yes, you already mentioned that. Take a deep breath and count to ten. OK, admittedly we don't know the guy's habits, but he'll turn up soon. Even if—and it's a long shot—even if something happened, this has nothing to do with you. You took him out for a drink, and whatever he got into later is not your responsibility. Frankly, it's not even any of our business. I, for one, am not going to lose sleep over whatever mess he created for himself."

His lifeless eyes had crossed her mind, but as she'd done each time earlier that day, she replaced the image with his victims' faces. Her anger flared. "Can we move on from this guy? I'm already regretting getting into business with him; he's becoming a hassle."

Savin seemed relieved. "OK, yeah, sure. I just freaked out for a moment."

"I noticed," Celeste said, laughing to lighten the mood and assuage her own anger.

The next few days brought more speculation about Nico, but no one had any clues to provide. Enzo relayed over breakfast on Friday that he wanted to keep the disappearance out of the press.

"Between us, this isn't the first time Nico has taken off, and I certainly don't want the fact that he's disappeared again to impact our portfolio."

Celeste had looked at Savin as if to say, "I told you so." Out loud, she said, "Enzo, we'll take your lead. We want your family's privacy to be protected, so if that means involving the authorities—or not—you let us know what's best."

"Celly, guess who's crashing your little Caribbean party?" Jack's voice boomed through the FaceTime app on her iPad. "I'm sure it could use a little adventure anyway!"

"So I guess Sav told you about our retreat, then?" Celeste asked.

"Yes, and honestly, my feelings were hurt that I wasn't invited," Jack said, his face twisted in a comical frown.

"Oh, babe, of course you're always welcome. Are you sure it's your scene, though? Sav and I will be working most of the time, and I'll have my fiancé and my future in-laws to entertain as well."

"You're so grown up, Cell," he joked, then sipped the umbrellaed cocktail in his hand.

"Where are you?"

"Peru." Jack recounted his past two weeks, hiking through the Amazon in neighboring Ecuador and then participating in a Peruvian Ayahuasca retreat. "I've found my true self, Celly," he concluded.

"I can only imagine what you have in store for the rest of us now that you've achieved samadhi," she retorted. They laughed, then Jack turned serious.

"I've been meaning to ask you, Cell…"

Uh-oh.

"What's been going on with you? Like, what was that gash on your stomach really? Is something wrong again?"

Again. She thought back to a night many years prior when Jack had discovered bruises on her wrists from Omar. "Oh, that little thing?" she said nonchalantly. "That's healing quite nicely. Theodore's been sweet, helping with the bandages. I'm as good as new now."

"And everything else is OK?"

Celeste despised it when the men in her life patronized her. *Of course it's OK because I'm handling it all.* "You're starting to freak me out, Jack. Is there something I should be worried about? You're not taking back the villa and making me cancel the wedding, are you? You're explaining it to Theodore if I have to call it off—he won't take it well."

Jack laughed and then tossed back his drink. "Of course you can still use the house. You've just seemed a little distracted lately is all. You haven't been busting our balls nearly as much as usual."

"Note to self: Be bitchier to my friends. Got it," she teased.

"That's better!" Jack said, and the tense moment passed. He rambled on about how he had processed all his generational and karmic trauma during the cleanse and marveled about the many different snake species that had slithered into his tent while hiking in the rainforest.

"Eww, sounds horrifying," Celeste said, her skin crawling at the thought of reptiles wriggling around the room while she slept. She was relieved at the change in subject, though. Jack had always been there for her when she needed him, but he wasn't one to pry. He seemed a little tipsy as he continued on, bouncing from topic to topic.

"OK, darling, you've had one too many of those Long Island iced teas, and I need to be ready for dinner in a matter of minutes."

"Just tell me one thing," Jack said, seeming to instantly sober up. "Was it you?"

There was no way Jack could know anything.

Could he?

"Was what me?"

"Are you the one who ordered... wait, hang on—" Jack must've set his phone on the bar because the screen went dark, though she could still hear him talking. She strained to listen.

"Yeah, yeah, I took care of it," she heard him say. He was apparently talking on another phone because she only heard his side of the conversation. Then background noise as he picked up the device she was on.

"Sorry about that, Celly. One of my ladies was missing me," he said, laughing at his own joke. "Now, where were we? Ah yes. So was it you? Were you the one who gave the orders?"

Celeste held back a frown and swallowed. "I give a lot of orders—you're going to have to be more specific," she replied, hedging.

"My entire garden has been dug up and replaced! The landscapers blamed it on your 'vision'—said you demanded they comply."

She laughed, relieved. "OK, if this has anything to do with the wedding, your villa, and someone claiming their vision requires the landscapers to work overtime, it has Meredith written all over it."

"Apparently, the perfectly fine lilies were not an adequate backdrop for the—and I quote—'wedding of the century.' My guys were told there *must* be wild poppies, or we may as well call the whole thing off."

"Yes, that's *definitely* Mere. So I'll see you in Cayman in"—she calculated the dates in her head—"in less than two weeks?"

"Yep."

With that, Jack hung up and was off to other things, and she was left with her thoughts. She'd just returned from a session with Anne Marie, and Theodore would be home any minute for dinner. Celeste had realized in speaking with her therapist about non-Nico-related things that she felt no remorse. In fact, it was quite the contrary. She was confident she could pull off everything she'd planned, and without sounding any alarms. When Anne Marie asked how she was doing, she'd been honest—she felt victorious—though, of course, she attributed it to the acquisitions. *Partially true.*

Her phone rang with an unknown caller. "Hello?"

"Mizz Dono—er, Celeste. It's Gabriel. Can you talk?"

"Sure, but it has to be quick. I'm expecting Theodore any minute."

"Your acquisitions were smart. Because of your insights, we've gained access to networks that we had no previous knowledge existed. But I'm still concerned about your circle. You're sure your fiancé isn't compromised?"

"Of course not!" Celeste exclaimed.

"Well, keep things close to the vest for a week or two. We must get to the bottom of this. It could jeopardize everything."

Oh yes. I'm aware.

"We'll all be together in Grand Cayman soon. Staying for a week. Is there—" *I can't believe what I'm about to say.* "Is there anything you need me to do?"

"Stay safe and stay out of trouble. How's your abdomen?"

Celeste explained that the cut was healing nicely and that Dr. Smythe, her plastic surgeon, had performed a procedure to ensure there would be no scar. "Though I have to keep it out of the sun until it's fully healed."

"I was more worried about an infection than a scar. Let's meet when you return. I should know who the leak is by then."

AFTER SHE HAD dinner with Theodore that evening, Celeste excused herself, claiming she wanted to soak in the tub with a good book. She'd chosen a lighthearted rom-com to take her mind off all that was going on. Within the first five pages, there was the stereotypical meet-cute. Her mind wandered back to that night at Savin's when she and Theodore had had their own rom-com opener. He'd made eye contact from across the room. Not casual eye contact, either—a bold stare. She was disconcerted by his presence when he'd followed her to the terrace, and to assuage her nerves, she had taken a cigarette when he offered it, then coughed awkwardly from the smoke. Her most important decision back then was whether to invite him back to her place that night or wait until the next night.

The first time I put much thought into fucking on the first date. It wouldn't have mattered when they slept together. Her pull toward him was magnetic, even in the beginning.

And now Gabe was asking her to examine everyone, and memories she'd been otherwise too distracted to process before came to the forefront of her mind. She recalled being told by one of the many doctors she'd seen that she may have post-traumatic amnesia. Were there things she'd missed because her memory had blocked important details?

14

A RECKONING

The gentle breeze ruffled Celeste's locks as she stared out across the infinity pool and, beyond that, the Caribbean. Poppy was scolding Theodore for not stopping by to say hello when he'd been in London the last time. Had he mentioned that he'd gone to the UK recently? Celeste couldn't recall.

Getting rid of Nico had been largely anticlimactic. Thoughts of his death didn't even visit her when she slept. Instead, it was still the same recurring nightmares—Omar standing at the altar or Theodore dying by Omar's hand. No, Nico never crept into her dreams. Perhaps the goddesses and gods gave her a free karmic pass for ridding the world of Nico's toxicity. She and Michel had agreed that the longer Nico's brother waited to go public about his disappearance, the more distance it put between her and his body in the Hudson.

"Celeste, dear, when will you be able to join Theodore on a trip?" Poppy asked. "We'd love to take you to the English countryside sometime. It is breathtaking and beyond relaxing."

"I told you Mum would expect us to travel with her all the time once we opened Pandora's box," Theodore said to Celeste, grinning. "You're going to be occupied with these acquisitions until the wedding, aren't you, dear?"

Celeste nodded, and before she could reply, Theodore turned back to his mother. "Let's wait until after the wedding, Mum."

"Your mother just wants to spend more time with you two, and she's always wanted a daughter," Teddy explained with his usual fatherly warmth.

"Truly, we think of you just like you're our own, Celeste," Poppy chimed in. "Minus the complexities of a sibling romance, of course," she added, her English piety ever present.

Celeste and Theodore burst out laughing. "Yes, Mum, we guessed you weren't suggesting incest," Theodore teased as the server brought their meals.

The four sat on the patio at Blue, the prime restaurant at the Ritz, where they were staying. They'd come to Grand Cayman early to have time to themselves before Savin and the team arrived the following day. Celeste had orchestrated this in anticipation of her planned fact-finding missions. With Nico out of the way, she could move on to RH Global and Matthew, biding her time until the festivities the day before her wedding day, which was exactly two months away.

The hackers were at a loss with regard to the seed company. They each had come to Celeste with nothing new, perplexed at the cryptic origins of RH. She wasn't surprised in the slightest and became more committed than ever to digging up what she could on the trip. *Meaning my adorable fiancé and his parents are going to have to entertain themselves.*

"I forget how much I like conch until I get back to the Caribbean. Can't wait to try everything," Celeste remarked. They'd ordered a multicourse tasting menu and the wine pairing, so they were in for a long dinner.

"It's divine. I complain about the journey to the Caribbean but always enjoy the food, weather, and laid-back vibe once I'm here." Poppy dove into a story about the "marvelous villa" she and Teddy had stayed in during their last visit to Turks and Caicos. Poppy had an unrivaled ability to make life seem magical, a flair for storytelling that she had passed along to Theodore. He kept the chatter going with his parents, mostly him teasing Poppy. Celeste watched him and smiled. He was the perfect devoted son, and they were the doting parents. She loved being a part of his little family. It had been over twenty years since her own parents had died, and Celeste appreciated more than she could verbalize the two people who had raised the man she found so alluring.

As welcoming as he and his parents were and as wonderful as their relationship had become, she knew she had to ask Theodore some difficult questions soon. But what if, once she had the answers, she decided she hadn't really wanted to know? What if his responses revealed things that put all she loved about him in jeopardy? Would she stop loving him? Was love that fragile? For that matter, would he stop loving her if he knew how she had changed since they met? And this brought her back to the cyclical line of thinking she'd battled for a year. It was hard to imagine that he had done anything worse than she had, though. *Suck it up, Celeste. Get the information you need. Tonight.*

Celeste and the Prescotts consumed two or perhaps three bottles of wine at dinner—she had stopped counting. Back in their room, she and Theodore sat on the terrace listening to the ocean waves. Emboldened by the alcohol, she said, "You never really did tell me about that night on the boat."

"Omar's boat?"

She gave him a look as if to ask, "To what other boat would I be referring?" Out loud, she replied, "Yes, of course, Omar's boat."

"I'll tell you anything you want to know."

"How did you know I was there?"

"Because you texted Savin, and we geotracked you."

Celeste frowned. She'd always thought burner phones were untraceable, but then again, she had turned off the phone for fear of being traced. She made a mental note to ask Michel and the hackers about it.

"What else do you have questions about?"

"How do you know how to shoot a gun? I recall you being a pretty accurate shot, hitting Omar in the chest from long range."

"I explained this when you were in the hospital, and you didn't ask again—so I wasn't aware you didn't remember." He grabbed her hand and massaged it, a pained look on his face. "I grew up hunting with Dad; it's a very English way to spend the weekends. I became a pretty good shot. A couple of years ago, I began going to the shooting range occasionally—as the world becomes more and more unhinged, it seems only reasonable to know how to provide a modicum of protection for my family. And then I moved to the US to be with you, and the gun violence here is unprecedented. I don't always carry a handgun with me when we go out, but if we'll be walking around, I do."

She couldn't help herself; she had to know more. "Why haven't I ever noticed? When was the last time you carried it when we were together? When do you go to the shooting range?"

"I didn't want to scare you with a gun in the house. The last time I had it on me was when we met everyone for brunch."

Because the West Village is notorious for its gun violence. She resisted the urge to roll her eyes.

"I go to a shooting range in Brooklyn or there's one on Long Island."

She wanted to ask why she'd never seen him at the range she frequented in Brooklyn, but then she'd have to give herself up.

"Satisfied? Anything else?"

He had reasonable responses, as he always did. She just wasn't sure if she believed him, and any further questions could then provide an opening for him to launch into an inquiry of his own. She realized how tipsy she was and decided against pressing any further. "No, I'm good. For now."

"I will say I'm grateful that I took up marksmanship because otherwise I'd never have been able to get rid of Omar—at least for a little while." Theodore seemed to be weighing whether to say something. "He's back for real this time, isn't he? I've noticed you've been skittish lately. I was waiting for you to confide in me, but you didn't. I tried not to take it personally—though I wondered why you felt like you couldn't."

Suddenly, she wanted out of the conversation. She leaned over to kiss him and whispered in his ear, "You saved the day as you always do." Then she sat on his lap, straddling him and feeling his erection pressing into her. He kissed her hungrily, and she knew she'd successfully distracted him from the conversation as they made love in the shadows on their patio.

THE REST OF THE D&C team arrived late the following morning. There was a buzz of excitement when they gathered for lunch and Savin opened the meeting.

"We're here to work, but that doesn't preclude you from having a little R&R and some fun as well. Tonight we'll meet around five p.m. for a sunset sail on that boat over there." He pointed to a massive yacht docked at the pier. "In the meantime, enjoy lunch and spend a little time soaking in some vitamin D."

"We have a busy rest of the year, so take advantage of your time away," Celeste added, true to her role as disciplinarian. She noticed that Savin and Rani still kept their distance from one another for the remainder of the meeting. *They must not be ready to announce their engagement to the team.*

Once the group scattered after they'd eaten, Savin, fruity drink topped by an umbrella in hand, walked over to her. "Celly, I need you to run an errand with me tomorrow morning."

"Oh? What for?"

"I want to get Rani something special—a diamond necklace, perhaps. You know my motto is 'go big or go home,' but Rani may want a woman's touch. You have great taste in jewelry."

"And my motto is 'flattery will get you everywhere,' so of course I'll join. Jewelry happens to be my specialty."

The two made plans for the next day, and Celeste went to search for her future in-laws and fiancé. She found them relaxing at the pool and noticed that cocktail hour had already begun.

"It seems everyone is enjoying fruity drinks with umbrellas," she joked. She caught the pool boy's attention and signaled that she wanted the same. "Teddy and Poppy, I hope you'll join us tonight for a sail," she said genuinely.

"No, you kids have fun. I've arranged for me and my beautiful wife to dine under the stars by ourselves on the beach," Teddy replied.

"That sounds lovely and very romantic, Dad. Nice work. I'll try to get this one away for some romance, but when work beckons, it's nearly impossible to distract her." Theodore put his arm easily around Celeste's shoulders and kissed her forehead. Her body responded to his lips on her skin, but she ignored the sexual stirring deep inside of her.

"In my defense, we've recently acquired two firms, and I need to keep my team motivated for some disruptive changes." *Though not as disruptive as I had planned a couple of weeks ago now that Nico is out of the way.*

Teddy whistled. "Two firms simultaneously. Impressive."

"I have no doubt you can pull it off, dear," Poppy added.

"That remains to be seen, but I'm trying my damnedest. Keeping Savin focused, on the other hand, is quite the feat," Celeste replied, laughing. She changed the subject. "Poppy, I wanted to get your thoughts on the archway. Mere has given me so many options, and I have no idea what I'm doing. I figured you may be able to help." Celeste retrieved her iPad out of her bag and pulled up her photo album.

After some discussion of the wedding, it was time for Celeste and Theodore to shower before meeting everyone at the boat. They walked hand in hand back to the room, Celeste scheming about how to get away from everyone—and soon. She didn't want to squander the opportunity to get to the bottom of RH.

"Do we have time for a little action?" Theodore asked, smiling devilishly.

"I can always make time for that, my love."

Theodore led her to the bed. She lay down, and he removed her cover-up and bikini bottoms. *Will this man ever get tired of giving me head?* She hoped not. She groaned as her body responded to his mouth in between her legs and his fingers stimulating her clit. He stroked his erect cock with his other hand, and just when she couldn't take it anymore, he spread her legs wide and mounted her. *He even makes missionary sex exciting.* Everything was forgotten as the two made love. She wrapped her legs around him and lifted her hips so that he could go deeper. And then the magical feeling swept over her, followed by relaxation.

They took a shower, and Celeste put on a long, flowing dress and low-heeled espadrilles, while Theodore wore a white linen shirt and khaki linen pants. They met everyone at the dock promptly at 5 p.m. Celeste put Brett in charge of doing a head count. "Only Savin and Rani are missing," he relayed to her.

Just then, Savin strolled up.

"Where's Rani?" Celeste inquired.

"She has a bit of a headache, decided to sit this one out," Savin said quietly. *He's really committed to hiding this from the staff.* She looked at him quizzically and made a mental note to ask him questions the next day. *Now is neither the time nor the place.*

She mingled a bit with the group, leaving Savin with Theodore to discuss whatever it was they talked about when they were alone. *Futbol, no doubt.* Europeans and their soccer. Theodore came to find her above deck just as the sun was going down. The breeze ruffled her hair, and she pulled a pashmina over her shoulders when the air became chilly.

After watching the breathtaking sunset, the group sat down for a lovely dinner served by the boat crew. Celeste and Savin each spoke from the end of the table where they sat with Theodore, and then they watched as the team mingled. "This is quite a success so far, don't you think?" Celeste commented to her longtime business partner.

"It truly is. Great idea, and it was all your doing."

"Rani was instrumental in making this happen," she remarked. "By the way—a headache?"

"Yeah, she's a bit under the weather," Savin replied nonchalantly and shrugged.

Theodore was on his phone, typing furiously. He looked up to see Celeste watching him. "Sorry, darling, I'm almost finished," he said, appearing to hit Send on whatever he was crafting and then jamming his phone in his pocket.

A quartet came out and played as dinner was served, one mouthwatering course after the next. When the group had finished eating, the band left and a deejay set up. Celeste had allotted one hour for dancing before everyone headed back to the dock.

Lorraine was apparently the only one who wanted to hang out with Celeste and Savin. She sat down next to Savin. "This is just the best, truly," she said sincerely. "I've never worked anywhere with such a great group."

"Hey, would you like to grab another glass of Champagne with me out on deck?" Celeste asked Lorraine. She wanted to get Lorraine's pulse on the recent changes. Her protégé was sharp, and Celeste wanted to make sure Lorraine wouldn't go sniffing around. They walked outside together.

"So what do you think of the acquisitions? Do you anticipate the integration going smoothly?"

"As I've said before, selfishly, I like how it's nearly doubling our AUM," Lorraine replied, referring to the assets under management. "And TA Capital was a great move. But—" She seemed to remember she was speaking with her boss. "With all due respect, of course— what I haven't been able to understand is why you and Savin decided to acquire the Ricci Fund. The brothers have made huge gains at times, yes, but they're arrogant. They've had massive losses and paid dearly in the past. The very recent past in fact."

Celeste decided to be honest—or at least relay part of the truth. "Do you notice anything interesting about the timeline when they had their crash?"

"It was last year. Why?" Then things seemed to click in Lorraine's mind. "Ohh. So they know—" She looked around to see if they were alone and lowered her voice. "So they know Omar."

"Bingo. And the other time they lost significant value? Did you see that in your research?"

This time, Lorraine caught on right away. "The Biochrome short," she said emphatically. "Wait, no way!"

"Yep. I of course didn't see the connection until after the deal was done. I realized they had put out feelers for us, led us to their firm when we were looking to expand in the UAE and Europe. All along, I had thought *we* were pursuing *them*, but the opposite was really happening."

"Wow, that's wild. So what would you like me to do?"

"I know your current role keeps you quite busy. However, you are my best analyst, and I trust you implicitly."

Even in the dark night, Celeste could see Lorraine was blushing. "Thank you, Celeste. That means more than you know coming from you, a total mastermind."

Yes, yes, I am. "I'd like for you to monitor their transactions. Make sure Enzo and Nico aren't still dealing with shady funds like Omar's. I'm worried the others will miss anomalies, but you already know what to look for, given all that you did in the past. That is, if you're interested in taking on another project, of course."

Lorraine exuded excitement. "Yes, I'd love to!" she exclaimed.

Celeste shook her head. "That was your cue to demand more pay for having two jobs," she said, laughing. "This will come with a bump in pay. I'd really rather not answer Savin's questions, so I'll have my accountant make the transfers directly from my bank account to yours."

"Wow, OK. I'm in!" *She didn't even ask what the accompanying raise was. Women need to make the same demands as their male counterparts.*

"Great, we'll discuss specifics when we're back in the office. Let's get inside." They began walking, and Celeste looked over her shoulder and said nonchalantly, "Would you mind not telling Brett? I know you two work closely together these days."

Lorraine had the decency to blush and nodded her head affirmatively.

CELESTE AWOKE EARLY the next morning and went for a run on the beach. When she returned, Theodore was still asleep. She showered and got ready for the morning outing and subsequent necklace shopping with Savin. She carried a nondescript bag that was already packed with what she needed to transform from Celeste Donovan to a new alias, Brinn Horvat, a Croatian woman. Celeste had chosen Brinn just for this trip; she didn't want to burn Mia's identity if the banks she needed to visit made copies of the passport or anything about her visit triggered suspicion. After texting one of her hackers from her burner phone, she hid the phone in a pocket in her suitcase and hurriedly left the hotel.

She'd taken the time to study a map of the town on Grand Cayman. The first of the two banks was far enough away from the hotel that she decided to make herself over as Brinn at a coffee shop and slip out the back entrance. It had been a relief the previous week to discover that the Cayman Islands did not have CCTV anywhere. As long as she remained under the radar, she could come and go freely from the banks.

She walked to the back of the least noteworthy café she'd been able to find and entered the women's restroom, locking the door behind her. She changed quickly into a plain maxi dress with a buttoned-up sweater around her shoulders and a cheap pair of large sunglasses, all things that Celeste would never wear. Then she added a nose prosthetic and wig, redid her makeup, and emerged as Brinn, leaving out the back entrance as she'd planned. Keeping a steady pace, she walked to the bank, making the turns she'd mapped out in advance. Once inside, she asked to speak to a manager, and a teller (female, of course, because women always got the lower-paying positions) picked up a phone and relayed the situation.

A short, balding white man walked out of an office and motioned to her to come in. "How can I help you today, Miss—?" the man asked as he gestured for her to sit. His face had pockmarks, likely from teenage acne or too much booze.

"Miss Horvat," she finished, extending her hand. "But you can call me Brinn."

He shook her hand and smiled. His hand was sweaty, causing her to swallow hard, but she reminded herself she could wash her hands right afterward and smiled back. "OK, what can I do for you today, Brinn?" he asked.

She'd been practicing how to have a nondescript Slavic accent to ensure she could pull off any number of identities that Michel's passport forgery team could dream up for her. It seemed to be working. The man typed away on his computer, a massive Dell machine originating from the early 2000s, from the looks of it. *That dinosaur holds the key to so many things.*

"One of my business associates seems to have misplaced our account number." She rolled her eyes for effect and then added, "He is so irresponsible sometimes."

"And both of your names are on the account?" he inquired. *Thanks to hacker number two, they are.*

"Of course. Matthew Duncan, and you already know my name, Brinn Horvat."

He typed at a snail's pace. Celeste was in disbelief that the Caymans remained one of the financial capitals of the world with men like him running things.

"Ah, yes, I see it now. What is the name of the business entity to which the account is registered?"

"RH Global," she said confidently.

"May I see your passport for identification?"

She pulled Brinn's passport out of her bag and handed it to him.

"I have to make a copy of this. I'll be right back."

Celeste flashed a syrupy smile. "No problem." At the last minute that morning, she had put a burner phone she'd never used before in her bag. She felt it vibrating on her lap. She quickly pulled it out of her bag to read whatever communication had come through. Missed call from a local number. She called it back in an effort to communicate while she was alone.

"When the bank accessed the account, it alerted someone. There are some roughnecks en route to you. By tracking their location, I'd guess they're about five minutes away," Michel said, then ended the call. Celeste put the phone back in her bag just as the manager returned.

"Here's your passport." He handed it to her, and she dropped it in her bag as he began rattling off security questions—Matthew's hometown, his mother's maiden name. Celeste could answer the questions easily because she'd spent so much time studying him. Once they were finished, the manager said, "Great. Now that I've confirmed your identity, what is it you'd like?"

"The account number and the balance would be great, thanks."

The manager pulled a notepad out of his top desk drawer and began writing out the numbers. At that pace, she'd never escape before the men arrived. Finally, he tore off the piece of paper from his pad and handed it to her. She kept her face neutral as she read it, then stuffed it in her bag. "I really must be going, Mr.—I guess I didn't catch your name."

"Mr. Thompson, but you can call me Benjamin."

"Thank you, Benjamin." She looked at the clock on the wall behind him. "Oh shoot, I'm late. My brother is going to kill me. Thanks again."

With that, she rushed out of his office. She would've preferred to leave by a side exit, but she was certain he was watching and that would raise suspicion, when she'd been unmemorable up to that point. She walked through the front door and looked both ways once on the sidewalk. No one was in sight, but she knew she didn't have time to spare. She'd left the back door propped open at the café, so she made her way there from memory.

When she was a few blocks away from the bank, she saw two men running on the next street over out of the corner of her eye. They didn't see her, but she pressed her body against a building until they were gone anyway.

"Goddammit," she cursed once she reached the café and realized someone had closed the door. She hid behind a dumpster in a nearby alley, scrambling to remove her disguise before someone discovered her.

She estimated she had twenty minutes before she had to meet Savin at the jewelry store, which was about a five-minute walk away. Once she was back to herself and the disguise was stowed in her bag, she walked to a juice shop, where she ordered a smoothie, then asked for the key to the restroom.

The friendly employee, a teenage girl from the looks of it, smiled and said, "It's open for customers, ma'am." Celeste dashed in and quickly freshened her makeup. *Chill out. You got what you came for. The rest of the trip is gravy.*

But she couldn't escape the uncomfortable truth—someone was three steps ahead of her at every turn.

EVEN WITH THE RESTROOM DETOUR, Celeste would be a few minutes early to meet Savin. She walked while sipping her smoothie, trying to appear nonchalant. She had talked herself into believing—or at least pretended to believe in that moment—that it was the fictitious Brinn who was in danger, not herself. She'd been quite open about the trip, leaving a digital footprint every step of the way. Sometimes it was better to hide in plain sight, especially with forty employees, a business partner, a fiancé, and the fiancé's parents there to keep her company, as well as the security outfit arranged by Angelo to detect anything going wrong.

As she was walking, she noticed a man and woman across the street. The woman's profile looked familiar. *Rani?* Yes, it was definitely her. Celeste squinted to try to identify the man, but his face was turned away from her. Yet even from behind, he also looked familiar, with his broad, powerful shoulders and blond hair. She racked her brain. *That's it!* From behind, he looked like Alexsandr. *Alex talking to Rani? Here?* From Celeste's vantage point, the two seemed to be arguing.

"Celly! Earth to Celly! I'm over here," Savin called from outside the jewelry store.

She waved to him and looked back once more. The man and woman were gone. Had her eyes been playing tricks on her? No, she knew what she'd seen. Rani and the man who had kidnapped her from Riyadh were speaking to one another on a sidewalk in the Cayman Islands. She tried to remember Rani's facial expression. *Angry. She looked angry.* But no mystery was going to be solved right then. She didn't want Savin to notice anything was up, so she put on her brightest smile and told herself she had to let it go for the time being.

"Hi darling," she said as she approached him. "Let's spend some of your hard-earned money." Savin held out his elbow, and Celeste wrapped her arm through his. They walked into the jewelry store.

"And here come the vultures," she whispered as three salespeople raced toward them.

Savin waved them away. "I won't be needing any assistance today, other than this lady," he said, pointing to Celeste. "She can spot the perfect gift like no one else."

They strolled over to the necklace counter, Celeste trying to act the part of his relaxed best friend on vacation. Best friend, soon-to-be wife of his childhood friend, business partner, street fighter. *Gun owner. Murderer.* Her identity was ever evolving these days.

"OK, so what's the look we're going for with this? What's the vibe?"

"Something not too over the top but that says, 'I love you more than words,'" Savin explained. "And maybe something besides a plain diamond. Any ideas?"

"Rani's style is sophisticated and chic. If I were you, I'd go with either a solitaire diamond or something like this." She pointed to a gorgeous cushion-cut sapphire with a diamond-encrusted chain. "Set against her olive skin and dark hair, it will look stunning. She could wear it for special occasions, but it's even dressy enough for her— well, I suppose it's yours also—wedding day as her something blue."

Celeste made a mental note to get her own something blue. *I'm great at so many things but a disastrous bride.* She wagered that other women had everything for their wedding figured out by the age of seventeen, whereas she was still scrambling her way through the planning mere months before the day.

Savin grinned broadly. "Yes, this is the one. It's absolutely perfect!" He pointed to the female salesperson hanging in the back. "Excuse me, miss. Could you help me and my friend here?"

Celeste was proud that he was observant enough to notice that the salesmen had overshadowed the young woman when she and Savin had walked in. *I've trained him well. The pretty penny of commission she'll get from this sale will probably pay her rent for several months.*

"I'm Savin and this is Celeste. What's your name?"

"Dariana."

"Lovely to meet you, Dariana. Could you tell me a little about this necklace right here?"

When she began talking about the stones, Dariana came alive. Her knowledge of jewelry was evident as she rattled off the weight in carats and the origin of the stone.

"Do you know the meaning of sapphires?" Savin asked.

"They represent serenity and are believed to bring good health and peace of mind."

"That sounds perfect, as my lady seems a little troubled lately," Savin commented. Alarm bells went off in Celeste's brain. *Fuming. That's how she'd best describe Rani's face from earlier. What's troubling you, dear Rani? What are you mixed up in?*

Savin continued, "And how much for this beautiful work of art?"

Suddenly, Celeste's vision began narrowing, and she felt like a panic attack was coming on. When she thought Theodore was dead, she'd had them almost daily, so she was no stranger to the sensation.

"Excuse me for a sec. Dariana, could you point me to the ladies' room?" she asked in what she hoped was a nonchalant tone.

She rushed toward the back of the store. Once there, she splashed water on her face and then practiced breathing exercises to slow everything down in her mind. It wasn't the time to freak out. But it was hard to remain calm after what she'd found out at the bank.

The account balance was $94 million. Matthew was rich, but he wasn't the kind of wealthy that would have nearly $100 million lying around in an offshore account. What was he involved with that would generate that kind of money? Was he blackmailing someone? Was it a slush fund for Omar? Would there be a big withdrawal intended for some horrible evil? Her thoughts were jumbled.

And what she'd found out about Rani was also upsetting. Celeste knew one thing for sure—it was time for a reckoning. That woman was keeping secrets, and with so much access to Celeste and Savin, Rani was way too close for comfort. Sharing her suspicions with Savin, though, would break his heart. Celeste couldn't bear to upset him unless and until she was certain Rani was involved in something concerning. She vowed to get to the bottom of it before they left the island known both for its seven-mile beach and for concealing ill-gotten money.

Ninety-four million fucking dollars.

Celeste's breathing slowed back to normal. She could and would figure out what was going on, and she wouldn't let it disrupt her months of planning. After touching up her makeup, she returned to the sales floor just in time to see Savin slide his black card across the counter to Dariana, who was beaming from ear to ear.

"She's going to love it," Celeste said when she was at Savin's side. She lowered her voice and added, "Thank you for making her day—and her month."

"Worth every penny to see those assholes put in their place and to know that her life will be a little better," he replied.

Celeste was no stranger to the evils of the world, yet she still had hope that good would prevail. *Ironic that I'm the heroine in this story.*

CELESTE NEEDED to sneak away to call Michel and her hackers, but Savin insisted that they have lunch together.

"C'mon, we're going to be with those D&C fuckers all week. Have lunch with me."

"Those fuckers are our employees, and we promised them an inspirational trip."

"We promised them free rooms and the ability to get drunk on the D&C tab."

Celeste laughed. "Fair enough."

They stopped at a casual hotel restaurant on the water about half a mile from their hotel. Once they ordered their lunch, Celeste wanted to do a little digging.

"Have you decided when you'll give Rani her gift? She's going to love it!"

"I was thinking I'd take her to dinner alone on the last night. I agree—she'll love it."

"Does she know anyone on the island? I could've sworn I saw her walking earlier before I met you."

Savin was taken aback by the question. "No. Why would she know anyone here?"

"Yeah, I didn't think so. Must've just been a woman who resembled her, the dark hair and all." Celeste shrugged and changed the subject to D&C business. She didn't want to raise any suspicion.

"Sur-prise! I'm here!" came a loud singsong voice from behind her that she'd recognize anywhere. *Jack.*

"Does he ever show up at a planned time?" she asked Savin.

"Never. At least not in the twenty years we've known him."

Jack plopped down in one of the extra seats at their table before they had time to stand and greet him. He began chattering away immediately.

"I flew here on my own. Made it in one piece even!"

"That is truly remarkable," Celeste commented—and meant it. Jack was extremely capable but quite reckless. She still couldn't believe he'd been granted a pilot's license in the first place.

"OK, so let me get this straight. You guys *voluntarily* convened a trip with all the nerds you employ? Sounds like a barrel of laughs," Jack teased.

"They are pretty dorky," Savin admitted.

"You two sound like high school bullies. We have the best and the brightest, and they make us a lot of money," she said in defense. *But the guys are right—I'm sure this is the coolest thing that's ever happened to most of them.* She realized that she'd get no intel on Rani during lunch.

Savin changed the subject. "So Mere tells me we're going deep-sea fishing tomorrow?"

And I'm going to do a little recon when you're out of my hair. "Yes, you, Jack, and Theodore are going, and some of the guys from the firm are golfing. And I'll have a lovely break from everyone."

"Don't sound so excited to get away from us," Savin said, chuckling. "Yes, that's the plan. Theodore apparently does this sort of thing all the time. I've asked Rani for advice on what to wear—seems so barbaric."

"You're such a pussy," Jack said, then howled with laughter. "You'd never make it alone in the wild."

"What situation would present itself where I'd ever need to make it in the wild? Life isn't a Crocodile Dundee episode."

"Crocodile Dundee isn't your best example," Jack said sardonically.

Celeste's patience was wearing thin while they waited for their food. She was itching to get back to her RH research, and if she didn't get it done on the trip, she wouldn't have time to sneak away again to the Caymans before the wedding.

Ughhh.

While the guys were droning on, Celeste joined a VPN, then opened her maps to see where the other bank she needed to visit was located. After the run-in earlier, she needed to be more careful. *Was Alex here? And how is he entwined with Rani? Why would they be arguing?*

"Earth to Celly," Savin said, jerking her from her reverie. "You just completely checked out on us."

"Oh, sorry. I realized I totally forgot to tell Mere to order flowers for my, uh, bridal shower."

"So just text her," Savin suggested.

Celeste pulled out her iPhone. "No, I need to catch her on Face-

Time." She feigned annoyance. "You two would never believe how much planning a wedding takes."

Jack giggled. "There's zero chance you've done any planning of it."

You're right—I've spent my time planning other things.

"I have to dash back to the hotel." She gathered her bag and took the last sip of her sparkling water. "So glad you joined us, Jack. Have Sav show you what he dropped some coin on today. See you for dinner, darlings." With that, she turned on her heel.

It was early afternoon. To cover her tracks, she would head to the hotel and actually call Meredith, and if she had time, she'd stop by the other bank. She decided to walk along the beach from the café to her hotel. Slipping off her sandals when she reached the sand, she walked to the edge of the water and toward her hotel. Her new burner phone rang.

"That was a close call," Michel barked by way of greeting.

"A little too close. I saw two large men running when I was only a block away. Who tipped them off, and why are they involved?" As an afterthought, she added, "By the way, who tipped you off?"

"I have my sources. I'll report back on what I find out. But I thought there was something else you should know."

The now-familiar feeling of dread that accompanied those words washed over her. She took a deep breath and exhaled it out loudly. "What now?"

"I created a trail to suggest that Nico returned back to the UAE on a PJ the morning after... well, the morning after. Enzo believes the information that's been passed along to him, so Nico's disappearance will go public soon. Hopefully, it won't attract much attention."

Nico on a private jet to UAE takes me right off the suspect list. "Let's hope. But there's something else. Spit it out."

Michel sighed heavily. "I hesitate to even bring it up, but you'll find out one way or another."

"Out with it!" Celeste nearly shouted, then looked around as though noticing the children splashing in the water nearby for the first time. "Just tell me."

"Nasrin was lying."

Her heart sank. She'd really begun to like Nasrin and felt that they would've been friends under different circumstances. "I'm going to need a little more information than that."

"Someone *did* kill Zari because of his connection with you. Probably Omar's men once they tracked you down. But she didn't want you to be riddled with guilt."

"So her brother's hatred was well-founded?"

"I wouldn't say validated, but it was based on the correct assumption that someone murdered Zari to get to you."

She processed the information for a moment, biting back tears. It was just as she'd suspected. Zari's children would grow up without their father because of her. "Well, it's not exactly what I wanted to hear, but thanks for letting me know. I have to go."

She put the burner back in her bag just as she heard her iPhone ringing. *What now?*

"Mizz—er, Celeste, rather. Do you have a minute?" *Fucking Gabe.*

"Yes, I have *a* minute, then I have to go." She watched her feet making imprints in the sand and the water washing them away. The chorus of kids squealing in the background and their parents calling after them to be careful was distracting her. *What a bullshit day this has become.*

"I found the leak. It was as we suspected. It's someone one degree away from the core illuminati group."

Please don't say Theodore. I can't handle any more bad news today.

"Who is it?"

"Rani."

Mic drop.

The first thing that came to mind was the necklace. If Savin returned it, Dariana wouldn't get her commission. *Jesus, Celeste, focus.*

For the second time in five minutes, Celeste said, "Thanks for letting me know," without meaning it at all.

Changed my mind. I don't want to get to the bottom of any of this shit. I want to sit on a chaise and get drunk off fruity drinks while ordering a pool boy around.

Gabe hung up and Celeste put her phone back in her bag. As she walked the rest of the way, she tried to shake off the feeling of impending doom. When she got to the Ritz pool on the way to her villa, she was less than enthusiastic to see about ten of her analysts soaking up the sun. She plastered a smile on her face.

"Hello, everyone! I'm in a rush, but I'll see you at dinner tonight." She hurried away before one of them could stop her with "I was wondering if you could take a look at my…"

Once in her room, she flung her bag on the bench at the end of the enormous bed and lay down spread-eagled. She was exhausted, and it wasn't even 2 p.m.

"Hello, my love," Theodore's voice called from the terrace, startling her. She stood up and walked out there.

"Oh, hey, babe, I didn't realize you were here," she said, sitting down on the empty chair next to his. She leaned over to kiss him on the cheek, then asked, "How has your day been?"

"Better than yours, from the looks of it."

"Sav and Jack were their usual overbearing selves at lunch, and I've remembered one thousand things I have left to do for our wedding—"

"Ladies and gentlemen, she called it a wedding!" Theodore said, mimicking a commentator.

Celeste laughed, then turned serious. "To be fair, when you call it a wedding, it really ups the ante. Then people start expecting it to be perfect, and with the acquisitions and all the travel—well, I just feel it will be less than."

"Nothing done in the spirit of celebrating our love could be anything less than perfect, honey," Theodore said.

She considered that in light of what she was planning. *I sincerely hope you're right.*

THERE WAS no time that afternoon to run to the second bank after she and Theodore had sex and then showered. Instead, she had to find Rani and confront her. But she couldn't let Savin know. The thought of hurting him when he was happy for the first time ever was almost too much, so she'd have to make sure he never found out. Or at least not until Celeste had the evidence she needed to prove Rani was the rat. She had relayed the information Gabe had shared to Michel and then texted Rani, proposing a pre–cocktail hour walk on the beach. Celeste had to know the truth or she'd go mad. The two agreed to meet at the tiki bar on the beach at the end of the hotel property.

While she was walking across the resort grounds, Celeste scolded herself for being so blind as to what—or who—had been right there all along. Rani had had a front-row seat to her and Savin's lives for years. *Years.* It was time to assess the damage.

Rani was waiting for her, leaning casually against the bar. She wore a lime-green tank polo shirt, a white tennis skirt, and a rattan visor, with her dark hair in its usual tight, sleek ponytail. She looked as though she'd just finished a fitness photo shoot, her bronze skin glistening in the sun. In her hand was a pink smoothie with a straw.

"Celeste, you are always so chic. Love the flowy sundress—perfect for a day like today," Rani commented, nodding to Celeste's Charro Ruiz number.

"Thanks!" Celeste ordered a bottle of cold Fiji water and settled her check. She turned back to Rani. "Were you out on the courts?"

"I was indeed. But not without a huge hassle." They began walking, and Rani became animated as she dove into a story. "Get this. I went into town this morning to look for a racket. I was a little early, so I decided to walk around a bit." She took a sip of her smoothie and continued.

"Cutest little town. Anyway, I felt as if someone were watching me. You know how you can tell? When your intuition gives you shivers or something? It was exactly like that. So I walked fast and then hid in the shadows. When I heard the footsteps coming, I jumped out and demanded that the person tell me why he was following me."

"Holy shit, that sounds scary. What happened?"

"He was carrying a camera. Said he had me confused with some B-list celebrity. I demanded he give me the memory card. Oddly, he handed it right over and slithered back into the shadows. I mean, seriously. Paps on vacation. My word." Rani rolled her eyes and then looked at Celeste.

"Should we file a police report? What did he look like?"

"IDK, do you think we need to? I wasn't going to make a big deal of it. He was a tall, blond brute. Everything about him was sharp angles—his jaw, his nose, his forehead. I just remember thinking he looked sharp," she said and laughed.

Definitely sounds like Alexsandr.

"He would've been hot, but he ruined everything when he opened his mouth. He had the most twangy Southern accent, which as you know is not my thing."

Celeste, the anglophile, admitted, "It's not mine either." *Guess it's not Alex.* She thought back to other times she'd been suspicious of Rani, determined to get to the bottom of it.

"I'm sorry that happened to you. Let me know if there's anything I —we, the firm, Angelo, et cetera—can do. It's very important to me that everyone is safe, especially on a work trip."

The two walked a bit in the hot afternoon sun, gabbing about the island's shopping. Celeste suggested they enjoy a glass of wine at the next spot they saw to get into the shade. They wandered up to a resort Celeste hadn't visited before. It had a terrace with a bar right off the beach.

"Perfect! What would you like?" Celeste asked as she waved down the bartender.

"Sancerre."

Celeste ordered two glasses. She kept the conversation light until they were on the second round.

"There's something I need to ask you," Celeste said, looking pointedly at Rani.

"Of course. Fire away."

Taking the risk, but Celeste plunged in. "I thought I saw you on the street a few months ago in Paris, but when I asked you about it, you said you hadn't been in a while. I could've sworn on my life that it was you, though."

Rani suddenly looked sheepish. "I told Sav it was silly to hide all this from you." She took a sip and continued, "So on one of your business trips—when you and Savin went to Paris, I tagged along. We stayed at—"

"You stayed at the Plaza Athénée." Celeste recalled Savin ducking out of their time together a few times on one of their trips and with vague excuses. "That makes sense. He was acting strange that entire trip. You're saying it's because he was harboring you in his hotel room?"

Rani giggled. "Yes, he was hiding me, his fugitive coworker girlfriend. But I don't regret going. Wow, Celeste, it was my first time at that hotel. It is beyond gorgeous!"

"Yes, it's quite opulent." *The story checks out.* Celeste toyed with the idea that Gabe could be mistaken about Rani being the leak, which seemed as unlikely as Rani lying to her face right then. She artfully changed the subject to ensure she did not alarm Rani. "So what do you think of our making these acquisitions?"

"It seems very exciting! I always knew you and Savin would do big things. You're such visionaries. You especially, but if you tell my beloved I said that, I'll deny it until my dying days!"

Celeste had an idea. "I see you taking on more responsibility at the firm—that is, if you'd like to."

Rani's eyes lit up. "I wanted to talk to you about the same thing. Now that most everyone knows Sav and I are together, it would be great to transition to something—not right away, of course, but sometime before the wedding—where I'm not working so directly and on display with him."

Celeste recalled a morning not long before when Rani and Savin had seemed unhappy with one another. She was glad that her and Theodore's laundry wasn't aired in front of an audience—and at work, no less.

"How would you feel about transitioning to operations? I envision you overseeing functions like your current role. You could choose and train your replacement. Well, probably replacements plural. Yours are big shoes to fill."

"Thanks, Celeste, that means a lot."

"Savin and I have been discussing how we will expand our core enabling functions. Now that we're taking on these huge firms, I'm getting a little skittish about our cybersecurity. Would you be interested in heading up the integration? We'll need everyone on the most secure VPNs with encrypted applications on their phones. Because we'll be spread out across the globe, it's even more imperative that we have an airtight network. You could set up the technology department and recruit a chief technology officer. How does that sound to start?"

"Yes, these are great ideas! I adore Savin, but it will be nice not to have work be about power plays. It was fun banter in the beginning, but having the finance bros looking on all the time is annoying, to say the least."

"Oh yuck, I hadn't really thought of that. Yes, absolutely, I'll talk to Savin, and we'll make this transition happen. It will be accompanied by a bump in pay and equity, of course."

"Even better news!" Rani said.

"Cheers," Celeste said, clinking her glass against Rani's.

"To a bright D&C future," Rani replied.

A promotion and raise for her and direct access to her impenetrable devices for my hackers. Everyone wins.

THE NEXT COUPLE of days were much less eventful. Most of the group either fished or golfed the following day, and Celeste was able to sneak off to the second bank in much the same way as she had with the first. The second bank account balance was lower. *"Only"* *fifty million.* It was beyond Celeste's comprehension how Matthew could have so much cash moving through his accounts. She intended to get to the bottom of it.

When she told Gabe that Rani didn't appear to be the leak, he was perplexed and promised to follow up. "Maybe she doesn't know her devices are compromised?" he pondered aloud.

"That's possible and seems more likely than her being involved in an underhanded plot to ruin us," Celeste concurred.

By the end of the week, Celeste was more than ready to return to New York with Theodore. She relayed as much as they packed on their last night.

"Yes, it's been beautiful, dear, but it's time to be back home," her fiancé agreed. "Can we just stay in the West Village until it's time to get married?" he joked.

"Yes, please," she said, laughing as he pulled her into an embrace and spun her around.

"One more quick dip in the hot tub before bed?" he suggested.

"Also a yes, please!"

They changed into their robes and went onto their private terrace. After Theodore arranged a little music and opened a bottle of wine, Celeste could finally relax a bit.

She and Theodore descended into the jacuzzi, and she turned on the jets. The starlit sky illuminated the terrace, and she could see Theodore's expression. He looked relaxed and in love.

But I can't get too comfortable. Celeste had a sneaking suspicion that the weeks leading up to the wedding were going to be interesting, indeed.

15

NEXT STOP: MARRIAGE

"Enzo's finally pulled the trigger, I take it," Savin said, charging into Celeste's office the following week. He thrust a newspaper at her. "Look! The police think he made it back to UAE before disappearing. It can't be my fault, then, right?"

Oh, for fuck's sake, Savin. "Sav, no one ever thought it was your fault. You're always dying to be more important than you are," she said and laughed heartily.

Savin made a comical sad face. "That's not very nice. I'm extremely important in some circles."

"You know what I mean. No one thought you made Nico disappear."

"Maybe it was you, Celly! Maybe that's why you're so nonchalant about all of it," he said.

He doesn't know anything. Relax. "Oh, Sav, what are we going to do with you and your imagination?"

"You're right. On to more important things than our missing business partner. Hell, even his brother is over it, so we should be too. Now, I think we need to have a spring gala. D&C Philanthropies had its inaugural fundraiser last year, and we need to carry on the tradition."

"Savin, I'm getting married in a little over a month. In what world is a hastily thrown together gala within this time frame a good idea?"

Savin grinned sheepishly. "Who says it will be thrown together in haste?"

"What have you done?"

"Well, we didn't want to bother you, so—"

"So you planned the whole thing and you're just telling me now?"

"In my defense, it wasn't just me."

Celeste groaned in frustration. "I don't even have time to shop for a dress or help with planning. We just bought two companies, or did you forget? Am I the only one who remembers such things these days?"

"I don't tell you often enough, but you're doing an exceptional job. You're an inspiration to me and to everyone who knows you," Savin said in a saccharine tone.

"Now I know you're full of shit."

"Why is it so hard to believe—"

"OK, cut it out. When is it?"

"Let's see. Today is Tuesday. Theodore had Rani and Mere block off your calendar for Saturday. So, yes, it's this Saturday."

"My fiancé is in on this scheme as well? Goddammit."

"Yes. You can work out the details with the ladies and my mate. Oh, and we have lots of guests. The usuals, and Mark, Jin, Jack, Sam and Roberto, even Fred and a plus one, ya know."

"Are the Ricci brothers and Tarek and team making the trek?"

"Did you already forget I told you Nico is still missing?"

"Oh, shit, yes, sorry. You've caught me so off guard. Forgive me for being a little disoriented."

"Disoriented or not, you're scheduled to give another inspirational speech to top last year's, and you have four days—Celly, are you listening? Four whole days to write it! A piece of cake."

"You know how I hate surprises—and more than that, I hate

secrets!" *Ironic since I'm harboring so many.* "Is that all you wanted? To dump this on me?"

"Yep. Well, that and to tell you it appears there is only one Ricci brother to deal with now."

"And Tarek et al.? They're definitely in?"

"Indeed. Matthew, Kaya, and Tarek will be there."

"What's the venue?"

"It's fancy."

"Well, at least you've done something right. If you're going to blindside me with an event, it had better be black tie and red-carpet worthy. Let me get my life sorted today, and then I plan to yell at you some more for giving me like two days' notice."

Savin wasn't bothered in the least by her scolding. "That's my cue," he said, grinning widely. He left her alone in her office.

Matthew on US soil. An interesting development. She had to keep him around to find out more about RH Global, and perhaps an evening out with him would be the perfect way to get him to talk.

Celeste scrolled through her encrypted inbox. She usually loved Tuesdays. It was when Omar's sidekick would send her status updates. He'd become invaluable, and she was confident everything was falling into place with her plan after his email that morning. Her mood had turned dark, though.

What troubled her was beyond Omar for once. Knowing that Nasrin had lied to protect Celeste brought with it a familiar heaviness and wave of guilt that she thought she'd been able to shed. Omar had killed Zari, and now Nasrin would spend her days devastated by the loss of the love of her life. Celeste was astonished that Nasrin was still concerned with protecting the woman responsible for her husband's death. Nasrin was a better person than she was, she supposed, considering that Nasrin had tracked down Omar's right-hand man and recruited him. Celeste vowed to find a way to make it up to her. She had considered inviting Nasrin and her children to visit the United States. *Kids, a trip to America—the consolation prize for losing your father! And the lady he died to protect is paying for it!* It hardly felt like an appropriate offering.

"I have her."

"Does she know?"

"She knows nothing."

Nasrin had explained away those cryptic texts that had plagued Celeste, but now with fresh eyes, Celeste realized that she still had so many unanswered questions. She vowed to get to the bottom of things right after the wedding.

∾

"WE HAVE A PROBLEM," Tarek's voice boomed. Celeste was seated in Bryant Park, attempting to enjoy a latte before her late afternoon happy hour with Fred and Savin. *But duty always calls.*

"What is it?"

"My head of IT alerted me to something that may be of interest. Matthew's requested a new hard drive and new devices. Said he suspected his security had been compromised."

"That seems a little strange. Wouldn't he know that IT's first call would be to you?"

"He wanted me to find out. To send a message. Is it possible he knows that we have access?"

Celeste thought back to the men running toward the Cayman bank. Had she tipped her hand too aggressively? *No.* She had the information she needed, whether Matthew moved the money to new accounts or not. She wasn't in the same position she'd been in two years prior. Now she had a wealth of contacts on the dark web and bad guys she could hire to do any sort of dirty work. She'd get to the bottom of RH regardless of Matthew's attempts to hide what he was doing. She had spent months gathering evidence to put Omar away, and ultimately, he'd ended up protected by the very government that had committed to protecting her. No, she wasn't interested in that path again. She wouldn't be framing Matthew and his kind. They would meet a much darker fate.

∾

"YOU BARELY HAVE time for us these days," Ty whined.

"She's probably downgraded to some Insta-famous glam squad with no talent," Patrick countered.

Ty, her needy hairstylist, and Patrick, her bitchy makeup artist, were getting her red-carpet ready for D&C's gala. They were the most talented in the city, in her opinion, and before her life had derailed, she loved to have their company before events. It hit her how much she missed the people in her life. With the secret life, the late nights, she barely had time for anything else besides work these days.

Celeste's normal routine the morning before a gala was to work out, eat a healthy breakfast, and spend the day grooming. As a reflection of how much her life had changed of late, she had a double session with Zed that day and spent the rest of the morning taking a long subway trek to pick up the supplies she would need in Italy from a shady character Petey had unwittingly helped her identify.

Petey. The poor guy thought he had a budding friendship with Mia Blosch, a woman who didn't exist. Instead, he was helping Celeste transition into a successful criminal. *Can't say that I'm mad about it.* And it wasn't her fault that he mistook her willingness to learn from him as a sign that she wanted to sleep with him. *Read the room, buddy.*

Now the men scrambled to finalize her look while Meredith was bustling in and out of the room, steaming Celeste's dress, setting out her shoes and jewelry, and packing her clutch and a backup bag in the event Celeste and Theodore decided to grab a room at the hotel venue.

"What would I do without all of you? Sav sprang this event on me on Tuesday, and you've managed to make it seem as though I've been preparing for months. You're the best in the biz!"

"Careful, Ty will get a big head if you compliment him too much," Patrick said.

"That reminds me. God, I'd love some good head right now. I know exactly where I'm going tonight after this. On the prowl," Ty interjected.

"Gross, you two!" Mere said. "Drink up, Celly. You look better than a few weeks ago, but still not your best self." She handed Celeste a green juice.

"Thanks!" Celeste said. *Not surprising that I look like shit given the late nights. I need to keep up my strength for the next few weeks, that's for sure.*

Once the guys had finished, Mere helped Celeste into the dress she'd chosen, a long, red silk number with a sweetheart neckline and a cape around the shoulders.

"Is that a bruise?" Mere asked Celeste, pointing to what was most certainly a contusion on her midsection from her Thursday night session with Zed. She'd told Theodore that she was at spin class that night.

"Yes! Ugly, isn't it? My trainer had me doing abdominal crunches with a weight, and it left this gross thing. Thank God it's not somewhere more prominent." To distract them from asking more questions, she pointed to the abdominal scrape caused by Gabe's window, which had nearly healed. "I told you what happened with this, right? Dropped a fucking plate in the kitchen. Theodore came running and had to bandage me up."

"Mere is right; you need some self-care. Dropping dishes? Doing abs with weights? You're basically a zombie," Patrick said.

"Excuse me for a moment." She walked into the living room and retrieved a bottle of Champagne from her wine refrigerator, attempting to balance the bottle with four flutes and a tub of ice.

"Honey, let me grab that for you," Theodore said, appearing from her office. *My office?* Theodore never went in there.

"Did you find what you were looking for?"

Theodore looked confused for a moment, then seemed to understand. "Oh yes. I misplaced my iPad charger and grabbed one of yours." He pulled a charger from his pocket, then stuffed it back in. He took the bottle, glasses, and ice from her and handily carried them into their bedroom. She followed him.

Ty, Patrick, and Meredith broke out into cheers.

"Champagne! Let's see if she's grabbed the good stuff." Ty took the bottle from Theodore's hand. "Not bad, a 2006 vintage." He popped the top.

That'll stop the inquisition. She exhaled and distributed the drinks, putting on a happy face for her friends.

CELESTE STOOD by the stage and took in the lavishly decorated event space. Ivory spring blooms adorned the cocktail tables, and the Champagne waterfall was a hit. Meredith and Rani had outdone themselves with event planning yet again. *And Meredith managed to pull this all together with a wedding mere weeks away, no less.* Celeste made eye contact with her beau from across the room. Theodore looked like a movie star in his Tom Ford tuxedo. He winked when she waved, then he turned back to Roberto and Sam.

Savin was set to meet her any minute, and they'd address the crowd together. The most important movers and shakers from their industry were in attendance, if for no other reason than to try to understand what the hell D&C was up to. She could hear their whispered conversations, speculating on the bold moves. "How did the Ice Queen ever get Tarek on board?" "How insane does one have to be to go into business with the Riccis?"

"You've got quite a turnout, Celeste. A shining example of how our industry can and must do better," Fred said from behind her. "You've really grown into a force these past few years. And wedding bells too? I'm happy that everything is coming together. You deserve it."

Celeste turned around to see Fred and his date. He always looked a bit disheveled and out of shape, even in a tuxedo. Tonight he was beaming ear to ear.

"Hello, I don't believe we've met before. Celeste Donovan." She extended her hand, and the woman, a striking blonde beauty in her mid-fifties, shook it firmly.

"Elizabeth Kennedy," the woman said warmly. She was wearing a tasteful black Oscar de la Renta peplum gown and understated diamonds.

Fred looked at Elizabeth with stars in his eyes. He was clearly smitten. "I told Elizabeth about all the good work D&C Philanthropies has been doing."

"I've been following what you and Savin have been up to," Elizabeth said. "Your strategies to build up infrastructure in targeted developing countries isn't only innovative but has also been extremely effective. I'd like to get involved."

"Fantastic. We're quite proud of it. I'll arrange some time for us and Lorraine. She runs our foundation."

"That's what I mean. Innovative from the ground up. What a spectacular idea to bring the younger generation into the fold and so early in her career. Brava, Celeste!"

Just then, Savin scurried up behind Fred, looking frazzled.

"Savin, meet Elizabeth," Celeste said. "We're meeting with her soon to discuss potential partnership ideas."

Savin smiled broadly, but Celeste could tell something was up. "Lovely to meet you, Elizabeth. I look forward to toasting future endeavors after dinner."

"We have taken up too much of your time. We'll let you get back to hosting," Elizabeth replied. She hooked her arm into Fred's, and the two walked away.

Celeste leaned her head in close to Savin's. "What's going on with you?"

"Gabe called. He has information regarding Ni—"

Out of the corner of her eye, Celeste saw a man approaching. *Gabe showed up here? Tonight? Was nothing sacred to this man?*

"Celeste, I trust Savin has gotten you up to speed."

At least he's appropriately dressed in black tie. "Actually, no, he hasn't. What's so important that it is derailing our annual fundraiser?"

"It's Nico."

Celeste kept her expression neutral. "Oh?"

"Remnants of his cell phone were found in lower Manhattan

recently. We were able to check cell phone towers, and we now have reason to believe that he never left New York."

She stared at him blankly, waiting for him to proceed. It seemed wise to avoid saying anything incriminating. *Of course he never left. Get on with it.*

"If I had to guess, Omar was behind his death, and while I haven't been able to verify it, it's possible that Omar could be in New York as we speak."

"Gabe, did you have regularly scheduled business in the city today?"

"Not beyond delivering this news and meeting with some of my guys on the ground."

Celeste was touched. Despite the shit she gave Gabe, he did have a good soul. "Thank you for coming all this way to relay the news and ensure we were appropriately on alert."

Gabe had a hint of a blush.

"Please stay tonight," Celeste suggested. "We have airtight security and an exciting evening planned. We'll find you in a little while to discuss things further."

"Yes, I had planned to stay. I can't allow another—mishap where Omar is involved. Not on my watch."

Celeste wondered if Michel's guy and his sloppy cleanup would be a problem for her, but she decided not to worry. She wasn't concerned about Omar, but she believed she convincingly appeared to be. She knew from her communications earlier that week that he was bouncing around the Caribbean in his yacht. *Enjoy it while it lasts, asshole.*

D&C raised record dollars that night, thanks to Lorraine's hard work, and Celeste pulled her aside after dinner to tell her so. Lorraine's cheeks were flushed from excitement and Champagne.

"Congratulations, Celeste!" she said and hugged her boss. *Yep, a little tipsy.*

"This is much more a reflection on you than it is on me and Savin. You blow me away on a regular basis, Lorraine. I'm continually impressed by your ingenuity, drive, and passion to do the right thing." To Celeste's surprise, her eyes welled up with tears. *Not so much the Ice Queen these days.* "Truly, I hope you know the magnitude of your impact."

"Lorraine, you've outdone yourself tonight," Theodore said, appearing at Celeste's side and slipping an arm around her waist. "What an incredible testament to your dedication. Now, would you mind if I whisk my soon-to-be bride away for a dance and a smooch?"

Celeste rolled her eyes and laughed along with Lorraine. He was the only man who could pull off using the word "smooch" while still sounding sexy.

"Of course, and thank you both—it means so much." With that, Lorraine walked away. *Probably on her way to find Brett.*

"Who was the guy that approached you and Savin earlier?" Theodore asked. "Savin looked upset."

"Oh, Savin's always hysterical. Can't ever assume he's got a grasp on reality," Celeste said nonchalantly. She hadn't ever expected Gabe to be in the same room as Theodore, so she wasn't prepared with an answer. "Remember how I told you we were looking into everyone in the office and in our newly acquired offices for security breaches? That guy is one of our consultants." She lowered her voice and moved in as though she were telling a secret. "Don't look now, but we're concerned it's the Italian firm. One of the brothers is here, so G—Glen is checking him out."

"Makes sense. Glad you guys have found someone you trust."

Wouldn't go that far. But it was a nice gesture to come and warn me in person.

"Babe, I have to make a few more rounds, then we can call it a night."

"Of course, darling." Theodore kissed her on the lips and went to look for a Scotch refill and Savin, no doubt.

Celeste had purposely waited to get a pulse on the new guys until they were a little liquored up. She grabbed a glass of Champagne off a server's tray and looked around the enormous room for Matthew. As she suspected, he looked quite drunk. She beelined to him, smiling and giving casual hellos along the way to donors.

"Matthew, how lovely to see you in New York. I trust your trip was uneventful. Are you enjoying the city?" She smiled widely, batting her lashes and flashing her dimples. *A little flirting to destroy Omar never hurt anyone.*

Matthew responded immediately to her vibe, completely unaware that Celeste thought he was a drunken slob.

"It's been nice so far, but perhaps you could show me around a little tomorrow," he offered suggestively.

Gross. Celeste resisted the urge to roll her eyes. He was so sexist and arrogant that he didn't realize how inappropriate it was to proposition his new boss.

"Perhaps. So tell me, how is the integration going in Dubai?"

"Kaya and I don't know what you've got on Tarek, but it must be good because otherwise he never would've gone into business with —" He finally seemed to realize that it was his boss he was talking to and sobered a little. "I don't know where I was going with that, but it's great. The team you've sent out has been really helpful."

"And do you feel the benefits are clear? That the cybersecurity is running adequately?" A flicker of concern crossed his face. *That's all I needed to know.* She couldn't wait to destroy that man, but she needed him until she uncovered the RH connection.

Tarek walked up then. Celeste almost didn't recognize him in a tuxedo, though he was still wearing his headpiece.

"This event is fantastic, Celeste. Thanks for including us. And thanks for the generous donations to some very important causes close to our hearts at TA."

Matthew laughed drunkenly. "You mean, pet projects."

"I think it's time for you to go home, Matthew," Tarek instructed.

Celeste was surprised when Matthew acquiesced. He pulled out his phone and appeared to order a car to pick him up.

"Where are you staying, Matthew?"

"The St. Regis."

"And you're staying for our Monday meeting, right?"

"Yes, I'll be here through Tuesday. My car is here."

Matthew couldn't get out of there fast enough.

"You blackmailing him or something?" she asked, prodding Tarek.

"I was testing him. Believe me, he usually makes a complete ass out of himself if there's a bar around. It was an anomaly that he left, which means he's up to something." *He sure as hell is, and I haven't seen Kaya all night. Maybe she's in on it.*

Celeste walked through the room, attempting to connect with as many people as she could as quickly as possible. By the time she made her way to the other side of the ballroom, her cheeks hurt from the fake smiles.

"Dear, things are winding down, at least for the people our age. Shall we go home?" Theodore inquired.

"I'd like nothing more."

"CELLY, it's time! You have to acknowledge you have bridesmaids! And that I've chosen the most perfect dresses for them."

It was the following morning at 10 a.m., and Celeste would've preferred to have a lazy Sunday in bed instead of being subjected to Mere's annoying enthusiasm. *Like I've had a carefree Sunday any time in the past few years.* The two sat on the floor in Celeste's living room, Mere's giant binders in front of them.

The wedding was only a month away, and they planned to arrive in Italy a week before the festivities. Meaning Celeste had only three more weeks to train, to finalize the plan, to gather supplies. For better or for worse, the time was fast approaching for some sort of resolution. Either Omar would prevail—or she would.

Savin had promised to work with Rani and Mere to plan what he called "a robust itinerary" for the Tuscany trip. Celeste was certain this meant she'd be exhausted by the end of the second day after hitting every great restaurant within a fifty-mile radius. As far as she could tell, everything with the wedding planning was running smoothly, though she usually zoned out when Mere began discussing it. She was obsessed with coming up with the worst-case scenarios. What if things didn't go as anticipated? What if she spent all the time researching and scheming, only to discover that Omar had found a way out or Matthew had burned the RH Global trail? But she mustn't give in to her anxiety.

She pulled herself back to the present. Mere had been working double time to pull off the wedding of the century. The least Celeste could do was pay attention.

"OK, I'm listening. Give me the deets."

"You're wearing a beautiful champagne—well, you know what kind of dress you'll be wearing. I mean, I hope. You haven't exactly been focused on wedding planning to date, and we're leaving in three weeks."

Anything to avoid her looking that sad.

"You've got my undivided. Who are my bridesmaids and what are they wearing? Did anyone say no?"

Mere burst out laughing. "You asked them already, and I don't think they said no. Sam and Rani, remember?"

"Haha, I get it. OK, what else?" Celeste sighed as she heard one of her phones vibrating. "Hang on, this will be quick."

She answered it and walked into her office. "Hello?"

Michel began speaking in a rush, his voice heavy with emotion. "My daughter was mugged, and I can't prove it, but I'm almost certain it's Omar-related. You should see her bruises. It was extremely scary. We went to the police, even though I have little faith that anything will be done."

He continued, "Part of me wants to talk you out of what you're planning, but the more rational part of me knows that we can't live like this anymore. He has to go."

Celeste had never heard Michel sound anything other than authoritative, and now he sounded near hysterical. She needed him to pull it together because he'd become her rock. "I'm so sorry,

Michel. Please keep me posted and let me know if there's anything I can do."

"I have to get back inside the hospital to see my daughter. Take good care."

Once Michel hung up, Celeste padded back into the living room and spent the remainder of the day talking weddings with Meredith.

Next stop: marriage.

16

─────────

HOW TO GET AWAY WITH MURDER

It was almost time to leave, yet Celeste felt unrushed. She sat on the tranquil terrace overlooking the idyllic Tuscan countryside, sipping tea. She'd awoken before the sun to meditate—she needed to be clearheaded for the day ahead.

The sky was a brilliant explosion of pinks and yellows as the sun peeked over the horizon. Rows of pristine Cypress pencil pines dotted the meticulously manicured rolling hills, on the highest of which lay the town of Montepulciano.

Even at this early hour, the staff below bustled about in the courtyard preparing the already immaculate grounds for the week's festivities. The air of old Hollywood romance that Jack's villa provided was the perfect backdrop to marry the love of her life. Only one thing—or person, as it were—stood in the way of the new life beckoning her. *Omar.*

Despite the passage of time and a lot of therapy since his abuse, she could still hear the *crack* of her wrist echoing across the Mediterranean. She shuddered at the metallic taste of her own blood as if it were happening in that moment. With Omar alive, no one she loved was safe, as her recurring graphic nightmare of Omar killing Theodore reminded her.

And there it was—the constant motivation to keep moving forward with this plan. She couldn't wait for the Feds to get it together; she wouldn't risk Theodore's life. The time to act was now. She stood up resolutely. *Omar will never hurt anyone again.*

Back inside, she dressed quietly in a camel tank dress and espadrilles, adding an Hermès scarf and wide straw fedora. Her soon-to-be husband was snoring softly in the lavish California king bed. *He deserves his rest after last night's performance*, she thought, smiling devilishly. She'd slept soundly also, her usual nightmares at bay.

"Good morning, beautiful," Theodore murmured sleepily. "Can't we stay in bed all day?"

She learned over to kiss his cheek and laughed when he pulled her on top of him. He gave her a heady kiss.

"Don't tempt me, sexy man," she said when she felt his morning erection against her body. "I'll be late for my pampering."

Celeste had told everyone she was spending the day at a lavish spa to assuage wedding jitters. Even after so many lies, she still hated deceiving Theodore. But some things a woman must do on her own.

He let out an exaggerated sigh. "I guess I'll have to keep myself busy without you," he said with a grin.

"I'm positive Savin will keep you entertained," she replied. "And you know how irritable I am when I miss a massage!"

Celeste slipped into the en suite bathroom before he asked more questions and locked the door. The Chanel tote she'd hidden in the vanity the previous day was still there, seemingly untouched. She rummaged through its contents to make sure nothing had been disturbed.

The last time she had dressed as Mia was the morning of the recent D&C Philanthropies gala. She had used her dark web contacts to find a source for the deadly substance she'd need to carry out her plan. She'd met a man whose face she'd never seen in a camera-free shadowy alley behind Columbian Presbyterian hospital on Manhattan's Upper West Side. She didn't know what motivated him to sell lethal substances to people like her, people with nefarious, though justified, intent, but after what she'd been through, she was sure most people had their reasons. It was surprisingly easy to obtain all sorts of contraband right on the streets of New York City, as she'd learned listening to Petey's stories. And she'd covered her tracks well. After Petey had unknowingly taught her how to get away with murder, she was confident she could move undetected.

My final day as Mia. Hopefully.

She returned to the bedroom. Theodore had already dozed off again by the time she was ready to leave. She made her way through the sprawling villa to the foyer and out to the Alfa Romeo waiting to take her to the heliport a few miles away. A handsome young man tipped his hat to her and rushed to grab her bag. She pressed it possessively against her.

"No, thank you," she said, waving his hand away and slipping into the back seat.

Celeste stared out the window, lost in thought, not fully seeing the rolling hills and lush greenery. She mentally walked through the agenda Michel had laid out for the day. There was no room for error, but they'd paid off enough people to have confidence that everything would go well.

When her driver began chatting, she replied, "*Il mio italiano è pessimo,*" and he promptly snapped his mouth shut.

The car ride was quick, and in no time, she had exchanged pleasantries with the helicopter pilot and was buckled in with her headphones on.

"Our flying time will be about forty-five minutes, miss," he said. "The weather is perfect."

And it's a perfect day to put an end to this nightmare, indeed. "Yes, it does look that way, doesn't it?" she replied, at once feeling at peace.

She and Michel had scoured over every detail for months, leaving no room for error. They kept their circle small—only three other people knew of their plan. He'd urged her not to be there in person when everything took place, but after a shouting match (she shouted, he chimed in and then finally relented), it was decided that she would have an active role, if for no other reason than her own peace of mind. After all, this wouldn't be her first murder. She was confident she could handle Omar as well as she'd handled Nico.

Once they landed at Urbe, Celeste climbed into the back of the awaiting Mercedes Sprinter with blackout window tint. The driver would not arrive for another ten minutes, so he would not see her before the transformation into Mia.

She scrambled to change her clothes and rummaged through the black case that held everything she needed to ensure it was in order. She had checked it obsessively since leaving New York because she knew its contents would be nearly impossible to replace in Rome. She wouldn't risk any deviation from the plan.

Celeste tucked the last of her golden locks into the wig cap and retrieved a chic brunette wig, purchased at an upscale boutique in Brooklyn (rumored to be the artist behind Bey's locks), and a nose prosthetic from her bag. She added silver Chanel eyeglasses, then secured the final touch of her disguise into place just as she saw the driver walking up. *Here we go.* She took one more cursory look in the rearview mirror and frowned at her reflection. *Safe to say I'll never be getting bangs IRL.* The driver only nodded in greeting and let her sit in silence for the fifteen-minute drive to the hotel.

She had reserved a suite at Hotel de Russie for the week as a home base. It was the place where Michel had brought Omar. Theodore and the others had no idea that she'd slipped away as Mia to Rome once already since they'd arrived in Italy the week before. Everything had needed to be organized. *Good luck is when opportunity meets preparation, as they say.* No one could ever accuse her of being unprepared for this moment.

It had been a long journey. Unbeknownst to her friends and colleagues, she'd broken ranks with the illuminati once she found out Omar was a protected asset of the US government and had been planning this all along. As usual where Omar was involved, the only way to get anything done was to do it herself. *Well, that's not entirely fair.* Theodore and his associate *had* rescued her from Omar's captivity in St. Tropez. But she would've found a way out eventually.

She stood looking in the mirror of the master bath in her hotel suite, ensuring her disguise was still in place. Once she was certain she was unrecognizable, she smiled to herself.

Voilà! Celeste Donovan becomes nondescript Swiss woman once again. It amazed her how easily she could transform into an entirely different person. She'd had a lot of practice of late. A glance at the hotel room clock indicated it was time to go downstairs. She checked the contents of her bag for the final time, ready to face what the day had in store for her.

She slipped the Do Not Disturb sign on the outside door handle, closed the door tightly, and walked down the hallway to the elevator. Once in the lobby, she walked out to the Jardin de Russie, where Michel was seated.

"It's about fucking time," he growled when he spotted Celeste strolling up to him at a carefully curated, casual pace. He was also incognito, but not in full disguise. A bottle of sparkling water had been opened and poured for them.

She rolled her eyes. But she didn't mind his outbursts—they were nothing in comparison to her recent meltdowns. "Oh, fuck off, it's barely nine a.m."

"Are you sure you have everything?" he continued. "We only get one shot—" She and Michel had gone round and round about her bringing the contraband to Rome. He thought for sure it would get confiscated. Celeste, however, had no fear lately, especially given that there'd been no blowback from the Nico situation. Now she felt only the rush that came from knowing Omar would be out of her life for good.

"Yes, for the fortieth time, I brought it all, and I am fully aware that this is it," she interrupted. "Believe me." She turned to the server when the woman reached the table. "Cappuccino, *per favore*, and nothing else." She turned back to Michel. "Everything will go well, and this will be over by nightfall." She looked at the time on her phone. "And now we wait."

Omar was captive upstairs in a room not far from hers. He'd been there for two days, tied up with restraints. At 10 a.m., a security guard that they had paid would switch off the cameras that would otherwise get footage of Michel and Mia going to his room together.

Michel had been shooting up Omar with a steady stream of heroin since he'd brought Omar to the hotel. Celeste had brought the smack from New York, along with some uncut cocaine in a nasal spray bottle. They wanted as many drugs in Omar's system as possible. Given his history, death by overdose was believable.

Celeste had known for months that she was going to kill him, that he would die by her hand while she watched the breath leave his body. She could see no other way to move on because the world was not big enough for the both of them. She would feel no remorse. She would feel free.

And so Celeste accepted the repercussions, whatever they may be, of the irreversible act she had resolved to commit. After she and Michel worked out the logistics, she wasn't even afraid of getting caught. She'd learned long before from watching how Omar operated that one could get away with nearly any crime with enough money and organization. When she first decided to take his life, she feared Omar would be too difficult to track down. He had disappeared for months after he fell off the boat. But Hadid and Nasrin had solved this for Celeste by connecting her with Omar's henchman, so that she'd been able to keep tabs on him. It was only when the wedding planning was well underway that everything had come together. So she had been forced to be extremely patient over the past few months to wait until they were in Italy to take her revenge. It wasn't necessarily a bad thing, because she had been able to prepare, prepare, prepare. Everyone mistook her distraction lately as related to wedding planning. Instead, she'd been laying the groundwork for Omar's disappearance.

I do not want the news to break until after *my wedding.* Chet and Gabe would certainly tell the illuminati, basically her entire guest list, what happened, and calling a last-minute meeting would be annoying. Omar would not get to ruin her day. Alas, it was the only part of their plan that they could not control, and it made Celeste uneasy. But it couldn't be helped. The circumstances were ripe, and they wouldn't have an opportunity like this again.

"Do you think he knows what we have in store for him? That I'm behind it?" Celeste asked.

"Nah. He's been too out of it. Though I did let him sober up a bit from last night to this morning so he can actually realize what's happening and feel the pain."

"Spoken like a true sociopath."

"My daughter still hasn't recovered. He'll pay for her suffering. I figured you'd also want him lucid."

"You guessed right." She glanced down at her phone. *It's time.* She motioned to the server for their bill. She took out a few euros from her bag, aware that credit cards were too easy to trace. The calm feeling she'd had at sunrise had carried through the morning. She wasn't anxious, only excited that in mere hours she could truly exhale for the first time in well over a year, knowing that Omar would never hurt anyone again. *A life for a life, isn't that right?* She and Theodore would be married the next day in the most beautiful of places with their closest friends and family. But first, retribution.

MICHEL SWIPED the key card to open the suite where he'd been holding Omar captive. "He's in the smaller bedroom," he said and led her there.

"Well, well, well, what a nice view!" Celeste remarked, walking into the room and taking in the scene.

Omar was tied to the bed with leather bondage restraints around his wrists and ankles. He had used rope to tie her up when he abused her years before. She chose more sturdy restraints because she knew they would create painful burns on his joints when he struggled to break free, even more so than rope would. She stood at the end of the bed, assessing him. Crust had gathered in the corners of his mouth, which was bound with a gag. His lips were dry and cracked. His beard was scruffy, and he had dark circles under his eyes. Both of his arms were lined with track marks, as were his feet and hands. He was even more repulsive than normal, which was a high bar.

Celeste removed her wig and smiled. Omar's face registered shock when he realized it was her. He tried speaking, to no avail.

"Omar, darling, we *must* stop meeting this way, with one of us tied up and all that. It is *so* lovely to see you. Too much time has passed. Theodore and I were so happy to hear you wanted to attend our wedding. But of course, Michel and I here have other things planned, dear. So much better suited for you."

Celeste stood patiently, enjoying his struggles. She thought of the lives he'd ruined, the innocence and dignity he'd stolen from her. She had spent the past year mourning everything she'd lost, how Zari's children would grow up without a father, Nasrin without a husband, Chet widowed, now Michel's daughter traumatized. Yes, this was justice, and this was what had to happen to put an end to his evil. She and Michel watched in silence as Omar pulled against the restraints until his wrists were bleeding. He maneuvered his head until the gag covering his mouth slid down enough for him to speak.

"Celeste, Celeste, my love," Omar's words spilled out. "I'm so sorry you have to see me this way, but I'm so glad you're here. I knew you'd come for me. You see, this was all a misunderstanding. If you'll just untie me—"

She laughed and laughed. "Oh, sweetie, how cute. You thought I came to rescue you? No, no, we're just getting started, dear. Did you really think I wouldn't come for you after the last time? You thought you'd get away scot-free with brutalizing women, with ripping Zari away from his family, with murdering Chet's wife? Thought you'd cuddle up to someone in the US government for immunity and just walk? Oh, no, darling," she said, sneering at him. "Oh, no, I couldn't allow any more of this destruction. Your time is up.

"And Michel here and I... oh, forgive me, where are my manners? This"—she gestured to Michel, who had taken a seat in a chair by the window—"is my colleague Michel. He's helped me come up with a way to rid the world of your disgusting and vile presence. Is that why you had his daughter mugged? Because you knew he was working with me? Regardless of your reasons, I guess you've gotten to know each other a little over the past few days. Hope you're enjoying the smack. We read in the *Post* that heroin was your drug of choice lately, so we tried to oblige.

"Speaking of, you're looking a little ragged, Omar dear. Your benders seem to be catching up with you. Well, if I'm being completely honest, you look worse than ragged. You look like absolute shit. It's not going to be hard to convince anyone your cause of death is an overdose."

"Dea—Celeste, we can work through this. No need to do anything rash." *Ten, nine, eight, seven, any second now...* The rage that was always lingering just beneath the surface with Omar could erupt with little provocation. She watched the fury rise in his body, even bound and gagged. His cheeks became bright red, and he pulled his arms and legs against the restraints with more force. "Listen here, you fucking whore, you untie me this minute—"

Michel had been standing by the window, taking in the scene with an expression of mild curiosity, but when Omar started shouting, he moved over to the head of the bed.

"Michel, darling, could you pull his gag up again?" She looked at the bedside clock. *Still ahead of schedule.* They had to time everything just right.

"I've waited so long for this moment. It took us a while to come up with an effective trap. Did you know Michel and I set you up? Turns out your right-hand man wasn't so loyal after all. He was more than willing to plant some seeds to manipulate you, convince you that the wedding was the perfect opportunity for whatever you were planning. And you fell for it. Brilliant, huh?

"I must ask, though. Did you really think I'd let you ruin my wedding day? After you nearly killed me and tried to kill my fiancé? Omar, c'mon," she said and then laughed. "You always underestimate me. I think it's good to give you a little time to think about your actions. Because your time of reckoning is here, Omar." She looked at

Michel. "Could you keep an eye on him for a few minutes? I'll be back."

She went to the restroom at the other end of the suite, grabbing a bottle of water from the minibar on the way.

The truth was, being in the same room as Omar again wasn't as easy as she'd anticipated. She was no longer afraid of him, per se, but his very presence brought back so many memories she had hoped she'd forgotten. She had invested a lot of time in therapy to process what had happened, but the fact remained—some fragments of trauma would always be there.

They would still move forward with the plan—of that she was sure. But it may not be as easy to detach as it had been with Nico.

Inhale, one. Exhale, one. Inhale, two. Once the mindful breathing had calmed her nerves a bit, she was ready to go back in. *Just one more hour.* She and Michel both had wanted to draw out Omar's suffering, but it wasn't worth blowing her spa outing cover.

Omar's eyes were bulging when she returned to the room. She recognized the panic reflected on his face because she'd felt that fear more than once.

"He's starting to feel the effects of the strychnine."

"Fun! Omar, get this. Michel and I researched so many different ways to kill you. Of course, there was the easy way out—we could've just hired someone to get rid of you. Shoot you or slice you open from your balls to your neck and let you bleed out. Have someone beat the shit out of you. That one could've been nice so you could feel the way I did, ya know? Seven surgeries, Omar. Did you know I had to go under the knife seven times to repair the damage you caused? And can you imagine the pain and trauma I endured? The feelings of guilt I carry around every day because Zari's children are growing up without a father? How I feel when I think of the other women you've harmed? The chaos you've financed by giving weapons to terrorist groups around the world? You are a rotten motherfucker, this much is true. So yes, admittedly I want to see you suffer. Maybe that makes me no better than you, but I like to think that I have a more humanitarian angle—to stop you from hurting anyone else.

"So here's what we came up with. The heroin has been laced with strychnine—it's not super common, but it does happen with street drugs in New York. We cut it with just enough so you will die slowly. You see those spasms you're experiencing? They'll continue to get worse, much more painful.

"But this is my favorite—have you ever heard of halothane? No? Michel was kind enough to recommend to me the perfect antidote to the misery and pain you spread. You're a cancer to humankind, a despicable coward preying on the vulnerable. But no more, Omar. That ends today. And tomorrow I will marry Theodore despite your best efforts to destroy us.

"In the meantime, here's what's going to happen. I, of course, want to be transparent every step of the way because we've come up with the perfect cocktail to ensure you'll die with maximum suffering and enough consciousness to think through all the crimes against humanity you've committed.

"First, I'll inject this halothane and you'll be paralyzed, completely paralyzed, but you'll still feel pain and be aware of what's happening. Then it'll be time for another fun one—ricin—to kick in. I particularly like the effects of this one. Only a tiny bit, making it nearly untraceable, and your insides will feel like they're burning from the inside out. You see, the poison will cause your organs to fail, but slowly enough that you'll feel the pain. You'll finally pay for what you've done. We've timed things just perfectly, so we expect this to be over in the next half hour. It'll feel like much longer for you."

Omar's eyes bulged as she walked over to the side of the bed.

"Once we shoot this into your leg, voilà! You'll vomit, you'll seize, you'll spasm, you'll shit your pants. Your lungs will fill with fluid as your organs fail. And you'll want to beg for it to be over. The best part for me, though, is that you won't be able to speak, only to think about what you've done, all the suffering you've caused. Maybe you'll find peace with your maker, although I suspect there's a special place in hell for someone like you.

"If you're not suffering enough, we'll add a little more. And finally, we'll top it off with more heroin, but not until you've fully appreciated the pain. The genius of our plan is that it'll look like a heroin overdose. And you'll die in the undignified way in which you lived, your legacy nothing more than a cliché.

"Your sendoff will be knowing that tomorrow I will marry Theodore, and we'll live the happily ever after we were always destined to. You'll be long forgotten by the time I get back from my honeymoon. How magnificent is that? This has been such a good talk."

She thought about Petey. Had it made him happy to take the lives of the bad guys? She wanted to feel happiness in this moment. The fact that Omar was alive and well had left her unsettled for over a decade. Now she would finally be able to sleep without being afraid he'd hurt someone she loved.

"Goodbye, dear Omar. I'd let you say a few last words, but yours don't deserve to be heard." She opened her Chanel bag and pulled out the black case with the remaining syringes and substances. While she was preparing the halothane, she said, "On second thought, I would like to hear what you have to say. Well, maybe. Michel, would you mind letting him speak one last time? He'll probably be in too much pain in a couple of minutes."

"Of course. Anything to say for yourself, scumbag?" Michel asked while removing the gag.

"Celeste, Celeste, hear me out. Maybe I'm not the best guy. I've made some"—he winced in pain from a muscle spasm, then continued—"mistakes, especially with you, Celeste. But don't fool yourself. The man you're about to marry is no better than me. Why don't you ask him what he's been up to lately?" His breathing was getting a little raspy, and his body jerked again. He yelped.

"I'll always love you, Celeste, even though you've betrayed me in unspeakable ways and cheapened our love by not obeying me, forcing me to act rashly. I've made peace with it." He was having trouble speaking but seemed determined to release his last words. "One last thing: Who the fuck"—he paused as his body began seizing and he writhed in pain—"is Zari?"

Celeste narrowed her eyes. *Desperate words from a desperate man.*

The fact that he couldn't keep track of all the people he'd killed only confirmed she was doing the right thing.

She'd had enough. She flipped the needle and then stabbed the meat of his thigh with the syringe as Michel had trained her. She kept eye contact as she slowly released the clear liquid into Omar's bloodstream, the poison working its way through his body. By the time the syringe was empty, his body continued to seize, and his breathing was getting more shallow.

For her peace of mind, she needed to see the poison take hold, to know Omar was really gone and couldn't hurt anyone she loved. His eyes were darting around in panic, like he was trying to scream, but no sound escaped.

She and Michel sat wordlessly for some minutes, united in their pain but lost in their separate sorrows of all Omar had taken from them. A single tear slid down Celeste's cheek. She mourned for Zari's wife, Nasrin, and for that young woman she herself had once been. She recalled the pain she'd felt during those months she thought Theodore was dead, still able to call it to the surface of her consciousness readily.

This was the way it had to end.

Michel cleared his throat, drawing her out of her reverie.

"I'd like to give him another dose along with the smack. At this point, it will get pretty ugly. He won't die peacefully. Are you sure you'd like to stay and watch? It's up to you, but it can be quite traumatic to witness."

She checked the time. She still had an hour before she had to leave.

The tears welling in her eyes began to fall. *Look what he's made me become.*

"I have to stay."

"OK, it won't be much longer now. Believe me, he's suffering."

It happened just as Michel had explained. The seizures became more violent, and Omar lost control of his bowels. He was foaming at the mouth. She swallowed the bile that was rising in her throat, nauseous from the stench of his body breaking down.

And then it was over. She watched the life escape his body and heard his last breath. It was just as she had imagined, except for the unexpected and inexplicable sadness that she felt. She began to sob. Michel embraced her and led her into the adjacent sitting room.

"There, there," he said in an uncharacteristic moment of empathy. "It's always upsetting and even more so the first few times."

"I thought I would feel happiness, relief, vindication. But... I feel... nothing." The tears continued to fall, and she sniffled. *Get it together.*

"This is the difference between you and someone like him. He took pleasure in hurting other people, causing chaos and confusion, leaving behind a trail of loss. You—you love. You endured his torture, spent countless nights believing Theodore to be dead. You did this for your loved ones, for all the other women he intended to hurt, for Nasrin. You feel pain when you see other people suffering; he didn't." Michel shifted in his seat, suddenly seeming a bit uncomfortable.

"I should clean this up, and you need to get going. Things will... the odor will be unbearable soon."

"We really wrecked this room, didn't we?"

"Don't worry. Once my cleaner finishes, no one will ever know what happened."

Celeste went to the bathroom on the other end of the suite because she didn't want to see the body again. She refreshed her makeup, and soon any sign of her tears was concealed. She pulled the wig back into place.

"Michel," she called out. He appeared within a few moments. "It's time for me to go. I—I can't thank you enough. I don't know that I could've done this without you."

"I'll be in touch." He patted her on the arm and awkwardly left the room.

Now. Now the rest of her life could begin.

17

———

WEDDING, INTERRUPTED

"You look radiant!" Ty exclaimed. "Look at these golden Hollywood locks, coiffed to perfection. I'm incredibly talented, ya know."

"There has never been a more exquisite bride," Patrick murmured softly while applying the final touches to Celeste's makeup.

How did I let Theodore talk me into this? Celeste watched as the two men critiqued her from all angles, making sure every hair and lash was styled to perfection. The magnitude of the day and everything that had led up to getting her here were not lost on her. *Please don't let the news break today.*

Earlier that morning, Celeste Donovan had stood on the terrace overlooking the Tuscan estate where her wedding would be held in a matter of hours. Seven stories below, uniformed staff bustled about, finalizing arrangements. She had let out a squeal of happiness and clapped when she spotted the enormous, flowered arch under which she would wed the love of her life. Standing nine feet tall, it was made of over one thousand blush peonies. She'd savored the silence, anticipating what was to come.

She was grateful she'd had those final moments alone, which she'd craved since she and her friends had arrived in Italy a week before. The dinners, the sightseeing, laughing and celebrating with the people she loved most in the world—her last week as a single woman had been dizzying. *And now I'll be one half of a whole or some bullshit married women are reduced to.*

Now, she moved as though she were gliding over to the mirrored platform for one final hair, makeup, outfit check. Ty had delivered on her request for sleek red-carpet-worthy waves, and Patrick had painted her as a glowing goddess, the circles under her eyes expertly camouflaged. And the dress. She'd never seen one more beautiful. The off-the-shoulder trumpet style accentuated her small waist and lean figure, while the layers of handmade lace with embedded crystals gave the dress a romantic, ethereal feel.

"Knock, knock," Savin called out, peeking his head through the doorway of the bridal suite. "The maid of honor is allowed in for a moment with the bride, right?" Without waiting for a response, he charged in.

"How many times do I have to tell you you're not my MOH?" Celeste asked, then laughed.

"I lost out fair and square to my old lady, but truth be told, I'll never let it go," he joked as he walked over to the vanity where Celeste was now sitting. He let out a low whistle.

"Wow, Celly, you are... you look... you're quite a vision," he continued. "My mate is one lucky man." Savin nodded to Patrick and Ty. "Could you two excuse us for a moment?"

"Yes, but you gotta make it quick. I still have so *much* to do," Patrick said. He grabbed his iPhone and turned on his heel to leave. *Why are the men in my life so dramatic?*

"What is so important that you kicked out my glam squad on my wedding day?" Celeste asked.

"Theodore wanted me to check in and make sure you weren't planning to leave him at the altar," Savin said. "Mark doubled down on you as Runaway Bride, while I wagered that you'd take the more conventional route and be hitched in under two hours. I've got fifty grand on this. Don't fuck it up." He winked, then sat down on the sofa nearby.

"Yes, you said as much at the rehearsal dinner last night. I've got no plans to dash, if you'll recall. Though I hardly expect you would after downing so much Scotch."

"But seriously, is it a crime to see how my bestie is doing on her wedding day?"

"Of course not. I love you for stopping by."

"I'm over the moon for you two. I can't think of anyone who deserves true love more than... Theodore." He jumped back as she stood and made a move as though to slap his arm.

"Ahem." Jack stood at the door with his head peeking in, loudly clearing his throat. "Let someone else have a turn, jackass."

It's hard to be in a funk with these two around. They always managed to lighten the mood with their banter.

"OK, OK." Savin walked over to Jack and fist-bumped him. "Don't disappoint. Fifty grand, remember?" he said over his shoulder to Celeste, then left.

"Hey there, gorgeous." Jack let out a whistle when she stood up to hug him. "How you holdin' up? Ready to get hitched?"

"Of course! I got the scaries out of the way yesterday." *The truest thing I've ever said.*

"Glad the spa day treated you well while we hung around here, ensuring everything is perfect for your perfect day."

Patrick and Ty came back into the room. "Helloooo? We still have two hours' worth of work to do in a half hour. I'm going to have to ask you to postpone the rest of this convo and be on your way," Patrick said.

"Do you see the abuse I put up with? I'll see you out there, darling," she said to Jack. He kissed her on the cheek and left.

"OK, you two. Let's pick up the pace. I don't have all day, ya know," she teased, knowing it would set Ty off.

"Ungrateful brides!" he retorted. "I must say, you're the most beautiful but also the most insufferable."

"I'll take that as a compliment," Celeste said. "Seriously, though, thank you for making this day exactly what I'd always dreamed of."

Patrick and Ty looked at each other and burst out laughing. "We knew your Ice Queen ass would get weepy and sentimental on us today," Patrick said.

"I, for one, am here for it. You found love—and with such a fox too," Ty said dreamily.

While the pair continued their last-minute touch-ups, Poppy walked in. "Hello, my dears," she said. "Oh, Celeste. Oh my. You are exquisite. My son is a lucky man, and his father and I are so grateful to be gaining a daughter. I told Teddy he wasn't allowed back here, but he sends his love. I hope I haven't been too overbearing." Poppy was wearing an elegant Monique Lhuillier tulle strapless gown in a blush color that set off her dark hair nicely.

"Poppy, you've been quite the opposite of overbearing. It was so nice to have you around throughout this planning. I'd have been lost without you."

"Meredith and I took care of the something old, something new, something borrowed, and something blue." She reached for her ivory Chanel wallet on a chain and pulled out a pair of gold bobby pins encrusted with diamonds. "Once we confirmed you weren't wearing a veil, we knew these bobby pins would work for your something old and something borrowed. Your mother wore them at her wedding. Your brother was able to track them down, and I had them cleaned."

Celeste was floored. It had been so many years since she had looked at her parents' wedding photos, and she had been consumed with so much other than her wedding that she'd forgotten about the tradition.

"Wow, Poppy, I—I don't know what to say. This was so thoughtful."

"It was Mere's idea to track down something of your mum's. I was just the connector because no one, not even a slouchy brother, can say no to an old lady. Now I'm off to say some last words of congratulations to my only son. I'll see you out there." With that, Poppy left in a cloud of Chanel No. 5.

"Ha! You weren't aware of the clips, but I knew. I'd been saving a space in this beautiful Hollywood coif for just this very moment to put these pins in." Ty carefully placed one of the pins on each side of Celeste's hair. "Voilà!"

"So you were all in on it? This is just... well, wow. Thank you, they look lovely."

"Don't you want to know what the something new is?" Patrick blurted. "I'm not great at keeping secrets, Celly, so just say yes!"

Celeste laughed. "OK, yes, of course I want to know what the something new is!"

Patrick stuck his hand in his pocket and pulled out a small Harry Winston box. He opened it to reveal stunning teardrop earrings. "Theodore said he was saving these for the perfect day."

"It's... these are gorgeous." She removed her diamond studs and inserted the new earrings.

Finally, the two men were satisfied with their work and stepped aside when Sam and Rani came in, carrying a bottle of Champagne and flutes.

"My god, you are glowing," Sam said. "Breathtaking."

"My man's got fifty gees on this and wanted me to make sure you plan to show up. I figured getting you a little tipsy is my best bet," Rani said, and everyone laughed. "This is for the most beautiful bride," she continued, handing Celeste a glass of Champagne.

"And we've got the something blue," Sam said. She pulled a baby blue silk garter from her clutch. "Let me help." Celeste knew well enough now to accept assistance when offered while she was wearing a wedding gown. Sam bent down and slid the garter into place, then stood once more.

Celeste took a sip, processing all the love from her friends, these people who were like family.

Everything it's taken to get me here—it was worth it to be surrounded by so much love.

"Wait, is my brother here?"

"Mere checked in on him a few hours ago. He and his fam are running a little late, but they'll be here."

Typical. Of course he'd make my day about him.

"Mere is here to save the day!" Meredith said, moving breezily into the room. "It's time for everyone to go to their places and leave me alone with the lady of the hour. Move along! Off you go!"

Celeste laughed at the theatrics as her friends exited the room.

"How are you?" Mere asked. "I can't wait for you to see how perfect everything, and I do mean everything, turned out."

"With the staff of forty you've hired, I imagine it will be. And how's my groom-to-be? Has anyone spoken to him?"

"He is a bundle of nerves but as handsome as can be."

Suddenly, Celeste only wanted to be in his arms, somewhere far, far away. *A few more days and it'll be just us.*

"Is it almost time?" she asked.

Meredith downed her Champagne and looked at her phone. She squealed and clapped her hands, jumping up and down. "You're getting married, Celly! In thirty minutes!"

"Knock, knock." Celeste looked up to see Angelo coming in. "Everything looks good from my end. Everything is in place." He took a step back. "My, my, my, would you look at that? You look incredible, Celeste. Don't worry, today we've got you covered."

"Thanks, Angelo."

"Is that all? If so, shoo, shoo! Be gone! It's time for me to get this lady to the altar!" Meredith scolded.

Angelo obeyed, leaving the two alone once more.

Celeste walked over to the three-way mirror one last time. "This dress, Mere, you've done so much to make this day special for me... I don't know what I would've done without your help." Celeste's eyes welled with tears. "Oh, I think I... must have something in my eye." She reached for a tissue.

"Aw, Celly, it's OK to be emotional on your big day. All the best people are."

"Well, at least I know two people who will be weepier than me— Sav and Theodore."

Both women laughed.

"All right, you ready to do this?" Meredith extended her arm to Celeste.

"As ready as I'll ever be," she said and took Meredith's arm. They walked through the hallways of the villa, down the massive staircase, and out onto the garden terrace.

There stood Jack and Savin, waiting to escort Celeste down the aisle. The quartet began playing "All of Me" by John Legend.

"I believe it's time for you to marry my mate, Celly," Savin said.

"There's never been a more beautiful bride," Jack remarked.

She smiled at each one, then looked beyond them. To the naked eye, it was simply another upscale Italian wedding. But she knew better. She spotted Angelo close to the house, barking whispered orders into his earpiece. She also knew there were two snipers on the roof and plainclothes *polizia* on the periphery of the land, as well as Angelo's guys strategically placed.

"Snipers, Angelo, really?!" she'd exclaimed when he suggested it. She was overruled by her entire wedding party, including Meredith. "Mere, I thought for sure you'd be on my side. I mean, nothing screams romantic Tuscan wedding like snipers with AR-15s!"

They'd insisted it was for the best. "Safety first!" Jack, never one to give two shits about safety, had even chimed in.

"Fine, whatever. But they'd better not make it into any photos." *Can't argue too much or they'll be suspicious.* She knew they were over-compensating because she'd been kidnapped in Paris the previous year. *C'est la vie.*

Now, she took in the scene around her, the beaming faces of twenty-five of their closest friends and family members. Then she spotted Theodore. In that moment, his eyes locked with hers, and the music, the guests, the sunshine faded into the background. Only the two of them remained, as though a magnetic force drew them together. She'd stopped trying to explain it because the connection was too difficult to verbalize, or perhaps it was too ethereal. She would fight for their love with everything she had.

It was worth it, baby. All of it. And now it's just me and you. Timeless.

Theodore broke into a wide smile that lit up his entire face. She fought the urge to run to him.

"I think it's time," she said, hooking elbows with her two escorts.

"You pussy," Jack muttered under his breath to Savin, who had tears streaming down his face.

"Sav, pull it together," Celeste said. "At least you've gotten your fifty grand sewed up nicely."

He sniffled. "Mark's going to be pissed. He thought for sure you'd bail."

The three laughed as they made their way to the altar, Celeste nodding hello to the guests as she passed by.

There's not a dry eye in the house. Well, except for me. Patrick will murder me if I mess up my makeup. She took inventory. *Everyone made it here OK. Wait, my idiot brother and his wife and kid...* She scanned the faces but did not see them anywhere. *It figures.* She never saw him unless he wanted money.

Roberto waved from the second row, holding up his and Sam's infant daughter, who was precious in her pink lacy gown and matching headband. Jin, Mark's wife, and their daughter were seated with them. Jin, always looking sleek and glamorous, was wearing a stunning terra cotta slip dress that popped against the simple white floral arrangements on each row.

The expressions on Poppy's and Teddy's faces could only be described as pure pride and joy.

Meredith was across the aisle with Patrick and Ty, beaming. Her hard work had paid off. "You're amazing," Celeste mouthed to her. Patrick stuck out his tongue, and Ty blew a kiss.

And finally, she was standing next to the love of her life. Savin and Jack kissed her on the cheek and went to stand next to Theodore. She turned to the two women who had become true friends to her and smiled. "Thank you for everything," she said and handed Sam her flower bouquet. Both Sam and Rani were dabbing the corners of their eyes.

"Celly, you deserve this," Rani whispered, squeezing her hand.

Celeste turned back to Theodore and locked eyes, and again everyone around them disappeared in an instant. He put his hands out and took hers.

Mark cleared his throat. "We are gathered here today to celebrate," he began. And with that, it felt as if the past were wiped away, giving Celeste and Theodore the fresh start she'd been wishing for since the whole mess started. Then it was time for their vows.

"Celeste, sweet love of my life," Theodore began, "you are my sun when I rise, my moon when I sleep, my North Star. In short, you are my everything. I knew I loved you the moment I saw you. I found this little poem that puts into words exactly how I feel about you." He withdrew a small notebook from his jacket pocket.

Of course he did. The most romantic, over-the-top gesture imaginable.

Theodore cleared his throat and began reading.

> "And when I saw her there,
> waiting for me
> in the window,
> I knew that I was the luckiest man
> in the universe,
> and that the gods had graced me
> with a goddess,
> and a grace
> beyond time and space,
> and I knew
> I must have done something right
> in this lifetime
> to deserve
> such a gift as this."

Now it was Celeste's turn. "Theodore, my darling, no one was more surprised than me that I said yes when you asked me to marry you." The crowd let out a collective chuckle, Theodore's sexy baritone laugh louder than everyone else's.

"Until you came along, it never occurred to me that I could meet someone I would want to spend my days and my life with, who could love me so perfectly, be so attuned to my needs. But then I met you, and your actions, your love proved to me that everything I thought I knew about love was wrong. I always thought it was fragile, given but then taken away when things didn't go as planned. You've taught me how wrong I was, how I misunderstood what it means to love and be loved. You see all the parts of me, good and bad, and you still wake up every day and choose to love me despite my shortcomings."

Celeste could no longer hold back her tears. Without consciously realizing she was doing so, she deviated from her prepared vows. "I wish I could stand up here and say I couldn't imagine life without you. But I can. I can because I had to live day after day, week after week, thinking you were gone forever. I had to experience what life was like without you. While I wish I could've figured it out in a much less painful way, losing you and then getting you back was the reason I could confidently say yes to spending the rest of my life with you. Because there was no way I could say no. Life with you is a grand adventure, and I am so happy we've gotten our second chance.

"I am deeply, madly—as our neighbors can probably attest to when they hear me yelling at you—crazy in love with you."

Tears were streaming down her face, and Theodore's eyes mirrored her emotions. Behind Theodore, Savin was sobbing and blew his nose into a handkerchief.

"Excuse me for a moment. Sav, can you pull it together? I was just getting started," Celeste said.

"Who would've thought the Ice Queen could bring anyone to tears?" he retorted.

When the laughter died down, Celeste continued, "As I was saying, Theodore, darling, you're the most special man I've ever met, and I feel so blessed every day to have your love. I promise to make you sleep on the couch only when absolutely necessary and to love and cherish you always and forever."

"Theodore, do you take Celeste as your lawfully wedded wife, to have and to hold, as long as you both shall live?" Mark asked.

The groom nodded affirmatively. "I do. A thousand times over, I do."

"And Celly, er, Celeste, do you take Theodore as your lawfully wedded husband, to have and to hold, as long as you both shall live?"

"I do."

"Then my work here is finished. I now pronounce you husband and wife. Theodore, you may kiss your bride!"

Theodore embraced Celeste Hollywood-style, dipping her, and then they kissed. A long, passionate kiss that left them both heady and aroused.

"Get a room!" Jack said through cupped hands.

It was everything Celeste had wanted and more. When the two came up for air, Mark said, "May I introduce you to... well, I would introduce you to Mr. and Mrs. Prescott, but Celeste is keeping Donovan, so I'll introduce you to the happy couple."

Hand in hand, Celeste and Theodore turned to the crowd. He whispered to her, "We made it, baby! We made it together."

"Yes, we did indeed."

Out of the corner of her eye, she saw a flicker of movement. She perused the lawn for anything unusual. The guests were all smiles, standing and clapping. Angelo was at his perch, wearing his usual on-duty, don't-fuck-with-me expression.

And then she saw what had caught her eye. One of the security guards was dashing toward the house through the trees bordering the lawn. Celeste groaned. *Wedding, interrupted.*

"Babe, did you just see tha—"

But Theodore wasn't listening. He was looking back at Jack. The two of them made eye contact, and Jack gave a firm but almost imperceptible nod. Then Theodore turned back to her.

"See what, honey?"

She gestured to... no one. The running guard was gone. Everything appeared as it had only minutes before.

"Let's get this show on the road so we can get out on the dance floor!" Rani said. "Sav, honey, no more tears, OK? You know how it makes Celly uncomfortable when people display emotions."

The entire wedding party laughed.

"That's our cue, darling," Celeste said to Theodore, and the two walked back down the aisle as newlyweds. *Husband. I have a husband now. Wow.*

After the ceremony, Meredith and Sam helped Celeste out of her massive gown and into an ivory silk slip dress. She bent down and fastened her Aquazzura crystal heels, then straightened up again.

"I feel so free, like I've lost fifty pounds," Celeste remarked.

"Because you have," Ty said. "I'm surprised you lasted this long in that thing. I hope you didn't pay per yard of fabric." Everyone laughed. "But it is beautiful, even I have to admit," he added.

Ty put a few fresh curls in Celeste's hair, while Patrick touched up her makeup, and then it was time to enjoy the reception.

SAVIN CLINKED his Champagne flute until he had everybody's attention. "I'd like to make a toast to the bride and groom. Now, I'd be lying if I said I haven't been waiting for this moment since Celly and Theodore went on their first date," Savin said. "I knew they were destined to be together from the moment my mate called me up, asking me all sorts of questions about Celly."

"You'd also be lying if you said you didn't stay up late writing your best man speech that very night, snug in your jammies," Jack commented. Laughter spread across the patio where everyone sat awaiting the main course.

The evening was unseasonably warm, the usual spring chill at bay. Festive string lights twinkled along the terrace railing, and tealight candles lined the tables, illuminating everyone's faces in a soft, romantic glow.

"Ignore the guy in the cheap seats," Savin said. "Celly, Theodore, I can't tell you how thrilled I am that you two found—well, if we're being honest, that I orchestrated—this most perfect love connection. It's obvious to anyone observing you that you two have a once-in-a-lifetime love, the kind many can only dream of. I've watched you grow from two, some might say cynical, people committed to the single life into a team committed to doing what's best for you as an 'us.' I know I'm not alone when I say that I am elated to see the two of you"—he paused, dabbing his eyes with his handkerchief—"Well, we watched you go through so much when... Theodore was away and when Celly was... sick, and..." His voice broke from the lump in his throat. "It's just wonderful to see you two finally getting the happiness you deserve. *Saluti!*"

It had been a whirlwind week, especially with the Rome detour, but Celeste finally allowed herself to exhale and enjoy the moment. This moment was what she'd been fighting for all along, what she'd killed for. "I love you," she mouthed to Theodore and softly kissed his lips while the others clinked glasses and whistled.

"Well, I hope you didn't think we'd let Savin show us up," Sam said. She, Rani, and Meredith stood together, Sam holding a fork like a microphone to the small group. "Celly, watching you and Theodore fall in love has been such fun. For those who don't know, I met Celly the same night Theodore did. I asked Roberto who was the James Bond type following Celeste around like a lost puppy. I could tell he was smitten even then, and I'm blessed to have been able to watch their love blossom as it has. You two are unstoppable." She handed off the fork to Mere.

"I'm speaking collectively as your glam squad because Ty would make it all about him, and we know better than to ever give Patrick a mic," Meredith began.

"Is this a roast or a toast?" Patrick said, playfully pouting.

She smiled and rolled her eyes. "Anyway, Celly, while you've always been a radiant beauty with more brains than half of Wall Street combined, being in love has made you glow from within, what we coined the Theodore Glow. Hence, we've been secretly referring to your life as pre-TG and post-TG. We wish you a lifetime full to the brim with adventure, laughter, and love!"

"OK, OK, it's my turn," Rani said, taking the fork. "It was so hard to keep dating Sav a secret because we had a front seat to watching our favorite couple, Celly and Theodore, fall madly in love. Cheers to a lifelong partnership of all the things. Love, laughter, doing everything together in life and nothing on a rainy Sunday afternoon."

Rani's sincerity could be heard in her voice. There was no way she could have nefarious intentions when it came to Celeste and Theodore. *Could she?* No. She'd cleared her name when she came clean about Paris. *Hadn't she?* "Thank you, everyone," Celeste acknowledged, clinking glasses with Theodore. "We are so grateful to have you in our lives."

"And I'm the luckiest man on the planet," he replied for only her to hear.

The quartet resumed playing while everyone enjoyed dinner and drinks. "Mere, I don't know how you pulled this off with the millions of other things I ask for occupying your time, but it's exactly what I've always wanted," Celeste remarked to Mere when she came over to check on Celeste. "Every detail is perfect."

When the keyboardist played the first few chords of "By My Side," Theodore took that as his cue to whisk Celeste over to the makeshift dance floor. They danced cheek to cheek in comfortable silence. *I never knew it was possible to feel this much love.*

"I fall more in love with you every day, my beautiful wife."

"I was just thinking the same thing, my darling husband. Who could've predicted I'd ever get hitched?" They shared a laugh.

"Hey, what were you and Jack worried about earlier?" Celeste asked.

"Worried?"

"I thought I saw—"

"Do you mind if I cut in for the next song?" Savin interrupted.

"The man who brought me together with the most magnificent woman alive? But of course, dance away."

Savin reached for Theodore's hands in jest and spun him for a twirl. "Oh, sorry, you meant a dance with your lady. My bad!" He grabbed Celeste's hands and led her in a waltz around the terrace.

"So? How is it? Being married and all?"

"Well, I don't have a ton of experience, but if the last hour has been any indication, I'm sure it'll be lovely."

"Smartass. Truly couldn't be happier for you two."

"Well, looks like you and Rani are on the way to a fabulous love story yourselves." She joked about Savin's track record and affinity for heartbreak, but deep down, she'd always felt protective of him and hoped he would end up with someone wonderful. Like Rani.

"I was promised a dance with the best man," Rani said, appearing when the song was winding down.

"He's all yours," Celeste replied. "I'm in need of a little more Champagne anyway." She left the couple and asked one of the servers for a refill. Everyone was having a great time on the dance floor and at the bar.

She wandered over to chat with her new in-laws, who had their heads tucked together giggling at a nearby table.

"Am I interrupting anything?" she asked as she approached them.

"There's our beautiful daughter," Teddy remarked, pulling out a chair for her and giving her a kiss on the cheek.

"We're never too busy for you, dear," Poppy said warmly. "I remember our wedding like it was yesterday. How does it feel?"

"It's been such a whirlwind of a week!"

"Yes, Savin definitely kept us busy, didn't he?"

I had some of my own things to tend to as well.

"TODAY WAS PERFECTION. It was—*you* are—everything I've ever dreamed of. I've never known happiness like this," Theodore whispered in her ear as he caressed her breast through her teddy. They were back in their palatial suite later that evening. Candles flickered around the room.

"It was exquisite," she murmured. "Except lugging that dress around all night. You know that thing weighed like twenty pounds, right?"

He stood behind her, and she could feel how aroused he was against her body as his hips swayed with hers.

"Shh, no more talking. Tell me about it tomorrow," he replied softly. Theodore lifted her into his arms and carried her to bed. They made love, at first furiously and then sweetly. Afterward, Celeste laid her head against his chest, drifting in and out of sleep while he told her the story of the night he fell in love with her. The last thing she remembered hearing him say was "Baby, we made it. Together."

One or the other of them awoke an hour or two later, and within seconds, they were intertwined once more.

If this is what marriage is like, I shouldn't have waited so long.

"Darling, darling," Theodore said, gently rousing her from sleep. "I have a surprise for you, babe."

Celeste peeked at him through half-shut eyes, trying to decide if whatever her husband was talking about was worth disrupting the best sleep she'd had in years. "Mm, but I was sleeping so well. This surprise had better be worth it, Mr. Prescott." She stretched and opened her eyes. The early morning sun shone in through the sheers, and she could see the exquisite countryside from bed.

"I'm whisking you away to Capri for a few days. You're going to love it. Everything is already arranged, and we're leaving in half an hour."

"Wait, what? We're missing the wedding brunch?"

"Yes, sweetie. I wanted to get an early start. The chopper is already waiting for us."

"But I'm not—"

"Packed? Mere packed a separate bag for you that we stored downstairs. Let's take a quick shower and just grab the necessities. Passport and such."

He picked her up and carried her into the bathroom, then set her down on her feet.

"I should travel like this more often," she said. She looked in the mirror at the two of them. Disheveled, sleepy, wearing matching grins. *It was all worth it even if just for these moments.* Fleeting images of Zari, Nico, and Omar slipped into her conscious mind right then. She shook them off and brushed her teeth while Theodore started the shower.

The two quickly rinsed off, dressed, and then gathered what they needed for the trip. Celeste packed her Chanel bag, now much lighter without the supplies, and a large leather tote of things she'd need that Mere hadn't packed in the bag downstairs–her extra passports, burner phones, and cash. *You just never know.* Now that she'd had time to process the idea of a surprise trip, it seemed fortuitous to leave the mainland before the news broke. She hoped she'd have a chance to check in with Michel before they began their journey to the island.

"OK, my love. I'm as ready as you can expect me to be with a moment's notice," Celeste called. Theodore was waiting for her in the sitting room and, as usual, was typing on his phone. He looked up at her and smiled.

"I can't wait to have you entirely to myself, Mrs. Prescott."

"Oh, we're not doing that. I remain Mizz Donovan, betrothed to one Theodore Prescott," Celeste said. They laughed. The pronunciation reminded her of Gabe. She wondered what he would do when he found out about Omar. *That can wait until we're back in New York. Hopefully.*

"It was worth a shot," Theodore said and picked up her bags. They walked quietly through the villa so as to not wake anyone at the early hour. Celeste was sad to miss out on brunch but was looking forward to Capri. It was one of her favorite places to visit.

When they arrived on the back terrace, Angelo was waiting with a golf cart loaded with luggage.

"Good morning, Angelo. Well, technically, it's still night, I suppose."

Angelo nodded by way of greeting and placed their bags on top of the many bags already stacked.

"I guess Mere *did* pack well for us," Celeste observed while getting situated in the cart. She marveled that Mere had managed to keep the clandestine escape a secret.

"C'mon, let's get going. The chopper is waiting."

"We aren't going to the heliport in town?" Celeste inquired.

"No, I arranged for something a little more convenient this time,"

Theodore explained, sitting next to her and taking her hand. He nuzzled her neck.

They were on their way. She turned to look back at the villa for the last time. *That's odd.* The lights were on in one of the bedrooms. From her vantage point, it appeared that Jack was in a heated discussion with a dark-haired woman whose profile was vaguely familiar.

Theodore and Angelo were discussing something inane, but Celeste was only partly listening. Her mind was racing, as she weighed whether to alert Theodore to what she'd just seen.

"Babe, babe," she interrupted him, tugging on his sleeve. "Look!" She pointed to the window where she'd seen the light. But it was dark now.

"What is it, dear?" Theodore asked patiently.

"That's weird, I thought I saw a light on in Jack's room. It looked like he was with a strange woman."

"I don't know Jack that well, but from what you and Sav say, that sounds very on brand for him, right? Perhaps he has someone local he meets with when he's here," Theodore reasoned.

Celeste considered it. *But to invite her to the villa on my wedding night?* "I suppose it's possible."

Moments later, they arrived at the edge of Jack's property, where a helicopter awaited. Angelo and the pilot loaded the bags.

"I don't want this feeling to end," Theodore murmured.

"I think you're stuck with me forever, honey," Celeste replied, kissing his nose.

"I can't ever lose you," he whispered.

"OK, everything's on," Angelo said.

"Thank you, Angelo," Celeste said.

He embraced her in a tight hug, whispering cryptically, "I get the feeling you're in trouble. Let me know how I can help."

Celeste pulled back and looked at him quizzically. "Safe travels back to New York. See you very soon!" she said nonchalantly. She accepted the pilot's hand and got into the helicopter.

Once they were buckled in, they ascended over Jack's property. Celeste took one last glance at the immaculate grounds. To say she was grateful that she and Theodore had been able to celebrate their union with the people they loved most in the world was an understatement; she had thought it was an impossibility only one short year before.

I finally got my happily ever after.

EPILOGUE

The pristine white villa set high above the town of Anacapri had the perfect atmosphere for the newly wed lovers. Celeste and Theodore had taken lunch alfresco on the sun terrace, surrounded by manicured foliage, and now Theodore softly snored in a chaise by the pool. Celeste gazed at him.

Yes, my love, it was all worth it to get us here. She caressed his cheek and then walked over to the cliff's edge to admire the calm sea below, glistening in the sunlight. She savored the moments of serenity that the last leg of their honeymoon adventure provided, though what awaited her upon her return was nagging at her subconscious.

The haste with which they'd departed Jack's villa the morning after their reception had left little time for planning, so Celeste had been sneaking in hushed, untraceable conversations with Michel. She'd expected that the skulking would end once Omar was out of the way. To the contrary, the situation was now heating up on several fronts. As Alex had once alluded to, there were others besides Omar who considered her a person of interest, including her own government.

Gabe's incessant calling was perhaps one of the more surprising fallouts. She'd decided the day before the wedding that she'd have to keep him at arm's length until Omar's death was ruled an overdose.

As planned, the *polizia* received an "anonymous" tip (from Michel) after the wedding, informing them that a stench was coming from one of the Hotel de Russie suites. Upon investigation, the *polizia* had found Omar with the track marks and the smack and nothing to suggest foul play. Michel and the cleaner had staged the scene well, and the autopsy revealed a host of illicit drugs but no traces of anything else they'd administered to Omar. It was a relief for her and Michel when the *polizia* determined Omar's was a clear-cut overdose case.

He died in the undignified way in which he lived.

Maybe Gabe disagreed with the Roman cops, because he'd been blowing up Celeste's phone to such an extent that she'd decided to shut it off for the remainder of the five-day honeymoon.

You had your chance to take care of all this on your own terms, Gabe, and you squandered it. You figure out how to tell your bosses they fucked up by siding with that monster.

Gabe wasn't the only challenge. The advantage—and disadvantage—of slowing down and taking a break from work was the additional time she now had to think and process. Omar's vitriol toward Theodore hadn't been surprising, but his words replayed in her mind at inopportune times. Even in his last living moments, Omar had tried to exert his ability to get inside her head, and he'd made it no secret that he had it in for Theodore.

Still, Celeste was no fool, and some things didn't add up. How could Omar not have remembered who Zari was? All those months, she'd been sure that Omar had Zari killed, and Omar had even alluded to it in the past.

If Michel was right that Nasrin had been lying to her about an alternate reason behind Zari's death to spare her feelings, then it seemed only natural that Celeste's original hypothesis held true—Omar had hastened Zari's death by ordering his murder. Conversely, if Omar *had* been responsible for Zari's death, he surely would have been able to recall it. Omar was always manipulative, sure, but he had been desperate in those last moments when he was fearful for his life. Celeste would have expected him to be agreeable, apologetic even, if he thought it would buy him some reprieve.

Yet Celeste now believed it was possible that he hadn't caused Zari's death based on his reaction. *Back to square one on Zari.*

Celeste had begun doubting whether she'd actually cleared those in her circle because the fact remained—there had to be a rat. She vowed to become more vigilant when she got home; it was imperative that she assess everything with a clear head. *I guess it's not time to retire my Mia alter ego after all.* There were other gaps, too—important ones.

But Celeste did not intend to waste another moment of her honeymoon on these things—they could wait for her return to the States. Now, in the most beautiful of places, she and Theodore were celebrating a transcendent love, a love she'd been willing to kill for, with a breathtaking view of the Mediterranean and one of her favorite cities. She pushed the dark thoughts aside.

"Babe, shall we eat at L'Olivo tonight?" she asked when she was seated next to her napping husband.

"Mmm, that sounds amazing, but only if I can have dessert here first."

"Done," Celeste said, moving over to his chair and lying against him. She traced her fingers up and down his abdomen for a few seconds until he was aroused, then they sneaked inside for a decadent nooner.

"Mrs.—" the butler began, standing in their boudoir doorway after frantically knocking. He was a distinguished Italian man, immaculately dressed, with a full head of salt-and-pepper hair neatly in place.

"Please call me Celeste," she interrupted while tying her robe tightly. Theodore was in the shower out of hearing range. "Is there something I can help you with?"

He frowned. "You have a phone call. On the house line reserved for the locals, which is a bit unusual." *On my honeymoon, no less. Ughh.*

"Hmm, OK. Can I take it in the staff quarters?"

He looked at her quizzically, probably trying to figure out protocol for an American who received a house call. "Follow me, *signora.*"

As they made their way through the massive villa, Celeste grew more and more furious. How dare they—whoever it was—disrupt the only time she'd taken off in ages?

"What?" she said sharply into the phone in the villa's library. She gave the butler a look suggesting that he make himself scarce, and he quickly scurried away, closing the door behind him.

Michel's voice boomed, fraught with worry. "We have a situation."

"I turned my phone off so I could enjoy the last bit of my honeymoon. This couldn't wait until I'm stateside in a matter of days?"

Just then, there was a knock at the door, as Michel replied grimly, "No, it can't. In fact, it may already be too late."

TO BE CONTINUED

ALSO BY RACHAEL ECKLES

Continue the Celeste Donovan Series

Trading Secrets, Book One

Blind Trust, Book Three

ACKNOWLEDGMENTS

If my debut, *Trading Secrets*, was a group project, the sequel, *Risky Assets*, was largely a solo affair. I began writing it a few months after the global pandemic began as a project to keep me busy, alone in my apartment with my pup at my feet while the world waited for life to "get back to normal." What strange times we live in. I've grown as a woman and a writer since the first book, largely because I've had so much time for self-reflection during the past two years. My hope is that it made me a better version of myself. Time will tell.

I'm grateful first and foremost to my readers, the people who kept me going when I was certain I had only one book in me. Your enthusiastic check-ins asking when you could read the next installment of Celeste Donovan's adventures are what kept me inspired, excited, and ultimately motivated enough to bring the second book to fruition. Thank you. This one's for you!

Thank you, Joyce Bond, for making this story so much stronger and for your love of and commitment to Celeste's character. You make me a better writer, and together, we got this book into the world under the strangest of circumstances, right down to the wire and with all sorts of unexpected challenges. We did it!

Claudia Carravetta, you're always my number-one cheerleader and my Wendy Rhoades performance coach. Thanks for your unwavering encouragement and belief in my talent. It means the world to me.

Swami ji and Roxanne, you have each provided so much support for me on my journey to become a better version of myself. Thank you both for your commitment to my growth and for feeding my soul, my intellect, and my heart with compassion and kindness.

So many people have provided me with endless support, friendship, love, and laughs while I've been locked away writing (and quarantining—I avoided Covid longer than Fauci, so I feel like that's something to be proud of). Kelly Campbell, Alex Borchard, Cordelia Kim, Sarah Yekinni, Mike Carter, Courtney Roberts, Denise Bissell, Kelsey Olson, Abby Hanemann, Kira Zalan, Jennivere Kenlon, Kern Briggs, Alena Amano, Katherine LaPointe and Peggie LaPointe, Francesca Danzi, Amy King, Kelsey Lang, Adam Taliaferro, Wasey and Kunwal Kheiri, Amanda Koziura Quick, Gary Meltz, and Chris Pernie, to name a few—you listened and kept me going in a way I'm not eloquent enough to pass along. Jenni Wagoner, you made my first release so much fun with our wine tastings with readers. Oksana Pali and Zakeyma Peterson, you gave me so many laughs and endless support over the past two years.

Lauren Saint-Louis, your reminders to take care of my physical health and continue my commitment to becoming stronger and more resilient kept me on track. There were many weeks during the past two years when you were the only person I saw in 3D, so you've had to listen to me babble incessantly and repeat "as soon as this book is finished" more times than either of us could count. Thanks for your commitment to my wellness.

Juan Pedro Liotta and Mia, the silver lab, you two made this book possible by keeping Sassy entertained while I wrote day and night. Mia, I believe your steady spirit is what drove me to name Celeste's alter ego after you.

Thank you, Grandma Ellie, for sparking my love of romance novels. My parents now know you let me borrow some steamy novels at a way too young age. I am grateful because it's one of the reasons I became such an avid reader.

Sassy, my sweet little pup, thanks for tolerating my twelve- to fifteen-hour days in front of my laptop. We have many long walks and pup cups ahead of us this summer.

Finally, to my family—Mom, Daddy, Jessie/Saster, Korey, and Jordan—thank you for believing in me, even when I didn't believe in myself. No matter what career path I dream up, your confidence in my abilities has always given me a deep foundation of support.

ABOUT THE AUTHOR

Photo Credit: Oksana Pali

An Indiana native, Rachael Eckles moved to New York City after law school. There she worked in the finance industry, her inspiration for the elusive Celeste Donovan world. She currently lives in Manhattan, where she is working on her next novel. Rachael donates a portion of her proceeds to local and global programs that empower women and girls through her foundation, Aphrodite Gives.

For more information, please follow Rachael Eckles at:
www.RachaelEckles.com